PRAISE FOR

SONG OF THE BLACKBIRD

"Debut novelist Michaels, a doctor herself, brings verve and veracity to this smooth-flowing hybrid romance/suspense tale. Emma's clinic scenes, which showcase both prisoners' manipulations and their mitigating circumstances, are particularly realistic and resonant. Michaels also weaves in lovely, literary through-lines . . . a captivating story. . ."

—Kirkus Reviews

"There are plenty of romances on the market and plenty of novels about prison experiences; but combining the two under one cover in a prison romance is a different approach, indeed, and so *Song of the Blackbird* provides a powerful saga of the unexpected."

–D. Donovan, Senior Reviewer, Midwest Book Review

"With compelling characters, a unique setting and a sweet love story, Michaels introduces her debut series, Albatross Prison. The characters are skillfully crafted, drawing readers in with their opposing opinions, belief in their actions and strong familial values . . . this is a gratifying tale of forgiveness, compromise and love."

–Romantic Times Review Source

DB Michaels

Song of the Blackbird

For Poppy

CHAPTER 1

Prison at last.

A trickle of fear slid down Emma's spine as the metal gates slammed shut behind her. She swallowed down her anxiety. For years she'd been waiting. She couldn't back out now. Beyond the entry gates, long vertical steps shot toward the top of the hill. She climbed up, remembering the general layout of the prison from the tour last week. The main clinic lay down on the other side of the hill, a full fifteen-minute walk away and the sooner she got there, the better.

At the top, Emma veered left and hiked yet another slope to a locked gate. As she opened the gate, a shrill whistle pierced the air of the Sensitive Need Yard. A horde of guards seemingly from nowhere stampeded toward a dilapidated building to her right. The guards ran, clutching their batons, screaming, "Down! Down!" to the men wearing blue loitering in the yard.

The inmates dropped to the ground, their eyes riveted to the commotion. Emma cowered back, her heart racing. *Should she follow them? Better to head straight to the clinic.* Suddenly a loud cheer burst forth with chants of "Kill him! Kill him!"

Someone was being beaten. *What if it was Sam?* Emma followed the last guard around the corner of the building and screeched to a halt. A massive grim-looking man in a blue suit was stomping on a frail elderly inmate on the ground. At least twenty guards surrounded the group, urging the huge man on.

"Kill him!"

"He deserves it!"

"Harder! Harder!"

The man in the suit seemed oblivious of the jeers. He was enormous, at least six foot four inches tall with a wide, muscular body. His set mouth and grim face twisted in savage satisfaction as he repeatedly kicked the man on the ground. "You have a death wish? Get up or I'm going to beat the hell out of you," he said to his victim.

The old man's body jerked a few times before he stopped moving altogether.

"Get up, you filthy bastard," the huge man yelled. He lifted his boot to deliver another blow.

"Stop it," Emma shouted, running into the group. The attacker's head swiveled in her direction, his eyebrows flying together in a deep frown.

Up close, he looked younger than she'd thought, perhaps in his late thirties or early forties at most. Black hair framed a formidable, stern face. The man's strong square jaw jutted forward and his mouth compressed into a thin line.

"Who the hell are you?" he asked, straightening to his full intimidating height. His bright eyes glared down at her, their silver color accentuating his striking face.

"Please stop hitting him." The inmate lay motionless on the ground. *Was he already dead?*

"Stay out of this," the brute said, clenching his fists.

"He needs help." Emma dropped to the ground to check on the poor victim.

"Don't touch him." A grip of steel clutched her arm. For a big man, he moved as quickly as lightning, for there he was, kneeling right beside her. A tag with the name Chambers was clipped to the front of his suit jacket.

"Please, let go of me." Emma shook off the man's grip and grabbed a stethoscope and penlight from her bag. She listened to the victim's chest. Breath sounds were present but faint and slow. His pupils were a little small but reactive. A jagged scalp laceration oozed out a steady stream of blood. Emma pulled out a handkerchief and pressed down hard on the wound.

"So you're a nurse?" Chambers's silver eyes bored into hers.

"No. I'm the new doctor." Emma shook her head. The poor man may be dying right now and all because of this brute. "Listen, he needs help. Can you call an ambulance?"

Someone snickered behind her. Emma turned. A sea of blue, at least fifty inmates, kneeled at the periphery of the crowd.

"Code 1 already called," a guard yelled.

"Is that 911?" Emma asked. The handkerchief was already soaking a deep red color, emitting a faint metallic smell. "He needs to go to the emergency room."

"No hospital," Chambers said. "You'll take care of him here."

"He needs the hospital. They can do a CT to make sure there's no head bleed."

"I said no hospital. My orders."

"Call 911, please." Emma turned toward the nearest guard. "We can't let him die here."

"Sorry, Doc." The young guard flicked a nervous glance at Chambers. "You heard what he said. No 911."

Emma waved the bloody handkerchief in front of Chambers's face, deciding more action was needed. "This man is hurt, Mr. Chambers. Who's in charge here? Can I talk to him?"

A muffled roar of laughter erupted from the group of inmates behind them. The young guard coughed into his hand and gave her a sympathetic look.

Chambers's silver eyes hardened into a slate gray. He pulled out a clean handkerchief from his pocket and pushed it into the young guard's hand. "Smith, hold pressure until Code 1 comes. Looks like the doctor is forgetting some basic first-aid training."

Another roar of laughter rose from the crowd of inmate spectators. Emma knelt next to Smith, too upset to give the brute a piece of her mind. At least the bleeding seemed to have slowed somewhat with the new handkerchief.

"Get those inmates out of here." Chambers shot up from his sitting position. "Where the hell is that Code 1 team?"

The majority of guards dispersed to clear away the sea of blue. One by one, each inmate filed out in a single row, some of them darting covert glances Emma's way. All of them wore identical light-blue shirts and pants with the California prison logo imprinted down the front of the right pant leg. Emma scanned the crowd for Sam's face and bit back a sigh of frustration when no one looked familiar.

The poor man on the ground groaned, drawing Emma's attention.

"Am I in heaven?" he asked in a hoarse voice.

"No." Emma felt his racing pulse. His breath became shallower and quicker while his skin remained cool and clammy. *Was he bleeding internally? Why wouldn't they call 911?* "What's your name?"

"Roberts," the man croaked out. He raised his arm to try to touch her hair.

"Hands down," Chambers ordered from above.

"It's okay." Emma squeezed the man's hand. "Do you know where you are, Mr. Roberts?"

The inmate cowered away and curled into a fetal position. "Don't hurt me," he whimpered.

"He needs some space, Mr. Chambers." Emma tried to be as polite as possible but Chambers only stepped closer and glared down at his pathetic victim.

"No one is going to hurt you, Mr. Roberts," Emma stressed. "I won't let him hurt you."

Chambers's grim look darkened even more. He glowered at her, his silver eyes glinting like bullets ready to raze her down. "Stop being so naïve, Doc, or you'll be the next one on the ground."

"Are you threatening me?"

Chambers's eyes widened a fraction before they snapped together in a ferocious frown. "Don't tempt me."

Emma shivered and leaned back. *He wasn't going to harm her, was he?*

"Oh, for God's sake, woman. I was talking about your precious Roberts down there. He's the one who would hurt you, not me."

"He's unconscious, Mr. Chambers. I don't think he'll be doing anything right now." Emma checked on the wound again.

An ambulance's siren suddenly pierced the air. Emma smiled up at the guards, thinking they'd obeyed her after all. Chambers clearly wasn't as in charge as he wanted to be. Her smile fell the instant she saw the ambulance, or what passed for an ambulance. The rickety vehicle that rolled up the hill sounded like an ambulance but looked like a faded rescue van from the 1950s. And to make it worse, instead of EMTs, two middle-aged women in scrubs came out, each slowly moving along at a sedate pace.

"Hello, Mr. Chambers." The woman in pink smiled, showing uneven white teeth. "How are you today?"

"Good." Chambers looked even tenser than before. "Where's the rest of the Code 1 team?"

"There's another code down the hill," the other nurse said, batting her eyelashes. "You need help, sir?"

"Yes," Emma interrupted. *Were they flirting with the man?* Emma shook her head in disbelief. A more uncaring beast she'd never met. "I'm Dr. Edwards, the new prison physician. Can you help me over here?"

"The new doctor," the nurse in pink exclaimed. "We're so glad you're here. I'm Ms. Bryant and this is Ms. Carter. We're the Urgent Care nurses."

"Oh, great." Emma swallowed down her anxiety. *How the heck were these two women going to help her load the patient into the van?* They were old, older than her mom had been when she'd died. She shook their hands and prayed for a miracle. "Can you check his vital signs? I need an O2 sat and an ACCU-CHEK too."

A moment of silence stretched to a few seconds too long. "I'm afraid we can't do that," the nurse named Ms. Bryant finally said.

"What?"

"We have to bring him down to the treatment area," Ms. Carter said. "Our portable blood pressure machine isn't working right now."

Emma swallowed again. *How backward was this place?*

"Smith. Jones. Load the inmate in the van," Chambers ordered. "Quickly, so they can stabilize him."

Emma's jaw almost dropped. *This coming from the man who had savagely beat her patient?*

"What?" Chambers's silver eyes flashed at her. "I want him out of my yard, Doc. The sooner, the better. Less commotion to stir up the rest of the inmates."

"Of course." She should've known. All he cared about was the perfect order of his yard. *Who the heck was he?* Some bombastic yard supervisor, no doubt.

Emma followed the two officers into the ambulance. Inside she didn't find any IV set or equipment except for an AED machine and an oxygen tank with a mask. She fastened the mask on Mr. Roberts's face as he lay strapped on the stretcher. The two nurses got into the front of the van. Emma settled in the back, sitting alongside the stretcher with Officer Smith.

A few minutes later, the ambulance arrived at the bottom of the hill next to a group of old bungalows. Several wild black cats lounged close by. On the opposite side of the bungalows lay rows of dilapidated buildings labeled with the numbers 200s and 300s, which Smith pointed out as inmate dorms.

"Come this way, Doc." Ms. Bryant led Emma up a ramp into the nearest bungalow. Inside to the left, at least five officers sat laughing and chatting with one another. They congregated around a large wooden desk facing a room labeled *Men's Clinic*.

"Another Code 1?" A large dark-skinned guard flicked sunflower seeds out of his mouth as he stood to see Mr. Roberts wheeling by on the stretcher. "What is it? Seizures or another 7219?"

"Altercation." Smith grinned. "With the boss himself."

"Shoot, man," the dark man said. "How many is that? The third this month?"

"Hey. Whatever works." Smith cracked his knuckles before heading into the clinic. Emma rushed after him and helped lift Mr. Roberts onto an empty gurney.

"Okay. I need an IV, monitor, and some O2." Emma stripped off Mr. Roberts's shirt to look for further injuries. "Someone get the vitals."

Ms. Bryant plopped her heavy frame into a chair and wiped perspiration from her forehead. "I need a break. Carter, you want to do the honors?"

Ms. Carter rolled her eyes and dragged herself from the portable AC unit. She slapped on the blood pressure cuff and shoved a temperature probe into Mr. Roberts's mouth. He coughed and snapped his eyes open, flailing his arms and legs.

"What the hell?" he mumbled.

"Relax." *At least he was moving all extremities.* Emma put a restraining hand on his shoulder. "We're trying to help you. Does anything hurt?"

"Go away. Wanna sleep." The man began snoring within a few seconds.

"Track marks." Ms. Carter lifted the inmate's arm, revealing two faint red pricks. "Better get the Narcan ready."

"Remind me to order some more. We're almost out." Ms. Bryant heaved herself out of the chair and pulled up some Narcan in a syringe.

Emma shined a light into the patient's eyes. The pupils were now pinpoint. His breathing had slowed and some goose bumps appeared on his arms. *Amazing. An opiate overdose.* Maybe these nurses weren't so bad after all.

"Good job." Emma flicked the two nurses a grateful glance. Over the next half hour, Roberts continued to breathe on his own without the need of Narcan. Emma cleaned and stapled the head laceration. Other than a few bruises on his chest and thigh, he wasn't as injured as she had feared. No need to call 911, as his neuro exam was pretty normal. After giving him two liters of saline, she took a brief tour of the Urgent Care.

A crash cart with a defibrillator lay on one side of the room and an old monitor screen dangled over the gurney. Several signs about what to do in a code hung on the faded peeling walls. Adjoining the main clinic was a small inner room, the doctor's office, housing a desk and a large computer.

"I know. Everything looks a bit run-down," Ms. Carter said. "The state has no money for renovations."

"Must be different where you're from, Doc," Ms. Bryant said as they settled down around the gurney. "What made you decide to work in a prison?"

"I like working with the underserved. And the government is paying off half of my student loans for being here." *At least she could tell the truth about that part.*

"You're kidding me, right?" Ms. Bryant pulled out a granola bar from her coat pocket. "I never heard of that."

"The feds want more doctors to work in public service jobs, so they assist with the loans," Emma explained. "It's a great help."

"Well, we're glad you're here." Ms. Bryant beamed. "We really need a new doctor now that Dr. Cassidy is retired."

"And Dr. Ross is cutting back his hours, too. Something to do with his family," Ms. Carter said before tossing her empty coffee cup in the nearby trashcan.

"Chop, chop. Get to work, ladies." A tall, chubby bald man in a white coat bustled into the room, rubbing his hands together with waterless soap. "What have we here? Another OD?"

"Dr. Brown." Ms. Bryant smiled. "Glad you're here. Clinic wasn't that bad, was it?"

"Bad enough." He grinned, turned Emma's way, and slapped a hand to his forehead. "Oh, my God, you're the new doctor, right? I totally forgot you were coming today."

"It's okay." Dr. Brown looked young, his friendly ruddy face dominated by a large nose and an easy smile. She gave him a firm handshake. "Emma Edwards. Nice to meet you."

"Julien Brown. How do you do?" His light-blue eyes smiled at her. "I'm the chief. I think you toured while I was on vacation."

Mr. Roberts suddenly emitted a loud groan before falling back to sleep.

"What's up with him?" Dr. Brown pointed his large shiny head toward the patient.

"Elderly inmate beat up by one of the staff here," Emma said. "Vitals stable, getting fluids. Probably shot some heroin too."

"Custody beat him up?"

"Custody?" Emma asked.

"The guards. That's what they're called here. You know, the men and women in green."

"Oh. I'm not sure if Chambers is Custody, but the man is way out of control."

"Chambers?" Dr. Brown asked with a quizzical expression.

"Yeah," Emma said. "Tall, rude brute. Really rough around the edges. You know him? Who's his supervisor?"

A delicate cough came from the nurses' corner. Dr. Brown's face changed into a peculiar shade of red as he stared at the open entranceway.

No, it couldn't be. Emma groaned to herself. She turned around and sure enough, the big brute from earlier stood glowering at her from the doorway. Two men in green Custody uniforms flanked his side.

"I assume you two have met," Dr. Brown said in a strangled voice.

"Dr. Edwards, nice to see you again." A pair of familiar silver eyes flared at her. "If you have a complaint about me, call the governor."

"Of California?" Emma asked, her spirits dwindling as fast as air from a popped balloon.

"Of course. What other state would we be talking about?" The man extended his hand. "Maxim Chambers. Your warden."

CHAPTER 2

Emma closed her eyes and prayed it was all a dream. But alas, the gods were not on her side. *Of all the luck.* He had to be the warden. No wonder the guards kowtowed to him. Suddenly she found her tiny hand swallowed up in a warm paw. "Emma Edwards, nice to meet you," she squeaked out.

Chambers shot her a nasty look before dropping her hand like a hot potato. "Who hired her?" he barked to Dr. Brown.

"Headquarters, when you were on vacation, sir. She's very well qualified. Graduated the top of her class from UCLA."

"Knew I shouldn't have taken that many days off," Chambers muttered, shaking his head. He strode toward the gurney and flicked a glance at the monitor. "Vitals are good. How's the inmate? Ready for transfer yet?"

"No." Emma hurried over. "He's barely awake. He needs more time."

"At this rate, he'll be here all week." The warden's frown deepened. "I want him gone as soon as possible."

"Then maybe you shouldn't have hit him so hard," Emma mumbled half to herself.

"Excuse me?" Chambers whipped his head toward her. "Do you know what this man did, Doc? Last year he pulled a knife on a nurse. Yesterday his heroin killed another inmate. And guess what? He tried to stab me today when I confronted him about it."

Emma bit her lip. *Jesus Christ. How could she have been so fooled?* Roberts had seemed so harmless.

"Smith!" Chambers suddenly bellowed. "Where the hell are you?"

Poor Smith had just returned from a bathroom break and rushed over. "Here, sir."

"Didn't I tell you not to leave her alone with him?"

"Yes, sir."

"What's wrong with you, Smith? Can't you follow a simple order?" Chambers shook his head and cast his wolf-like silver eyes toward Emma. If she didn't know any better, she'd think he was checking her out. *Fat chance of that.* The man probably thought her a nuisance and wanted her out of his sight as soon as possible. She shivered, dreading what he'd do next. He acted like a beast. A handsome beast, if you liked the tall, dark, menacing type. Thank goodness she was immune.

"Where's your alarm, Doc?" Chambers finally ground out.

Dr. Brown stepped up and gave a placating smile. "Sorry, sir. I haven't shown her how to get the alarm yet."

"She needs a whistle, too." Chambers swung his penetrating eyes back to her. "You can't forget it. Ever. Use the whistle or press the alarm whenever you feel threatened by an inmate. That's the fastest way to get help. Got it?"

"Yes." *Jeez, he had a point, but did he have to be so rude and overbearing?*

"Remember. Alarms and whistles on at all times, every-one. I know some of you are complaisant and don't think you need it, but we work in a prison. Always be vigilant." With that, Chambers nodded and exited the room with his two minions in tow.

"Whew." Dr. Brown wiped a hand over his forehead. "That was a close one. I thought he'd never leave."

"Is he always that bad?" Emma asked, finally breathing easier.

The two nurses got up from where they were sitting, looking surprisingly unfazed. "His bark is worse than his bite," Ms. Carter said.

"All the staff respect him. He's just strict," Ms. Bryant added.

"And I heard something horrible happened to his family," Ms. Carter said. "It made him really bitter."

Suddenly the patient on the gurney swung himself up and began retching.

"Hey! Watch my new sneakers." Ms. Bryant grabbed a pink basin and shoved it under Mr. Roberts's mouth.

Emma took advantage of the patient's upright position to get a good listen to his chest. *Good.* It was clear, no signs of aspiration. But the smell of vomit was overwhelming. Emma coughed and hastily stepped back. "Mr. Roberts, I'm going to give you something for your vomiting."

After the intravenous Reglan, the patient settled down again and got transferred to the infirmary down the hall. Dr. Brown told her it was called the Outpatient Housing Unit, or OHU for short. It had twelve beds, mainly for patients needing observation or those requiring intrave-nous antibiotics or fluids.

He led Emma to room one, where a small twin bed lay

wedged against the right wall. A thin, jaundiced man rested on top of it, his face gaunt and his mouth slightly open as he slept. A stale, sick patient smell permeated the room.

"This is Mr. Nash, metastatic liver cancer with cirrhosis. Not a candidate for surgery."

"How long does he have?" Emma asked, knowing the prognosis couldn't be good.

"Less than six months. We're trying for compassionate release but I doubt he'll get it."

"Compassionate release?"

"Yes. The state's trying to save money. Any terminally ill inmate can apply for release."

"You don't think he'll get it?" The poor man looked like a skeleton, probably weighing no more than a hundred pounds at most.

"I doubt it. Depends on what crime he committed."

"What did he do?"

"Don't know and don't really want to know." Julien led her back to the main nursing station.

"Maybe it's not as bad as you think," Emma said. She knew what Sam did was justifiable. His sentence had been way too harsh. She needed to find him as soon as possible. Speaking of which, now seemed as good a time as any to start. "Dr. Brown?"

"Please call me Julien." The chief stood next to an overgrown stack of charts at the center desk of the nursing station. A thin, middle-aged secretary with curly brown hair sat at the front desk, filing her fingernails, while a young nurse in pink scrubs was pulling up some medicine in a syringe. "This is Dr. Edwards. Lexi, our secretary and Ms. Macky, our RN," he introduced the two women to Emma.

"Hi." Emma pulled a chair next to Julien and sat down.

She could feel her heart rate pick up and tried to calm down before she ruined everything. "Julien, how do you keep track of patients here?"

"We have the green paper charts for now. But electronic health records are going to be mandatory soon, so Sacramento is phasing in a new computer system," Julien said. "It's pretty good but we still depend on the paper charts a lot."

"So how do you look up a patient?" Emma tugged at the pendant on her necklace, hoping her mom was looking down on her. She needed whatever help she could get.

"Usually by the CDC number…but you can do it by last name, too." Julien logged on to the nearest computer and started punching in some numbers.

"CDC number?" Emma tried to contain her excitement. Any minute now, she might find out where Sam was.

"Yes. California Department of Corrections. R for rehabilitation if you want to use CDCR." Julien rolled his eyes. "Not that there's much rehab going on in here."

"Okay…so you can look up by last name, too?" Emma asked, trying to sound as nonchalant as possible.

"Yes. Here, I'll show you." He pulled out the nearest chart. "This is Mr. Nash. See? Type his full name in and then a CDC number will pop up. Make sure you check it's the right birthdate."

"Thanks." Emma clicked through Mr. Nash's history and tried to ask the appropriate questions, but the pounding in her heart became stronger by the minute. Her ears were beginning to pound too. "Can I play with the computer for a while? I want to get familiar with the charting."

"Sure." Julien smiled. "I'll be down the hall, rounding. Let me know if you need help on anything. We'll go see the different clinics later."

Emma blew out a deep breath and wiped her palm on her pants. She glanced to the left and then to the right. The nurse had left and the secretary was still typing. She lifted her fingers and clicked in "Sam Morris." *Yes!* There were four listings, with only one that matched the right birthdate. The roaring in her ears escalated. *308-35U.* That was it. All those months of planning and there he was. She assumed the dorm number was 308; 35 must be the bed number. She wasn't sure what the *U* stood for, but it didn't matter. She was so close. Her mouth felt dry and she forced down some saliva.

"Ready?"

Emma jumped up and swung around, careful to block the computer screen. Julien stood behind her, his face in a half-smile. "Let's go around and see the other clinics."

"Sure." *Darn. Her voice came out too high.* Emma cleared her throat and logged off the computer, repeating the dorm number in her mind several times.

"Oh, before I forget." Julien pulled out a document from a nearby station. "This is a 7410 that you'll have to fill out a lot. It's an accommodation chrono."

"Chrono?" Emma glanced at the form.

"Yes. The inmates need doctors' orders to get a lot of stuff. You circle what they need. Cane, crutches, braces, whatever." Julien pointed to the top right corner of the form. "But their favorite is a lower bunk. We don't have enough bunks for everyone, so Custody doubles them up. Most of the inmates hate to be on top. So they finagle all sorts of reasons to get the bottom bunk."

"What are the legit reasons?"

"Seizures, if they're over sixty, or had surgery within six months, or broke a limb." Julien handed her another paper.

"Here's the list of reasons. Don't give them the chrono unless they qualify. Most of them make up a bunch of crap to try to get one. Back pain's their favorite, even though they do tons of exercise every day."

"Okay." Emma looked at the paper and tried to get familiar with the top reasons.

Julien showed her some of the other commonly used sheets, and the rest of the morning passed in a blur learning about the prison. Unit 1 and 4 clinics were up the hill near the Eagle gate where she'd entered that morning. Units 2 and 3 were near the Urgent Care next to the infirmary down the hill. Julien informed her the prison covered almost one hundred acres, with health care facilities arranged both at the top and bottom of the hill.

After greeting the doctors of Unit 2, two very nice men named Dr. Tran and Dr. Parker, and saying hi to Dr. Pan of Unit 3 whom she'd already met last week, Emma walked up the hill with Julien to tour the other two clinics. She was surprised to see how free-flowing the inmates were. They mingled with the staff like regular people, distinguished only by their blue clothing.

"Takes some getting used to, doesn't it?" They passed a crowd of inmates hovering in front of a small bungalow.

"Yes. I always thought prisoners are locked up in cells," Emma said.

"Only at the high security facilities. Albatross Prison is medium security. We're open dorms with perimeter fencing."

A couple of black cats crossed their path. "What's up with them?" Emma pointed to the cats. "I saw a couple earlier. Do they run wild here?"

"Yup. Keeps down the rat population." Julien laughed at her horrified gasp. "Just kidding. We don't have rats, but we have a lot of cockroaches. And at least half a dozen raccoons."

"Ugh." One cat looked pretty plump as it darted out of their way. "They look pretty well fed. I don't think they eat roaches, do they?"

"No way." Julien laughed again. "There're several food stations in the prison. Our cats don't have to do any hunting at all."

"You're kidding me, right? Someone brings them food here?"

"Yes. The warden apparently has a soft spot for cats." Julien grinned. "Custody brings them food and water regularly."

"Interesting." *That big, gruff man had a soft spot for animals? Maybe he just wasn't a people person.* Several men in blue walked by carrying huge clear trash bags filled with ramen noodle packages, Twinkies, chips, and various other junk foods.

"What are they doing?" Emma asked.

"Buying their monthly canteen food."

"Anybody can buy the food?" *Did Sam ever buy anything? He used to love chips and Cup-o-Noodles.*

"If they have money, they can buy it," Julien said.

Something squeezed tight in Emma's chest. Why had Sam refused all her offers of help? Why had he sent back her letters and money? He'd refused her visits, too. He'd been unhappy at first but had accepted his situation more by the second year of his incarceration. She hadn't seen him in almost a year. The last time they talked on the phone was six months ago. And she hadn't heard from him since. He'd cut off all contact with her. She hadn't even known he'd transferred from Delano to Albatross until she'd visited his first prison and found out about the transfer.

"What happens to the guys who don't have enough money?" Emma asked. "Do they get enough food?"

"Twenty-nine hundred calories a day the state provides." Julien rolled his eyes. "Don't worry. They get plenty of food. And free medical, mental, and dental care. Some of them don't even want to parole. They have it pretty good here."

Maybe prison life wasn't that awful. Still, she desperately wanted to confirm for herself that Sam was okay. Emma scanned the crowd of blue, hoping to see that familiar lanky form with the frizzy black hair and gentle brown eyes. Would Sam be mad to see her? He'd told her to be patient and wait for his parole date but how could she when she hadn't heard from him in ages? She needed to make sure he was all right, needed it as much as the air she breathed.

After several fruitless minutes of searching the crowd, Emma caught sight of the pristine scenery extending far beyond the barbed-wire fences. They were near the top of the hill by now so she had an unobstructed view of the terrain. She'd been too busy worrying about Mr. Roberts earlier to notice the view.

Stretches of blue mountains spread across the horizon, and nestled outside the prison gates was a lush green golf course surrounded by tall, sweeping palm trees. In the distance, rows of windmills spun their blades majestically in the cool crisp autumn air. It was hard to remember they were only an hour away from the congestion of Los Angeles. The sun shone like a beacon in the sky, illuminating all the glorious beauty of nature. It looked like paradise until one saw the barbed-wire fences and the imposing towers dotting the prison's exterior.

"This used to be a private horse ranch of a reclusive billionaire in the 1950s." Julien pointed to a tall building on top of the hill to the left. "There's the Albatross Hotel, where his guests used to stay. The state took over the land in the seventies and converted it into a prison."

"So Unit 1 patients are housed up here?" So much history lay behind the beat-up old prison. *Did Sam know any of it?* Emma was sure he'd find the prison's history fascinating.

"No. The hotel isn't earthquake-safe. We stopped using it as a dorm years ago."

"So where do the inmates stay?"

"In those bungalows next to it." Julien waved his hand to the left. "I know, it's a lot of climbing to get back and forth to the different clinics. If you want, you can wait for a golf cart."

"Golf cart?"

"Yes." Julien pointed to a cart heading down the hill. "The heads of the departments get golf carts. Someone's bound to be going back and forth and usually they'd offer you a ride if you need it. Although sometimes you can't find a cart. They break down and take a long time to fix."

"How come there's such a delay to get things fixed?"

"It's the state." Julien shrugged. "Everything here takes forever. No funds and slow staff. We didn't have a working phone for Dr. Tran for about six months, can you believe it?"

"That long?"

"Get used to it," Julien warned. "The prison is over forty years old. Things break all the time. If you need anything repaired, let me know and I'll put in a work order. They'll eventually get to it. But prepare for a long wait."

"Okay. Thanks for the warning." By this time, they'd reached the top of the hill. Julien didn't appear quite as out of breath as she was. Emma realized she should definitely hit the gym again. The last few months, she'd been too preoccupied with Sam to do much. She inhaled the cool fresh air and resolved to do better. Suddenly, a shrill call of a blackbird greeted them.

On-ke-kaaangh. On-ke-kaaangh. The bird perched on a low-lying branch of an oak tree close to the spot where Mr. Roberts had been beaten that morning. His pitch-black wings had two bright red patches. Emma leaned forward. White streaks bordered the red. *Oh!* She felt a surge of excitement, sure this was a good omen. He was the rarest of birds, the tricolored blackbird, Sam's favorite ever since they'd gone bird-watching together as children.

On-ke-kaaangh. On-ke-kaaangh. The bird let out another call before spreading his wings and flying away. Sam used to look that way, confident and bold. What did he look like now? Would he be downtrodden and despondent or would he be like the blackbird, proud and free, ready to fly and sing despite what life dealt him? How she longed to see her brother again.

CHAPTER 3

Maxim Chambers took off his suit jacket and folded his long body into the oversized office chair. *What a morning.* He shook his head and grimaced. Bloody stupid Roberts almost got him with that knife. Maxim flexed his shoulders and felt his muscles tighten with tension. It was a close one, almost too close, but that was what he lived for. He remembered the rush of satisfaction when Roberts had fallen as flat as a pancake. He would have kicked him harder except for that annoying doctor.

She stood no taller than his shoulder but man did she pack a punch with that mouth. A rude brute, she'd called him. He guessed technically she was accurate on both counts but did she have to sound so disgusted? Her green eyes had spit fire at him. He'd never seen eyes that green. Coupled with her black hair, she looked like a bewitching cat. *Bewitching.* What the hell was he thinking? Some men might find her elfin, slender looks attractive but he preferred the tall, buxom type. Yet, those eyes. Maxim rolled his shoulders back and rubbed a hand behind his neck.

Emeralds. That was what they reminded him of. Too bad the rest of the package didn't match up.

Regionals had been fools to hire her. She was too young and too petite. How was she going to hold up with these godforsaken inmates? All the other doctors were men. It didn't bode well to throw her in among the prisoners. *Damn.* He'd have to keep an extra eye out for her, another problem to add to his plate. As if he hadn't enough problems already.

Back on the tour, Julien informed Emma that the inmates who needed extra protection stayed in Unit 4, the SNY or Sensitive Need Yard.

"Extra protection? From whom?" Emma asked.

"From other inmates," Julien said, leading her out of the SNY facility. "The SNY guys are, you know…the child molesters, transgender patients, anyone who might be picked on. They're all in this unit. Especially the ones who snitched on their gangs."

They went out to the yard, climbed up several steps and reached another locked gate.

"Key number 527." Julien held up his set. "It opens all the outdoor gates. And by the way, be really careful with your keys. They're assigned to you and you have to check them in and out every day."

"Yes. They told me that during the tour. What happens if you forget and bring them home?"

"The guards at the gate will make you bring them back, even if it's the middle of the night."

"That's a little excessive, isn't it?"

"It's for the security of the prison. They want all the keys accounted for to make sure none goes missing. And it's how they keep track of who's here and who's not." Julien shook his set of keys. "If you don't return them, they'll assume that you're still here on the grounds somewhere, especially if they can't reach you at home. And if you ever lose your keys, you have to report it immediately."

"Immediately?"

"Yes. They'll shut everything down to find them. No one wants an inmate to get a hold of them."

"That's good to know." Emma reached into her pocket to make sure her keys were still with her.

Julien unlocked the gate. "We're leaving SNY and going to the admin building."

"Does this lead to the outside parking lot?" They'd taken so many turns, she was losing her orientation.

"No. We're still in a restricted part of the prison." Julien locked the gate after them. "You can leave the prison by only two gates. The Falcon Port way down the hill on the west side and the Eagle gate up here. You entered the Eagle gate this morning, right?"

Emma nodded. "It's close by, isn't it?"

"Yes." Julien gave her a sympathetic look. "I know, it's confusing but you'll get used to it. From the Eagle gate, you have to climb up a flight of stairs to reach Units 1 and 4 and then down a hill to reach Units 2 and 3. Anyway, now we're heading to the White House, as some people call it. That's where the head honchos sit."

"You mean the warden?" Emma's stomach knotted. She wasn't looking forward to spending any more time around Maxim Chambers.

"The one and only. He likes to attend our meetings,"

Julien said. "We have meetings every day to talk about patients. Dr. Kaye, the CMO, will be there."

"CMO?"

"Chief medical officer. Didn't she interview you?"

"No. Only Regionals interviewed me."

"No worries. I forgot they're shifting power to Regionals now." Julien rubbed his bald head and kicked a small pebble out of the gravelly path they were on. Locked gates still surrounded them but they were now in a separate fenced off section next to the SNY yard.

"What does Regionals do exactly?" Emma asked.

"Sacramento wants to hire more qualified doctors, so they set up Regionals to do the hiring," Julien said. "Used to be the CMOs could hire anyone they liked, even if the person wasn't that good. Now only the regional departments get to do the hiring. It makes everything more uniform among the thirty-three state prisons."

"I guess that's a good way to get better doctors." Emma followed the chief up a ramp into an old office building.

"Yes, but Kaye is probably upset Sacramento took the hiring power from her so don't be surprised if she's a little snippy." Julien lowered his voice. "And before I forget, I wouldn't go bad-mouthing Chambers around Kaye."

"They're pretty tight?"

Julien nodded. "She believes he walks on water. Major crush on him. But you didn't hear it from me." The chief winked and pressed his lips together with his fingers. He motioned for her to proceed down a long hallway. "And you should know Kaye is in charge of medical but Chambers is in charge of all of us. And the man's a stickler for protocol. Wants everyone to be on time."

Julien led Emma down a dim-lit hallway into a large

conference room. The room was at least twenty feet long, with an elongated oak table in the middle flanked by an array of soft blue chairs. All the chairs were taken except for the two closest to the front.

"You're late." Chambers glanced at his watch and frowned from the head of the table. "Well, what are you waiting for? Come sit down."

And a good morning to you, too. Emma walked behind Julien and clenched her hand as she sat in the only vacant seat left. It was clear no one wanted to be next to the warden. He loomed like a mountain sitting on her left side. She pushed her chair back and tried to look inconspicuous.

"You must be Dr. Edwards." A gorgeous woman with long blond hair appearing to be in her late thirties sat across the table. Her ruby red lips stretched in a thin smile as she extended her hand. "I'm Dr. Kaye, the CMO. Don't be late next time."

"Sorry." Emma's left hand inadvertently brushed Chambers's arm. He stiffened up like a board. She jerked her hand back and shoved it under the table. *What was it with the man?* Waves of palpable tension emanated from him.

"Why don't we go around and introduce Dr. Edwards to everyone?" Julien suggested.

Seven men took their turn introducing themselves. She had met everyone except for Dr. Cam and Dr. Churchill. Dr. Cam was Asian with a narrow face, kind eyes, and black hair tinged with silver. Dr. Churchill was younger with blond hair, a muscular physique, and shrewd brown eyes. He headed part of the team at Unit 4. The other physician in Unit 4 was Dr. Yee, an older gentleman with glasses and a gentle demeanor. They had been at a pharmacy meeting earlier when Julien and Emma had toured so she hadn't met them. Apparently, Dr. Ross was still missing.

Emma made the appropriate responses, all the while sensing Chambers's impenetrable silence as he sat as still as a statue next to her.

"Why don't you tell us a little bit about yourself, Dr. Edwards?" Julien proposed.

The mountain moved his chair back. Emma met a penetrating pair of silver eyes. She looked away and cleared her throat. "There's nothing much to tell. I grew up in Southern California and went to UCLA for med school and residency."

"So this is your first real job." Julien clapped her on the shoulder. "Welcome to Albatross. Glad to have you here."

"Okay. Let's move on," Dr. Kaye interrupted, flicking back her golden mane. Her long fake nails tapped a light tattoo on the table.

"Exactly. We're wasting too much time." Chambers shuffled through some papers. "Let's start with the patients in the hospital."

"Mr. Nash was discharged last night," Julien began. "We saw him this morning. He's stable, not getting worse but definitely not getting any better."

"Any recent family visits?" Dr. Churchill asked.

"His daughter came last weekend."

"Are all the compassionate release papers filled out?"

Chambers snorted. "I wouldn't even try if I were you. He shot a man four times in the head in cold blood."

"Why did he shoot?" Emma asked.

Chambers glared at her. "Who cares why? It wasn't in self-defense, that's for sure."

"Maybe he had a good reason," Emma said.

Chambers's eyebrows drew together. "Don't be so naïve. All the inmates deserve to be here. Every one of them committed a crime."

"Have you seen him lately?" Emma felt compelled to speak up for the poor man. "He's barely able to get out of bed. Maybe he's had enough punishment."

"So now you're an expert on the law?" Chambers asked. "The man killed someone. His sentence was twenty-five years. He's only served five. He's not going anywhere."

"That's too bad."

Chambers's right hand twitched beside her. "Enough about Nash. Any inmates in the hospital?"

Julien began rattling off some names. *Thank goodness Sam wasn't one of them.* At least not this time, but had he been ill before? They'd always been close. Something horrible must have happened to him. Maybe he'd been beaten up and lay hurt somewhere all these months. But then there was the 308-35U. Surely if he was hurt, they wouldn't have assigned him to a dorm?

One of the side doors to the conference room opened and several inmate workers lifting large boxes entered. One carried two huge boxes. His face was partially obscured but when he turned, Emma's heart almost stopped. That uplifted nose, the frizzy hair, the lanky build. She squeezed her eyes shut and snapped them open again, sure her mind was playing tricks on her. But no. There he was. He turned and suddenly caught her eye. His whole body stiffened. That was it, a momentary tenseness. Nothing else. No smile, no spark of recognition. He put the boxes on the cart and followed the group of inmates out the door.

"Excuse me." Emma hastily stood. "Sorry. I'll be right

back." She rushed to the door, registering Chambers's and Kaye's identical expressions of disapproval. But what did it matter? She'd seen Sam. Her darling, beloved Sam. She flung the door open. *Where the heck were they?* They couldn't have gone far. She bolted down the corridor, turned left, and caught a glimpse of blue going around the next corner. She ran after them. There they were, exiting the building farther down the hall.

Emma sped outside. The four inmate workers stood in a single line near the locked gate she'd entered with Julien awhile back. Their supervisor opened the gate with his set of keys. They were at least fifty yards away but Emma had no problem identifying Sam. His gait was the same. The usual swing to the arms and the mild dragging of his left foot. Courtesy of his cursed father who'd started this nightmare. Sam never turned around as the group disappeared from sight. Either he was mad at her or maybe he'd lost his memory? Had he had a concussion from some head trauma? He had to know her. There must be a reason for him to ignore her like that.

Suddenly, a blackbird's call rang in the air. *On-ke-kaaangh. On-ke-kaaangh.* Then a short pause and another. *On-ke-kaaangh. On-ke-kaaangh.* Sam's voice definitely.

Emma's heart soared. She put her hand to her mouth and prayed she still remembered. "*On-ke-kaaangh. On-ke-kaaangh.*"

It didn't come out as polished as when they'd practiced it long ago camping in the woods but it was enough. Dear God, it was enough. Tears rushed behind her eyes as the familiar birdcall echoed back to her. She swallowed several times and wiped the wetness from her cheeks. She'd found her brother at last.

CHAPTER 4

"Brown, go check on Dr. Edwards." Maxim glanced at the clock one more time. It'd been nineteen minutes since she ran out of the room. Just ran out. *Didn't the woman have any manners?* She'd pushed her chair back to stay as far away from him as possible. Even then, her slight rosewater scent had drifted over to him. Light yet sweet. Delicious. *Damn it. What was wrong with him? Since when did he fantasize over a woman's perfume?*

He hadn't been thinking straight since she stormed into his life that morning. She was aggravating, rude, naïve, and too cursed young. *What the hell was she doing in his prison?* Maxim shook his head and stretched his tight collar.

"Relax, Maxim." Kaye laid a hand on his arm. "I'm sure she didn't get in any trouble."

Maxim lifted his arm out of the way and bit back a sigh. One date all those months ago and Kaye was on him like white on rice. "I am relaxed. Let's move on. Is the flu clinic all set up?"

"Yes. Everything's ready." The CMO smiled, fluttering her long eyelashes.

Such flawless beauty. Too bad it was only skin deep.

Only two female doctors on his team and he was cursed with the both of them. One couldn't get enough of him and the other thought he was a rude beast.

"We need more inmates to take the shot," Maxim said, trying to clear his mind of female doctors. "Last year was a disaster."

"Only because they didn't want to wait in line to sign the consent forms," Brown spoke up from the doorway as he reentered the room.

"Where's Dr. Edwards?" Maxim tried to contain his ire. Clearly Brown hadn't understood his instructions.

"I don't know. Maybe she went to the bathroom." The tip of Brown's ears turned pink. "I couldn't go in there to check."

"Of all the stupid excuses." Maxim bolted out of his chair. "Your doctor has been missing for almost half an hour now and all you can say is maybe she's in the bathroom? Where's your head, Brown? We're in a damned prison. She doesn't even have her whistle on."

The silly woman might have been mauled by an inmate by now. Maxim's hands clenched into fists. Just as he was about to activate the alarm, the doctor walked through the door, looking like she didn't have a care in the world.

"Where the hell have you been?" he demanded.

Instead of cowering or making excuses, her face lit up in a smile. And it was directed at him. Maxim's heart lurched. A queasy feeling stirred in his stomach. Like the initial time he rode on a roller coaster. First, the emerald eyes and now that smile. Maxim tugged at his tie and tried to regain his equilibrium.

"I'm so sorry." She smiled again. "I had to go to the bathroom. I didn't mean to take so long."

She was good. Maxim had to give her that. He would've been fooled except for those eyes. They had wandered away at the last minute. "You were in the bathroom all that time?"

"It's a little embarrassing." Her skin flushed a light pink color. The woman had freckles, the biggest one near the corner of her upper left lip. "I'm sure you don't want me to go into details."

"No. Of course not." *How the hell did they end up talking about what a woman did in the bathroom? And why did she have to have freckles?* They were damned distracting. Maxim silently cursed and sat back in his chair. "Next time, you have to tell us where you're going, Dr. Edwards. It's part of the safety protocol." He fished in his pocket. "Here's a whistle. Don't go anywhere without it."

"But that's yours," she protested. "I can't take it."

Noble and naïve. She was going to be the death of him. Maxim forced his eyes to look above her left shoulder. "I'll get another one. Besides, you need it more than I do."

"Okay, thanks."

Her hand accidentally brushed his as she took the whistle. An electric jolt ran up Maxim's arm and he jerked back, feeling as if he'd been scorched. *Damn it. What was happening to him?* She was naïve and rude. Barely out of training. And a liar to boot. Nothing to be worked up about, except as a duty to protect. She was in his prison and he needed to make sure she was safe, that was all. Still, when was the last time he gave an employee his whistle? Maxim shook his head in disgust and sat through the rest of the meeting, trying hard not to think about freckles.

After the meeting disbanded, Maxim spent the rest of the afternoon catching up on emails and correspondence before leaving work. Evening was his favorite time of the day. There was nothing he looked more forward to than getting in his Porsche and cruising back home after a hard day at work. Sure, Palos Verdes was over an hour away but the long drive never bothered him. But today was Monday. Visiting day.

He switched on the car's ignition and leaned back against the leather seat. Out of nowhere, the doctor's smile suddenly flashed before his eyes. He hastily turned on the audio system and pressed a couple of buttons. Soon the calming lyrics of Walt Whitman's poem reverberated in the car.

The words never failed to soothe him and they worked their magic again that night. By the time he exited the freeway, Maxim's mind was more at peace. Another day without a death. He should be thankful for that at least. So what if a disturbing doctor had invaded his space? It was nothing he couldn't handle.

"How's it going tonight, Mrs. Olsen?" Maxim greeted the charge nurse on the second floor of the nursing home a few minutes later.

The nurse tapped her clipboard and smiled at him from behind thick glasses. "Good so far, Mr. Chambers. Everybody tucked in right and tight. They all just had their dinner."

"Good." Maxim tasted the bile in his throat. *Dinner. What a joke.* Still, what else could they have called it? "Can I go see him?"

"Of course. Go ahead. I think he's watching TV right now."

"Right." He walked down the hallway and knocked on room number nine. *Why was he even knocking?* It wasn't as if he was expecting an answer.

His father was in the usual position, lying on his side and staring out the window. His thin white hair lay damp and neat, combed back from his high forehead. He wore the familiar threadbare brown pajamas, the same pair he possessed for fifteen years now. The nurses said he'd throw a fit if they tried to put anything else on. He stayed still most of the time but when he had his fits, he'd thrash around. One time, he almost fell off the bed when the nurse had forgotten to secure the railing.

"Hi, Pops." Maxim bent and kissed his father's sunken cheek. It felt rough and cool and the slight bristles tickled his chin. He inhaled the familiar soft scent of baby shampoo and lifted the shirt a tad to make sure the gastric tube wasn't leaking. "How are you doing today? Nothing new, huh?"

His father stared straight ahead, not blinking. It was the usual silence. No moans or grunts today either. Maxim sighed. *Did Pops even know he was in the room?* Years ago, the doctor had told him there was irreversible brain damage, so Maxim's hopes weren't high. Alas, there wasn't anything he could do except take it one day at a time.

Maxim walked across the room, picked up a loose blanket from the floor, and straightened the stack of books on the nightstand. "Any requests tonight or should we do the usual?" The TV in the corner was blaring *The Biggest Loser*. Maxim switched it off. His father had never been a fan of TV. He didn't know why the nurses kept insisting on turning it on every night. Something about routine and not disrupting it. A bunch of BS if he'd ever heard any.

Maxim pulled out the top book from the stack on the nightstand. "You know, I was listening to Walt on the way here, Pops. Do you want the same CD? Mrs. Olsen can play it for you when I'm not here."

Silence. Utter silence. Maxim pulled a blanket over his dad and leaned close. He heaved a sigh of relief when a breath finally fanned his cheeks. "So do you want your favorite?"

The favorite it was, Maxim decided after getting no answer. He pulled out a chair and sat across from the bed, making sure not to block the window. He began reading and didn't stop until long after his father's eyes closed.

CHAPTER 5

"Why do TV shows always overdramatize the ER?" Riley asked. "You know, most of the time, my job is pretty boring."

"Hey. It's whatever sells," Emma said to her best friend as they finished watching Emma's favorite TV show, *Grey's Anatomy.*

"I wish I could save a life every day." Riley sighed and flicked back her long brown hair. "Instead all I get are back pain patients and snotty kids. Nothing exciting has happened to me in ages."

"You want to work in the prison? I can check if they need another doctor." Emma scooped up the last of her tom yum soup and flipped channels to Lifetime, hoping to catch one of their romantic comedy specials. A commercial was running so she muted the TV. They were sitting on the couch in her studio apartment, eating Thai food after her first day at the prison.

"But there's no ER there, right?" Riley asked as she twirled her Pad Thai noodles with a fork.

"No. But you're double boarded. You can do internal medicine."

"No, thanks. I don't like clinic." Riley took a bite of the noodles. "And I'm not sure how you can work with criminals. Isn't it scary?"

"There're guards everywhere. I feel pretty safe and my loans are being paid off. And besides, I like working with the underserved." Emma turned off the TV when the commercials ended and a cop show appeared.

"Speaking of the underserved, are you sure you can't join Doctors Without Borders?" Riley took a sip of her iced tea. "You told me before you wanted to go."

"Sam needs me more right now."

Riley scoffed. "He's twenty-four, Emma. He's not a baby anymore."

"I'm all he has. I need to make sure he's okay." Emma tugged on her pendant.

"Did you get the chain fixed?" Riley pointed to the necklace.

"Of course. I'd never want to lose it." Her mom had given it to her before she'd died. It was Emma's most precious possession, not for the necklace per se but for what lay inside the locket. She rubbed the smooth border of the heart-shaped pendant. "My mom would've wanted me to do this."

"Your mom's gone, honey." Riley's brown eyes shone with sympathy. "You have to think of yourself now. God knows you've spent enough time taking care of your family."

"My mom was sick. I had to take care of her."

"I know. I'm not talking about when she was sick, Em. I know she needed you then, but even before she was sick, you helped out a lot." Riley pointed an accusing chopstick in the air. "You were busy all the time. Never free to do anything. Always studying or babysitting your brother. Your parents really dumped a lot of responsibility on you."

"Larry was a truck driver. He was never home." *Why the heck was she defending her stepfather?* Still, Riley's accusations were a bit unfair. "And my mom was working three jobs to support us. We didn't have money for a babysitter, Ri. It was only me. And I love Sam. I keep thinking it's my fault, that I could've prevented the whole thing somehow."

"Don't be silly." Riley leaned over and squeezed her arm. "Larry is the culprit, no one else."

"I know. But you know how it is." Emma forced out a smile, trying to forget the past but that awful day flashed through her mind like it'd happened yesterday.

She'd come home to Anaheim early from medical school that Christmas break. Mom was having a good day. The breast cancer hadn't metastasized to her spine yet, so she was still able to walk around. And Sam was nineteen and finally out of juvenile hall, getting ready to restart his life. He'd been there for cocaine abuse and swore to them that he'd stopped using. They were sitting around the Christmas tree, sharing stories and opening presents, like the old days before Larry had gone bonkers. Emma could still see Mom's shocked face when the door crashed open and Larry had charged into the room.

They'd known he was drunk by one look. His clothes hung loosely on his thin frame and his eyes darted wildly around the room before finding their target.

"There you are," he yelled as he staggered over to Sam. "Get up, you idiot. Face me like a man. This is where you've been all this time? Staying here with your worthless mother?"

"Get out of my house," Mom shrieked. Emma rushed to her side but it was too late. Larry had turned their way and was charging at them full speed. In one hand, he waved the poker he'd grabbed from the fireplace.

"This is my house, woman. You stole it from me!"

"Stop, Dad, or I'll shoot." Sam pulled a gun out of his waistband, his eyes wide with fear, his hand shaking.

"Don't, Sam!" Emma shouted.

Larry rushed at them with the poker. Emma stepped in front of her mom and raised her arm to ward off the blow. Two loud pops rang in the air. Larry fell on top of her, his eyes still open as blood seeped through the hole in his chest. It was disgusting, the alcohol fumes mixed with the scent of fresh blood. She never forgot the smell.

The police believed Emma and her mom about Sam defending them but he had a bag of crack cocaine on him and was carrying a gun without a permit. With his juvie record, he wasn't allowed to carry any firearms. Sam swore he wasn't using the cocaine and was only trying to sell it for some money to help with their mom's medical bills. Emma howled her rage at the injustice of it all. Sure, her brother shouldn't have possessed the drugs and selling it was wrong, but his intent had been good. The judge didn't care, however. Sam had been just another black kid with a bad record. He got sentenced to seven years, and their mom had died one year into his term. Her poor mom, who had only ever wanted the best for her children.

Emma wished with all her heart she could relive that time. Maybe she could have calmed Larry down that day. Or if she'd tried to talk to him more when he'd called, demanding to see Sam. Sam had just been released from juvie, and Emma had thought she was protecting him by keeping his father away, but obviously she'd been dead wrong.

Looking back, Larry hadn't been all that bad in the beginning, when he was sober and taking his medications.

Her father had died before she was born, so Emma had been happy to get a stepfather when her mom had remarried. She and her mom were white, so they got a few strange looks from their conservative neighbors when Mom had married a black man. But Mom hadn't cared. She was more concerned about Larry's bipolar state, but he'd been stable on meds when they'd married.

Emma had been five when Sam was born, and she too, like her parents, fell in love with the cute little boy who charmed everyone with his smile and mischievous nature. He was happy all the time, always laughing and whistling, as if the world were his oyster.

Larry turned all his attention on his son, but Emma hadn't minded. Sam was her little brother and her best friend. She'd cheered wildly when he'd taken his first step. She kicked his first soccer ball with him and read tons of books to him when he was a kid. He loved birds from the beginning. She remembered his first drawing was of a mockingbird they'd seen on one of their frequent family camping trips.

The tricolored blackbird, though, became his favorite. He loved its stark colors and its mysterious birdcall. They'd practiced the distinctive birdcall many times together when they were younger. Their mom was a Buddhist and had taught them about reincarnation. Emma thought the whole concept kind of fanciful but Sam loved the idea of coming back to life in a different form. He'd even told her he wanted to be a blackbird in his next life so that he could fly in the open sky. Emma had laughed, thinking he was being silly but Sam's obsession with birds continued. He drew them incessantly and loved to talk about them to anyone who'd listen.

They'd been a happy family until Larry started drinking and stopped taking his meds. He had an extramarital affair, swearing to her mom it was only a one-time thing, but Emma had her suspicions. He'd gone into wild mood swings as well, lashing out at them for no particular reason. He hit her mom a couple of times but her mom hadn't wanted to leave, had wanted to support him. Until the day Larry had hit Emma. Had slapped her across the face when she'd been seventeen for talking back to him.

The divorce was quick but nasty. Her parents had shared custody of Sam, who'd just turned twelve. Larry moved to Compton, and Sam was shipped back and forth from Orange County to LA every weekend. Larry bad-mouthed her mom and her to Sam every chance he got. He continued drinking and soon lost his steady job. Sam always denied it but Emma was sure his father must have struck him sometimes. After all, a leopard didn't change its spots. Child services never found any evidence and Sam only had praises to sing about his old man during his visits. Gradually her brother grew apart from her and started to hang out with the wrong crowd at school.

Gone was the happy little boy of Emma's childhood. Over time, Sam became surly and withdrawn and didn't want to be around her anymore. She wasn't cool enough and was too white. He soon got expelled from high school. Then he got arrested for drug possession one summer while staying with his dad.

At juvenile hall, thank goodness he cleaned up his act and spent his free time drawing again. He mostly focused on birds he'd see from the detention center's grounds. He got clean and sober and earned his GED. Emma taught him to drive and they soon became close again. She'd planned to help him with his college applications that Christmas. That dreaded Christmas when things had gone so wrong.

"Hey you." Riley tapped Emma on the arm. "You have to let it go, Em. I can see the memories are killing you."

"I know." Emma sighed and bit her lower lip. "I just want my brother back."

"Hang in there. Two years and he'll be free." Riley leaned over and gave her a much-needed hug.

"Thanks," Emma said, glad her friend was around. She was going to miss Riley when the Doctors Without Borders group left for Vietnam. "And thanks for bringing over the takeout. You know I can't cook for the life of me."

"I don't know how you can eat like that and keep your figure." Riley's lips curved down at the corners. "It's so unfair. I watch everything I eat and look at me. Lucky I get to wear scrubs at work. They don't show much."

"At least you have curves." Her friend had the perfect hourglass figure. "I'm like a scarecrow. All sticks and bones."

"You look like a model and you know it." Riley threw a pillow at her.

"Yeah. Right. I don't even have boobs."

"You do, too. But you should dress up more." Riley sipped on her iced tea. "Who knows? Maybe Prince Charming is right around the corner."

"Right." Emma shook her head and laughed. "My warden is certainly no Prince Charming."

"Really? That bad, huh? Old and fat? Or my favorite, balding with nose hairs?"

"No. He's actually the opposite." Emma made a face. "He's very fit and kind of handsome. If you like the tall, dark, silent type."

"Ooh." Riley wiggled her eyebrows and shot Emma a suggestive look. "That sounds intriguing."

"Yeah, maybe." A shiver chased down Emma's spine. *Darn, but the man did radiate a certain magnetism.*

"So you might be interested in him?"

"His manners are atrocious." Emma shook her head to chase away her whimsical thoughts. No way could she be attracted to such a brute. She carried the dirty dishes to the sink. "He's too grim, Ri. I'm glad I didn't have to face him during the initial interview."

"Aw. Too bad he's such an ogre. How did you get that job anyway?" Riley finished her tea. "Didn't they do a background check or something? They don't know Sam's your brother, do they?"

"We have different last names. And he's really dark-skinned. I'm white. I don't think anybody's going to suspect anything," Emma said as she loaded the dishwasher. "And you know how I got the job. A lot of patience, scanning the government website every day. Finally one of their doctors retired and in I came. Lucky I just finished residency, too. I have a good resume, you know."

"Good resume, right." Riley scoffed. "You could have gone to Harvard. Yale. Stanford. All the academic hospitals wanted you."

"But Sam isn't there."

"I know. Promise me you'll be careful."

"Of course I will. Don't worry." Emma poured the liquid soap into the dishwasher tray. She turned on the machine and wiped down the counter before checking the fridge. *Yum. Just what she was looking for.* "Want some chocolate cake?" she called over her head. "I got one from Marie Callender's."

"No, thanks. Those extra calories are going to kill me." Riley glanced at her watch. "I have to go, Em. My shift starts at seven tomorrow morning. I'm the only ER doctor on. Text me if you want to chat."

"I can't from the prison. They told me no cell phones. They're considered contraband in there."

"Okay. No worries." Riley put on her coat and grabbed her purse from the counter. "Next time, my place, okay? I'll make sure to lock Hunter in the garage."

"But I feel so bad you have to do that for me. I should be over it by now, don't you think?"

"Don't worry about it." Riley was sympathetic as usual. "Different people have different phobias, Em. Yours happens to be dogs."

"Not all of them. Only the monster huge ones."

"I know. So next time, my place. Hunter will be out of sight." Riley gave her a hug before waving good-bye and heading off.

Emma turned on the radio to her favorite soft rock station before heading back to the small kitchen to cut out a piece of chocolate cake. It'd been good to catch up with Riley. It would have been nice to travel with her to Vietnam but maybe next time. After Sam paroled.

Emma bit down on the delicious chocolate cake. It was sweet, decadent, and rich, exactly as she liked. Her favorite song, "Saving All My Love for You" by Whitney Houston started playing and Emma couldn't help but sing along. Sure, she sounded horrible but no one was around so she didn't mind. Sam was the crooner in their family, a talent he'd inherited from Larry. Did her brother still enjoy singing? She couldn't wait to catch up with him.

The next morning as she approached the prison,

Emma's heart hummed with anticipation. *Respect. Fairness. Accountability. Leadership.* The words were imprinted on large signs posted along the drive up the hill to the parking lot. *How nice to work for those goals.* Maybe there was some rehabilitation at Albatross after all. She parked the car, walked through the parking lot and up a ramp where she opened a single door that led into the Eagle gate checkpoint. There was only one guard stationed behind the paned glass window on the left at the moment, an older man with graying hair and the nametag of Vasquez.

Emma showed Vasquez her state ID and her bag, which he inspected and then after exchanging a chit with him, she was able to get her set of keys. The chit was a coin a little larger than a quarter on which her name was engraved. Julien had warned her she couldn't get her keys without giving up one of her assigned chits. Then at the end of the day, she'd get her chit back when she turned in her keys.

Vasquez buzzed Emma through another door where she waited in a fenced-in area the size of her small living room. After making sure the door behind her was securely locked, the guard buzzed open a wired sliding gate, which finally led her into the prison. So much work for entering and exiting the prison but Emma supposed that was how they made sure things were secure.

A dark-brown and gray bird with bold streaks down its white chest greeted Emma with its song as she climbed the seventy-five steps up the hill. *Nice.* There were so many birds around. And she got free exercise as part of her job. This, on top of having Sam around. Who could have asked for more?

Halfway up the steps, Emma spotted Chambers talking with Dr. Kaye. The CMO was standing a shade too close to the warden, her long, bright red talons on his arm. He didn't seem too pleased by the conversation but maybe that was his usual look. The man always seemed to have a scowl on his face.

"Good morning, Dr. Edwards," Chambers called out to her as she passed.

"Good morning, Mr. Chambers," Emma said, silently cursing her luck. Now she'd have to make conversation when she was already in a hurry to see Sam. Dr. Kaye gave her a fake smile, revealing perfectly straight white teeth. Today she had on a figure-hugging red dress more fit for a party than a prison. Her four-inch heels coupled with her tall physique made her only a few inches shorter than the warden. They made a striking couple: he dark like a fallen angel and she as fair as a Barbie doll.

Chambers left Dr. Kaye's side and homed in on Emma. If she hadn't known any better, she would've thought he was a bit relieved to see her. "You have orientation today, Dr. Edwards. It's starting in a few minutes. Come. I'll take you there."

"No need to take her, Maxim," Dr. Kaye said, her greedy eyes following him. "I'll do it. It's on my way."

"I'll do it. I have to be there anyway to give the first speech."

With that, he indicated for Emma to walk back down the stairs.

"Do you think we can reschedule the training?" She wanted to see Sam, not be in some class. *And did the man have to be so tall?* She had to tilt her head all the way back to look at him. "I have patients to see."

Chambers frowned again. "You can't see patients until you go through the orientation. Didn't Brown tell you?"

"What's the orientation about?" Emma raced to keep up as he headed down the steps.

"It's called IST. Institutional Safety Training." Chambers slowed down only a tad. "It's an annual class for all employees. It teaches you things like prison policy, proper behavior around inmates, how to file a complaint. Most of the people there will be retraining. It's an all-day class, so come on. We don't want to be late."

He sped down the steps with his hands clasped behind his back, never turning around to see if she followed. "We don't have all day."

Emma stomped down the steps, cursing her luck. It looked like there wasn't going to be any time to see Sam today. At the bottom of the steps, they had to exit the main gate and go out again into the parking lot. "Where the heck is the meeting?"

"Back before you make the first turn into the parking lot."

"Way back there?" Emma bit back a groan. "But that's at least a ten-minute walk. Is there a golf cart?"

"Ten minutes is too far for you?" Chambers's eyebrows rose all the way to the top of his forehead. "You're kidding me, right?"

"Just go." *Did he have to sound so superior?* "I'll follow you."

She trekked behind the big brute and soon was out of breath keeping up with his long strides. "Come on," he called after her. "We don't want to be late."

By the time they entered the training building, she was sweating and it was only eight in the morning. The room resembled a big gym, with many long tables laid out in horizontal rows facing a blackboard in the front. A few dozen people were waiting for the class to begin, most of them Custody. Their general chatter crashed to a halt as soon as Chambers entered the room.

Immediately, two men in green jumped out of their seats and sidled up to them with ingratiating smiles. "Why didn't you call? We had the golf cart all ready."

So he did have a taxi. Emma glared at the warden and brushed a hand over her damp forehead. "Where can I sit?"

"Any table is fine." Chambers didn't look too pleased at her sweaty appearance.

Well, tough. You should have slowed down a little, pal. Emma shook her head and bit back a sigh of frustration.

"Rogers, get Dr. Edwards some water," Chambers ordered the man on his left.

"Yes, sir."

"I don't need water." Emma found the farthest table back and wedged herself between two burly officers. There were more open seats up front but no way did she want to be that close to the warden. Rogers immediately brought her a bottle of water.

"Thank you, everyone." Chambers's deep voice boomed from the front of the room. "I want all of you to meet Dr. Emma Edwards, our new doctor."

Emma waved from where she sat, cringing when all eyes turned her way. *Drat the man.* She looked sweaty and unkempt, and of course he had to focus all the attention on her.

"Now, let's get started. How do you know an inmate is lying?" Chambers paused and looked around the room before announcing, "Because his lips are moving."

The crowd burst into laughter and heartily cheered him on. Emma's temperature spiked along with her heart rate. "What a horrible thing to say," she blurted out in a loud voice. A deafening silence blanketed the room.

CHAPTER 6

Chambers whipped those freakish silver eyes to her. "Care to repeat that, Doctor?"

"Yes." Emma stood up. "How can you say something so derogatory?"

"But true." Chambers's commanding voice rose a notch. "I was making a point. Never trust an inmate."

"I'm sure you can trust some."

"How long have you worked in corrections, Doctor?"

"That has nothing to do with it." Emma raised her voice. "What about those signs I saw on the way up here?"

"Signs?"

"Respect. Fairness. Accountability. Leadership," Emma said. "What is leadership without accountability? Without respect? Without fairness? Is it fair that you call all of them liars? That's not good leadership, is it?"

Emma swore she could have heard a pin drop in the room. Sure, she might have gone too far but she was tired of people treating inmates like dirt. Her brother didn't deserve this.

"Enough," Chambers bellowed. "Believe whatever you want. No one really gives a damn. The only thing I care about is your safety. And the safety of every single person who enters this prison."

"Hear, hear, Warden." Shouts erupted from the room. "You go, Mr. Chambers."

An encompassing warmth suffused Emma's face. Chambers clearly was a crowd favorite. The man was rude, arrogant, and prejudiced, but all his minions apparently loved him. She couldn't win here. She sat down and tried to focus on Sam. No need to get riled up over things she couldn't change.

Thank goodness Chambers left after the first hour. The rest of the day was filled with videos and lectures about carrying your whistle and alarm at all times and not having relationships with inmates. Sexual harassment had to be reported and supervisors shouldn't date their employees. Coworkers could date but must keep their relationship at home and not carry it into work.

It all seemed like common sense. Emma didn't understand why they couldn't say it in five minutes instead of eight hours. At last the torture ended and she drove home with a migraine.

The next morning, Emma walked into work determined to see Sam again. She figured the best place to find him would be to work in Unit 3, which would cover his dorm. *Perhaps the current Unit 3 doctor would call in sick?* She got her wish, for Dr. Pan did call in sick but unfortunately Dr. Ross was also a no-show.

"You'll have to cover both Urgent Care and Unit 3," the evil Dr. Kaye told her at their doctors' morning meeting.

"But that's a little too much, don't you think?" Julien tried to defend her. "It's her first day seeing patients."

"Didn't you say she had a top-notch education?" The CMO's red lips thinned. "Let's see what she can handle."

"No problem." Emma forced out a smile. *Anything was worth it for a chance to see Sam.*

Two hours later, she found herself running between the Urgent Care and Unit 3 clinic like a headless chicken. Three men had gotten admitted to the Housing Unit overnight and as the Urgent Care provider, she had to cover them, too. This, in addition to taking care of Mr. Nash, the liver cancer patient, almost tipped Emma over the edge.

"Don't work so hard, Doc," Mr. Nash said in his thready voice when she stopped by to see if he needed anything. Today the poor man looked grayer and frailer than before. The sharp contours of his ribs were visible beneath his worn shirt.

"I'll try not to." Emma pulled out a chair to sit next to the dingy bed. She shivered and hugged her white coat closer. "You want me to turn on the heater for you, sir? It's so cold in here."

"It doesn't work." Mr. Nash tugged a thin blanket halfway up his chest.

"Really?" Emma stood up. "I'll call maintenance right now. They have to fix it. You'll freeze in here."

Her patient reached out a bony hand and scratched at his blanket. "They called already, but you know how it is. The state takes forever."

"Well, let me get you a couple of extra blankets at least." Emma stepped out of the room. *Surely she could make his last days more comfortable.*

"Hey, Doc." Vincent, the charge nurse, interrupted her halfway down the hall. "Inmate Jones wants more pain meds. He's the one who had the hernia surgery. And we have a code brown in room four. Toilet backed up. Could be norovirus. Did they talk about it this morning in your conference? We need Public Health."

"No." Emma shook her head. "Nobody said anything about diarrhea. How many patients?"

"Four so far, admitted last night. You want me to call Public Health?"

"Sure. They need contact isolation. Can we do that here?"

"We can try," Vincent said as he headed back down the hall. "Inmate crew is cleaning up the mess."

"Wait." Emma hurried after him. "Is somebody going to fix the toilet?"

"Yes, we called maintenance already."

"Ask them to fix the heater in room eight, too. It's freezing in there. How do I get Mr. Nash some blankets?"

"Ask Lexi, the clerk." Vincent headed toward room four. "And Doc, don't forget hernia man."

Emma nodded and entered the nursing station where she found the clerk in her usual spot. "Lexi, Mr. Nash needs some extra blankets."

"Mr. Nash?"

"Yes. Room eight."

"Oh. I thought he was still in the hospital." She shrugged her shoulders and gazed back at the computer screen. "Sure. I'll get them in a minute."

"Now, please." Emma gritted her teeth.

"Oh, all right." The secretary heaved a big sigh and dragged herself out of her chair. "I don't think we have any extras. Let's ask the porter."

"Oh, for heaven's sake, I'll check myself. Where do I look?"

"Closet farthest down the hall on the left." Lexi settled back in her chair again. "But Morris can check for you."

Emma stumbled as her world tilted. "Morris?"

"Yes. The black porter. The other ones aren't free right now." Lexi pulled out a bag of pumpkin seeds and started snapping on one. "He's probably down the hall trying to clean room four. Want me to call him?"

"Uh, sure," Emma said, her heart rate picking up a notch. *Calm down.* It was a common name. No way could it be her Sam. But Lexi had said black. But at least half the inmates were black. She shouldn't get her hopes up.

"You called for me?" *His voice.*

Emma whipped her head around. There he was, in the flesh, holding a mop in one hand and a bucket in the other. His beautiful, sad, brown eyes gazed back at her.

"Yes." Lexi snapped through another pumpkin seed, her eyes glued to the YouTube video playing on the computer screen. "Get Dr. Edwards some blankets, will you?"

"Yes, ma'am." Her brother shot her an anxious look before walking down the hall.

Emma hastened after him. "Sam," she breathed out when she got close enough. "How are you?"

He shook his head and kept walking. Emma paced beside him, oblivious of everything, even the stench emanating from room four.

"Let's talk," she said.

"Not now," he whispered.

They reached a large supply closet at the end of the hall. Sam opened it and reached for some blankets. Emma stepped inside the room and pulled him in after her, slamming the door shut. The tears clogged at her throat. *After all this time.* Emma threw her arms around her brother and held on tight. He felt so thin. Much thinner than before.

Sam hugged her for only a few seconds before pulling back. "Emma, what are you doing here?"

"I came to see you, of course." She touched his cheek.

"I'm in a prison, Em. You can't be here."

"I was worried. You stopped writing." *She could hardly believe it. Sam. She was never going to let go of him now.*

"Em, if they see you with me, you're gonna get in trouble. You gotta get out of here."

"And miss a chance to spend time with you? No way."

"For God's sake, Em. Trust me. You don't belong here." He combed a hand through his frizzy black hair. "You're going to get hurt. These guys are vicious."

"Did the other inmates hurt you?" Emma anxiously scanned his body for signs of injury. "Is that why you stopped writing?"

"Come on, Em." Sam held her face between his hands. Her throat felt tight. "If they catch us together, you're toast. They'll fire you and might even take your license away."

"Don't worry. I'll tell them the truth, nothing bad about that."

"Don't ever do that." Sam covered her mouth with his large hand. "Don't let anyone know about our relationship. We can't be seen together."

Emma pulled off his hand. "Why not? It's not like I'm trying to spring you from prison. I just want to know you're okay."

"I'm fine. If they know about us, they'll separate us for sure. Probably transfer you to a different prison."

"What?"

"Yes. They're really strict about these things."

It took a moment to digest the unwelcome news. "Fine,

I won't tell anyone." Emma squeezed his hand. "But we can talk, can't we? If you work here, I'll see you every day."

"Don't let them think there's anything between us." Sam wrapped an arm around her shoulder. "I'm going to make it out of here. Don't worry. I gotta go."

"Okay. I love you." Before she had a chance to hug him again, he'd slipped out. *If only they had some more time together.* She swallowed a couple of times and then exited the closet.

"There you are." Vincent stared at her from the other side. Her heart thundered. *Had he seen Sam, too?* "We've been looking for you."

"Sorry." Emma lifted the blankets and forced out a smile. "I finally found the blankets. What's up?"

"Hernia guy's still whining. Can you see him?" Vincent took the blankets from her. "I'll give these to Nash."

Emma gazed down the hall. Sam was picking up a mop and bucket a few yards away. *Her baby brother. Safe.* She blinked back some tears. He seemed okay. Maybe he'd been busy the last few months. Maybe he hadn't had time to write. But busy in prison? Doing what? Something must have happened to him and she needed to know what it was. He didn't look like her easy, care-free brother. There were shadows underneath those eyes, a certain somberness to him she hadn't noticed before. Was he afraid of something? What could it be? But the important thing was he was alright. And she was going to make sure he stayed alright for the rest of his sentence. But there was no time to dwell on that now. The hernia patient was still waiting.

Mr. Jones turned out to be a twenty-five-year-old obese man with a huge nose and dull blue eyes hidden behind spectacles. He lay on the bed picking his nose while reading a magazine, looking quite comfortable until he saw her.

"Where have you been, Doc?" he asked in a whiny, nasal voice. "I'm dying in here."

"You must be Mr. Jones. I'm Dr. Edwards." Usually she would have extended her hand but the nose picking killed that idea. "Where do you hurt?"

"Everywhere," he moaned, pointing a chubby finger from his head to his toe. "I need some Vicodin or something. The Motrin ain't doing nothing."

Emma did a quick exam. Everything was normal. She reassured him of this, but he kept demanding narcotics. She agreed to give him some Tylenol #3 but back at the nursing station she learned that he was an "N" number, a narcotic commitment, someone incarcerated due to drug addiction. Not wanting to foster his addiction, she cancelled the T3 and told him he'd get Motrin instead.

"I already know it doesn't work," Jones whined as soon as he heard the news. "I need the T3, Doc. Come on, be nice for once."

"Believe me, I'm trying to do what's best for you." Emma escaped before the man could say anything else.

Out in the hallway, at least twenty inmates sitting on the wooden bench stretched against the wall were grumbling about the long wait.

"Are all those patients waiting to see me?" Emma asked her LVN, a Filipino man named Bill who was holding a tall stack of green charts by her desk when she entered Dr. Pan's office.

"Yes." He placed the charts on the desk. "The outside waiting room is full, so Custody brought the men back here. Ready for your first patient?"

"Sure." Emma sighed. *It was going to be a long day.*

The office was large, about twenty by twenty with an old, wooden desk laid out in one corner, an exam table against the wall to the right of the desk, and a sink to the left of the entrance. An old-fashioned heater spewing out hot steam lay between the desk and the exam table. Some electric cords from the EKG machine stretched across the heater on their way to the plug near the desk. That didn't look safe at all.

A loud clanging explosion suddenly rang out. Emma ducked and covered her head with her hands.

CHAPTER 7

"It's okay, Doc," Bill said in an amused voice. "It's the heater making noises. No big deal."

The loud clanging burst out again. It sounded like someone hammering on metal right next to her head. At least it hadn't been the electrical fire Emma had feared. She pointed to the cords. "Are you sure that's okay? They're so close to the steam."

Bill shrugged and pulled out the plug. "No worries. I'm sure it's safe but if it makes you feel better, we'll pull it out."

"Alright." *Clang. Clang. Clang.* Emma rubbed her temples. "Does that go on for a long time?"

"Usually not." Bill handed over a green tome that looked like a phonebook. "Let me get your first patient. He has liver problems from hep C. It's pretty common here."

The enormous chart belonged to Mr. Barkley, an older man recently discharged from the county hospital who was sixty but looked more like eighty. He had cirrhosis with abdominal swelling, intermittent confusion from his end-stage liver disease, as well as recurrent vomiting up blood, the reason he stayed in the hospital recently. She flipped through the mostly illegible chart, which was at least four inches thick. And that was only the fifth volume. The other four lay stashed in a box by her feet. Emma shuddered and took in a deep breath.

"Do you know why you're here, Mr. Barkley?" she asked.

"What?" The man's rheumy eyes closed as he nodded off. *Clang! Clang! Clang!*

"Yes?" Mr. Barkley snapped his eyes open. "Who's shooting?"

Emma glanced at the vital signs. No temperature recorded. But blood pressure only eighty-six. His huge abdomen protruded like a swollen balloon under his shirt. His belly probably needed to be drained again. The man could be septic for all she knew.

Clang! Clang! Clang! Emma squeezed the bridge of her nose. "What's your name, sir?"

"Gary," he mumbled, nodding off again. She felt his forehead and winced. He felt as hot as that heater.

Emma darted out of the room, trying her best to ignore the sea of angry faces glaring at her from the bench as she dashed into the nurse's office. "Bill! Mr. Barkley's really sick."

"What? He was fine a few minutes ago." Bill flipped another page in his car magazine. "The guy's confused sometimes. No big deal."

"Get a wheelchair to move him to Urgent Care. Why didn't you take his temp? I think he's septic."

"Are you sure? He always looks that way." Bill finally abandoned the magazine and accompanied her across the hall.

"He's hypotensive with a fever. Come on, help me move him." Emma touched the man's forehead again. *Damn.*

She should have seen him earlier. But she hadn't known he was that sick. She reached for his wrist. *Thank goodness.* The pulse was thready but at least present.

"Here's the wheelchair, Doc." Sam stood in front of her.

Emma couldn't help the relieved smile that came to her face. "Thank you. You're Morris, right?" She remembered at the last minute to pretend not to know him.

"Yes, ma'am." With the help of another inmate, they transferred Mr. Barkley to the wheelchair. "You want him down in Urgent Care, Doctor?"

"Yes, please." Her hand brushed over Sam's during the transport. An image of Sam moving their mom into a similar wheelchair flashed before her eyes. Her mom had been so slight, probably half the size of Mr. Barkley here.

"Him, again?" Ms. Bryant scowled as soon as she saw them. "That's the fourth time this month."

"Fifth if you count the ER visit the other day," Ms. Carter added.

"I need an IV stat. And 1L normal saline bolus. And hook him up to a monitor," Emma ordered, hurrying over to examine Mr. Barkley as soon as Sam and the other inmate laid him on the gurney.

"You know he drank like a fish, right?" Ms. Bryant clucked her tongue. "He's never getting a new liver. Might as well let him die in peace."

"Nobody's dying. Not on my watch." Emma pressed on the patient's protuberant abdomen, eliciting a loud groan. "Call an ambulance. He probably has an abdominal infection, SBP. Where's my IV?"

"No veins," Ms. Carter announced. "Last time we had to put one in his foot."

"Look at least. You don't know 'til you try."

The nurses took their time gathering their IV equipment. Blood pressure now eighty. Emma grabbed a nearby tourniquet and tied it on the man's left arm. *Damn it.* No vein. And none on the right arm either.

"Careful, Doc." Sam spoke up from her left. "He has hep C."

"Nobody asked for your opinion. Get out of here, Morris," Ms. Carter snapped.

Emma gave Sam a sympathetic look as he left. She tilted the gurney down so the patient's head was more toward the floor. *Yup, worked every time.* There it was. The external jugular. She wiped the area with an alcohol pad and slipped in a sixteen gauge. It flushed beautifully.

"Wow." Ms. Bryant beamed. "I haven't seen an EJ done in years. Last time I think was when Mr. Chambers did it."

"The warden?" Emma hung the normal saline and squeezed in the first bolus. Surely her ears were playing tricks on her. *What did that beast of a man know about IVs, least of all where to put them?*

"Yeah. The man was an EMT before he went into corrections," Ms. Carter said. "Can you believe it? He's so talented."

"He beats up inmates." *Nice. Blood pressure was going up now.* Maybe she shouldn't talk about the warden with them but somebody had to bring him down a peg or two.

"Only when the inmates deserve it," Ms. Bryant said as she got off the phone. "Ambulance is on its way."

"He looks so handsome when he knocks them down." Ms. Carter wiggled her eyebrows. "All tough and manly."

"For goodness' sake." Emma rolled her eyes. "Handsome? Are you kidding me? The guy is like a barbarian."

"Don't hold back, Doc," a sarcastic voice came from the doorway. "Tell them how you really feel."

Damn. She couldn't mistake that deep voice. *What was it with her luck today?*

She was sure her face was as red as a beet. "Hello, Mr. Chambers." He looked as formidable as ever in a pristine blue suit with a silver tie that matched the exact shade of his unusual eyes.

"Doctor." He nodded his head. The two minions by his side stepped back a notch to let him enter the room. "Didn't you learn anything during orientation yesterday? No gossiping at work."

"We weren't gossiping. I just put in an EJ and—"

Mr. Barkley suddenly flailed out his right arm.

"Hey, watch it." Emma pushed the arm down. "Don't pull out the IV, sir. You need it."

"Get it off." With surprising strength, he flicked her hand off and dove again for his neck.

"Stop him." Emma grabbed his arm with both hands. The old man tried to spit at her, but luckily she dodged in time. "You got any Ativan? Give him one milligram stat," she yelled at the nurses.

"You heard the doctor. Get the Ativan." Chambers was at her side in an instant. He pushed down on Mr. Barkley, who was now thrashing about like a fish out of water.

"Step back, Doc." Chambers's warm breath feathered her cheek. Up close, his eyes looked more gray than silver. "You'll get hurt. Move." He shoved her out of the way.

Emma staggered back, reeling. *Couldn't the man be more civil?* She had the situation under control. All she needed was the Ativan, which Ms. Bryant was pushing in right now.

Chambers's two minions in green jumped forward in unison. "Sir, you want us to tie him down?" the shorter one asked.

"No." Emma put out a protesting hand. "The Ativan is going to kick in in a minute. We don't need restraints."

"Sir?" the taller guard questioned from the foot of the gurney, where he was holding down the legs.

"Just get them ready." Chambers's eyes swung to the monitor.

At least the blood pressure wasn't low anymore. Luckily the ambulance crew arrived at that moment and took over. Emma sighed in relief and briefed them on Mr. Barkley, who slowly but surely began to calm down.

The older EMT held onto the neck line to make sure it was secure as they lifted the patient onto the ambulance gurney. "Glad you guys got the IV. We couldn't get it in last time. The ER doctors had to put in a central line."

"Dr. Edwards did it in one go." Ms. Carter flicked a glance at Chambers, who looked as disapproving as ever. "She reminded me of you, sir."

"Is that meant to be a compliment?" Chambers asked.

Surely he was joking? Emma caught his eye and grimaced. She should've known. The man's face was as straight and stiff as a board.

"Can I help you with something?" Emma tried as hard as possible to sound gracious but man, did he push all her buttons.

The paramedics pushed their now sleeping patient out the doorway.

"What's going on with the diarrhea cases?" Chambers asked, his silver eyes piercing down at her. "Is it norovirus?"

"I don't know." Emma took off her gloves and tossed them into a nearby red trashcan.

"You don't know?" His voice raised a notch. "That's your best answer?"

"Yes." *Damn.* She'd totally forgotten about the code brown. She wiped a hand across her sweaty forehead and flicked a resentful glance at Chambers's still pristine suit.

"When will you know?"

"When I get some tests back."

"When will that be?"

"I have to see the patients first." She turned her back on him.

"You haven't seen them yet?"

"No." She shoved her hands under the sink and switched on the water. *Couldn't the man leave her alone?* She'd see the diarrhea cases now and order some stool cultures, if the brute would stop with his endless questions.

"Look, I'll go check it out right—" Emma turned and slammed into what felt like a brick wall. *Why was Chambers standing so close?* Her foot slipped and his arms swallowed her up in one swoop. A brief, all-encompassing warmth surrounded her. Like an electric blanket.

"Watch where you're going." Chambers pushed her back as if she were contaminated.

Emma scoffed. "You're the one who's in the way. Can't I get some space around here?"

"The nurses were moving the gurney." He cocked his head to where the gurney lay wedged against the corner.

"Right." *The clinic was way too tight, and what was that wonderful smell she'd inhaled in his arms? Coffee beans. Her favorite drink.* Emma turned away in a hurry. "I'll be down the hall in room four."

"I need you to see the diarrhea cases."

"I am. They're in room four." *Good thing he didn't seem to notice her discomfiture. Why did he have to smell so warm and inviting?*

"Good. Report to me when you're done."

"I have a whole clinic left to see. We'll send stool cultures. They won't be back for a couple of days."

"A couple of days?" His eyes drew together in a frown. "That's too long."

"That's the way it is." *Coffee or not, the man still was downright overbearing.* "Don't worry. They'll be in isolation until then. So no one else can catch it, even if it's norovirus."

"Not good enough," he insisted. "We need to know today. Last time, several dorms got sick and an inmate almost died."

"We'll isolate all new cases." *Drat.* Maybe she'd misjudged him. He seemed to care for his inmates after all. "Public Health is on board. We only have a few patients so far."

"Headquarters won't like it. They want this thing resolved now."

"Headquarters?"

"Sacramento. They've been calling me all morning, wanting answers."

Something in Emma's chest deflated. *She should've known.* He didn't really care about the patients. No, not at all. Mr. High and Mighty was more concerned about his image, about how he looked to his bosses. "Well, tell them whatever you want. But we won't know for sure for a few days." She left and went down the hall to room four.

Pathetic. She was pathetic. One warm, incredibly nice hug (if she could even call it that), and she was about to forgive him for all his sins. Maybe she needed more human contact. It'd been a year since she'd dated John, and he'd been her only serious boyfriend. Her medical school and residency schedules had been too packed to go out much.

"Hey, Doc." A heavily tattooed, angry-looking man on the bench raised his beefy arm. "When are you gonna see me? I've been here since nine o'clock."

"Yeah. Me, too."

"We've been waiting for hours. We didn't even have lunch yet," someone else added.

"Sorry, gentlemen." Emma checked the time. Two twenty already. No wonder they were upset. But the diarrhea cases had to come first.

She spied the stack of yellow gowns and gloves outside room four and donned both of them before entering the room. The four patients were in their respective beds, watching TV. *General Hospital, of all things.* Grown men watching soap operas? She'd never believe it if she hadn't seen it with her own eyes.

"Aw, Doc," the youngest patient said when she switched off the TV. "That was the best part. We're about to find out who the father is."

"Sorry. I need to talk to you. I'm Dr. Edwards." Emma adjusted her gloves. "When did you start having diarrhea?"

It turned out their symptoms began two to three days ago. Some had abdominal pain and vomiting. Some hadn't. They resided in different dorms but all had attended the same substance abuse program together. After examining them, Emma asked for stool samples whenever they went again. She flipped the TV back on, disposed of her gown and gloves, and walked out, relieved that at least the men's symptoms weren't too bad. Back at the nursing station, she washed her hands and wrote orders for stool cultures and strict contact isolation.

"Where's Vincent?" she asked a middle-aged nurse sitting at the main desk.

"He's left already. His shift's from six to two." The woman slurped down some won ton soup from a plastic bowl. "You must be the new doc. I'm Ms. Marcs."

Emma's stomach grumbled. The sizzling soup smelled heavenly. Her packed lunch lay in the cabinet in Urgent Care. She could get it and wolf it down in two minutes, but the grumbling escalated outside. She downed a cup of water from the dispenser instead and prayed for patience.

"Mr. Ransom?" she called out.

The heavily tattooed man stood up. "About time, too."

He was almost twice her size, topping her by over a head. She ushered him into the office and closed the door. Goosebumps popped up on her arms. He looked aggressive. Tattoos littered not only his face but also his neck and ears.

"Have a seat," she said, trying hard not to look at the curse word tattooed across his forehead. His hair was oily and slicked back with some slime, his arms huge, bulging with muscles. "I'm Dr. Edwards. I'm covering for Dr. Pan. You saw the nurse recently?" She tried to read his chart simultaneously to save time.

"I saw the fucking nurse. Not that she did shit for me."

"Hey, tone it down with the language," Emma said, feeling for her alarm. Thank goodness she'd remembered looping it around her belt this morning. The guy gave her the creeps with the way he was staring at her, like Hannibal Lector come to life.

"Or else what?" He stretched his lips, revealing uneven yellow teeth. "What are you gonna do? Give me a time-out?"

"What can I do for you today, Mr. Ransom?"

"Pan never gave me the low bunk." He leaned over the desk and stared hard at her. "I need it."

"Why do you need it?"

"Because my back hurts. Every day." He cursed again. "Write it and I'll be out of your way."

"Do you have seizures?"

"No."

"Did you have any surgeries recently? Are you visually impaired?" Emma recited the list she'd learned that morning.

"No. Do I look like I'm blind?" His face turned red. "Give me the fucking chrono."

"Calm down." *Jesus. He was as angry as hell.* Emma moved her index finger over the alarm button. His beady eyes took in her gesture, and he settled back in his chair. She breathed out a sigh of relief. "Don't make me use it."

"Alright." He held up his hands. "Like I said, write the chrono and I'll get out of your way."

"Tell me about your back pain."

"Nothing to tell. Just give me the chrono." His face flushed red again as his hands clenched into fists.

"Calm down, Mr. Ransom. I can't give you the chrono until I examine you first."

"No. You're not examining me." He shoved his chair back. "Give me that chrono."

"I can't. You need a good reason to get one."

Suddenly he lurched forward and grabbed her wrist. His meaty hand squeezed like a vise. Fire danced up her arm. Just like with the pit bull years earlier. She fumbled for the alarm with her other hand and pressed hard. A loud buzz rang out.

"You fucking bitch! I'll show you a good reason." Ransom flung her wrist away and lunged for her neck. Emma ducked. She tried to stab her pen into his neck, but it missed and bounced off him like a Ping-Pong ball.

"Help!" she screamed. "Someone help!"

CHAPTER 8

A slew of bright stars flashed behind Emma's eyes as Ransom slammed her against the wall. Her head exploded with pain. Suddenly a horde of officers rushed into the room. Someone yanked the brute off of her. Emma collapsed to the floor, dazed, her hand throbbing. She shut her eyes tight and put her head between her legs.

"Are you okay?" The gentlest of hands were prodding at her.

"Sam?" She groaned and forced her eyes open.

Chambers's stark face frowned back at her. "Did he hurt you? Are you okay?" His formidable face radiated with tension yet his eyes had the most peculiar light in them. He was kneeling on the floor, his body almost touching her but not quite.

"I'm fine." Emma shook her head, trying to chase away the roaring in her ears. At least half a dozen other officers were in the room but she didn't see Ransom anywhere. "Where is he?" she asked, her voice trembling.

"He's at the tank, on his way to the hole," Chambers said.

"Hole?"

"Isolation over in Chino. We don't have it here. Don't worry. He's in a holding cell right now and is never coming back."

"Thanks." Emma forced out a smile. She felt the strangest desire to throw herself into his arms and feel that warmth again. The blow must have affected her more than she thought. She rubbed her head. The fire started again in her arm. "Ow."

"What is it?"

She stood and Chambers immediately extended his hand. "Careful. You shouldn't move 'til the paramedics get here."

"What? I don't need an ambulance." Emma plopped into the closest chair. Her wrist throbbed like crazy but all she needed was an X-ray, not the ER.

Clang! Clang! Clang!

"What the hell is that?" Chambers asked.

Emma rubbed her temple with her good hand. *Yes, definitely a full-blown migraine.* Zigzag lines crisscrossed in front of her eyes.

"It's the heater," Ms. Marcs said from the doorway. "Are you okay, Dr. Edwards? You want us to wheel you to the Urgent Care? You can wait there. The ambulance should be here any minute."

"I'm fine." She winced as another clang burst out. "I have a migraine. And my wrist hurts."

"Where?" Chambers gently prodded her wrist and asked her to wiggle her fingers. "They can get the X-ray in the ER."

"I don't need the ER," she said again as another clanging sound erupted. The noise was going to kill her. She had to get out of here. Emma stood and took a tentative step. A wave of light-headedness slammed into her, almost knocking her over. Before she knew it, Chambers had swung her up in his arms like a sack of potatoes.

"What are you doing?" she shrieked, twisting in his arms. "I can walk. Put me down."

Chambers only grunted and kept going. The other officers hurried after them as he carried her down the hall to the Urgent Care.

"Where the hell is that ambulance?" Chambers bellowed as he placed her gently on the gurney in the main treatment room.

"They said ETA is fifteen minutes." Ms. Marcs wrapped a blood pressure cuff around Emma's arm.

"I'm going to the tank." Chambers shot a peremptory look at the nurse. "Don't let her get out of that gurney."

"Never saw him this worked up before." Ms. Marcs shook her head as Chambers exited. She handed Emma an ice pack. "Ransom is going to get the beating of his life. Poor Mr. Chambers is probably going to get suspended."

"What?" Emma's heart slammed against her chest. "Suspended? Why?"

"He likes to take justice in his own hands." Ms. Marcs clucked her tongue. "Last time he beat up an inmate, they gave him a warning. This time I'm sure it's going to be worse."

"Please call him back."

"He's not going to listen."

"Well, he should." Emma slid out of the gurney. She grabbed the railing as a wave of light-headedness hit her. "I'm not going to sit around and watch him get in trouble on my account. Where is he?"

"You can't leave, Doc." Ms. Marcs rushed to her side. "He'll kill me if he sees you out there."

"Then go find him." Now her brain felt like it was on fire. *Why was she still hearing that clanging sound when it was back in the other room?* "Tell him I'm going to go look for him. Unless he comes back right now."

"Just stay in that gurney." Ms. Marcs helped her lie back on the stretcher. "I can't promise anything." The nurse clucked her tongue again before heading out.

The ice pack felt cool and refreshing against the soreness in her wrist. *Clang! Clang! Clang!* Emma winced and closed her eyes, wishing she'd asked for a Motrin. *Oh, God.* She hoped Chambers wasn't going to lose his job because of her.

"Em, are you okay?"

Emma opened her eyes.

Sam stood next to her, his eyes lit with concern. "What did that bastard do to you?"

"It's just my wrist. I'm fine."

"You don't deserve this." He darted a glance at the doorway and squeezed her arm. "Find another job, Em. You shouldn't be here."

"It's only a sprain."

"Listen." He shot another look to the entranceway. "I gotta go. My shift ended already. Custody will kill me if they find me here. Promise me, Em. Go home and don't come back. I'll write, I promise."

"I'm not leaving."

"What the hell is going on in here?" Chambers loomed in the doorway, his fulminating glare directed straight at her brother.

"I called him to get me another ice pack," Emma said hastily. "Thanks, Morris. You can go now." She tried to reassure her brother with a smile.

"Yes, Doc." Sam bent his head and scurried out of the room.

Poor boy. She hoped he wasn't going to get in trouble over this.

"You're okay?" Chambers asked, his breath a little short, as if he'd run all the way here.

"Of course. Why?" Emma forced out a smile.

"She said you passed out, that she couldn't wake you up."

"Oh. Sorry." Emma swallowed. The guy looked like he was about to explode. "Please don't get mad at Ms. Marcs. I told her to get you. You didn't do anything to Ransom yet, did you?"

"No. I was about to but that damned nurse came in, swearing that you were unconscious." Chambers's scowl deepened. "Now the guy's on his way to the hole, with his nose and face still in place. Damn it. He almost killed you."

"So he'll be punished. He's going to the hole, right?" Emma licked her lips. So much raw rage emanated from the man. "Ms. Marcs said you may get suspended if you do anything to him."

"That damned nurse should keep her mouth shut."

"Excuse me. The ambulance is here," Ms. Marcs said in a small voice. She flicked a nervous glance the warden's way and stayed clear out of his path. Luckily he didn't seem to pay her any attention, his eyes fixed on the EMTs entering the room.

It turned out to be the same crew who had transported Mr. Barkley earlier, Robertson and Garcia.

"Hey, Doc. You hurt?" Garcia asked, his friendly face filled with concern.

"Only my wrist." She held up her right hand. "How's Mr. Barkley? Is he okay?"

"Abdominal infection, like you called it. He's in ICU, but doing okay, last we heard."

"ICU? Why? Is he on pressors?" *The poor man.* Pressors didn't bode well.

"Not sure if his blood pressure needed the pressors. But probably. It was really low when we left him."

"I don't know who the hell Barkley is and I don't want to know," Chambers said. "Stop wasting time and take her to the hospital."

"I only need an X-ray," Emma insisted. "Is there an urgent care walk-in clinic close by? Too bad I can't order my own X-ray here."

"She got slammed against the wall." Chambers stepped closer and gave her his usual scowl. "She's been complaining of a headache and can barely walk."

"I have a migraine. I don't need the hospital."

"Let's do a quick exam, shall we?" Robertson shined a light in her eyes and asked her a few simple questions. "She looks all right to me," he pronounced.

Chambers emitted a low, disapproving growl.

"Can you stand up and walk?" Garcia asked hastily.

"Sure." Emma sat up slowly, knowing she'd better pull this off. *Good, the pain had subsided a lot.* Her head no longer felt like a pressure cooker. A few more steps and then she'd be home free. She took a deep breath and put one foot in front of the other. A wave of nausea swept over her. She grabbed the closest object, which happened to be Chambers's arm. He steadied her with his hands, and the next thing she knew, she was retching all over his pristine suit.

"Oh, my God." Her face felt like a furnace. "I'm so sorry." She tried to wipe the slime away, which unfortunately only made it smear even more. Her cursed stomach chose that moment to heave again.

"Here." Someone shoved a kidney basin her way and luckily Chambers's suit was spared another attack.

"Sit down," Chambers said in a flat voice. "You're going to fall."

And Emma was sure he wouldn't catch her this time. Not if he dared risk another slime attack. She lay down and closed her eyes, eternally glad she didn't have to look at him. At least the nausea subsided a little bit.

"Can somebody please just take me home?" she asked, not caring that her voice came out in a whine. "Maybe Dr. Brown? I need to sleep it off. I'll take the X-ray tomorrow."

"Brown left early today. His kid's sick," Chambers said. "Pack her up, gentlemen. You know she needs to go."

"Uh, Doc." Garcia's voice sounded close to her right ear. "I'm afraid your boss is right. Better be safe than sorry."

"Alright. Fine." Emma kept her eyes closed. There was no point arguing. Chambers was never going to leave her alone until she complied, and God knew he probably wanted to go home to change as soon as possible. That was the least she could do for him.

"Something wrong with your eyes?" Chambers's voice sounded only a foot away.

The stench of vomit was overwhelming. She turned her face away and held her breath. *Dear God, could this day get any worse?*

"The light hurts." It was partially true but the main reason was looming right next to her. "Please go away. You stink." *Damn. Had she just said that out loud?* Emma groaned in mortification.

The stench receded, but she was definitely not going to open her eyes. Chambers probably thought she was a major catastrophe. A major *rude* catastrophe.

She felt the paramedics lift her onto another stretcher. They strapped her down with some belts and began rolling her out of the room. They halted near the exit to say something to the guards. Emma didn't smell any more vomit. Probably safe to open her eyes now. *Drat.* Chambers's silver eyes stared right back at her. He'd shed his jacket and was in a blue long-sleeved dress shirt.

"Why are you still here?" Emma squeaked out, knowing her face was probably as red as a lobster.

"Close your eyes. The lights are pretty bright out here."

"You okay, Doc?" Ms. Marcs stood on the other side of the gurney. She gave the warden a wary glance. "All the patients are asking about you. Wishing you the best."

"The patients?" Emma couldn't help but smile. *At least she wasn't a complete disaster.* "Who are we talking about?"

"Well, all the guys in room four, and even grumpy hernia man. And Mr. Nash too."

"Mr. Nash." She reached out a hand. "Is his heater fixed? It was freezing in there this morning."

"Afraid not." The nurse shook his head. "Maintenance takes forever sometimes."

"But it's so cold in there. I don't think the blankets will be enough." Emma tried to get up but the belts were too tight. "Can you move him to a warmer room?"

"All the rooms with heaters are full."

"He can't be in that room." Emma chafed against the belts. "Give me the list of patients. Maybe I can discharge someone so you can transfer him."

"Stop moving." Chambers stilled her hands with his big paw. He seemed remarkably unfazed for a man she'd thrown up all over on. "You're not discharging anyone. We're going to the hospital, remember?"

"But he'll freeze in that room. And I'm feeling better already. A few more minutes isn't going to hurt."

"Smith," Chambers bellowed. His familiar minion magically appeared. "Call Maintenance and tell them I want Nash's heater fixed. Today. And tell them to get rid of that infernal clanging sound, too."

"Yes, sir." The man dashed off, eager to do his duty.

"Ready to go?" The EMTs pushed the gurney outside, where a medium-sized ambulance greeted them. *Odd.* She thought it was evening already as so much had happened, but the sun was still bright.

"What's the matter? Does the sun hurt your eyes?"

"No. I mean, only a little bit." Emma hated how one lie spiraled into the next. "Sorry about your suit. You don't have to go with me. I'll be fine."

"It's policy. One of us has to go with you." His eyes blazed at her. "And how could you worry about my suit? That bastard almost killed you. I'll follow in my car." With that, he abruptly left and the paramedics loaded her into the ambulance.

After a short ride, they finally arrived at the emergency room. Some techs wheeled her to the trauma suite, a huge freezing room with monitors everywhere. Emma was fishing for a pen in her massive purse to fill out the paperwork when Chambers entered.

"Has anyone seen you yet?" He loomed over her.

"No." *Damn.* The pen was nowhere in sight and her hand was hurting again.

"Here, use mine." Chambers handed her a fancy engraved fountain pen and kept looking at her with his strange eyes.

Why didn't he say anything? Maybe he wasn't in a chatting mood. Come to think of it, she wouldn't be either if she'd been vomited on and forced to go to the ER for an employee who wasn't even that sick. She tried to concentrate on the paperwork.

"Ow." Emma dropped the pen. Her hand hurt like hell.

"Give it to me." Chambers grabbed the paperwork and sat down next to the gurney. "I'll fill it out for you. Emma Eve Edwards, right?"

"Yeah." *How the heck did he know her middle name?* Right, he had access to her personnel papers. He must've looked her up to make sure Regionals hadn't committed some grave mistake in hiring her.

"Age?"

"Twenty-nine."

"Marital status?"

"Single."

"Phone number?"

And so it went. On and on. The guy did it without complaining, recording everything precisely in his bold, distinctive handwriting. When they were done, he flagged down the nurse and handed over the paperwork as well as her insurance card and driver's license. He stayed by her side the whole time except for when the doctor stepped in to examine her. It was strange having him in the room. He worked on his laptop but checked on her once in a while to make sure she didn't need anything.

Thank goodness the ER doctor, a man named Dr. Aikins, cleared her for discharge after a few hours of endless waiting. Her head CT turned out fine, just as Emma had predicted. Her wrist was sprained, but not broken. Dr. Aikins applied a tight ACE bandage around it and told her to take it easy for a few days.

"I can still work, right?" Emma asked. Her nausea and headache were gone now that they had given her some morphine and Compazine.

"I'd take the next couple of days off if I were you. You won't be able to use that hand for a while."

"It's not broken. I'll be fine." And besides, Sam would be worried to death if she didn't show up tomorrow.

"Let's see how you feel tomorrow," Chambers suddenly said out of the blue. She hadn't known he was paying attention to the conversation, so absorbed did he seem with his laptop.

"Your boyfriend's right. You should take it easy."

"He's not my boyfriend."

"No, definitely not," Chambers said, all too readily in Emma's opinion. "I'm her boss."

"Oh, sorry." Dr. Aikins cleared his throat. "You were so involved with her care, I'd just assumed."

"Wrong assumption." Chambers snapped his laptop shut. "Can we go now?"

"Sure." The doctor gave him a wary glance before leaving the room. They were about to follow when a familiar sight greeted Emma's eyes. She silently cursed her luck.

"Emma." Her ex, John, hurried to her side. "Are you okay? Why didn't you call me? You know I work here."

Damn. She'd completely forgotten. John looked as dapper and handsome as ever with his wavy brown hair, light-blue eyes, and easy smile. The long white coat only added to his appeal. She turned away to gather her things.

"Emma?" John reached for her arm.

"Who the hell are you?" Chambers's face was as grim as ever.

Emma hastily stepped between them. "John, this is Mr. Chambers. Mr. Chambers, Dr. John Carmichael, an old friend of mine."

"Are you dating him? Is that why you haven't returned my calls?" John asked.

"What? No. He's my boss."

"From UCLA?"

"No, from Albatross."

"That godforsaken prison?" John cursed and threw her an accusing look. "I can't believe you went through with it. Why are you in the ER?"

"I sprained my wrist."

John glanced at the tape on her arm. "Then why did you need an IV?"

"I had a headache. You know, my migraines."

"Are you getting enough sleep? You know that always sets you off."

"What is this? The Inquisition?" Emma said, sick of all the questions. Her wrist throbbed and all she wanted to do was go home and go to bed. "Good-bye, John. I have to go."

"Wait, Em." He grabbed her arm. "Can we talk? Please?"

Emma pulled back. *Couldn't the guy take a hint?* Her day had been tough enough. She didn't need this right now.

"Please." John reached for her again.

"She said no." Chambers's big paw shoved John's hand away. "Leave her alone." He ushered her out. John's eyes seemed to bore into her back all the way to the exit.

"What a mess." Emma shook her head when they

reached the parking lot. "This is definitely the worst day of my life."

"Tell me about it." Chambers's big body seemed to vibrate with tension. "Come on. My car's this way."

Emma hesitated. She didn't want to intrude on him more than she already had. "Can you call me a cab? They can drive me to my car, and I can take it from there."

"Don't be ridiculous. You can't drive. You just got morphine."

"Oh. I forgot." The man's silver eyes bored into hers, sending a shiver up Emma's spine. It wasn't quite fear she felt, but something else. A sense of danger. Excitement even. *Was the morphine getting to her?* "The cab can take me home." *Now why was she feeling a little breathless? It must have been the medicine. Or was it because of those silver eyes? They were downright striking.*

"Where do you live?"

"In Corona."

"That's right on my way. Hop in."

They'd reached his car by now, a sleek black Porsche. He held the door open. It'd be silly to insist on waiting for a cab. Emma slid into the car and gave him her address, which he plugged into his cell's navigation system. Chambers's huge body dominated the entire front of the car as soon as he sat. His massive arms seemed strong enough to rip the steering wheel off its stem. Strangely enough, Emma no longer found his size intimidating.

CHAPTER 9

What a day. For a moment there, she could have been toast. Emma sighed and leaned back against her seat. Off went the hairclip…her head was hurting enough already and she didn't need the clip's hard edge digging into the headrest. The enormous sky stretched above them like black velvet. Thousands of brilliant diamonds twinkled down on them. She'd always loved looking at the sky at night. Even with all the ugliness in the world—the violence, the poverty, the misery—there was still so much beauty out there.

Emma took in a deep breath and settled back in her seat. She'd spent many nights star-gazing with Sam in the San Bernardino Mountains before he went to live with his father. Before he slipped off the straight and narrow path and became who he was today. She shook her head at the memories and tried to find Orion, Sam's favorite constellation.

"I can't believe how clear the sky is tonight," she said, half to herself.

Chambers's arm twitched next to her but he didn't say anything. Somehow Emma didn't mind. She felt more relaxed and carefree than she'd been in a long time. The morphine must definitely be kicking in.

"Do you like star-gazing?" she asked, knowing she shouldn't but she couldn't help herself. The silence was getting to be too much, and she didn't mind starting a conversation, even if it turned out to be one-sided. "I love it. I find it so mind-boggling. Can you imagine? There may be life out there, people just like you or me. Wouldn't that be strange, meeting your other half in another galaxy?"

"Another galaxy?" Chambers shook his head. "I doubt it. There's probably no life out there."

"How do you know for sure?" Emma asked, surprised he'd finally spoken.

"I need to see it to believe it." He sounded relaxed and calm for the first time since she'd known him. "But you're right. The stars are beautiful."

"I love looking at the constellations. I never can find the chair in Cassiopeia. But I can see the *M* sometimes." She pointed to the *M* as the sky was especially clear tonight. "I like the Canis ones, Major more than Minor. Draco the Dragon is nice. But my favorite is Andromeda. I think it's so romantic that Perseus rescued her, don't you? And they got married and had children and are now forever in the sky together."

"How's your head feeling?"

"Fine." *Had he heard anything she'd said? But it didn't matter, did it?* Just hearing his deep, masculine voice was enough. It was definitely better than his gruff tone at work. "Thank you for coming with me today, Mr. Chambers."

"No problem. And you can call me Maxim. Chambers sounds so formal."

"Alright. Thanks." *Maxim.* She liked the sound of it. It suited him, strong and tough. "Please call me Emma."

"Okay." They continued on in silence for a while until he flicked on a CD. Beethoven's Fifth Symphony floated over the audio.

"You listen to this stuff?"

"Yes. It's my favorite. What? Why the strange look?"

"It's just..." Emma bit her lip. "Classical is so refined."

"And?" His voice had become steely again.

"You're in charge of inmates. You run a prison. You're so..."

"What? Crass? Crude?"

Emma squirmed in her seat, not knowing how to apologize. Luckily his cell rang, saving her from a response.

"Chambers," he said over the Bluetooth speaker.

A man's friendly voice sounded from the other end. "It's me. Can you talk?"

"Sure. Hold on a minute." Chambers looked at her, his eyes somber. "Sorry, do you mind? This shouldn't take long."

"Go ahead. I don't mind." *Not at all.*

"What's up?" Maxim asked.

"I know it's last minute but we had to move Kyle's birthday party to tomorrow evening. Lani's mom can't make it on Saturday. Can you come?"

"Pleeeaaase. Uncle Max. You have to come," a boy's eager voice chimed in.

"Sure, Big Boy." *How indulgent he sounded. Definitely different from the tone at work.* "You're turning three, right?"

"Yup. You and me play airplane."

"You got it."

"And me want rocket for present."

"A rocket? I can manage that. Anything else?"

A woman's laughing voice suddenly interrupted.

"Come on, Maxim. Don't spoil him so much. He has a million things from you already."

"I can't help it. He's my only godson, you know."

"Are you going to the charity gala next weekend?"

"Which one is that?" Maxim frowned. "It's hard to keep track of all of them."

"The CVU. It's your favorite."

"Oh. Of course. Thanks for the reminder. I've been really busy lately."

"I know. You work too hard." The woman's tone softened. "We never see you anymore. Come by for dinner sometime."

"Okay. I'll try."

"Bye, Uncle Max. See you tomorrow."

"Bye, Big Boy."

Maxim clicked off the Bluetooth and turned toward her. "Sorry about that."

"No worries." *What a surprise. He'd sounded so gentle.* The man clearly loved his godson. And he did charity work, too. Emma felt even more awful about that Beethoven remark. "What's the CVU?" she asked, trying to lighten the mood.

"It's an organization that supports victims of crime."

"That's nice of you." *And noble, too.* "How did you get involved?"

"It's kind of personal," he said after a short silence.

"Oh." He sounded terse again. She looked out the window and tried vainly to think of a different topic.

"Is your head okay?" Maxim suddenly asked.

"Yes. I think so."

"Good. You could have been really hurt." His huge hands tightened on the steering wheel. "I wish I'd beaten the crap out of Ransom. An eye for an eye. We should do that to all the criminals."

"Not all of them are bad, you know." *Definitely not Sam.*

"Of course they are. Ransom almost killed you today."

"Yeah. Ransom was bad. But he doesn't represent all of them."

Maxim scoffed. "You're too naïve."

"And you're too prejudiced." Emma sighed. Here they were, back to their old disagreements again.

Maxim's face closed up. "This is your exit, right?"

They finished the rest of the ride in uncomfortable silence. He walked her to the door without saying much when they finally arrived at her place.

"Thanks for the ride." Emma touched her pendant.

"No problem. Get some sleep. You look exhausted. Take the day off tomorrow."

"My car." She suddenly realized her predicament. "It's still at the prison."

"I'll have someone bring it back for you. Give me your key. You have a spare, right?"

She handed him the key and told him where her car was parked.

"Good night." Maxim's face was as expressionless and formidable as ever.

"Thanks for all your help." He'd done so much for her today. *Too bad there was this tension still festering between them.*

"No problem." He glanced at the door. "You have a deadbolt? Make sure you use it, okay?"

"Sure." *What an odd thing to say.* She waved good-bye and stepped over the threshold. He was full of surprises, the warden. One minute gruff and overbearing, and the next protective and even considerate. It'd been a horrible day but being with Maxim had surprisingly made it more tolerable. She fell asleep dreaming of the stars and of his deep voice.

CHAPTER 10

Pound! Pound! Pound! Maxim slammed his fist against the punching bag. Since four in the morning, he'd been at it. He should break off to do his usual five-mile run but the memory was too fresh. *Pound!* She'd looked terrified. *Pound!* She'd been wedged against the table and the wall. *Pound!* That bastard had had his hand around her throat. She'd collapsed on the floor and he'd never felt more terrified in his life. Except for that one time fifteen years ago. *Pound! Pound! Pound!*

The sweat poured off his face like water but he didn't feel it. His hands were probably cracked and bleeding through the gloves but he didn't feel them either. He was numb all over. Emma had been so brave at the hospital, insisting she was fine when any other woman would have broken down by then. *But no, not her.* The woman was amazing. Stupid, naïve, stubborn, reckless: she was all those things. But also simply amazing.

Pound! Pound! Pound! The bastard could've killed her. That beautiful little fool. He should have ripped

Ransom to pieces right away instead of escorting her to the Urgent Care. But she'd insisted on walking on her own and would have fallen without him. How slight she'd felt in his arms, like a small, injured angry bird. She'd been mostly bones and he'd been afraid he'd crush her with his massive arms but somehow she'd survived their encounter. *Too bad he hadn't.*

Maxim ripped off his gloves in disgust and yanked open the back door. He flung himself out into the cool morning air and raced along the familiar path that curved around his house. He jogged down the steep cliff where the path ended and soon found himself at his favorite location, running along the beach. Seagulls pierced the early morning stillness with their cries while the sun was trying to peep above the horizon.

He'd run like this every day for the past ten years, and the exercise usually relaxed him but not today. Today all he could see were Emma's frantic emerald eyes, her swollen wrist, the white bandage on her arm at the hospital. All he could hear were her screams for help. His body broke into a cold sweat. Somehow he had to make sure she didn't get hurt again.

Two hours later, Maxim arrived at the prison knowing what he needed to do. His body was sore but at least his mind was more at peace. She wouldn't be here today, so he could rest easy on that account. She hadn't looked so good when he'd left her last night. It was as if the strain of the day had finally caught up with her. Maybe he should ask Brown to check up on her.

The doctors were all waiting around the table in the conference room when he entered. *Damn.* He'd never been late before. *It was all that woman's fault.* He shook his head in disgust and resolved to keep her out of his mind. As soon as he shared the news with the group.

"Good morning." He sat in his usual place next to Kaye. "Some of you may have already heard. Dr. Edwards was assaulted yesterday afternoon in the Unit 3 office." A rumble went up among the group. He waved down their questions. "She's okay. Just a sprained wrist. She's resting at home today and may need the next few days off. Brown, I want you to check up on her later."

"He doesn't need to. I'm right here." Emma's voice spoke up from the doorway.

Unbelievable. Maxim braced his hands against the edge of the table. *What the hell was she doing here? Didn't she ever listen to advice?*

She came into the room dressed in her usual tasteless outfit of brown pants and a loose-fitting shirt. Her thick, long, black hair was clipped back again in its staid pony-tail. At least her wrist still had on the ACE bandage. *Thank God for small favors.*

"Why are you here?" Maxim asked, praying for patience. "Didn't I tell you to take the day off?"

"I don't need it," the woman replied in her usual blunt manner. "I'm fine. There's nothing to do at home anyway."

"Do? You're not supposed to do anything." He gripped the table harder. "You're supposed to be resting."

"Are you sure you're okay?" Brown asked.

"Yes. My wrist's a little sore. But I'm fine."

"What happened?" Kaye said, looking none too happy to see her either.

"An inmate got unhappy and grabbed my wrist." She had a slight tremor in her voice. Maxim didn't think anybody heard it except for him. "He pushed me against the wall. I pressed my alarm, and a group of officers saved me."

"Group?" Dr. Parker spoke up. "I heard it was Mr. Chambers who did all the rescuing. Before the other officers could do anything, Ransom was already flat on the floor."

"Oh." She turned her eyes toward him and smiled. "Thank you again for your help."

Maxim turned away and cleared his throat. *She was going to kill him with that smile.* "Don't mention it. I would've done that for anyone."

"He definitely would have." Kaye rubbed her hand on his arm. "Maxim, you're so brave. I love that about you."

Dear God. Could the woman be any less subtle? He yanked his arm out of the way. "Brown, help the doctor fill out a 115. Ransom isn't going to get off easy. I'll make sure of it."

"Yes, sir." Brown nodded. "All the doctors are here today. Dr. Edwards can take it easy. She'll have a lot of time to fill out the paperwork."

"But I want to get back to work," the contrary woman said, kicking Maxim's temperature up a notch. "Can I go back to the Urgent Care?"

"Sure, if you want," Brown said. "But Dr. Ross is here today. His wife is no longer sick. Maybe you can help with the infirmary patients."

"I have a better idea. We have a huge backlog of chronos that need to be filled out," Kaye said. "She'd be perfect for the job."

"Her hand's still sore. She won't be able to write," Maxim said before the evil witch could think of more chores for Emma. *What was it with the CMO?* She seemed out to get the new doctor. *Must be a female thing.* She'd ruled the roost for so long it was probably hard to share the spotlight with anyone else.

Kaye pasted on her fake smile and agreed to have Emma be the extra doctor in the Outpatient Housing Unit. *Time to announce his executive decision.* He'd thought long and hard and it was the only solution that'd let him sleep at night.

Maxim cleared his throat. "From now on, whenever Dr. Edwards sees a patient, I want an officer in the room with her."

"What?" Both Kaye and Emma spoke up at the same time.

"I don't need an officer."

He should've known the stubborn woman wouldn't agree to anything he suggested.

"She's right," Kaye said. "You're overreacting. It was a one-time thing, Maxim. We've never had any staff assaults until now."

"That's because we never had a female doctor before."

Kaye spluttered and shot him an injured look. "I've been here for years."

"You don't count." Kaye's face reddened. "You don't see patients, that's what I mean." *Him and his big mouth.* Maxim bit back a groan. That was a bit tactless, even for him.

"So she'll have her own personal bodyguard? Is that what you want?" The CMO whined in that nasal tone he detested.

"I don't need a bodyguard." Emma was giving him her usual contemptuous look. "Patients need their privacy. They're not going to open up to me if there's an officer in the room."

"Well, that's too bad. Damn their privacy." Maxim slammed his hand down. "You're working with inmates, for God's sake."

"They're still patients. They have rights, too."

"Rights? Are you kidding me? They're criminals. Stop being so foolish."

"Stop being so biased." She glared at him. "You know how I feel. Not all inmates are bad."

"Excuse me," Brown said to his right. "It's eight thirty. The doctors have to go to their clinics."

"Let them go. Not you, Dr. Edwards. You stay. Brown and Kaye, too." Maxim waved Emma over to a seat. She looked like she wanted nothing more than to bolt and get away from him but by God, he wasn't done yet.

"Sir," Brown said. "I think your intention is good. But it's not very practical. I don't think there's a spare officer available to protect Dr. Edwards."

"Of course there isn't." Kaye's red lips thinned. "We don't have the money or the resources to hire a personal bodyguard for her. If she can't handle working in the prison, she should quit."

Maxim paused, his whole world stilling. Finally, a ray of light. *Why didn't he think of that before?* The woman didn't belong here and he was going to go mad worrying about her if she stayed. It was the perfect solution, but he had to be careful. The last thing he needed was a lawsuit accusing him of pressuring her to quit.

"Dr. Kaye is right. Your credentials are great, and you can probably find a job anywhere." He took pains not to sound too hopeful. "I'll even write you a great reference."

"I don't need a reference." The doctor leaned over, two spots of color appearing on her pale cheeks, her freckles in stark relief. Maxim felt a queer tremor in his chest. "I'm not quitting." Her emerald eyes flashed like fire. "And you can't make me."

"Fine." He focused on the spot above her right shoulder. "But if you stay, you have to have a guard with you whenever you see patients. That's not negotiable."

"What officer? I thought you didn't have one."

"Officer Smith."

"But Maxim. That's your personal assistant." Kaye put a hand on his arm.

"Now he's Dr. Edwards's." Maxim pulled his arm away. "They give me too many damned assistants. I don't need all of them."

"So now I'm stuck with one of your minions?" Emma had the audacity to ask.

"Minions?" He had the strangest desire to throttle her. That or kiss her until that smart mouth stopped talking. *Now how the hell did kissing get in the picture?* Maxim shook his head. Emma was clearly driving him mad.

"Yes. Minion. Personal slave to a taskmaster."

"Yes, you get my minion," he said, his temperature rising faster than a speeding bullet. *How dare she call him a taskmaster?* "If you see a patient without Smith, you're fired. Just so we're clear," he added.

"Fine." Emma flashed those amazing eyes at him again before stomping out of the room.

Maxim brushed a hand through his hair and tugged at his tie. Brown threw him a strange look and Kaye pouted her too-red lips at him. He walked out and slammed the door, clenching and unclenching his fist. *Why the hell did that woman always rub him the wrong way? And why did she have to have those freckles?* Tomorrow he was going to have to add another hour to his morning jog.

CHAPTER 11

"I can't believe he forced Smith on me."

Emma fumed silently as she watched Sam mop the floor at the Urgent Care. Her two nurses were on lunch break and Dr. Ross was down at the OHU admitting a new patient, a man with possible flu. Dr. Ross was older and distinguished-looking with a kind face and bushy eyebrows. He had insisted on Emma not seeing patients so that she could recover from yesterday's ordeal.

"I think it's a great idea." Sam wrung the mop with his hands. "But better if you'd taken his other offer and quit. Jesus, you could've died, Em. It's dangerous in here."

Sure, working at Albatross was a bit risky, but what place was truly safe these days? Wasn't it the other day some crazy guy had killed a urologist in Newport Beach right in his clinic? And what about that angry family member shooting the doctor at Johns Hopkins Hospital a few years ago?

"There's violence everywhere," Emma said. "Don't worry. I'll press my alarm more quickly next time. I'm sure it was a one-time thing. Chambers is going overboard with this. I'll never be able to see you in private."

"We're talking now, aren't we?"

"That's not enough." She fiddled with her pendant and checked the doorway. Lucky for them, no one had come back yet. "Sam, I want us to catch up. Can we meet somewhere?"

Her brother glared at her and kept on mopping, his long arms rhythmically moving up and down. "Don't be stupid, Em. Do you want to get fired or something? We can't meet."

"We could if you were my patient. But now that stubborn, arrogant man ruined all my plans." She couldn't believe she'd thought Maxim considerate last night. The morphine must have totally gone to her head. "Why doesn't he mind his own business?"

"He's trying to keep you safe. That's why there's a lockdown today."

"Lockdown? What's that?"

"It's when Custody restricts us to our dorms. No one can go anywhere except to chow hall and medical appointments." Sam dumped the dirty water and filled the bucket with fresh water from the sink. "Didn't you notice the yards were empty? Everyone is locked down today."

"Because of what happened to me?"

"Yes. They always do that after a fight or an assault." Sam scanned the entranceway and resumed mopping. He was on the last row of tiles now. "I'm only here 'cause I'm the porter. They let some of us out."

"Hey, you're doing a great job." She grinned. "Much better than when you were living with us. Wanna clean up my place when you get out?"

"You wish." He wiggled the mop at her and she laughed. Thank goodness there was still a trace of that mischievous boy left in him.

"Dr. Edwards." Officer Smith suddenly appeared in the doorway. "You shouldn't be alone with an inmate. Warden's orders."

"He's the porter." Emma jumped down from her seat on the gurney. *How much had Smith heard?* Hopefully he hadn't been there long.

"Doesn't matter, Doc." Smith gave Sam a frosty stare. "Are you done yet? No loitering if you're finished."

"Yes, sir." Sam pushed the bucket and mop to the hallway.

"So you're going to be my shadow?" she asked the guard when they were alone.

"I know you don't want me around but Mr. Chambers insisted." Smith gave a self-conscious smile but straightened his shoulders.

"I know, but I only need you when I'm seeing patients," she said. "And since I'm not seeing any patients today, you have the day off. Go do whatever you want."

"Sorry. He said to always be around. In case you need me."

"Oh, for heaven's sake. I don't need you with me all the time. It's overkill."

Smith shuffled his feet and adjusted the badge on his shirt. "Like I said, sorry. Mr. Chambers's orders."

Emma bit back a groan. But it wasn't Smith's fault. He was only doing his assigned task and the man probably did a ton of errands for the warden in the past, no matter how unpleasant some of them must have been. Take driving her car from the prison back to her studio last night. She was sure he had better things to do with his time than be at the beck and call of his boss.

"Hey," she said, knowing she should have said it earlier.

"Thanks for driving my car back for me last night. I really appreciate it."

"What? What car?" Smith gave her a blank look.

"You know. Mr. Chambers said he'd have you drive the car back for me."

"He asked me to move his car, but he didn't say anything about yours." The officer slapped a palm to his forehead. "Oh my God, did he tell me and I forgot?"

"No," she hastened to reassure him. "I don't think he actually said your name, now that I think about it. No worries."

Maxim must have driven her car back himself. How strange he didn't have one of his minions do it for him. Before she could think more about it, Julien came down to help her fill out the 115 form, a report of the assault. The chief assured her that with the 115, Ransom would definitely get his sentence prolonged. After that, it was time to check on Mr. Nash. Today the old man looked stronger and was sitting, watching TV with a thin blanket wrapped around his spindly legs.

"How are you doing today, sir?" The room was a lot warmer than before. "Looks like your heater is working again."

"Sure is, Doc." He tapped her hand. "Thank you."

"You're welcome." She squeezed his hand and smiled. "Anything else I can do for you while I'm here?"

"Not really." He stiffened when he saw the officer by the door. "Am I in trouble?"

"Of course not." She signaled with her head for Smith to move out of the room but the man didn't budge. "He's here to watch over me. Don't worry. He's not going to hurt you."

"Okay, that's good." Mr. Nash swallowed a couple of times before bursting into a prolonged coughing spell.

Emma held his hand through the attack and after it was done, she poured him a cup of water from the pink plastic container on his nightstand. Next to the container was a small Bible with a picture of a little girl taped in the front.

"Is that your granddaughter?" She pointed to the picture. The girl was beautiful, with curly blonde hair and clear blue eyes.

"Yes. That's Sarah." Mr. Nash showed her the picture. "She'll be eight next month. She lives with my daughter Amy in Visalia. You know where that is?"

"Central California, right?"

"Close, near Sequoia National Park." The frail man brushed his index finger over the picture. "Last time I held her, she was only three years old. She's grown up so much since then." He swallowed and clasped the book between his hands. "She's healthy and growing up safe. That's all I've ever wanted. I don't regret it one bit."

"Regret what?"

"My son-in-law was an alcoholic. He beat up my daughter so many times I stopped counting. She wouldn't press any charges." He coughed again and took another sip of water. "There was only so much I could take. Then he started hitting Sarah, and I had to do what I had to do. I don't regret it one bit, even if it landed me here."

"Maybe you'll get the compassionate release." How odd that his story was similar to Sam's. But Sam was young. He was going to parole in a couple of years. He wasn't going to die in prison all alone like Mr. Nash. She had to help this old man get his freedom somehow. How could the justice system not release him early to spend time with that beautiful granddaughter? He'd shot to save another life.

"Doctor!" Smith suddenly yelled from the doorway. "They need you stat in room five. Patient's coding!"

"What?" Emma rushed out. Room five was Mr. Jones's room. The man who'd had the hernia repair.

She raced in and found Dr. Ross doing CPR on Mr. Jones, who was lying still in his bed, his face deathly pale. Sam stood by their side, holding the AED machine. Ms. Bryant and Ms. Carter arrived at the same time as Emma.

"What happened?" Emma sprang forward to check the man's carotid pulse.

"Don't know. Porter found him unresponsive a few minutes ago," Dr. Ross huffed out.

"Morris? Hold CPR for a second." Ms. Bryant ripped up the AED pads and slapped them on Jones's chest.

"Lift him to the ground." *Damn. No pulse.* "The bed's too soft. Morris, lift him with Smith. Now, please." Sam's face was filmy with sweat but she couldn't stop to reassure him in any way.

The two men grunted and lifted Jones's sizable form off the bed to the floor. "Anyone call 911?" Emma asked. "Smith, you do it. Ms. Carter, bag the patient. Ms. Bryant, I need an IV. Check a sugar, too. Yes, Dr. Ross, keep doing CPR. What's on the monitor?"

"Wide complex tach, Doc." Ms. Bryant poked Jones's finger with a lancet. "ACCU-CHEK one hundred."

"Hold CPR. Is there a pulse?"

Ms. Carter shook her head. "So it's PEA?"

"Yes."

"What's that?" Sam asked.

"Pulseless electrical activity. Push epi one milligram.

No IV yet? No veins? Where's the IO kit? You don't have one?" Emma felt frantically for a femoral pulse. "Get me the central line kit!"

"I need help here," Dr. Ross said as his arms slowed.

"Morris, switch with Dr. Ross. You know CPR, right?" Emma dimly recalled showing him how to do it on one of her breaks from medical school.

"Thanks," Dr. Ross said as Sam kneeled on the floor and took over the CPR. Someone shoved a central line kit at Emma and she ripped it open. She doused the bottle of Betadine on Jones's right groin and blindly inserted the needle, guessing where the vein might be. No rush of blood back. She shook her head and angled it more medial. A twinge of pain shot up her wrist but she held the position until blood flashed in the bevel of the needle. *Thank God something was going right.* Emma threaded in the catheter and secured it with a couple of stitches.

"Any pulse?" Emma asked.

"Still in PEA," Dr. Ross said.

"Give him one milligram of epi."

The femoral line flushed beautifully but after several rounds of epi and CPR, there was still no pulse.

"Hang me a bag of fluids," Emma said. "Any ideas of what else we can do, anyone?"

"Ambulance is on its way," Smith said as he ran back into the room.

"Excuse me, Doc." Sam's eyes met hers over Jones's chest. "I think he OD'd on something."

"What, porter?" Dr. Ross demanded. "What the hell are you talking about?"

Sam kept silent and continued pushing up and down on Jones's chest.

"It's okay, Morris. Tell me," Emma urged.

Sam swallowed. "I saw him holding a syringe this morning."

"Why didn't you say anything?" Ms. Bryant's beady eyes narrowed at Sam. "Or did you give it to him? Been dealing drugs, porter?"

"No, ma'am," he said softly, looking down again.

"That was uncalled for, Ms. Bryant. Thanks, Morris." Emma tried to smile at Sam, but his eyes were glued to Jones's chest.

"Get the Narcan," Dr. Ross said as he took over bagging the patient.

"Fresh track marks." Smith lifted Jones's left arm and showed them the pinprick holes in the antecubital fossa.

"Give him two milligram of IV Narcan," Emma ordered.

All eyes turned to the patient as Ms. Bryant pushed the medicine. Jones remained unresponsive.

"Check another pulse. None? Resume CPR." Emma flipped open Jones's lids and shined a flashlight into his left eye. She swung the light over to the right eye. Pinpoint, both of them. *Damn.* Another OD. Sam was right. It was probably heroin.

"Asystole," Dr. Ross said, his eyes on the monitor.

That was never a good sign. "Give me another one milligram of epi."

The paramedics arrived at that moment and intubated the patient. They continued the code for another ten minutes but Mr. Jones never recovered.

"Time of death, 12:05 p.m." Emma ripped off her gloves and wiped a hand over her forehead. Except for some post-op pain, the man was as healthy as a horse yesterday. How could he be lying as stiff as a board today? A horrible sinking feeling gnawed at her guts. *She'd denied him the T3.* Was that why he'd used the heroin? To treat his pain? The logical part of her knew she wasn't to blame for his death—that he pushed the drug on his own. He was an addict, an *N* number. But did she contribute to it somehow by refusing him the narcotic?

"I have to notify the warden." Smith covered Jones with a white sheet. "There'll be an investigation."

Sam gasped and turned deathly pale underneath his dark skin. He stumbled out of the room. Emma rushed after him.

"Morris. You did really well. Thanks for telling us about the syringe." Too much staff was nearby for her to reassure him more.

"It didn't help." Sam lifted a trembling hand to his forehead. "You don't think I'm in trouble, do you?"

"No. Of course not. The warden told me another inmate died of a heroin overdose last year in SNY."

"The nurse—"

"Forget about Bryant." Emma placed a hand on his arm. "I can't believe she said that to you. Don't worry. You're not in trouble. You tried to save him. Your CPR was great."

"Dr. Edwards."

Emma let out a silent groan. Kaye, Julien, and Maxim were striding down the hall toward her. None of them looked too happy. Maxim was scowling at Sam, and she hastily took her hand off his arm. Her brother cast her a worried look before limping down the hall the opposite way.

CHAPTER 12

"I can't believe you're chatting with an inmate," Kaye said as soon as she got close. "A patient died. Why aren't you with him?"

"The code just ended." Emma rubbed her temple. Another headache was definitely coming on. "I was thanking Morris. He helped with the CPR."

"You let an inmate do CPR?" The CMO's voice rose. "What the heck were you thinking? They can't be in a code. Where were the nurses?"

"Managing the airway and pushing meds. What do you want me to do? Let the patient die rather than ask an inmate for help?"

"What the hell happened?" Maxim demanded. "Why did he code?"

"He OD'd. There were track marks. His pupils were pinpoint. We tried everything but nothing worked." Emma rubbed her hands up and down her arms, ignoring the mild pain in her wrist. She felt cold all of a sudden. Jones's dead face suddenly floated before her vision. Only yesterday, he was pleading for more pain medications. Goose bumps popped up on her arms. She swallowed and rubbed her hands harder. "I'm sorry. I need a minute."

She dashed into the staff bathroom across the hall. Her stomach roiled and she doubled over and vomited twice into the toilet. She stumbled to the sink and splashed cold water on her face. Some of it sprinkled onto the mirror. It was no use. Jones's dead face kept staring at her whenever she closed her eyes.

"Dr. Edwards, are you okay?" Julien's voice called through the door.

"Yes. I'm fine." *Did she have to look so pale?* Whatever makeup she'd applied that morning had rubbed off. She pinched her cheeks and bit down on her lips, trying to give them some color. Taking a deep breath in, she opened the door and almost barged straight into Maxim.

"Are you all right?" he asked, his silver eyes scanning her face.

"I'm fine."

"You don't look fine," Julien said. "Come on. Let's sit down in the office. Have you had lunch yet?"

"Where's Dr. Kaye?" There was no sign of the blonde.

"She's on the phone with headquarters." Julien touched her arm. "Relax. It's okay. She won't be back for a while."

"Hey. What happened?" One of the Urgent Care officers, a burly elderly man with a balding head and a trim mustache, rushed up to them.

"Sergeant Peterson." Maxim patted the officer on the shoulder. "Just the man I need. Find out what's going on. Room five OD'd."

"I thought with Roberts gone, things would've been better. We swept through SNY yesterday. No drugs. Want me to set up some cameras around the prison?" The sergeant rubbed his bald head. "That will monitor them more."

"That's a good start. Come. I want to see if there's any evidence in the room." Maxim's penetrating eyes flicked Emma's way. "Take the rest of the day off, Doc. You look awful."

Gee, thanks. The man was as charming as usual. Yet a part of her craved the warmth he radiated. She shivered and rubbed her hands on her arms again as Julien led her back to the Urgent Care.

"You look pretty shaken up." Julien placed a cup of water in her hands as soon as she sat down. "Here, drink this."

She gulped down the water and took in a deep breath. At least she wasn't shivering quite as much. "I think I may have killed him."

"How?" Julien's eyebrows rose as he scoffed. "Did you give him the drugs? Did you draw it up for him or help push it in his vein?"

"No, of course not."

"Then how did you kill him?"

There was nothing but sympathy on the chief's face. *God, she was so lucky to have him as a supervisor.* "I didn't give him the T3 yesterday," she confessed. "He wanted it, said he was in a lot of pain. But he looked so comfortable, Julien. Lying there, reading his magazine. I was going to give it to him but then I changed my mind."

"Forcing him to turn to heroin and therefore making you an accomplice in his murder?" Julien shook his head. "Don't be ridiculous, Emma. You had nothing to do with his death."

"You don't think so?" The gnawing sensation eased in Emma's gut.

"Of course not." Julien squeezed her shoulder. "Every year we have an inmate or two die of an overdose. We're in a prison. There're addicts all around you. You're not responsible for how they behave."

"He was so young."

"He was an adult. He knew what he was doing."

"I guess you're right." She felt marginally better, but only a little bit. "I should get back to work."

"You work too hard. It's the state. Relax. Where's your lunch? Is this it?" Julien handed her the brown paper bag he located in the doctor's cabinet.

Emma opened the bag and took a bite of her peanut butter and jelly sandwich. It tasted like sawdust. She grimaced and forced down some water.

"Hey. Come on, it's not that bad." Julien patted her shoulder again. "Wanna come to my son's birthday party on Sunday? Mary would love to meet you."

"Sure." *Something outside of work to focus on, just what she needed.*

Emma dragged herself through the rest of the day, trying hard not to think about Jones's sightless eyes. That night, Riley reassured her she did the best she could, but her doubts lingered. She called an old friend who was a drug counselor and felt a little better hearing it confirmed drug overdoses were sometimes inevitable. Curious, what finally lifted the weight off Emma's chest though was seeing her friend the blackbird again at the top of the hill near the administration building the following morning.

The bird perched on a branch, spreading his glossy black wings wide and scanning his territory with pride. Other than him, she hadn't seen a tricolored one in years. They were endangered. In fact, the last one she saw was on that camping trip with Sam when he was fifteen, before he'd been arrested. She had to tell him about the bird. It would definitely cheer him up, especially after what he'd been through yesterday.

"Good morning," she called to her brother as soon as they met in the Urgent Care. The nurses were getting their coffee down at the nursing station, and Sam was stacking boxes of gloves into the supply cabinet. Sergeant Peterson stood supervising with a cup of coffee in his hand.

"It's okay, Sergeant." Emma smiled at the kind-looking officer. "I'll watch over Morris. You go and enjoy your coffee."

The sergeant returned her smile. "Thanks, Doc. I'll be over there at the station if you need me."

"Sure." Emma closed the door to the clinic.

"What are you doing?" Sam whispered. "He's still watching us."

"There's a bunch of dirt I see behind the door here, Morris." Emma raised her voice. "I can't hang my white coat there. Can you mop it up, please?"

"Yes, Doc." Sam spoke loudly before dropping his voice. "Don't get us in trouble, Em."

"I'm not," she whispered. "How are you doing? Are you still thinking about what happened?"

"Did they find the drugs?" Sam slammed the mop back and forth against the door.

"No, I don't think so."

"It's bad in here, Em." He gripped the mop hard and squeezed his eyes shut. "Promise me something."

"What?" She touched his arm. "You're scaring me. What's wrong?"

"Don't trust anybody," he whispered. "Even the officers. They're bad too."

"What do you mean?" Emma pulled at her pendant.

"I can't tell you. Can you quit? Please? I don't want to have to worry about you."

"You worry too much. Remember, I have Smith to shadow me."

"He can't be with you everywhere." Sam leaned his chin on top of the mop handle. "And who knows if you can even trust him?"

"What's wrong with you? Why are you so paranoid?"

Sam gave a humorless laugh. "Because I'm triple C. Didn't you know that?"

"Triple what?"

"Triple CMS. Correctional Clinical Case Management System. It's for the crazy patients."

"I don't understand. You're not crazy."

"The meds make me tired so sometimes I spit them out," Sam said. "But most of the time I take them to help me sleep. It's not too bad. They're heat meds so I get AC in the summertime."

"What are you talking about? You're taking meds? Which ones?" *Had he slipped back into using drugs?* He wasn't making any sense at all.

"Don't worry. It's all legit. The psychiatrist prescribes them."

"What are they?"

"ZOLOFT and ABILIFY."

"But ABILIFY is an antipsychotic," Emma said, horrified. "You're not psychotic."

"Maybe I am." Sam's face turned sullen. "What? You can't handle it if your brother is crazy?"

"That's not what I mean." Emma bit her lip. "Are you okay? You don't need them, do you?"

Sam sighed and shook his head. "I don't think so. But sometimes the flashbacks get pretty bad. The meds help me sleep."

"Is this about your father?"

"I wish." Sam looked down. "No. It's worse. Much worse."

"Why didn't you tell me?" Emma forced him to face her. "Tell me what's wrong. Maybe I can help."

"Nothing you can do." He banged the mop back and forth again against the door. "Remember what I said. Don't trust anyone. It's for your own good."

"You done in there?" Peterson pounded on the door. "The nurses want to get back in. There're patients out here."

"Sure." Emma gave Sam a warning look before opening the door. "Thanks, Sergeant."

"No problem, Doc. Ready for your first patient?" The sergeant smiled at her before turning to Sam. "You, go to room four. The toilets need cleaning in there."

Sam shuffled out, his chin to his chest. Prison had changed her brother so much. Even at juvenile hall, he'd been happier, more confident. Now he was a shadow of his former self. He needed some TLC. *Darn, she'd forgotten to tell him about the blackbird.*

"Here's your first patient, Doc." A new nurse she hadn't met before brought in a thin young man who was wheezing. "Mr. Cavendish, twenty-one-year-old with asthma exacerbation."

"Thanks." The nurse was short, about her height. "What's your name? I don't think I've met you yet. I'm Dr. Edwards."

"I'm Madison. Nice to meet you." The nurse looked to be in her mid-twenties. Without makeup on, her face was plain and unassuming, though her eyes were a remarkable golden brown color. Her brown hair bobbed behind in a ponytail as she handed Emma the patient's chart.

"He's been doing well, no inhaler use for months and suddenly it hit him yesterday."

"Hey," Emma said. "How are you doing?"

"Okay." *Huff.* "Ran out of my inhaler." *Huff.*

"Give him a nebulizer." Emma lifted the man's shirt and put a stethoscope to his chest. Her heart rate picked up a notch. "He's not moving any air. Five milligrams of albuterol and five hundred micrograms of Atrovent. Stat, please. Hook him up to some oxygen." She rushed him to the gurney.

The man gripped both hands on the bed and sprung his torso forward. Deep pockets indented his collarbone as he gasped for air.

"He's retracting. Where's that nebulizer?"

Madison brought over the breathing treatment and soon a steady mist blew into Mr. Cavendish's face. He gulped in the air, his eyes wide with anxiety.

"Easy. It's okay." Emma laid a hand on his back. "Take it easy. In. Out. Nice and slow. Don't worry. In. Out. That's it. Keep going."

Emma reapplied the stethoscope. *Good, finally some air was flowing.*

"No past medical history except for asthma." Madison flipped through the chart. "Been intubated once when he was sixteen. Triggers are cigarette smoke, exercise, dust, and cats. Been at Albatross for six months without any attacks."

"Are you doing better?" Emma asked.

The man nodded and took the nebulizer tube out of his mouth. "A lot. Thanks, Doc."

"Keep going. We're not done yet." She put the tube back

in his mouth and watched the indentations around his collarbone disappear. He was breathing slower, too. The mist eventually stopped airing and Emma removed the tube. "So what happened? How come you had an attack?"

"I don't know." He rubbed the back of his neck. "It came out of the blue."

"Did something set it off? Were you exercising or around dust?"

"No, not really." His eyes shifted around the room and out the door to across the hall where the officers were sitting. He saw Smith in the corner of the room and swallowed. "I ran out of my inhaler, that's all."

"But you hadn't had an attack in a long time." Feeling something was off, Emma went over to Smith. "Can you step out of the room for a sec? Madison is with me. I need to ask the patient something."

"But, Mr. Chambers—"

"Will not mind because the nurse is here. I'm not alone." With that, she pushed Smith out of the room and shut the door. Madison smiled and gave her the thumbs-up sign.

"So tell me, Mr. Cavendish. What happened?"

"What do you mean?"

"I've seen young patients like you die of asthma. It's a horrible way to go." Emma looked him in the eye. "What set it off? Anything I can help you with?"

Cavendish dropped his eyes and fidgeted with his hands. "Okay. Don't tell anyone I said this but it's the cigarette smoke. They moved my bed last week closer to the bathroom and my asthma got a lot worse." He looked up and grimaced. "They're going to kill me if they find out. Please don't say anything."

"They smoke more in the bathroom?" Madison prodded.

"Yes. A lot. Especially at night." Cavendish coughed into his hands. "That's when my asthma acts up."

"Isn't smoking not allowed in here?" Emma asked. "Let's tell Custody so they can put a stop to it."

"No." Little dots of perspiration popped up on Cavendish's upper lip. "Don't tell them. My bunkies are gonna know I snitched. And they're gonna get back at me."

"Custody is not going to let that happen." Emma gave him a reassuring smile. "You should trust them. They can probably even move you to a different dorm. You'll feel a lot better."

"Not likely." A mutinous expression settled over Cavendish's face. "Can I go now? I feel better already."

"Not yet." Emma handed him a peak flow meter. "You need another round. And some prednisone, too. Let's check your peak flow. You know it tells me how well your lungs are doing."

Cavendish blew into the meter. The little balloon flew up to three fifty.

"What's your average? Six fifty?" Emma said. "I thought so. You're way off track. Madison, could you give him two more nebs? And sixty milligrams of prednisone by mouth, please."

Emma racked her brain, trying to find a way to help Cavendish without risking his safety.

"Madison." She flagged the nurse over. "So what do you think? Do they really smoke in their dorms?"

"Of course." Madison rolled her eyes. "You didn't know? Oh, I forgot, you're new to the prison, right? Well, let me give you the lowdown. There's a black market in here. Whatever you want—cigarettes, drugs, pills, downers, uppers—you can get it all for the right price."

"But that's horrible." Emma reared back in shock. "Custody's not doing anything?"

Madison scanned the room. Cavendish was a good distance away. She leaned close and whispered, "There're some rumors going around."

"What?"

The nurse made a locking gesture over her lips. "Family and visitors bring in most of the drugs. But I heard some staff members may be sneaking them in, too. Nobody's ever been caught. But you didn't hear any of this from me." Madison gave a warning shake of her head before heading over to refill their patient's nebulizer.

Cavendish better not have heard what they were saying. Emma shivered. *Could some staff members be the suppliers? Or was it only a rumor? How could Maxim let that happen if it were true?* The man seemed to be a stickler for the rules.

"Hey, Doc. I'm done. Can I go now?" Cavendish took off the nebulizer tube. Emma handed him the peak flow meter, her mind still racing over what she'd heard. "Six fifty, Doc. I feel much better."

"Let me take a quick listen." Emma applied her stethoscope. "Good, loud and clear. Here's a new inhaler. And you'll need to take four more days of prednisone, fifty milligrams every day. I'll talk to Custody and get you moved."

"But not tell them about the cigarettes, right?"

"Don't worry. I won't tell them."

She waved good-bye to Cavendish. *Aha.* Mr. Peterson was across the hallway. She may have a plan. "Hi, Sergeant," she called the older man over. "Could you help me with something?"

"Sure, my dear." The officer smiled and entered the room. "What is it?"

"Could you move Mr. Cavendish to another dorm for me?"

"But why?"

"Because it's damp where he is right now. It makes his asthma worse." Emma thought it was a perfect excuse. "He needs to be farther away from the bathroom. The steam from there flares up his asthma."

"You're a softie, Doc. Write that on the chrono and I'll have him moved, stat." He pulled at his mustache. "I wish we had more doctors like you. You really care about your patients, don't you?"

"I try," she said, forcing out a smile. "Thanks, Sergeant. I'll give you the chrono in a second."

Whew. Emma breathed a sigh of relief. Madison gave her a thumbs-up sign. She wrote the chrono and handed a copy to the sergeant. Now, she had to figure out a way to tell Maxim about the cigarettes. It wasn't going to be easy. He'd look down his long nose at her and demand proof. All she had were Cavendish's words. And didn't Maxim believe that all inmates lied? *Great.* Emma sighed, already dreading their encounter.

First things first, though, she had to take care of the rest of the patients in the waiting room. A cold, a first-degree burn, a sprained shoulder, a broken finger, a gallstone attack, and someone with recurrent back pain. The morning flew by in a flash.

In the afternoon, Emma rounded on the OHU patients to make sure they were doing okay. The possible flu had no fever for the last twenty-four hours so she discharged him with strict instructions to come back if he felt worse. The four diarrhea men hadn't had diarrhea for the past twenty-four hours. Plus they were eating well and stool cultures were negative for norovirus, so she discharged them also.

Smith trailed her from room to room as she did her rounds, not saying much but keeping a wary eye on her.

"You know where I can find the warden?" Emma asked the officer at the end of the day. "I need to talk to him about something."

"Here's his office number." Smith pulled a business card out of his wallet and handed it to her. "And his cell is on the back. He told me to give it to you if you ever need it."

"His cell, too?" Emma raised her eyebrows. "Your boss is pretty available to his staff."

"Not to everyone. Only to you it seems." The guard winked at her and grinned. Before she could respond, he added, "So you're done seeing patients, right? My mother's birthday party is tonight, so I don't want to be late."

After sending Smith off, Emma dialed Maxim's office and arranged with his secretary to meet him the following Monday. Apparently he'd driven away to a conference in Fresno. She didn't know why he'd given her his cell. A warm feeling blossomed in her chest. *Could the man be interested in her?* He'd been pretty considerate in the ER. And there was something about him that drew her. Maybe it was his all-encompassing warmth. She'd always had a thing for electric blankets. *God, she was pathetic.* She needed to focus on Sam, not be mooning over his jailer.

Hmm. The office was empty. A perfect time to check up on Sam. There was the patient's privacy act to consider but this was her brother, for heaven's sake. She closed the door to the clinic before punching in Sam's name and date of birth. Out came his CDC number. Then she clicked open the medication tab and punched in his number. Out popped his list of medications.

ZOLOFT 100 mg po qd

ABILIFY 5 mg po qhs

Emma glanced over to the right of the medication reconciliation form. Dr. Stewart was the prescribing doctor. *Hmm. How was she going to find the doctor and discuss Sam, all without raising any suspicion?* She could pretend Sam was her patient, which technically he was because she was the float. Emma covered for any doctor who was off, right? That made her the doctor for all these patients. She shook her head, knowing it was a weak argument but hey, at least it was something. She couldn't very well announce to the shrink she was the crazy sister wanting the scoop on her equally crazy brother. No, she didn't think that would go over very well.

CHAPTER 13

"Again. Do it again, Dr. Emmy," the little boy shrieked in her ear, all the while bouncing up and down and grabbing her hand with his chubby fingers.

"Okay, Robby. Here goes." Emma lifted him onto her back.

"Hey. My turn." Robby's little brother Stevie tugged at her leg. "My turn to play horsie."

"No. Mine." Another brother pulled at the other leg. "Dr. Emmy, me up. Me up."

"Hold on, boys." Emma laughed. "I can only do one at a time. Horsie is tired. Horsie has a very small back." The other two boys flopped on their bellies and plucked at her ankles. "Hey? Did I just get shackles on my legs? Oh no, I'm a horsie prisoner."

Delighted giggles burst around her. Emma galloped several steps in the inflatable castle on her hands and knees, trying to keep Robby on her back. Julien's little boy was turning eight, but he weighed a ton. Her back was starting to hurt but the boys were having too good a time to quit. Robby leaned a little too much to the right and off she rolled onto her back on the bouncer, surrounded by little bodies everywhere.

It'd been a good idea to wear shorts and a T-shirt today. Otherwise she'd be baking in the castle. Someone pulled at her hair tie and out came her ponytail. A sticky hand squeezed her right foot. Someone else tickled her nose with a lock of her hair. Robbie tried to lift her shirt but thank goodness she was too quick for him. "Sorry, little boy." She laughed and flipped on her belly. "Can't oblige you there."

"Too bad for us," a lazy voice said from somewhere to her right.

Emma pushed the hair out of her face and blinked. A tall, well-built, blond Adonis stood in front of her. She shielded her eyes against the sun. No, she wasn't imagining him. He was perfect, from the tip of his shiny blond head to the tilt of his beautiful aquiline nose to the easy grin on his firm, masculine lips. Eyes of the deepest sea-blue sparkled down at her.

"Hi, there." She stepped out of the castle, bemused and a bit dazed. The man was drop-dead gorgeous.

"Hi, yourself." Mr. Adonis laughed, his beautiful eyes alight with mischief. "Have I died and gone to heaven? What's your name, Angel?"

"Behave, Stewart." Maxim suddenly loomed next to the man and clapped him on the back. "That's Dr. Edwards, our new doctor."

Emma blinked a couple of times. Yes, that was Maxim next to Mr. Adonis. *What the heck was he doing at Julien's son's birthday party? Wasn't he supposed to be in Fresno for a meeting?* He was dressed in a gray business suit, his silk tie perfectly aligned, his shoes polished and shining, just like every day at work. *Didn't he realize he was at a kid's birthday party?* He was looking at her with the oddest of expressions. Emma glanced down. *Yikes!* Half of her abdomen was exposed. She yanked her T-shirt down and forced out a smile.

"Hi, I'm Emma Edwards," she said, reaching out to shake Mr. Adonis's hand.

"Charles Stewart." The blond god raised her hand to his lips. Emma took a quick step back. *Was the guy actually going to kiss it?* It seemed gallant in the movies but in real life was kind of creepy, even if it came from an Adonis. Up close, he looked older than she'd first thought. There were fine wrinkles around his eyes, which appeared a bit dissipated and bloodshot on closer inspection.

"How do you do, Mr. Stewart?"

"Why so formal?" The man put an arm around her shoulders while his other hand cradled a wine glass. "Call me Charles. And I have to call you Emma. Such an enchanting name. It matches you perfectly."

"Thanks." The man's breath reeked of alcohol. "Do you work at Albatross?"

"Yes. He's one of the psychiatrists," Maxim said with a faint sneer.

"Psychiatrist?" Emma's breath hitched. "Doctor Stewart?"

"Yes, darling." He grinned and pulled her closer. "But I thought I already told you. Call me Charles."

"Charles." Emma held her breath. *Damn. Why did the man have to be a lush?* But no matter. It seemed the perfect opportunity to find out more about her brother. "I was hoping to meet you."

"Really, darling?" Charles laughed and tugged her flat against his body. His eyes grinned down at her. "The pleasure is all mine."

"I see you've met my ex-husband," a familiar voice said.

No. It couldn't be. But it was. Of all the luck. Kaye stood there glowering at her. *Yikes.* Emma jumped back from Charles by a mile. "Your ex?"

"Ex. Thank God. Come on, Maxim. Let's go. There's so much screaming, I'm getting a headache." She looped her arm around Maxim and dragged him away.

"Well, that went well, didn't it?" Charles twirled his wine glass, watching the red liquid spin, his face shadowed by a trace of sadness. "She's been in love with him for years. Maybe she'll finally get him now."

"Who? Maxim?"

"The one and only." Charles sighed. "The guy is filthy rich. That's all she's after. His money." He tried to grab for another wine cooler, but Emma handed him a bottle of water instead.

"Sorry." Charles grimaced, looking a little lost and confused. "I hate seeing the two of them together. And I can never hold my liquor on an empty stomach."

"Come on. Let's get you something to eat." Emma filled two plates with pizza and salad, and they made their way to a table where Madison, the nurse from the Urgent Care, was sitting.

"Mind if we join you?" Emma asked.

"Not at all." Madison's sunny smile wilted as soon as she spotted Charles. "Actually, I forgot I promised to help Mary with something in the kitchen." She abruptly stood and waved them a hasty good-bye.

"What was that?" Emma gave the psychiatrist a curious look as they sat.

"Beats me." Charles shrugged. "Maddy's kind of unpredictable."

"Maddy? You know her from before?"

"Yes. I've known her for years. Her brother is a good friend of mine." Charles twisted off the cap of his water bottle. "Anyway, let's dig in, okay? I'm starving."

"Sure." Emma bit down on the pizza, wondering what the nurse had against Charles. He didn't seem that bad. Come to think of it, most of the people she'd met today had been friendly.

Everyone seemed to be having a good time. Julien was blowing balloons for a pack of kids in one corner of the backyard while his wife Mary chased their youngest son, a toddler in the midst of a major tantrum. Dr. Churchill or Bryce as he told her to call him today was teaching Julien's five-year-old how to ride a bicycle. Little boys and girls ran around the backyard, blowing soap bubbles and waving pretend swords. The Star Wars theme was a clear hit.

Maybe someday she could have a fraction of her surroundings. Maybe a kid or two and a husband as devoted as Julien to share her life with. And of course, Sam would be there, roughhousing with one of her kids, drawing pictures of birds for them. He'd be free again and hopefully happy, too. She turned toward the psychiatrist.

"Dr. Stewart. I mean Charles," she began. "Do you mind if I ask you something?"

"Sure, Angel." She noticed how the smile didn't quite reach his eyes this time. "As long as it's not about my ex."

"Promise. It won't be about her." Emma swallowed. "Do you know a patient named Morris? Sam Morris?" Goose bumps spread on her arms. She took a sip of water.

"Maybe." He bit down on a slice of pizza. "I see so many patients, they kind of blend in to one another. Why do you ask?"

The psychiatrist didn't appear as drunk as before. She wondered how much of it had been an act for his ex. She had to jog his memory somehow. "He's our porter in the Urgent Care. You know, about twenty-something with dark skin, five feet ten or so. He has a little limp when he walks. Really tall and lanky."

"Oh. That Morris." Charles snapped his two fingers together. "He's one of my nicest patients. Always polite and respectful."

"You think so?" Emma's heart swelled with pride.

"Yes. Are you his medical doctor? 'Cause you know, the whole patient privacy thing."

"Yeah. I'm his doctor." Emma bit her lip, hating the lie. "He said he couldn't sleep sometimes."

"Yes. Poor guy got the crap kicked out of him."

"What?" Emma's hand gripped the edge of her seat.

"Yes. It was over a drug deal." Charles took another bite of pizza. "He was in the hole for a few months. He's doing a little better but doesn't want to talk about it much."

Her poor brother. No wonder he hadn't written. *How badly had he been hurt?* Obviously he looked okay now but he must have suffered a lot. And what was this about a drug deal? Sam had told her he'd stopped using. Was that since he was beaten up or had he been sober since juvenile hall like she'd thought?

Drat. Could Sam have lied to her? She certainly hoped not. She was going to dig it out of him somehow, and if he was back on drugs, she'd have to intervene immediately. Maybe Charles had some idea. She hated snooping on her brother, but desperate times called for desperate measures. She turned to the psychiatrist. "You think he's back on drugs?" she asked, her heart thumping hard.

"No. I don't think so." Charles took a sip of water. "No one has said anything. And you know Custody does random checks on their urine."

Thank goodness. "Do you think he needs the meds you're giving him?"

"Probably. He has mood swings and insomnia, too." Charles gave her a shrewd look. "You want me to wean one of his meds?"

"What? No. Why do you ask?"

"Just the way you asked. Are you that worried about him?"

"No." Emma shook her head and then sighed. *Who was she kidding?* She might as well speak her mind. Charles appeared like he cared. Perhaps he could help. "I mean, yes. He seemed a little paranoid when he talked to me yesterday. I want to make sure he's doing okay."

"I saw him a few weeks ago. He looked fine but if you're worried, I'll call him in and have a little chat. Make sure he's okay."

"You'd do that for me?" Emma felt like hugging the man.

"I've always been a sucker for a beautiful face." Charles shot her his Adonis smile.

Emma smiled back. *The man was a born flirt.* "Thank you. I really appreciate it. But can you keep this between us? For patient confidentiality, you know." She couldn't believe she managed that without choking on the words.

"Of course. You can count on me."

"Dr. Emmy." Robby ran over and grabbed Emma's hand. "Come on, we're cutting the cake. I want you to sit right next to me."

"Aw. How sweet, Robby. Thanks but don't you want your mom or dad or brothers to do that?" Emma asked. Julien and Mary beckoned her with their hands. Apparently she'd become their son's favorite after all those horsie rides. She trudged over to the cake table, holding Robby's sticky hand.

Maxim towered near the cake, looking as formidable as ever. He'd taken off his jacket and had loosened his tie. The sleeves of his shirt had been rolled back, exposing his hairy forearms. Emma swallowed. Her insides tingled. When had she ever thought a man's forearms were sexy? And this was the warden, for goodness' sake. She looked up and caught his full frown. *What now?* She hadn't opened her mouth yet and he already radiated disapproval.

Soon they all started singing the birthday song. Maxim loomed like a mountain, only a yard away. She stole a peek at his forearms and knew she was in trouble. How could she be attracted to the man? He was rude, arrogant, boorish. Opposite of what she desired in a partner. Yet he'd been there for her in the ER the other night. And he'd driven her car back for her. *And that body. Must he be built like a Roman conqueror?* Emma shook her head. *What was she doing?* Maxim was Sam's jailer. The less she thought about him, the better.

"Smith said you wanted to talk with me?" Maxim suddenly asked when the song was over.

"What?" Mary was cutting the cake and divvying up the pieces. It was chocolate, her favorite. Emma snatched a piece before it all disappeared.

"You wanted to talk with me?" His voice rang with impatience.

"Oh, right." Somehow she'd totally forgotten about the cigarettes. "I tried to call but you'd already left for your meeting."

"Didn't Smith give you my cell?" Maxim's eyebrows drew together. "You can always reach me there."

"Well, it wasn't an emergency." And they were at a party right now. Knowing his temper, it was probably better to wait. "Let's talk on Monday."

"Is everything okay?"

"Yes." Emma took a big bite of the cake. "Well, I mean, no, not really but it can wait."

"Why don't you tell me now? I don't like waiting for bad news."

"How do you know it's bad?"

"Your face says it all. So spit it out. Don't worry, I won't bite."

The corners of his lips curved up a tiny bit. Emma's breath hitched. *Was that a hint of a smile?* She shook her head and finished off the cake. First the forearms and now that potential smile. She had to pull herself together.

"So are you going to tell me?" Maxim prompted.

"Sorry, not now. Let's wait until Monday." *Why was he staring?* She wet her lips and Maxim's stare intensified. Suddenly he made an odd sound and grabbed the napkin out of her hand. He wiped her mouth with the cloth in one fell swoop.

"You had chocolate there." His tone was grim, almost accusing.

"You could have just told me." Heat rushed to her face. "I would've done it."

"More efficient my way." Maxim's gaze shifted. "There's still a smudge on the left side. You should eat more slowly."

"Gee, thanks." She was sure her face was as red as a lobster.

Her tormentor grunted and walked away. Emma wiped her mouth and tossed the napkin into the nearest trashcan. The man was rude to the core. She couldn't believe she'd been mooning over him a few minutes ago.

CHAPTER 14

*P*hineas. That was what she'd call him. The black-bird flitted from branch to branch, looking strong and brave just as his namesake in Emma's favorite novel, *A Separate Peace*. Sam had loved the book and also thought it a fitting him when she told him about it before clinic that Monday morning.

"I hope I can see him one day," her brother said as he stacked reams of copy paper into the filing cabinet.

"You were up the hill that day when I first spotted you, right? Take a look next time. He may be there." Emma sipped her coffee, wondering how to bring up what Charles had told her.

"That was a one-time thing. Another crew is delivering supplies up there now."

"Maybe he'll fly down here one day."

"Yeah, right. You know how they like staying in their territory. Did you see any nests close by?"

"Not inside the prison."

"They're probably close by. Wish I could explore with you." He gave her a crooked smile. "At least I know about him. Thanks for telling me. Hey. Did you hear about the latest comet?"

"No. Tell me about it." *So he still liked comets.* Emma smiled, glad a core part of her brother was still there.

"I heard on the radio. Holmes is supposed to be coming the twenty-third or twenty-fourth of this month and be really bright, even visible with the naked eye." Sam's eyes turned dreamy. "I wish I could see it."

"You can't look up there at night?"

"Are you kidding me?" Sam scoffed. "My bunk isn't even close to a window. And you know they don't let us out at night."

"I'm out there. I can take pictures for you, if you like."

"Would you?" Sam's brown eyes lit up. "You're the best, Em."

"Any time." She touched his arm. "Do you need money or anything? I can deposit some in your inmate account."

"No, thanks. Save it for your down payment."

"What down payment?"

"I thought you and Carmichael were going to buy a house."

"No. We broke up."

"Really? But I thought you said he was the one. You were raving about him and said you'd bring him for a visit." Sam broke off as understanding dawned in his eyes. "You guys broke up because of me, didn't you?"

"He was afraid his parents couldn't handle it." Emma cleared her throat. "They're in politics. It was all about projecting the right image."

"Sorry, Em." Sam's big eyes were doleful. "If it weren't for me, you'd be happily married by now."

"Don't be ridiculous." She squeezed his arm. "If he

couldn't accept you, then he couldn't accept me. I was sad for a while but I'm over him now."

"Good." Sam looked more upbeat. "I never liked him anyway. He seemed so snobby in your letters."

"Speaking of letters," Emma said, glad she'd found her opening. "Why did you stop writing?"

Sam was quiet for a few moments before turning to look out the window. "I got in trouble, Em. I can't tell you more but don't worry. I'm okay now."

"Was it drugs?"

"How did you—" He whipped his head to the left and right and seeing nobody proceeded. "Yes. It was drugs, but they weren't mine. I swear it, Em. I haven't touched the stuff since the day I got arrested."

"That's great." Emma touched his hand.

She was about to say more but Madison brought in a patient with abdominal pain at that moment and clinic started. She did a history and physical and concluded the man likely had gastritis from too much ibuprofen. Emma prescribed him omeprazole and warned him to stop his NSAIDS. She next treated a few "spider bites," big abscesses that she enjoyed incising and draining. Then came the usual upper respiratory infections and back pain.

Toward lunchtime, Emma called Maxim's secretary to confirm his availability for their three o'clock appointment. Unfortunately, one thing led to another and by the time three o'clock rolled around, Emma still had several patients left to see. She rushed through them but as she was wrapping up, a Code 1 was called over the radio system. Ms. Bryant and Madison ran to answer it.

"Man down, beaten in the bathroom," a fuzzy voice said

over Smith's radio. "He's barely breathing. There's blood all over. 911 already called. On way to Urgent Care now."

Oh, my God. Emma yanked at her necklace. Could it be Sam? His shift had ended a couple of hours ago. *Someone had beaten him earlier this year—had they done it again? Was it her brother who was barely breathing? Where the heck were they?* Emma rushed out of the clinic as the nurses were pushing in a stretcher. An inmate lay on top, his eyes swollen shut, his jaw misshapen. Half his ear was hanging off.

He was white. It wasn't her brother. Emma's heart started thumping again.

"IV, O2, monitor. Now please," Emma ordered, appalled at the bad shape the man was in. "What happened? Can you hear me?" The victim mumbled something incoherent. Emma seized her stethoscope, quickly performing the primary survey. "Airway intact. Trachea not deviated. Breath sounds decreased on the left. Pulse present in femoral, none in radial."

"Blood pressure eighty-five over forty-five, heart rate one forty," Madison shouted.

"What's the pulse ox?" Emma yelled back.

"Ninety percent on one hundred percent non-rebreather."

"IV in yet?" Emma asked. "I need two large bore ones."

"Sixteen gauge in."

"Hang a bag of normal saline." Emma listened to the man's chest again. "No breath sounds on the left." She ripped open the man's shirt. "Trachea deviated! Give me a fourteen gauge catheter!"

"Pulse ox fifty percent!" Ms. Bryant shouted. "He's crashing!"

Madison tossed her the catheter. Mid-clavicular line, left second intercostal space. Emma pushed. A loud hiss gushed out some air. *Thank God.* She removed the needle. Trachea now back to midline.

"Good call with the angiocath," Madison called out. "Pulse ox now ninety-five percent."

"You saved him, Doc," Smith said from the foot of the bed, his eyes wide.

"Thanks guys, but he's not out of the woods yet. Keep the oxygen going." Emma secured the catheter with tape and then listened again with her stethoscope. Yes, breath sounds now present on the left.

The patient twisted his head back and forth, mumbling something. There was something familiar about him. She leaned closer and held his hand. "It's okay. You had a collapsed lung and I had to push a small tube in your chest. Try to relax. The ambulance will be here in a few minutes."

The man cracked his eyes open. "You promised. You promised, Doc," he said, his voice hoarse.

Goosebumps popped up on Emma's arms. It was her patient staring back at her, the asthmatic she'd helped move.

"Mr. Cavendish?" Emma squeezed the man's hand. Her heart lurched as a thousand knives danced in her stomach.

"Why did you tell them?" His voice was barely audible. "You promised you wouldn't."

"I didn't tell them," Emma breathed out. "I didn't."

"They got me in the bathroom. So many of them I couldn't fight back." Tears trickled down his swollen cheek. "Am I going to be okay?"

Abrasions and cuts flayed his chest. His face puffed out like a swollen watermelon, and his left ear seemed to be hanging on by a thread. Emma bit her lip.

"Dr. Edwards did everything she could, Cavendish." Smith patted the patient's good shoulder. "The paramedics are on their way. Hang in there, buddy."

Emma tried to speak but couldn't come up with anything. Soon the paramedics arrived and whisked Cavendish to the local trauma center.

"It's okay, Doc." Madison's golden brown eyes were full of sympathy. "You didn't know he'd get hurt. You were only trying to help."

"I said his dorm was damp." Emma felt a wetness on her cheek and brushed it away. "Not cigarette smoke. Steam. How could they do this to him?"

"They can be pretty vicious. It's not your fault."

"I want them arrested." She caught herself and laughed, a small hysterical sound that burst forth. "But they're already in prison. What else can you do to them? Oh my God. I can't believe it. That poor boy."

Cavendish's bloodied face and half-missing ear flashed before her eyes. Had she played a role in the attack? She should've spoken with Maxim earlier. Should have told him at the birthday party. Maybe he could have intervened somehow. Sent out more guards to monitor the place better. Better monitoring might have saved Cavendish.

Something had to be done to catch the men responsible. She couldn't sit here and let the perpetrators get away. Emma shoved her stethoscope in her bag and ran up the hill to inform Maxim. Surely he'd want to know and help catch the assailants. *Please, please let him be in his office.* A few minutes later, she rushed into the admin building and flung open his door. *Damn.* No one was there. She knocked on the room next door and jerked it open.

"Is Mr. Chambers here?" she huffed out to the grim elderly woman sitting behind the desk.

"No." The woman's voice was as cool as ice.

"Ms. Lee, right?" Emma forced out a placating smile. "I'm Dr. Edwards. Can you tell me where the warden is?"

"Your appointment was for three o'clock. He's already left."

"Please. I need to speak with him."

"Didn't you get his message?" The woman glared at her. "I told him not to bother but he waited for over an hour for you to show up. He even called down there to try to talk with you."

"I was busy with patients."

"He's available tomorrow between one and two. If you're free."

"No, thanks." How could she wait that long? It was imperative she reached him today. Emma raced out the Eagle gate and was panting by the time she got into her car. *Where was that business card Smith had given her?* She flipped through her purse and finally found it wedged between two gum packs.

He'd told her she could always try him on his cell, hadn't he? Or was it something polite he spewed out to everybody? The guy probably was furious with her for making him wait earlier. But it wasn't her fault. She was busy taking care of his inmates. She punched the number in and waited. After the fifth ring, his distinctive voice came on the voicemail.

Just her luck. Emma rubbed her temple and waited for the beep. Cavendish's bruised and bloodied face flashed before her again, and she squeezed her eyes tight.

"Hi, Maxim?" *God, she sounded so pathetic.* She cleared her voice and wiped away the tears. "Sorry to bother you but it's Emma. Emma Edwards. I need to talk with you. Where are you? I didn't want to call but it's an emergency. You see..." She swallowed a few times. *What was she doing?* Cavendish was already in the hospital. Where was the emergency? There was nothing Maxim could do tonight. She sounded hysterical and needed to pull herself together. The talk could surely wait until tomorrow, couldn't it? She took in a deep breath. "Sorry. It's actually not an emergency but I need to talk with you. Can you call me back? Please?"

Emma pressed the Off button and threw the phone back into her purse. *Okay, it wasn't that bad, was it?* She'd seen trauma patients before. She'd rotated in the ER many times. And she hadn't told anyone about the cigarettes. She wasn't really to blame for the beating, was she? In any case, she couldn't do anything tonight. She was going to head home and take a long, hot bath. And tomorrow she'd tell Maxim about the beating. Surely he was going to help somehow. He could investigate, find out who the attackers were, punish them as they deserved. Her cell suddenly rang. *Was it Maxim?*

Emma fumbled in her purse and yanked out the phone.

"Hello? Maxim?"

"Emma? It's me. John."

"John." Emma let out a huff of air. "I can't talk right now."

"What's the matter? You don't sound good."

"I have to go."

"But Em. I want to talk to you. I'm sorry about every-thing."

"Everything?"

"Yes. So, your brother's a criminal. I get that. I can deal with it."

"You'll deal with it?" Emma gripped the phone harder.

"Yes. He's not going to get out for a while. We don't have to tell my family. You can even take me to meet him." She heard him swallow. "But there'll be guards around, right? I don't have to be alone with him, do I?"

"I can't believe I'm hearing this."

"I know. You can thank me later."

"You've got to be kidding me."

"What?"

"We're done, John. Finished. Don't call me anymore."

"What? Didn't you hear what I said?"

"Bye, John." She slammed the phone shut. *Why had she dated him for that long?* Riley was right. The guy was a total loser. As she was pulling out of the parking space, her cell rang again.

"Leave me alone, John," she yelled. "We're finished, can't you get that?"

"Hold on, Emma. It's Maxim. Are you okay?"

"Maxim?" *God, she should have checked her caller ID.* This was definitely not her day.

"Yes," he said, his voice a little frantic for some reason. "Where are you? What's wrong?"

"I'm about to drive home."

"So you're safe? You're not hurt?"

"No. I'm not hurt." *Was that why he'd sounded so worried?* She hadn't meant to scare him. "Something happened at the prison."

"What? Where's Smith? I told him not to leave you alone." His voice rose a notch. "Are you sure you're okay?"

"I'm fine. It's not me; it's one of the inmates. He got beat up pretty badly. Can I tell you about it?"

"Now isn't a good time." He sounded more than a bit frazzled.

"No? It won't take long." *Don't go.* He'd always seemed strong and indomitable. She wanted to throw everything into his capable hands and let him take charge. "Please?"

A long silence ensued. Emma thought he'd hung up until he spoke again. "I'm in the emergency room. I can't really talk right now."

"I'm sorry. Why didn't you tell me?" Emma said, feeling like a heel. "Are you okay?"

"I'm fine." She heard a long sigh. "It's my dad. He fell and they're doing some testing."

"Is he alright?"

"I don't know." Another sigh. "I'm waiting for the test results."

Maxim sounded broken, so different from the formidable man she knew. "What hospital are you in?" she asked, wishing she could help somehow. Cavendish would have to wait for now. No way could she dump problems at work on him at the moment.

Maxim named a famous hospital in LA.

"My best friend works there." *And Riley happened to be working that night, too.* "And I know some of the doctors. You want me to come? Maybe I can help." It was the least she could do after the hours he'd spent with her in the emergency room the other day.

He hesitated for a few seconds. "You don't mind? I don't want to impose."

"You're not. I'll be there as soon as I can."

She hung up and dialed another number. *Darn. The ER must have been busy for her friend not to pick up.* Emma texted instead, asking Riley to look out for Maxim's dad.

"Emma," her friend greeted her as soon as she arrived in the emergency room a while later. "Why didn't you tell me?"

"Tell you what?"

Riley wiped a hand over her forehead and glanced at her pager. "That you were talking about *the* Maxim Chambers."

"What? What are you talking about?"

"Chambers of the Chambers Neurology Institute."

"You mean…"

"Yes." Riley grabbed Emma's arm and leaned closer. "The guy donates a ton to the hospital. We even have a wing named after him."

"Shoot. I didn't know." *Unbelievable. Maxim was that rich?*

"Admin has been all over me. They want everything to be perfect." Riley frowned. "But I'm afraid some things can't be fixed."

"What do you mean?"

"I was about to go talk to him." Her friend pressed her pager to silence. "Admin is hounding me for the results of his dad's tests. That's them beeping me again. Come on. He's this way. His father's still in radiology, but admin wants me to brief him on what I know so far. Crap. I hate to deliver bad news."

Jesus. It didn't sound good, whatever her friend had to tell Maxim. She followed Riley down a long white corridor, a gnawing sensation beginning in her stomach. She knew Maxim supported charity but the Chambers Institute? *Come on.* It was huge, treating stroke patients from all over the US. She'd heard there were even branches sprouting off in the East Coast.

"I was in a trauma when you called," Riley was saying as she pressed a button to open up a set of double doors. "Yes. I know. Gawk all you want. It's our new VIP wing.

All private rooms with flat-screen TVs, gourmet food, the whole works. Nothing but the best for your Mr. Chambers."

"He's not mine."

"I know that. His wife and kid are with him."

"What?" Emma stumbled.

"His family's here." Riley took in a deep breath. "Good thing, too. He's going to need a lot of support right now."

"I don't think he's married." *Or was he?* She'd assumed he was single. *Had she been wrong all this time?*

"Maybe it's his girlfriend. They seem pretty tight." Riley checked her pager. "That's radiology about Mr. Chambers's CT. I'll be right back. They're in the room two doors down on the right."

Emma stepped forward and knocked on the room, her heart pounding.

CHAPTER 15

"Relax, Maxim," Lani said, squeezing his arm. "I'm sure she'll be here soon."

Maxim switched Kyle's sleeping body to the right side of his chest. His godson was at least ten pounds heavier since the last time he carried him. "It's been over two hours. Something bad may have happened to her."

"What? Dr. Washington was just here." Lani scrunched her eyebrows together.

"Sorry. I was talking about Dr. Edwards."

"The one from Albatross?" Lani's voice picked up. "She's meeting you here?"

"Yes. What? Why the strange look?" Maxim patted Kyle's back to soothe him back to sleep. "It's a sixty-mile drive. She sounded really distraught on the phone earlier. Maybe she got into an accident."

"Maybe it's only traffic."

"It's almost eight." Maxim checked his watch. "I shouldn't have let her drive."

"Let?"

"You know what I mean. She's my employee. I'd feel horrible if something happened to her." He groaned when he noticed the twinkle in Lani's eyes. "It's not what you think. She bugs the hell out of me most of the time."

"Hmm. Interesting. So what's she like?"

"It's complicated." *Women. Did they have to ask about everything?* Maxim looked at his watch again. *Where the hell was Emma? And where was the ER doctor anyway?* His father had been down in radiology for over an hour already.

A soft knock sounded on the door. Emma entered, wearing jeans and a pretty pink sweater. *Thank goodness.* She looked pale though, her eyes wide with anxiety and something else Maxim couldn't decipher.

"You came," he said, his spirits rising for the first time that day.

"Of course. I told you I would." Her eyes flew to Lani and then fixated on his godson. A brief, wistful expression passed over her face.

"That was over two hours ago." Something tugged in Maxim's chest. *Why did she look a little lost?*

"There was a lot of traffic." Her eyes focused back on Lani. "Hi. I'm Emma Edwards."

"Nice to meet you. I'm Lani Blair." Lani shook hands with the doctor and then pointed in his direction. "That's my son sleeping over there."

"Oh." Emma bit her lower lip.

"How long have you been working at Albatross?" Lani shot Maxim a significant look. "And more importantly, how come I haven't heard more about you until now?"

"Leave it, Lani." Maxim stood and delivered Kyle to his meddlesome mom. The boy let out a little protest before settling in her arms. "You want to sit down, Doc? You look tired."

A text beeped. Lani glanced down at her phone. "That's Alex. He wants some updates. I'll be right back, okay?" She headed out the door with Kyle.

Maxim took in a deep breath, a weight falling off his chest. Damn if it didn't feel good having Emma here. Strange as it was, her presence calmed and soothed him somehow. Maybe it was because he was in the hospital, her usual stomping grounds. She was smart and capable. She could help him through this. And she was damned attractive, too, in that pink sweater of hers. *Who knew the woman had such nice curves?* Maxim cleared his throat.

"Do you want me to go?" Emma suddenly asked.

"What?" *Where the hell had that come from?*

"I don't want to intrude. Your girlfriend may not like it."

"Girlfriend?" Maxim shook his head. "You mean Lani? She's not my girlfriend."

"She's your wife?" Emma's face paled.

"No. Of course not." He couldn't believe she'd think such a thing. *Didn't she know anything about him?* "She's my best friend's wife."

"Oh. Thank goodness." Emma brought a hand to her mouth. "I mean. It's okay, too, if you're married. I wasn't expecting it, that's all."

"I'm not married. Never have been. And I'm not dating anyone. Just to make things clear." Maxim groaned inside. *Good job, Max. Really smooth there.* What the hell was he doing? His father was sick and here he was babbling about his personal life.

Thank goodness Dr. Washington came in then with his father in tow. An X-ray tech was pushing the gurney. "How is he?" *Please let there be good news.* But no. His father looked worse, lying shriveled up in the center of the gurney, his left leg awkwardly bent outward at the hip. An IV dripped some fluids into his right arm and a mask delivered oxygen to his face. His eyes were closed.

"He broke his hip." Dr. Washington cast Emma a harried look. "And he has a bladder infection. We're giving him some fluids and antibiotics."

"Is that all?" *That better be all.*

"How did he fall?" Dr. Washington asked, her eyes somber.

"They were changing him. He wanted his favorite pajamas but the nurse was new so she put on something else." Maxim closed his eyes. *Pops must have felt so distraught. If only he could erase the last twelve hours.* "Sometimes they forget that he's only partially paralyzed. Anyway, he struggled and fell off the bed."

"It was ground level? He hadn't been standing, right?"

"No. The bed's only a couple of feet off the ground."

The two doctors exchanged a look that made Maxim's blood run cold. "What is it?"

"I just got the CT result. Your father has a large bleed in his head."

A giant vise squeezed down on his chest. "Can they fix it?"

"I don't think so." Dr. Washington fiddled with her pager. "The nursing home tells me your dad has been bedbound and nonverbal for years. I know it's hard to talk about but does he have a DNR order?"

"What the hell does that have to do with anything?" Maxim bit out. "Do everything you can. I want the best for my father."

"We do, too," Dr. Washington said. "Sometimes the best is to be comfortable."

"What are you saying?"

"Maybe it's time to let him go. We can make him comfortable."

"Let him go?" *How dare she?* "Have you spoken to a neurosurgeon yet?"

"Yes. He said he can operate but it's pretty risky. Your father may die on the table."

"But without the surgery, he's going to die anyway." Maxim clenched his fists. "I want the surgery. It's his only chance."

"Are you sure? Your father is very sick already." Dr. Washington, fool that she was, didn't seem to comprehend him. "Think about his quality of life. It's best to make him comfortable."

"Please get out." Maxim gripped the gurney's railing. "Call the neurosurgeon. I want to talk to him."

"Surgery won't help in the big picture," the stubborn doctor insisted.

"I said get out!" A red mist grew over his vision. Maxim picked up a nearby vase and before he knew it, it was on the floor, smashed to smithereens. His father moaned and twisted his head from side to side. Maxim rushed over. "Sorry, Pops. It was only a vase." He leaned over and brushed a hand over his father's cheek.

An ER tech in blue scrubs flung open the door. "Is everything okay in here?"

"Yes." Emma shot him a worried look. "The vase got knocked over. Could you help clean it up?"

Maxim turned back to his father. His old man kept twisting his head from side to side. "It's okay, Pops. I'm here. I'm not going to let anyone hurt you." *Not anymore.* He was going to protect his father at all cost. A brief memory of that night fifteen years ago flashed before his eyes. He could still see the two men in black masks as they pulled out their guns.

"Maybe we can get him some extra morphine," someone said from across the room.

Emma was still there; they were alone. The damned ER doctor must have finally listened to him and left. And the floor was clean again.

"He seems to be calming down," Emma said, her voice soft. She brushed a gentle finger down his father's arm. Something squeezed hard at Maxim's chest. She was so kind and patient. And lovely. He didn't deserve her compassion, big brute that he was. How could he have lost his temper like that?

"It's tough when someone you love is sick," she said, her eyes full of sympathy. "My mom died a few years ago. It still hurts. I carry her picture with me all the time. In this pendant." Emma showed him her necklace. "It's hard now but every day the pain eases one tiny bit."

How did she get to be so wise and brave, this little slip of a woman? Maxim cleared his throat and blinked a couple of times. "He was an amazing father."

"I'm sorry. I wish I could make it better for you somehow."

"Tell me they can fix his bleed. That's all I need to know."

"I'm afraid it's not that simple. Riley is a really good doctor. She only wants what's best for her patients."

"You mean Dr. Washington?"

"Yes. She's my best friend."

"How could this be happening?" Maxim dragged a hand over his face. "He wasn't always like this, you know.

He was a science professor. His mind was brilliant, full of bright ideas."

"What happened?" Her voice washed over him like a gentle wave.

"Some thieves robbed our house a couple of years after I graduated college, when I was an EMT." Maxim looked over, not sure if she'd want the whole sordid story. Her eyes were warm and encouraging. "They killed my mom and shot my father in the head. The bullet got the left side of his brain. He became partially paralyzed and mute. Sometimes I think he recognizes me but other times..." Maxim shook his head.

"And he's been that way since?" Emma nudged him on.

"Yes. That was fifteen years ago."

"How horrible."

"Yes." He dug a hand through his hair. "But you know the worst part? The bastards who shot them are still out there somewhere. I've tried to find them so many times but it's like they disappeared into thin air."

"The police couldn't help?"

"They investigated but nothing panned out." He sighed. "Sometimes I think maybe they're already caught. That they could be in my prison."

"Is that why you're so hard on the inmates?"

"What?" *Was that why? He'd never considered it.* "Maybe."

Her eyes shone with compassion. A wave of guilt washed over him. *Would she look at him like that if she knew the whole story?* He braced himself for her disgust and was about to tell her when Lani came back into the room.

"Hey. How's it going?" his friend asked, her hands full with Kyle.

"He's still asleep?"

"Yes. My nanny forgot the key to our house." Lani sent him an apologetic look. "Do you mind if I go let her in?"

"No. Go ahead." He pointed to his godson. "He needs to be in his own bed. Your arms are going to fall off if you keep holding him like that."

"I'll come right back. My nanny can watch him."

"Thanks, but you've done enough already." Maxim sent her a grateful smile. Alex sure got lucky in the marriage department. Lani was not only gorgeous but good through and through. Kind of like... *Good God*. No way was he going to go there.

"Okay, I'll go but any news yet?" Lani shifted Kyle to her other hip.

"His hip's broken and..." No need to trouble Lani about the bleed. She'd never get any rest if she knew. "And we're waiting for another specialist."

"All right. Text me with any updates. Alex says he'll call as soon as he lands back in LA tomorrow." Lani turned toward the doctor and smiled. "It was nice meeting you, Dr. Edwards. Hopefully, we'll meet again soon."

"Please, call me Emma. They only call me Doctor at work."

"Thanks. Bye, Emma." Lani left with a friendly nod.

Emma. The name suited her. Short and sweet. Maxim shook his head, knowing the futility of his thoughts. She was his employee and strictly off-limits. And yet right now with his father deathly ill, he didn't give a damn about policy. He couldn't imagine going through this ordeal without her.

"She seems really nice. I take it the boy is your godson?" Emma asked, looking slightly bemused for some reason. "You're pretty good with kids, you know that?"

"They're much simpler than adults." Maxim walked back to the bed. His father's mouth was open and his breathing slow but regular. He glanced at his watch. Thirty minutes already and still no neurosurgeon.

"Let me check if someone's coming," Emma said.

Amazing. She was reading his thoughts. Which didn't bode well for his peace of mind. Luckily the neurosurgeon came in at that moment, a short, older man with white hair and a long mustache. Maxim's heart thundered. *Please, let it be good news. Please say they can operate.*

"I'm Dr. Barrymore."

Maxim shook his hand. There was nothing but grimness on the other man's face.

"I'm sorry but we had a second neuroradiologist review your dad's CT." The doctor tugged at his mustache. "The blood is actually not only in the cerebrum but progressing into the brainstem also. I'm afraid we can't operate."

"How long does he have?" Maxim forced out.

"Hours. Maybe a day at most."

Maxim seized the bedrail. A cold sweat broke over him. The neurosurgeon said something else and left. *Hours. Only hours.* How could this be happening? He touched his father's face and felt some wetness on his fingers. *Was his old man crying?* But no. His father's cheeks were dry. And his leg still lay twisted. *Should they turn him on his side?* He'd always liked looking out the window and maybe he'd be more comfortable that way.

God. Pops looked so broken. Frail and almost lifeless. Maybe he'd died all those years ago. And it had been all Maxim's fault. Why hadn't he locked the door that night? His parents were always reminding him to lock up after himself but he'd been in a hurry. Rushing to a party.

Concentrating on having fun as usual when his parents were left alone with their door unlocked. The thieves had entered right through the door. It was almost as if he had fired the gun himself. *What kind of stupid idiot son would do that to his own parents?*

It was all his fault. If only he'd come home sooner. If only he'd locked the door. He had killed both his parents that day. And no matter how many criminals he locked up, how many bad guys he punished, it was never going to be enough. His parents were never coming back. *Oh, God.* Maxim fell to his knees and let out a howl of rage.

Suddenly gentle arms wrapped around him as a sweet rosewater scent filled his nostrils. Emma hovered next to him, her beautiful face lined with concern. He didn't deserve her sympathy, but he couldn't help himself. She was his savior. The one light shining in his dark world. He buried his face in her abdomen, unable to control the violent sobs that racked through his body.

Emma brushed a hand through Maxim's wavy hair, surprised at how soft it felt. There were sprinkles of gray at the temples but for the most part his hair was as glossy black as her bird's. The familiar scent of coffee with a hint of spice emanated from him. She clasped him to her, knowing how hard it was to lose a parent, even when death had been expected for a long time. *The poor man.* If only she could offer some comfort. The warmth of his embrace enveloped her and Emma pulled him closer.

"It's okay," she whispered. "Just let it out. It's okay."

"It's never going to be okay." Maxim's body shuddered. "I killed them that day. It was my fault."

"What? What are you talking about?"

"I didn't lock the front door." His face was racked with guilt. "The robbers had free entrance. I might as well have pulled the trigger myself."

"How can you say that? It's not your fault." Emma cupped his face between her hands. "The robbers killed your parents. You had nothing to do with it."

"How can you be so forgiving?" Maxim's silver eyes locked with hers.

How could she ever have thought him cold and unfeeling? His eyes shimmered with tears. He brushed them away and caressed her cheek with the pads of his fingers. Her face tingled. She leaned in, mesmerized by the tender look on his face. She touched the short bristles on his chin and bent her head closer. He sucked in an audible breath, tightening his arms around her before suddenly pushing her away.

"Sorry. I need a moment," he said, his voice hoarse. He stumbled to the nearest window and stared out into the dark night, his hand clenched.

Oh my God. She'd almost kissed him. What was wrong with her? The man was wallowing in grief and she was coming on to him. *How could she have been so foolish?* He was her boss, and she best remember that. Maxim's face was stiff and formal again when he turned back. *Good.* It was better to keep things platonic between them.

"Do you think they can turn my father toward the window?" he said, avoiding her eyes. "He needs his brown pajamas also. They're his favorite. And I need Walt Whitman's *Leaves of Grass.*"

"*Leaves of Grass*?" Emma asked, wondering at the choice. "That's his favorite book. I need to read it to him."

Of course she agreed to assist. *If only she could do more.* Maxim didn't break down again. For the most part he remained polite yet distant. Still, Emma couldn't believe she'd once thought him a brute. Underneath that fierce exterior beat a vulnerable heart. How glad she was to have caught a glimpse of the tender man inside.

In the end, an aide from the nursing home brought over the book and helped put on his father's brown pajamas. They turned his father toward the window, making sure the old man's bad leg didn't get in the way. Emma took over reading *Leaves of Grass* when Maxim's eyes drifted shut toward the early hours of the morning.

Maxim's father passed away as dawn broke through the horizon. Emma woke Maxim up when she knew the end was near. The old man's breaths had become more agonal and labored. His hands were cooler to the touch. His eyes drifted open as the sun's early rays filtered through the window. Maxim held his father's hand while Emma stood close by, gazing out at the dawn. As the old man exhaled his last breath, a cloud of blackbirds flew over the sky.

CHAPTER 16

"Dr. Edwards." Dr. Kaye's shrill voice jolted Emma out of her slump. "Wake up."

"Sorry." Emma rubbed a hand over her weary eyes. She might have drifted off for a few seconds there; she wasn't quite sure. She gave a self-conscious smile. The other doctors were shooting her concerned looks from across the table. "I had a really long night."

"Then maybe you should have stayed home," Kaye said, tapping her pen.

"Yes. Sorry." She rubbed her neck and tried to stretch her stiff shoulders. She'd gotten home an hour ago from the hospital. Maxim had stayed behind to take care of the morgue arrangements. Emma had been tempted to stay home but the fresh memory of Cavendish's attack was too raw to ignore. She needed to know how he was doing. And maybe she could discuss the attack with the doctors instead of going straight to Maxim. The poor man had enough on his plate at the moment without her bothering him. He'd probably take at least a week off. Which made it only more imperative that she tell Kaye or Julien now rather than wait.

So she related to them what had happened with the cigarettes. Including how she'd arranged for Cavendish's move and how afraid he'd been of retaliation.

"It's not your fault," Bryce Churchill reassured her immediately when she was done. "They're always fighting around here. Somebody's bound to get hurt."

"And maybe it wasn't even about the cigarettes," Dr. Parker pointed out. "Could be Cavendish owing some money. And his guy got tired of waiting."

"Or maybe Cavendish did something really bad to one of the other inmates," Dr. Pan chimed in.

"You never know," Dr. Yee said. "Cavendish could be lying about the whole thing and only wanted to get moved. Maybe he didn't like his bunkies."

"What are you talking about?" *Why were they so dismissive?* "He had an asthma attack. It was bad. I saw it."

"We know," Dr. Ross said. "But what triggered it? Was it really cigarette smoke?"

"Or maybe he himself was smoking," Dr. Tran said.

"And lied about the bathroom smoke just to get moved," someone else added.

"Lied about it? Why would he do that?" Emma shook her head, mystified. *How could they not feel sorry for the guy?* He was beat up because he'd snitched. She was sure of it.

"Because he's an inmate." Dr. Kaye shrugged her shoulders. "They make up things all the time. So the guy was beat up. Who cares? Custody will deal with it. It's out of our hands."

"They almost killed him," Emma insisted. "All because he told me about the cigarettes. And why are they even smoking in here? I thought it was illegal."

"It is." Julien leaned back in his chair. "But sometimes Custody doesn't catch them doing it. Or they look the other way."

"But that's wrong." Emma took in a deep breath. "Cavendish's asthma almost killed him. They should enforce the rules more."

"We're in a prison." Dr. Kaye's sneer was ever present. "Inmates are going to do what they're going to do. They're criminals. They can't help themselves. They lie, they cheat, they steal, they smoke and do drugs, they fight. It's in their nature. You can't change it. Just accept it."

"I can't accept that." Emma half-rose from her seat. "Criminals can change. They can rehabilitate. And I'm sure Cavendish didn't lie to me. We have to help him somehow."

"You did," Julien said gently. "You sent him to the hospital. Come on, Emma. You can only do so much. You can't fix the system."

The meeting disbanded soon after. Emma found herself in an empty room, too exhausted to move, both physically and emotionally. So none of them believed Cavendish. He was an inmate, so he was lying. And even if he were telling the truth, who cared, right? Inmates got hurt. They fought, they killed each other. *What did you expect?*

"Ugh...." Emma groaned. What was she going to do? What hope was there for Sam if he was judged only by the color of his uniform?

How she hated the blind prejudice so prevalent against inmates. There was nothing to do except pack her materials together and head down the hill for another day in the Urgent Care. Her friend Phineas was fanning his feathers and belting out another song on her way down. *On-ke-kaaangh. On-ke-kaaangh.* His sharp eyes darted her way and then homed in on a caterpillar crawling on an out-reaching branch. *Snap!* He gobbled up his breakfast in one go.

Where is your colony, little one? Had he belonged to that cluster of blackbirds that had flown over the hospital earlier this morning? If so, he was really far from his family, like most of the inmates here. How many of the prisoners would love to fly away and join their family?

Urgent Care proceeded briskly as usual. She didn't have time to talk with Sam and only managed a brief glance to make sure he was doing okay. Dr. Ross had to attend his annual safety training, so Emma was left to hold up the fort. Half yawning, she managed to wade through three upper respiratory infections, two ankle sprains, a wrist injury, one abscess, an ingrown toenail, two cases of gastroenteritis, and a chest pain. She also spoke to Mr. Nash, making sure his pain was adequately controlled. The man inquired about his compassionate release and she reminded herself to ask Maxim next time she saw him.

Maxim. If she concentrated hard enough, she could conjure up his wonderful spicy coffee bean scent. She remembered the soft bristles on his face, the tender look in his eyes. *Had he gotten any sleep yet? When was the funeral? Was he handling it okay on his own?* They'd bonded during the night. How she longed to see him again all of a sudden.

Before she left, the Urgent Care nurses informed her that Cavendish had had a chest tube placed and had suffered some broken facial bones but otherwise was going to survive. His ear had been repaired. He was admitted to the trauma unit but they expected him to be released soon to the administrative segregation unit over at Chino to protect him from being beaten again. *Good. At least it was something.* As for finding the assailants and bringing them to justice, Custody told her they could only charge the men if Cavendish pointed out who they were. And knowing how he feared for his life, Emma doubted there was going to be anyone charged.

How ironic it was that crimes could be committed in prison with much more impunity than if they'd been executed on the street. *Did Maxim know this and simply look the other way?* How disappointed she'd be in him if it were true. She expected more of him, needed more of him than the tolerant dismissive attitude she'd heard at the morning meeting.

"Hey, Emma," Riley called her as soon as she got home. "How are you holding up?"

"All right," she said, swallowing a yawn. "Thanks for your help with Maxim yesterday."

"Maxim?"

She could hear the teasing in her friend's voice. "Yes. That's his first name." She took off her jacket but was too tired to change out of her work clothes.

"I know that." Riley's voice sobered. "Is he doing okay? Admin is worried to death, afraid he'll blame us for not doing enough. That poor old man."

"I don't think he blames you guys." Emma sat on her bed and kicked off her shoes. "You were great with him."

"Until he threw me out. You're right. The man can be pretty nasty."

"He was stressed out, Ri." Emma slid off her hair clip and lay back on the bed. "He's actually not that bad."

"Not bad, huh? Interesting. Anything you want to tell me?"

"Don't even start. He's my boss." Emma checked the clock. Her eyes felt like lead. *Four p.m.* A quick nap would be great. "Sorry, Ri. I'm about to crash right now."

"Just make sure he's single."

"He is, but you're reading too much into it." Emma stretched and yawned again.

"If you say so. We can talk later. Get some sleep."

A loud buzzing sound shook Emma awake hours later. She tossed a pillow over her head and buried herself underneath the covers. She was so not going to get that. It was the middle of the night; whoever wanted her could come back in the morning. She pulled another pillow over her head. The buzzing became banging. Loud banging. *Oh, for heaven's sake.* Whoever it was better have a good reason for jolting her out of her precious sleep. Emma threw back the covers and stumbled out of bed. Her eyes still felt heavy. Her foot slipped. *Drat.* Had that magazine been on the floor last night? The banging escalated.

"Okay. I'm coming." She lurched to the door and flung it open, blinking at the sunlight flooding her vision. "Oh, my God. It's so bright."

"It usually is in the afternoon," a familiar voice said.

Emma snapped her eyes open. *No, it couldn't be.* Yes, it certainly was, her frantic brain concluded. For standing in front of her was none other than Maxim Chambers, dressed casually in jeans and a light-blue T-shirt. She wasn't sure which she was more surprised by: his appearance at her doorstep or his attire. She'd never seen him dressed in anything but elegant custom-made suits. "Hi," she croaked out.

"Hello," he said, standing stiff and upright.

"What are you doing here?" Emma brushed the hair

back from her face. *God, she must have looked a mess. And was that a wet saliva stain trailing down her left cheek?* She swiped it away and rubbed her eyes again.

"May I come in?" Maxim asked.

"Sure." He dwarfed her studio the moment he crossed the threshold. "Uh, sorry. I just woke up. Do you mind if I?" She pointed to the bathroom. *Great, Emma. Very eloquent there.* "Make yourself at home." She rushed to the bathroom and slammed the door closed.

One look in the mirror and she almost fell again. Her hair was a complete rat's nest, and her shirt and pants hung on her body like old unwashed laundry. She stripped off the clothes and jumped in the shower. It took only five minutes but she felt a hundred times better by the time she emerged. But darn, she didn't have a change of clothes and couldn't imagine getting back into the outfit she'd slept in. The old faded blue robe hanging on the back of the door would have to do. She tied it securely at the waist and didn't bother drying her hair.

Why was Maxim here? Whatever the reason, she was sure it involved the prison and… *Oh my God. Did it have something to do with Sam? Had he discovered that Sam was her brother?* That would've been her worst nightmare. Second only to having pictures of Sam around the house that Maxim could easily recognize.

Emma made a swift mental inventory of her studio and breathed a sigh of relief. None of Sam's pictures were up yet. She'd moved recently from LA to Corona right after residency and hadn't had a chance to hang them. The only thing she managed to tape up was a big drawing Sam had sketched of his favorite blackbird. Which was nondescript and common, nothing to identify him by.

"I'm back," she said as she opened the door.

Maxim stood with his back to her, studying the blackbird picture with some attention. She quickly went over and examined it. No, nothing incriminating there. Only a simple "To Emma, with Love" at the top of the drawing. *Good, Sam hadn't even signed his name.*

"It's a beautiful picture," Maxim said in that grave way of his, not looking up from the drawing.

"Yes, my brother gave it to me," she said. "He loves all birds, but the blackbird is his favorite."

"He's very talented."

"Thanks. You know, we have a blackbird at the prison." Emma flipped her wet hair back. "Have you seen him by any chance?"

"No. Can't say that I have." Maxim finally looked up. His eyes widened and he stared at her for several long seconds, not saying anything before clearing his throat and turning away.

"Sorry, I was in a hurry."

What the heck was wrong with the man? The robe covered her from head to toe but he was acting as if she were half-naked or something. *Men.* Emma groaned to herself as she grabbed some clothes from the closet and darted back to the bathroom to change. If she hurried, she'd have time for some breakfast on the way to the prison. *Wait.* Emma screeched to a halt. *Did Maxim say it was already afternoon? Yikes!* She snatched up her watch from the counter. Two thirty. She'd slept half the day away.

Emma dashed back to the living room. "I overslept," she said, picking up her keys from the kitchen counter. "I have to go. I'm so late. Evil Knievel is going to kill me."

"Evil Knievel?" Maxim's mouth twitched.

"Yes, Evil Knievel Kaye." Emma slid on her shoes. "You know how she is."

"I do."

"Then you know why I have to run," Emma said, a little distracted by the potential smile playing on his face. "I'll see you at work?"

"No, don't go." Maxim raised his hand. "I already called and told them you're taking the day off."

"What? You can't do that. What if they need me?"

"It's past two o'clock. The clinics are almost closed. And all the doctors were there today."

"How do you know?"

"I was there. When you didn't show, we called your cell but nobody answered." He gave her an accusing look. "We were worried. By policy, if an employee doesn't show up at work, we're supposed to locate them to make sure they're okay."

"That's why you're here?" Emma blinked a couple of times. "You could have sent someone else. Aren't you busy with stuff?"

"I wanted to come." He gazed down at her, a peculiar look in his eyes. "To thank you for your help with my father. You were there for hours. I really appreciate it."

"You're welcome. Sorry I couldn't do more." *Did he actually show up at work today? It was too soon. He definitely should've taken more time off.* "How are you doing?"

"Hanging in there. I have to collect his things from the nursing home so I should probably head off." He turned to go but suddenly swung around. "Before I forget, what did you want to tell me that day in the car?"

"Oh, that." Emma sighed. *Should she trouble him about*

Cavendish now when his father had just died? "Maybe this isn't the right time."

"Why?" he said in that abrupt tone of his.

Her stomach let out a loud growl all of a sudden. "Sorry, I haven't eaten yet."

Maxim frowned. "Come on. Let's get you some food. You can tell me what's going on over lunch."

"You're sure they're okay about me not coming in today?"

"Yes. Positive."

"What about the nursing home? Weren't you planning to go there?"

"It can wait. If it's about my prison, I'd rather hear it now."

"Okay, then. Lunch sounds great." *In every way. How nice to be able to spend some extra time with him.*

CHAPTER 17

Whatever time they had together, Maxim had to make it short. He hadn't planned for the lunch. No. It was supposed to be a swift in and out. Make sure she was okay, thank her for her help with his father, and then deal with whatever she had wanted to talk about when she'd called him in the emergency room. *So much for his good intentions.* When her stomach had grumbled and she'd looked near famished, how could he not suggest lunch? He wasn't going to have her starve, not on his watch. She was thin enough already.

And just because she was beautiful and generous to a fault, that didn't really concern him, did it? The intense connection he'd felt with her at the hospital had been a product of their environment. Nothing personal. He'd been overwhelmed with grief, kind of shamefully so. He'd even imagined her almost kissing him when she'd caressed his cheek. *Kiss him? Who was he kidding? She'd been showing him sympathy, nothing else.* Maxim shook his head. Hopefully, she'd forget about the whole episode.

For God's sake, Emma was his employee. He had no

business feeling anything for her. Least of all the consuming worry that had clawed at him when she'd been a no-show at work this morning. Had she fallen asleep at the wheels the day before? Panic had gripped him, thinking she was lying hurt somewhere. Of course he had to come himself to make sure she was okay. He was a responsible employer, nothing more. And his world was filled with bitterness and vengeance, a dark place he had no wish to drag her to. She was everything good in the world and deserved to be surrounded by sunshine and happiness.

If he'd dreamt about her last night, it was only a dream, nothing substantial. And this morning with that old robe on, surely it was only his recent lack of sleep that had him thinking it was the sexiest garment ever. That had him imagining sliding it off her, exposing her smooth, silky skin. She'd smelled like fresh clean soap and shampoo. When had soap ever turned him on? *Never.* Maxim's point exactly. Lack of sleep was addling his mind.

Thank goodness she'd changed quickly. But why the heck was she wearing those tight jeans and that close-fitting purple top? Where were her plain slacks and oversized dress shirts? Damn. He had to make it short, had to ignore the deep sense of contentment that seeped through him as she smiled at him from across the table at the restaurant.

"So, what's good here?" she asked, her stomach making another growl.

"Everything if you're hungry. What do you like?"

"Anything with pasta or seafood, but no fish."

"Okay, their angel hair shrimp scampi is really good. And also their seafood jambalaya." He perused the menu. "Spaghetti with meatballs is another good one."

"All right, I'll take them."

"Which one?"

"All three," she said, her gaze direct as usual. "You don't mind, do you? We can split the bill."

"No." He'd never heard anything so distasteful. Of course he'd pay. "I'll pay. It's just…you're sure you can eat all that food?"

"Trust me." She gave him a lopsided smile. "When I'm hungry, I can eat the whole house down."

And she meant it. *Fascinating.* He'd never seen anyone eat that much. She'd started with the scampi and cleaned the plate within ten minutes. Next she attacked the spaghetti with gusto, leaving only a few meatballs behind, and then the jambalaya had slowly but surely disappeared over the next hour.

"Where do you put all of it?" Maxim asked, still not quite believing his eyes.

"Fast metabolism," she said. "Is there any dessert?"

Maxim laughed and felt the unused facial muscles work for the first time in what felt like forever.

"Hey, you laughed," Emma said, her emerald eyes shining at him. "You should do it more often."

Damn. Those eyes were going to kill him. And what the hell had happened to keeping it short? Fool that he was, he'd been too distracted by her eating.

"What's wrong?" Her worried voice came across the table.

"Nothing," he said quickly.

"I'm such a pig, aren't I?" She screwed up her pert nose and curved her lips in a self-conscious smile.

"I don't mind," he said. And immediately winced. "I mean, you're not a pig."

"Gee, thanks."

He looked up, expecting censure. Her eyes were

instead warm with humor. A lightness seeped into his soul. "Got me, didn't you?"

"Two laughs in a row." Her eyes twinkled. "You should do it more often. It makes you look friendlier. Less intimidating, less…"

"Like a barbarian?"

She looked down and started folding her napkin. "Sorry. I did say that, didn't I?"

"What? It's true. I'm a big brute."

"Maybe sometimes." She smiled, abandoning the napkin. "But not all the time."

Damn if that smile didn't do queer things to his insides. *And those freckles.* Maxim shifted in his seat. "So what's this thing with work you want to talk about?"

Emma fiddled with her pendant. "Can I tell you what happened the other day?" she finally asked, her beautiful eyes filled with anxiety.

"Sure." *What the hell was making her nervous?* He wanted nothing more than to chase away her fears.

After she was done with her story, however, those eyes looked even more troubled than before. "So what do you think?" she asked in a small voice.

"Someone has to be responsible for that beating." *Damn his officers. They should have done more.* "I'll look into it and make sure Custody monitors the dorms better."

"You'd do that?" There was a weird note of wonder in her voice.

"Of course. Rules are made for a reason. No cigarettes means no cigarettes."

"Oh. You don't know how happy I am to hear that." She grabbed his hand and squeezed with her tiny fingers. "I thought you might blow over it. Not even care."

"Of course I care. It's my prison," he said, trying hard to keep his hand still. She was pure danger. Distracting him with those eyes, killing him with that smile, and now torturing him with her touch. Her hand was soft and smooth, perfectly nestled in his palm. As if it belonged there. *What the hell?* Maxim yanked his hand back, his heart racing. *Short. Damn it. He had to keep it short.* His sanity depended on it. He shook his head in disgust and pushed his chair back.

"Is something wrong?"

"No." *Did the woman have to be so observant?* "I have to go to the nursing home."

"You want me to come with you?" she asked.

No, of course not. "Sure. If you want to." He bit back a groan. Those eyes had bewitched him somehow.

They drove to the nursing home, her long, beautiful black hair whipping in the wind between them. It was weird but the deep grief and ache of his loss seemed to ease each minute in her company. She helped him gather his father's belongings: a stack of old books, an antique watch, some clothes, and a wedding photograph. She was silent during most of it, not saying much.

"When's the funeral?" she asked as they walked back to the car.

"Saturday at noon."

They got in the car and finally it was time to drive her home. Maxim should have been happy about it but why the hell did he feel all wrong inside? His sanity depended on them separating but his thick mind didn't seem to comprehend. "Thanks for going over there with me."

"No problem. Glad I could help." She gazed up at the sky for a second and then suddenly shrieked. "Wait.

What's the date? It's the twenty-fourth, right? Oh my God, I have to run. I've got to be somewhere."

"What? A hot date?" *Not that he cared one way or the other.* Still, the thought of her on a date curdled his stomach somehow.

"Yeah." Her eyes twinkled. "You can say that. Although he's not really hot. He's actually pretty cold."

"Cold?"

"Yeah, his name is Holmes."

"Too much information." He gripped the steering wheel. "Don't worry. I'll get you home as fast as I can."

"He's a comet." She chuckled, her eyes now dancing. "We can see him together if you like."

"A comet? You mean like in the sky?" Maxim felt foolish and lighthearted all at once.

"Yes. I heard he had an outburst a few days ago. And that starting today we can view him with the naked eye." Her emerald eyes shone with excitement. "I have to see him. I promised to send my brother some pictures. He'll be so excited."

"Okay, then." *Why not?* It was already past evening time. The day was almost over. He could handle another couple of hours in her company. As long as he had his defenses up, it couldn't be that bad. "Let's find Holmes. Where should we go?"

"Well, I was going to go to Skyline Drive near my studio. It's pretty high up, but traffic is a beast heading that way right now." Emma peered left and then right, shading her eyes with one hand. "We have to find some place high to climb. Away from the city lights. They're too distracting."

"I know of a place," he said, feeling it was perfect. "It's not far from here. Are you game?"

"Sure." Emma settled back in her seat and looked up at the darkening sky. A few minutes of silence ensued as he headed the car back onto the road. "What made you go into corrections?" she asked as he entered the freeway.

"After my parents were killed, I wanted to go into law enforcement." *He'd been willing to try anything to catch those bastards.* "Corrections was the fastest way. The training at the academy is only sixteen weeks long."

"You must have advanced really quickly." Emma tossed her hair back and gave him a quizzical look. "I always thought wardens were older. And you don't look a day over fifty."

"Fifty?" Maxim bit back a groan. "Do I look that old?"

"Just kidding." Emma laughed, a beautiful, merry sound that seeped into his soul, warming him up from the inside out. "How old are you? Forty-something?"

"Thirty-nine," he said. "I know, probably ancient by your standards."

"No. Not at all." Her eyes were thoughtful. "It's what's on the inside that counts. How long have you been warden? Was it hard to get there?"

"It wasn't difficult. But it took a lot of work." *So she didn't think he was an old geezer.* The warm feeling in Maxim's chest deepened.

"How do you become warden? Do you have to go to extra classes or training?"

"A little bit of both. I had a good mentor. Mr. Peterson, the sergeant at the Urgent Care, remember?" Maxim flicked the turn signal on to make a right lane change. "He showed me the ropes, what classes to take, what exams to sit for, how to get ahead."

"How many years have you been warden?"

"This is my second year."

"Seems like you really enjoy your job."

"It's kind of my mission in life," Maxim confessed, surprised he was revealing so much of himself. But then this was Emma. She made everything easier in a way. "Somebody has to punish the criminals and make them pay. Make sure justice is served."

"All the criminals, huh?" Her voice became small.

"As many as I can get my hands on." Maxim glanced over, loving the way the moonlight danced on her face. She seemed sadder for some reason, though. *And why the heck should that concern him? Why this urgent need to take away her sorrow?* He finally made it to the exit and after several minutes commenced the long climb up.

"Where are we?" she said, her voice brighter. "I feel like I'm at Yosemite or something. Why are we the only ones on the road?"

"Because it's private property," he said.

"No, really?" She was quiet for a moment and then suddenly clutched his arm. "We're not trespassing, are we? I don't want to sneak in just to see a comet."

"Don't worry." *How could her hand feel so soft?* He needed to concentrate here. The road had a lot of twists and turns ahead. Maxim pulled his arm away. "We're not sneaking in. The owner gave me permission to use this place a long time ago."

"Okay, that's good." She craned her neck out of the window. "It's nice up here. The air is so fresh. How high up are we? The road is so windy you can easily get motion sickness."

He pressed on the brakes. "Are you carsick? Do you want me to slow down?"

"No. I like the twists and turns. My brother is the one who gets carsick, not me."

"The one we're taking pictures for?"

"Yes. I only have one. We're pretty close." Emma's voice suddenly dropped. "Thank you for doing this with me. I know he'd appreciate it."

"You're welcome."

After another few minutes, he finished the ascent and pulled up into the driveway.

"Wow. What is this place?" Emma stared up at the house. "It's huge. You're sure the owner is okay with us being here?"

"Positive." He opened the car door for her and escorted her through the circular entranceway. "He even gave me a key."

"All right." She looked around nervously. "We should hurry. I don't want to miss Holmes. Is there a cliff we can climb?"

Maxim chuckled. "We are on a cliff. Come on, let's go out to the backyard." He led her through the foyer and down the long hallway to the back.

"How big is this place?" She gazed around, her eyes wide. "There're sculptures and paintings everywhere. Is that an original Van Gogh? Your friend must be super wealthy."

"No, but his parents were," he said. "I can give you a personal tour later, if you like."

"No, thanks. I've never been into big fancy houses."

Maxim stumbled a little and caught himself. "Why? I thought most people liked them."

"Not me. A little cottage is all I need," she said. "With a nice rose garden in the back. Maybe a couple of bedrooms and a porch to sit on to watch the sunset."

"I see." His heart did a little tumble. "I think we're here. You'll like the backyard."

He opened the French doors and accompanied her out into the brisk night air.

"This is perfect," Emma breathed out, her voice full of wonder as she took in the surroundings. "I love all the roses. Are those koi fish swimming underneath us? Oh my goodness, they're so beautiful." She sat down and trailed her fingers in the water, touching a lily pad along the way. "I've always liked goldfish but these are so much better. They're huge. Do you think they get to a maximum size or just keep growing?"

"I never thought about it." She was so beautiful—it took his breath away. That midnight black hair as it cascaded down her back, those gorgeous emerald eyes that a man could drown in. The woman had cast a spell over him.

"So are you ready to meet Holmes?" She stood and smiled at him.

"Holmes?" He blinked a couple of times.

"The comet. That's why we're here, remember?" Emma dashed to the farthest corner of the garden and leaned forward against the balustrade. "It's perfect. We're really high up and there're no clouds tonight." She shielded her eyes with her hand and looked up. "Shoot. I wish I had my binoculars. I can't see much. Only a couple of stars."

"I can't see anything either." *Not with you around. Good God. He was in serious trouble.* Maxim took in a deep breath. He had to keep his distance somehow. Before he knew it, though, she'd flitted to his side, her light rosewater scent washing over him. He clenched his hand on the balustrade.

"I still can't see anything." She kept gazing up, her

attention focused on the sky. "Wait. Was that it? Did you see it, Maxim?" She laid a hand on his arm.

His whole body stilled. *Must she touch him?* He felt totally off-kilter, like when he first stepped on dry land after a few days of sailing. She was driving him crazy and she didn't even know it. He forced himself to look at the sky. *Damn.* But was that a bright sphere popping up out of nowhere?

"That's it!" Emma shrieked. She whipped out her phone and started clicking. "I can't believe I'm seeing it. It's never been this bright before. Ever. It's almost half the size of the moon. My brother will love this. We saw Halley's Comet together but he was still small back then." She took dozens of shots before stopping to review them. "Oh, the images aren't very clear." Her voice dropped. "He won't even know what he's looking at. I should have brought a better camera."

A dull ache tugged at his heart. Emma looked devastated. He hoped her brother knew what a gem of a sister she was. "Hey, I remember my friend having a great camera upstairs," he said, glad of the chance to step away. Even if it was for a few minutes, it should be enough for him to gain back his equilibrium. "I'm sure he wouldn't mind us borrowing it to snap some photos."

"Really?" Her wide eyes brimmed with hope, and he knew he was willing to do anything to grant her those pictures.

Maxim ran up the stairs. *Sure, she was his employee and off-limits. But that didn't mean he couldn't please her in this one thing, did it?* He located the camera and brought it back in time to snap at least a dozen photos before the comet disappeared.

"Can I see them?" she asked, squeezing close.

Maxim's breath hitched. She was so near all he had to do was extend one arm and she'd be snuggled right next to him.

"Oh, it's a film camera." Her warm breath fanned his cheeks. "I guess I have to wait for them to be developed. Can you do it soon?"

"What?" *That rosewater scent was killing him.*

"The film. On second thought, maybe you can give it to me. I'll develop it and make you copies, if you like." Emma stepped back and he let out a long breath.

"No, I can do it for you," he said, finally catching on to what she was saying. "I'll get them for you soon. Promise."

"Great." Her eyes darted to the left and then to the right. She cleared her throat. "So should we go? I don't want to overstay our welcome. What if your friend comes back?"

"No. Don't worry. My friend works a lot. He doesn't come out here much."

"Isn't that crazy?" Emma spread her arms and breathed in the night air. In the distance, he could hear waves crashing against the shore. "How could he not love it here? If I owned this place, I'd be out here every night."

"And what would you do out here?" Maxim asked, knowing he was playing with fire but he couldn't help himself.

"I don't know." She gave a self-conscious shrug. "Maybe read or just look at the sky or enjoy the scenery. I bet the view must be gorgeous when it's light out."

"The view is gorgeous now." He stared right at her.

CHAPTER 18

Damn it. Had he said that out loud? Maxim turned away and tried to gather his thoughts. "I mean, it's gorgeous at night, too."

Smooth, Max. Really smooth. He shook his head and wiped a hand over his face. All those hours staying up with his father must finally be catching up with him. His mind flitted from one topic to the next, unable to come up with anything neutral to talk about.

"You look a little tired," she said. "Maybe we should go."

Suddenly something brushed against his leg. He looked down. King's light yellow eyes glowed back at him. "How are you, my little man?" He bent and scooped the cat up into his arms. "Did you miss me? Sorry I was gone for so long." He smoothed King's coat with his palm exactly the way the cat liked it. Sure enough, a loud purr soon followed.

"Your friend's cat seems to like you a lot," Emma said with a note of wonder in her voice.

"Yes. He does." Maxim bit back a curse. He shouldn't have lied about the house. Now it seemed like one lie only fed into another. *Why the hell hadn't he told her the truth in the first place?* He'd foolishly thought it'd keep some distance between them but he should have known. Nothing was effective at keeping her at arm's length.

"But he looks so much like the cats from the prison. Black coat, yellow eyes." She did a double take when she saw King fully. "But he's missing a leg. And half his tail is gone."

"The raccoons almost killed him a couple of years ago at the prison." Maxim rubbed King's tummy. It'd been a bad day. Thank goodness he'd come in time. The poor cat would have been chewed to pieces.

"You rescued him from the prison?" Her eyes shone at him with an odd light.

"Yes, awhile back. Those raccoons can be pretty vicious." King twisted in his arms. "All right, down you go. Did Ana give you enough food before she left? Are you still hungry?"

King let out a loud meow before limping away, throwing a curious glance back at the doctor.

"Ana?" Emma asked.

"My housekeeper." Maxim winced. *Damn.* He should have been more careful.

"So this means." Emma swallowed and threw him an accusing look. "This is your house, isn't it?"

He was totally busted. No way around it now. He straightened. "Yes. Sorry, I should have said so earlier."

"Why didn't you?"

"I don't know. I thought it might complicate things." He shrugged. "Does it really matter?"

"Of course it does." Emma stepped back and spread her arms wide. "My God. You live in this huge palace. I should have put two and two together. You have a neurology institute named after you, for goodness' sake. Of course you'd own a place like this."

"You say that like it's a bad thing." *How dare she criticize him for supporting the hospital? The woman was impossible to please.* "So I'm rich. Big deal. It's nothing to get riled up about."

"That's not the point." She stomped her foot. "You lied to me. You said this was your friend's house, and I believed you. I felt nervous the whole time, thinking we were trespassing."

"It was my father's house. He was my friend, so technically, I didn't lie."

"You did and you know it." She glared at him.

"Did not."

"Just admit it. You lied." She advanced on him, her hands braced on her hips.

"Why are you so upset?"

"Because I can't stand liars." She stood toe-to-toe with him.

"I'm not a liar."

"You did it again." She slapped him on the shoulder.

"You're too much, you know that?"

"I'm the one who's too much? You're the one who—"

He pressed his lips hard against hers, just to shut the woman up. It was either that or strangle her with his hands. It was meant to be quick. But one touch and he was lost. Her lips were soft, malleable. *Heavenly.* They molded against his and he gentled the pressure, surprised like hell she was kissing him back. She tasted sweet and innocent and so damned good. He licked her bottom lip and groaned when she let out a soft sigh. He wrapped his arms around her, pulling her closer.

She opened her mouth only slightly but that was the only invitation he needed. His tongue dipped into her mouth, tasting every sweet recess. Her soft moans drove him wild. He grabbed the tight seat of her jeans and lifted her off the ground. *God.* He was losing control but he couldn't help himself. She wrapped her hands around his neck and tentatively brought her tongue forward. A shudder racked through his body. He bit back a curse when she entwined her legs around him, freeing his hands to explore the rest of her sweet body. Her skin was as smooth as silk. She groaned when he brushed the underside of her breast. The woman was amazing, so responsive to his every touch.

A loud ringing suddenly sounded. Emma froze before jumping away from him, her hand clasped over her mouth. *Dear God, what had he done?* Maxim stared at her, horrified. *Should he apologize? She was his employee, for Christ's sake.*

"You should answer that." Her voice was shaky and she didn't meet his eyes.

"What?" he asked, dazed. "Oh, the phone. Right."

Maxim pulled the cursed phone out of his pocket. The caller's words washed over him in a haze. When he finally caught on, the haze disappeared in a flash. Of all the nights, it had to be tonight. He gave his instructions before hanging up. Emma had moved several paces away from him, her purse strap already around her shoulders.

"I have to go. It's the prison," he said, cursing his luck. "Are you okay?"

"I guess so." She fiddled with her necklace. "What's going on at the prison?"

"They found a stash of heroin near the Eagle gate."

"Really? They asked you to come in?" Emma still wouldn't look at him.

"No, but I want to. I told them to call if they ever find drugs." Maxim brushed a hand through his hair. Maybe the interruption hadn't been that bad, now that he thought more about it. *Dear God.* He'd almost made love to her a moment ago. Made love to an employee. Sure, she'd responded quite enthusiastically, but he was still her boss. Any relationship between them was impossible. He hoped she'd understand and not get too needy. He'd have to apologize for the kiss, though he didn't regret it one bit if he had to be honest with himself. She'd been amazing. *God. That body. Those lips. That mouth.*

Best kiss of his life and it had to be with an employee. Maxim bit back a groan. She'd expect an apology. That'd also be a good step to resetting the strict boundaries between them. Maxim ushered her out of the house and into the car.

"I'm sorry about what happened back there," he stated as soon as they began the climb down the hill.

"Sorry?" she asked, finally meeting his eyes.

"I got carried away with the moment."

"Hmm. Carried away?"

"Yes. You were yelling and I didn't know how to make you stop."

"So you kissed me to…" She frowned. "To shut me up?"

"I guess." He dug a hand through his hair and tugged at his shirt collar. *This wasn't coming out right.* "Listen, I hope you understand that can never happen again."

Emma looked away, silent. Finally she turned back, her face somber. "I know. I hate the yelling, too." She gave her head a little shake. "But you bring out the worst in me sometimes. I don't know why."

"I'm not talking about the yelling." *So he brought out the worst in her, did he? Ditto, my dear. Ditto.* "I'm talking about the kiss."

"Oh, that." She tossed her long hair back and focused on the road. "I got carried away, too. It didn't really mean anything."

"What?" *The most intense, hottest kiss of his life and she thought it meant nothing?*

"I mean it was nice," she said in a placating voice. "Don't get me wrong. I enjoyed it and all but I know it was a one-off."

"One-off?"

"Yeah. We're completely wrong for each other." She flicked at her fingernails. "You're the last man I'd ever want to date."

"What? Why?"

"Too many reasons to count."

"Humor me."

"Well, first you're my boss, right?" She patted him on the arm. "Don't worry. I won't tell anyone. We both got carried away with the moment. End of story."

"So you're not upset about it?" He should be relieved. She was taking it really well. Better than well. *But what the hell were the other reasons?* Their work relationship was the only thing he could think of that hindered them.

He should demand an explanation but a man's ego can only take so much. *Look at her. Playing with her phone, looking like she hadn't a care in the world. Maybe she kissed men like that all the time.* Now didn't that deliver a kick to his guts.

"Not really," she said.

"What?"

"I'm not upset," she said. "You're okay with it, right?"

"Right." He tried for a laugh but it ended in a croak instead.

"Good. So let's forget it happened. It's already out of my mind."

"Mine, too." *Right after he took a ton of cold showers.* But she didn't need to know that. The cursed woman seemed as cool as a cucumber while he was burning up like a volcano.

"So what are you going to do about the drug situation?" Emma asked as he exited the freeway.

"Investigate." It was pathetic. His mind was still on that kiss, and she was prattling on about drugs. *And he was supposed to be the warden here. God. He was in serious trouble.*

"Investigate? How?" She finally put the phone down.

"Bring in the K-9 units. Talk to the officers at the gate."

"K-9?"

"Trained dogs that detect contraband and drugs."

"I guess that's a good thing, right? I hope you can stop the drugs from getting in, Maxim." She touched his arm. "We're all depending on you. I don't want any more patients to die."

And there it was: the real reason why it'd never work between them. Maybe Emma had already thought of it but it hit Maxim now like a tidal wave. True, he was her boss but there were ways around that if they kept their relationship out of the workplace. No, it wasn't that. The real reason lay a lot deeper. It struck to his inner core. He was dark and bitter, living for vengeance and punishment. He aimed to catch the drug dealers to punish them, to make them pay, to bring justice to the world. Saving lives wasn't even on the list.

Emma, however, was the opposite. She was giving and kind, her generous heart intent on helping others. He couldn't drag her into his dark and vengeful world. She deserved better, much better than what he could give her. Better to realize that now before he did something foolish. Emma didn't say much when he dropped her off. Just a wave of her hand and a hasty thank-you. Maxim made sure he heard the turn of her deadbolt before he walked back to the car.

He arrived at work ten minutes later, determined to focus. Emma depended on him to do well here. The K-9 unit greeted him as soon as he crossed the gate. Prince, a Belgian Malinois, was sniffing around the modules near the stairs, his short tail wagging.

"He won't find anything there," Maxim said to Sergeant Banding, Prince's partner. "Those are staff offices."

"You never know, Mr. Chambers," the sergeant greeted him.

Maxim had always liked Banding. They were near the same age. Banding was responsible, hardworking, and took great care of the Malinois. The four-year-old shepherd tracked down contraband for their region, sniffing out some heroin a few months ago at Albatross.

"So tell me. What happened?" Maxim asked.

"The watchtower called us a couple of hours ago." Banding whistled and Prince raced back to him, settling by his side. "They found a suspicious parcel right next to the fence near the Eagle gate. It was on our side of the prison. Somebody must have dropped it off."

"How many bags were inside?"

"Ten. Prince went crazy as soon as he sniffed the heroin."

"So ISU knows?" ISU was the Department of

Corrections Investigative Service Unit. Maxim had spoken to them earlier about keeping an extra eye out for suspicious activities after the death of Jones, the OHU patient. So far they hadn't come up with anything.

"Of course. I told them immediately. Some of my partners are here now." The sergeant rubbed a hand over Prince's thick brown coat. "Prince searched all around the gate fencing but didn't find anything else."

"Can you bring him tomorrow?" Maxim swallowed back a yawn. "The dorms have to be searched. Starting with the 300s. That's where Jones lived."

"We already went through his dorm, remember? It didn't turn up anything."

"I know that, but this barely happened. Maybe they're connected somehow." Maxim stretched his stiff shoulders. "I'll have my officers do a bed-to-bed search, too. But your unit's good with drugs. Look for cigarettes also. Have you found some lately?"

"Two months ago but none recently. Prince is trained to sniff out heroin, not tobacco."

"Maybe you can bring in a K-9 unit that does tobacco?" *He'd promised Emma and those cigarettes were plain bad news.*

"Okay. I'll check with the others. I'm sure they'll help out if they're free." Banding fastened a leash around Prince's neck and marched off with a wave of his hand.

The ride back home took forever. Maybe he should have bought a place closer to the prison, but he'd always loved his parents' old house. Maxim rubbed his eyes and sighed, wanting nothing more than to sleep. To dive under the covers, close his eyes, and drift off into oblivion. *No.* He had to be honest with himself. He wanted all the above, plus something else. Or rather someone else. And his foolish mind was already conjuring up images of her. Nothing risqué or inappropriate. Just her sweet body curved up next to his. He'd wrap an arm around her waist and pull her close, breathing in her light rosewater scent. His heart ached at the impossibility of it all.

His father had barely died. He should be mourning Pops, not pining after a contrary doctor. Maybe in a way his heart was finally recognizing what his brain had known all along. His father had been dead all these years already. His old man's shell of a body had existed but his mind, his soul was long gone. Maxim had been grieving slowly all these years; the final death hadn't been unexpected. He just never suspected it would come with peace and dignity, and he knew whom he had to thank for that.

Emma was perfect in so many ways. Just not for him. She didn't even like him. The last man she'd ever want to date, she'd said. Too many reasons to count, she had thrown at him. *God.* He was such a fool. He should have kept it short this morning. Well, he knew better now. He wasn't going to torture himself being near her, yearning for the impossible. From now on, he'd steer clear of her path.

CHAPTER 19

"I never felt more embarrassed in my life."

"Don't think about it. It'll only make it worse," Riley said over the car's Bluetooth.

"Nothing can make it worse than it already is." Emma groaned as she drove to work the following morning. "Oh God, Ri. I was all over him. Like a starving maniac. Even with John, I never acted that way."

"He must have been one hell of a kisser."

And then some. Emma's body shivered at the memory. The kiss was hard at first, almost punishing in nature. She'd been mad as hell at him and was about to push back but then his lips had turned soft, persuasive, gentle. She'd leaned into his embrace, soaking in the beauty of the moment. And then he'd lifted her up as if she weighed no more than a feather. He was all power and strength and it had driven her wild. She'd climbed up on him like a crazed woman, forgetting everything but the need to be closer to him. The man had cast some sort of spell over her. Lucky the phone had rung when it did or else she might have given herself to him right there in his backyard.

"So you had a passionate moment with the man. Nothing to be ashamed of," Riley said.

"But he kissed me only to shut me up, Ri." Even now, her face flamed at the memory. "How much more embarrassing can it get? I was all over him while he thought it was no big deal."

"Didn't you say he kissed you back?"

"Because I threw myself at him. Not because he cared one way or the other."

"I wouldn't be so sure about that."

"Come on, Ri. He dismissed the kiss like it was nothing." Emma swallowed. "I was shaking all over and all he could talk about was going back to the prison."

"You wanted him to go back, didn't you?"

"I know. Of course I want the drug problem addressed." Emma sighed. "But did he have to be so anxious to get rid of me? He rushed me out of the house like there was no tomorrow."

"The man loves his job, Em. You already knew that."

"But he didn't have to be so blatant about it." Emma glanced at the clock. Seven fifteen already. She was still two exits away from Albatross, which would make her at least ten minutes late.

"So how did you leave it with him?"

"I had to pretend it didn't matter." *And God how hard that had been, what with her heart still racing over that kiss.* "Especially after he told me it could never happen again. As if he was warning me to stay away from him. It was so humiliating. I had to pretend to misunderstand him, tell him I thought it was about me yelling at him, and not the other thing."

"So he doesn't suspect anything?"

"I hope not. I put on a pretty good show about how I could never imagine dating him."

"Ouch. That must have hurt."

"Hey. I had my pride to salvage." Emma shook her head. "And Sam to think about. You know my brother would always separate us."

"Maybe. Maybe not."

"What do you mean?"

"Maybe you should tell him about Sam." Riley's voice rose. "I know. Hold on a minute before you interrupt. The guy seems pretty decent. He may not be so down on your brother."

"Yeah, right. He hates inmates, Ri."

"Do me a favor and think about it, okay? I have to run. I just got to the hospital. Call me tonight."

Her friend hung up, and now she was alone with her morose thoughts. The sad part was that she'd almost told Maxim about Sam last night. She'd wanted to trust him. Had thought that she could indeed trust him. He'd been rather wonderful the whole day.

He'd been attentive, feeding her all that delicious food, reassuring her he'd take care of the cigarettes, bringing her all the way to his mansion to take the comet pictures. How her heart had melted at the sight of him cuddling that poor misshapen cat. He was huge yet so gentle and caring to that tiny unfortunate creature. The cat was from the prison. He'd rescued it…the guy truly had to have a heart of gold. She'd wanted to tell him about Sam. Surely a man who cherished a deformed cat wouldn't be too harsh on her poor brother. *Would he?*

She'd been so tempted. Maybe they could finally explore this strange connection between them. However it had come about, she knew she was attracted to him. More than attracted, if she had to be honest with herself. She was drawn to him, drawn to his strength and power and to the underlying tenderness she glimpsed beneath his formidable exterior. And she thought he must have had some feelings for her. He'd called her gorgeous earlier. True, he was a little hesitant afterward but she'd seen his striking eyes following her around the garden. They had glowed with tenderness and something else she'd been too afraid to delve into.

But then it'd all fallen apart. He'd mentioned his housekeeper. He'd lied about the house. Which meant he could lie to her about other things. She couldn't trust him. Not enough to share Sam's secret.

And looking back, how could she have thought he was interested in her? He was a millionaire, for heaven's sake. He lived in a huge mansion on a hill. Women probably chased him all the time. She was just a doctor, a good one but nobody significant in his rich and powerful sphere. They'd treated him like a king at the hospital the other night.

She didn't belong in his world. Plus he didn't even want her in it. He'd looked horrified when she'd pulled out of his arms. As if he regretted the whole thing. Emma's face burned at the memory. *How was she going to face him now?* She dreaded seeing him again. Dreaded looking into those eyes and knowing there was no future between them. She had to be strong, had to stick to her guns and pretend the kiss meant nothing. *God, it was going to be hard.* Maybe, it'd be best to stay away from him. Out of sight, out of mind, and all that.

She arrived not ten but a full fifteen minutes late to the meeting. A brief glance showed her Maxim was already there, along with the other doctors. Emma braced herself for his rebuke, surprised when it never came. Luckily there were a couple of empty seats at the end of the table farthest away from him. Emma slid into one of them.

"Sorry I'm late," she said to the table at large.

"It's becoming a habit of yours," Evil Knievel said from her usual seat by Maxim's side.

There was nothing she could say to that, nothing in polite company at least, so Emma kept quiet.

"Okay, I have some news, everyone." Julien gave her a sympathetic smile. "Today we're going to try something new. Dr. Kaye and I have invited the psychiatrists to join our meeting. You know how a lot of our patients have serious mental health problems? Well, this is our chance to discuss those patients."

"Sacramento set it out as a new requirement. We'll focus on the patients who take more than ten medications," Kaye added. "Let's review their meds and see if we can wean some of them."

"And it'll help us understand our patients better." Julien tapped his forehead. "You know how the mind always affects the body."

The door opened and a young Asian woman and two men entered. One of the men she recognized as Sam's psychiatrist, Charles Stewart. Today he had on tan slacks and a blue silk dress shirt coupled with a brown tie. His light blond hair was a little rumpled and wavy, giving him the perfect Adonis look. *Funny how his good looks didn't affect her much, not the way one smile from Maxim could take her breath away.*

"Emma," Charles greeted her like a long-lost friend. "How are you? Mind if I have a seat?"

"Of course not." She smiled at his friendly demeanor. "Good morning."

Some chairs shuffled down where Kaye sat with Maxim. Hopefully Charles would behave today. She sure didn't want any more trouble with his ex-wife.

Julien introduced the other two psychiatrists, Dr. Wu and Dr. Samuels. Dr. Wu began by talking about one of her patients, a thirty-year-old on twenty different medications. *Good. It was a SNY patient from up the hill.* Emma didn't need to concentrate. Her mind was already frazzled enough with Maxim sitting there at the end of the table. *Must the man exude such raw magnetism?*

"I'm sorry," Charles suddenly leaned over and whispered.

"What?"

"Sorry for how I acted the other day," he murmured *sotto voce.*

"No worries," she said.

Dr. Wu kept on talking. Soon it was Dr. Samuels's turn to discuss his patient, a schizophrenic manic-depressive who also suffered from heart problems.

"Penny for them?" Charles whispered again a few minutes later.

"Shh. We're in a meeting," she whispered back.

Emma turned and met a familiar pair of silver eyes. Maxim looked tired, his hair a little disheveled, his tie crooked. Her heart lurched. *Didn't he get any sleep last night?* Something must have shown on her face because Maxim hastily averted his eyes and busied himself with his notepad.

"My patient is a twenty-four-year old African-American man with PTSD." Charles began talking in his pleasant baritone. He gave Emma a significant look. "His name is Sam Morris."

"Morris?" Her heart lurched. *Had she heard right?*

"Yes, Mr. Morris, the Urgent Care porter," Charles answered.

The lurching escalated into a full gallop. Emma gripped the armrest of her chair.

"He's only taking two medications," Kaye said. "He can't be that complicated. Let's move to somebody else."

"No. I want to talk about him," Charles said, giving Emma another pointed look. "I think he's very interesting. Previously, no mental health problems, incarcerated five years ago and never saw a doctor until he was assaulted and sent to the hole."

"Get to the point, Stewart," Maxim bit out. "We don't have all day."

Emma clutched her necklace and tried to focus on her breathing. *Her brother, discussed as a patient, exposed to everyone. Dear God, she hoped they didn't suspect anything.*

"All right, I'll get there." Charles flipped through some notes. "He had a broken jaw and broken nose. Was in the hole for three months."

"Why was he assaulted?" Julien asked.

"It was a drug deal gone bad." Charles tapped his pen on the table. "Morris was in the wrong place at the wrong time and got the crap kicked out of him. When he came out, he began to see things."

"What things?" Emma blurted out.

"Dead people. Blood."

Emma gulped down some water.

"And then came the nightmares and flashbacks. Any little noise would set him off. He had panic attacks regularly."

Her poor brother. Emma swallowed down the lump in her throat.

"Meds were started three months ago," Charles continued. "He improved but still has the flashbacks and panic attacks."

"Typical case of PTSD," Dr. Wu said.

"And you're bringing him up because?" Dr. Kaye asked with an impatient shake of her head.

"What happened to him?" Charles asked. "Why did he become like this? A totally healthy man suddenly afraid of his own shadow? I blamed the assault at first. But he told me that he's been beaten before, by his dad no less."

Emma stifled a gasp and almost dropped her glass of water.

"But he wasn't afraid until now," Charles continued. "Something happened recently that made his panic attacks worse. I don't know what it is. He won't tell me."

"There's nothing you can do then," Kaye said. "Just leave him alone til he's ready to talk."

"Isn't there some way you can encourage him to talk?" Emma slid her chair closer to Charles. *Her poor brother. How much suffering had he endured?* She must help him somehow.

"Yes. I'd like to do cognitive processing therapy," Charles answered.

"CPT? No way," Dr. Samuels said. "Too much time. Focus on his meds. That's the best course."

"He's been getting them," Charles said. "But he's getting worse. CPT's the next step."

"What the hell is CPT?" Maxim suddenly spoke up from the end of the table. He was glaring at Charles as if the psychiatrist had just committed some great sin or other.

"It's therapy to help a person focus on his or her current problems and how to solve them."

"Sounds like a bunch of mumbo-jumbo nonsense to me," Maxim said.

"My thoughts exactly," Kaye declared. "The state's not paying psychiatrists to do CPT. Can't you let the psychologists deal with it?"

"I've tried, but they don't know how to do it well," Charles said. "I've had special training in it and can do a really good job."

"It's experimental," Kaye said. "We shouldn't waste taxpayers' money."

"But it's been proven to work," Charles insisted. "It's standard of care in the community. If the inmate needs it, he should get it."

"It's too time-consuming," Dr. Wu chimed in. "We have a huge amount of backlog we're already not seeing."

"I agree." Kaye glared at her ex. "With limited resources, we can't do everything for everybody. We need to see as many patients as possible, not focus all our attention on one inmate."

"I'm spending time with the other inmates." Charles slid his chair back and crossed one leg over the other at the knee. "They're easy, not complicated. Morris is my most complicated guy. He developed PTSD recently. I think we can help him by tackling it now and not waiting until his symptoms are more entrenched. It'll only be nine to twelve sessions and I bet he'll get better."

"They're fifty-minute sessions," Dr. Samuels interjected. "It's too much time."

"Right. Time that can be spent with your other patients." Kaye slammed her clipboard down. "I don't want you to do it."

"What if I stay late, do it on my own time?" Charles asked.

Emma could have kissed the man, so stunned was she by his response. "You'd do that for him? Spend your own time to help an inmate?"

"Why not?" He flashed her his devilish smile. "I've always loved a challenge."

"That's wonderful." Emma readily returned his smile. Her worries about Maxim seemed trivial compared to this. So she made an embarrassing pass at her boss. No big deal. Maxim seemed to be moving beyond it just fine. There he was, writing things in his notepad. *Was he even paying attention to the meeting? It didn't really matter, did it?* All that mattered was Sam. She should get over herself and her hang-up with the warden.

Her brother had been suffering, and Emma hadn't even had a clue. She needed to help him and CPT seemed promising. A sudden idea came to her, a brilliant one if she had to say so herself. She couldn't wait to test it out. It made sense and would be the perfect solution. Couldn't she be there during the CPT sessions? It'd let her spend more time with Sam and she didn't need Smith because Charles would be with her. Maybe she could convince Charles to leave them alone during a session or two, giving her some much-needed alone time with her brother.

"Suit yourself," Kaye was saying, frowning at her ex. "But I expect all the other patients to be seen in a timely manner. No slacking off on the others just to help Morris."

"Aye, aye, ma'am." Charles saluted. He winked at Emma on the side.

The guy was a lifesaver. As soon as the meeting disbanded, she followed him out. Maxim and Evil Knievel were both glaring at the psychiatrist for no particular reason that she could see. He was doing it free of charge on his own time. *How much more generous can the man get?*

"Charles," Emma called as he was about to exit. "Can I talk with you for a few minutes?"

"Sure. It'd be my pleasure." He gave her a suave smile, looking incredibly handsome. He was like a model on a magazine cover, good to look at but too handsome to date. "So what can I do for you, Angel?" he asked, his eyes twinkling.

"Those CPT sessions," she said as the door swung shut after them. "Do you think I can join you guys?"

"You mean with Morris?" His eyebrows lifted. "I don't think so. It's usually very personal. He probably won't want anyone else there."

"Well, if he's okay with me being there, can I be there?" *Sam better not put up a fight. She was doing this for his own good.*

"Sure, if he agrees. Although I'm not sure why you want to attend. It's very structured and boring if you're the observer."

They began their walk down the hill. And there was Phineas sitting on his usual branch. It was as if he'd been waiting for her to come out to share her good news with him. And it was indeed good news. Charles was going to let her attend the sessions. She could hardly wait to tell Sam.

"It's a tricolored blackbird," Charles announced, stopping dead in his tracks. "I haven't seen one in ages. He's beautiful, isn't he?"

"Yes." *Amazing. He'd not only noticed the bird but known exactly what type it was.* "How do you know it's him?"

"My father and I used to go bird-watching together," he said, a faraway look in his eyes. "That was his favorite bird."

"It's my brother's favorite, too." Emma felt a sudden kinship with the man. "We used to go bird-watching together all the time."

"Your brother?" Charles's eyes homed in on her face. "He likes birds?"

"Yes, since he was a little kid. I told him about Phineas a few days ago, and he got all excited."

"Phineas?" Charles quirked an eyebrow.

"Yes, the blackbird." She gave a self-conscious shrug. "I had to name him something."

"You sure did." Charles let out a rich laugh as they ambled down the hill together. "I think it's a beautiful name, very proud and lofty."

"Thanks." She was liking the psychiatrist more by the minute. "So your father liked blackbirds, too?"

"Yes, a long time ago." Charles pulled at his tie. "He suffered from PTSD from the Korean War. Seemed like watching birds soothed him whenever he was feeling low."

"Is that how you got interested in CPT?" Emma asked, marveling at the similarity between Sam and Charles's father.

"Yes. It worked for him really well. I think Morris would benefit." He cast her a funny look. "Mind if I ask how come you're so interested in his care?"

Emma stumbled and forced out a nonchalant look. "He's my porter."

"I see. And you're interested in all your porters?"

"No." She tried to think of anything that might throw him off. "He helped me that day when I was attacked."

"Oh, Jesus." Charles touched her arm. "I forgot to ask you about that. How are you doing?"

"Okay." With all that'd happened, she hadn't thought about the attack in days. It seemed like months ago, not just last week. "Maxim assigned an officer to be with me when I see patients now."

"Maxim, huh?" Charles gave her a keen look. "Is there anything going on between you two?"

"What? No. Why do you ask?" *How did he suspect? Had she given out some inadvertent clue?*

"He kept staring at you during the meeting," Charles continued. "And when we were talking, I thought he was going to come over and rip me apart."

Emma let out a nervous laugh. "Because he didn't like the CPT idea."

"Maybe. But be careful, Emma. I wouldn't get involved with him if I were you."

"I'm not." *He'd made that plenty clear last night.* "But why the warning? He seems pretty decent."

"Hah!" Charles scoffed. "The guy has no heart. He dated my ex for a while and then dumped her without any explanations."

"You mean Dr. Kaye?" *That certainly left a sour taste in her mouth.*

"Yes. She's been mooning after him ever since." Charles sighed. "He can be downright cruel. I don't know why she's still into him."

"Have you talked to her about it?"

"Not really. We didn't part on friendly terms." Charles grimaced. "The divorce was pretty nasty."

So Maxim and Kaye had dated. *Was he still interested in Kaye? It wouldn't surprise her.* The CMO was tall and gorgeous with the perfect hourglass body. Was that why Maxim had been horrified when she'd thrown herself at him? She wasn't his type at all, if Kaye was the typical woman he dated. *Not that it mattered.* From now on, she was going to focus on her brother and stay as far away from the warden as possible.

CHAPTER 20

"That should be it," Madison said as she discharged the last patient later that afternoon. "Long day, huh, Doc?"

Emma rubbed her eyes. Yes, it'd definitely been a long day. Urgent Care had rushed by with patient after patient, most complaining of viral symptoms. But she also took care of some serious cases including an abdominal pain she had to send out. For lunch, she swallowed down a granola bar before several fights broke out among the Unit 3 patients and she had to tend to their injuries. Another lockdown was enforced, which elicited more grumbling among the inmates.

"Yes, the fights kept us busy." Emma stretched her shoulders. "Do they happen that often?"

"Here and there. Usually after being locked down for a while, little things set them off," Madison said. "Too many lockdowns drive them wild. They have to act out somehow."

"That's horrible." Especially since this time the lockdown included all the porters, too. She hadn't seen Sam all day. Hopefully he was okay. Sergeant Peterson had informed her only dorm 305 fought so at least she knew his dorm was spared. Still, it would've been nice to ascertain for herself that he was unhurt. Plus, she needed to discuss the CPT sessions with him.

And on top of all that, she'd spotted from a distance Maxim and his minions passing through the OHU a couple of times earlier in the day. He had ignored her, which was perfect for her plan of staying away from him. *But did he have to dismiss her so easily?*

Emma glanced at her watch, ready for the day to end. *Five o'clock already.* Smith came up and shook her hand, his usually friendly face sad for some reason. He'd been silent all day, acting even a bit surly sometimes.

"Is something wrong?" Emma asked as she took off her white coat.

"Today's my last day," he said. "I'm being transferred to RJD."

"But why? You've been here for years, haven't you?"

"Yes, but…" He cleared his throat. "My brother recently got transferred here from Solano. He's an inmate."

"Oh." Emma's breath came out in a whoosh. *Poor Smith.* All this time, he'd been in a similar boat as she was. "So they're forcing you to go?"

"Yes. Mr. Chambers is real strict about these things. As soon as he found out that Vic was here, he made arrangements to send me away."

"But you worked for him for so long."

"Believe me, the warden never lets emotion get in the way." Smith gave a defeatist shrug. "He follows the rules, no matter what. Lucky Vic paroles in six months. I'll be transferred back here before you know it."

"Where's RJD?"

"In San Diego. I'll commute for now and see how it goes." He shook her hand. "I wanted to say I really enjoyed working with you, Doctor. Gonzalez will take good care of you."

"Gonzalez? So I get another guard?" *So Maxim hadn't dismissed her entirely after all.*

"Of course." Smith smiled. "Mr. Chambers made sure I had a replacement before letting me go. Luckily Gonzalez was unassigned and he's one of our best officers, too. You'll be in good hands."

"Thanks."

"No. Thank you." Smith patted her shoulder. "It's obvious you care about your patients and that you don't think of them as inmates. That's really nice to see."

Emma gave him a quick hug before he left. She was going to miss him. He'd been her shadow for the past week, always there if she needed him. Hopefully she'd see him back by next summer. How could Maxim have dismissed him so easily? Clearly, he was a stickler for the rules. Thank goodness she hadn't told him about Sam.

"Emma." Charles stood at the doorway, looking at her with an odd expression. "I'm glad you haven't left yet. Can we talk?"

"Sure." Emma waved good-bye to Madison and gathered her things together. "What's up?" she asked as she joined the psychiatrist. It was dark outside and beginning to rain slightly. She took in a deep breath. *Aah.* She'd always loved the smell of the rain, especially when it first came down. Charles held out an umbrella and ushered her underneath the awning of the mental health building. He seemed preoccupied with something, unlike his usual jovial, charming self.

"Is everything okay?" Emma checked her watch. With the rain, traffic was going to be a killer. She wouldn't make it home until seven at the earliest.

"I want to talk to you about Morris."

"Morris?" she asked, her heart thumping a little harder.

"Yes." Charles scanned the deserted area before leaning in toward her. "Don't worry. Your secret is safe with me."

Goose bumps popped up on Emma's arms. "What do you mean?"

"I reviewed Morris's file today."

"And?" *Why didn't he just spit it out if he already knew?* She reached for her pendant.

"There were some notes from our earlier sessions." Charles's eyes bored into hers. "One of them said he loved blackbirds, that his sister and he used to go bird-watching."

Emma's breath stilled. "So? A lot of people like blackbirds. That doesn't mean anything."

"Come on, Emma, trust me." Charles put a hand on her shoulder. "I know Morris is half white, that he has a white sister who's a doctor. He told me during one of our sessions."

Emma bit her lip and pulled on her pendant. *Dear God. He knew!* And she couldn't prevent him from alerting Custody. By this time tomorrow, she may be on her way to a different prison, just like Smith. Tears pricked behind Emma's eyes. "Please don't tell anybody," she whispered.

"Never, I swear it." For once, the psychiatrist's handsome face was solemn and earnest. "Do you want to talk about it? It must be hard having him here."

"No. I mean it's not hard." *Hopefully he was a man of his word and wouldn't reveal her secret.* "I came here because of him."

"You're not planning on leaving with him, are you?" Charles asked half-jokingly.

"No. I only want to spend more time with him. It was so hard getting to visit him only once or twice a month the past few years. I missed him." She swallowed down the lump in her throat. "I get to see him almost every day now. Even though I can't help much, at least I can still see him."

"I understand. Come on, Emma. Don't look so sad. I promise I won't tell anyone. You'll still be able to see him."

"Yeah?"

"Of course," he said gently. "Actually, that's why I got you in the first place. Your brother's in my office right now for a CPT session. Want to join us?"

"Really?" Emma couldn't believe her luck. "He's there? Now? But it's way past clinic time."

"I know but that's the only time I had open. Come on. I think he wants to see you."

A steady bubble of hope blossomed as Charles led her into the mental health building and down a long corridor. All the office doors were closed except for the last one on the right. It was partially shut. Charles pushed it open. Inside Sam was eating an apple, sitting across from a desk and swinging his legs.

"Dr. Edwards." Her brother hastily put down the apple.

"Sam, it's okay." Emma rushed to his side. "Dr. Stewart knows about us, and he's going to try to help."

"Why did you tell him?" Sam rubbed his forehead, his eyes wide with anxiety. "Now you're going to get in trouble. All because of me."

"Relax." Charles raised his hand. "I'm not going to tell anybody. Your secret's safe with me. I promise."

"Yeah. Right." A haunted look came over Sam's face. "What's in it for you?"

"Nothing. You're my patient." Charles touched Sam's shoulder. "I want you to get better. That's all. And I want to help your sister. You know she loves you very much."

"I know." Sam's lips trembled and he let out a moan. "I'm sorry, Em. I wish I could be a better brother for you."

Emma pulled him close. "You're a great brother," she whispered against his chest. "Don't worry. Everything's going to be okay."

Charles exited the room and Emma let out a long breath. At last, they were finally alone. No guard, no other staff around. She made Sam sit with her on the most readily available seat, an old sofa pressed against the wall to the right side of the desk. They spent the next hour catching up on everything she could think of. He told her about how hard prison life was, especially when he'd been in the hole.

"How come you were sent to the hole?" *Please answer me.*

"You won't understand." The same haunted expression returned to his eyes. "I don't want to tell you, Em. Can we leave it?"

"No." *Definitely not.* "Dr. Stewart says you're not doing well. You're having panic attacks and seeing things and scared all the time. What's going on? It must be related to the hole. You were fine before you left."

Sam hunched over and buried his face in his hands.

Emma gingerly wrapped her arm around his shoulders. "Please, I want to help you."

"Okay." Sam let out a long, frustrated sigh. "But first I want to make sure nobody's around." He went to the door, opened it, looked up and down the hallway and shut it again. "You can't tell anybody, promise. Even Dr. Stewart."

"He's your doctor. Maybe he can help."

"Promise!" Sam's forehead beaded with sweat and his eyes darted back to the door.

"All right. Jeez, Sam, calm down. It's okay. I won't tell anybody."

He paced around the desk, gazed out the window, and then turned back to her. "You're right. Before the hole, I was pretty happy. Prison was bad but routine. And I had a friend, Peter. Besides for my bunkie, Peter was the only one I was close to." He paused and swallowed. "He was a little slow but nice, you know? He followed me everywhere. First timer like me. We hung out and became friends. He loved to play handball. And when his mom sent these huge packages, he shared them with me. Food, chips, books, anything. He had some developmental delay so a lot of the guys made fun of him, called him a retard and nasty stuff."

"I'm glad you're his friend."

"Not anymore." Sam threw himself on the sofa and slammed his fist on a cushion. "He died. He got murdered."

"What?"

"Yes. It was all my fault." Sam buried his face in his hands again. "Please don't make me talk about it, Em. I can't. I can't. Oh God! Make it stop!" He curled himself into a little ball on the sofa, his body trembling from head to toe.

Her poor brother. Was this his typical panic attack? "Sam. It's okay. Please, Sam, stop. It's okay. I'm here." She crouched down to hug him and accidentally knocked a book off the table. It crashed to the floor, making a loud slapping sound.

Sam catapulted out of the sofa and started screaming at the top of his lungs. "Stop it! Go away! You're hurting me!"

"Jesus. Sam, calm down." Emma reached out a hand, but he flung her arm away, all the while screeching at her to leave him alone.

Emma's heart thudded a mile a minute as she ran out to get help.

"Oh my God, Charles. Help! Something happened. He's screaming. I can't make him stop." She collided with Charles and dragged him into the room.

Sam was sitting curled up in one corner with his head between his legs, his hands over his ears, moaning incoherently.

"Sam, it's okay. It's Dr. Stewart," Charles said softly. He shook his head at Emma. "Remember our breathing exercises. Keep your mouth closed. Take a deep breath through your nose. Yes, that's it. Hold it. Now release it through your mouth. Do it again. It's okay. No one is going to hurt you. Breathe again. Yes, just like that. Keep breathing."

Luckily, Sam calmed down enough to make his way back onto the sofa. His eyes were bloodshot and tear-stained, and he looked like he'd woken up from a deep stupor. Emma stood frozen by the sofa, scared one wrong move on her part might trigger the agonizing outburst again. She glanced over helplessly at Charles. Thank goodness the psychiatrist seemed to know what to do.

"Are you all right?" Charles handed Sam some tissues and sat down next to him on the sofa. "That was another panic attack. Nobody's going to hurt you. Try to relax and do the deep breathing again."

Sam took several deep breaths. His lips quivered as

he turned her way. "Sorry, Em. That was a pretty bad one, wasn't it?"

"Yes. But I'm sure we can help." *She'd be willing to do anything.* "You're going to get better. Isn't that right, Dr. Stewart?"

"Yes." Charles clapped a hand on Sam's shoulder. "I know you feel bad right now. The meds haven't worked. We're going to try something new. It's called cognitive processing therapy, or CPT."

Sam looked up, a flicker of hope in his eyes. "You think it can help me?"

"I think so but it's a lot of work. We have to meet every week, sometimes twice a week, at least an hour each time. I'll assign you homework. Exercises you have to do." Charles squeezed Sam's shoulder. "Are you game?"

"Of course." Sam sat up straighter. "I'm sick of the flashbacks and nightmares."

"Flashbacks to what?"

"He'll tell us when he's ready." Charles shot her a warning look.

"I can't sleep, can't concentrate, can't even spend time with my sister without going berserk." Sam kept on talking. "I want to get better. You deserve a functioning brother."

"I just want you healthy." Tears pricked behind Emma's eyes. She smiled tentatively at Sam and despite it all, he smiled back.

For a minute there, it seemed to Emma that they were all connected by an invisible bond, a common thread that stretched from one to the other. It was a strange, comforting feeling. She had had it only a few times before, years ago when her mother had been alive and Sam was still living at home. The three of them would be sipping hot chocolate by the fire or playing a board game like Monopoly or Trivial Pursuit. They'd laugh at a silly joke and Emma would feel this deep bond stretch between them, just like now. But Charles wasn't her mom and Sam wasn't the carefree boy he'd been back then. Yet it was nice to catch a fraction of the deep love she used to share with her family. If only she could feel such kinship again.

"So let's get started." Charles seated himself behind the desk and motioned Sam to the opposite chair.

Emma chose to stay on the sofa, a part of her still reminiscing about the past when her mom had been alive.

"CPT can treat PTSD but I need you to tell me about what happened, Sam," Charles began. "We need to know what the trauma was. If you can talk about it, each time it should get a little better."

"I don't want to talk about it." Sam grasped the armrest of his chair.

"You have to." Charles tapped his pen. "That's the only way you'll get better."

"The only way?"

"Yes."

"Come on, Sam." Emma pulled a second chair to sit next to him. "You can do it. What happened with your friend Peter?"

CHAPTER 21

Several minutes went by. The clock ticked relentlessly forward. Emma grew antsy with the silence but Charles seemed not to mind. He gazed at her brother and then turned those brilliant blue eyes toward her. *How kind and wise he was.* She could never repay him enough for all his help.

"Okay," Sam finally blurted, his story coming out in a rush. "I'll tell you what happened. I see it all the time. Peter was so scared. He kept looking at me. The first kick knocked him down flat. But they kept kicking him, anywhere you could think of. His head, his chest, his arms, his legs. There was blood everywhere. I couldn't stop them. I yelled and screamed but nobody came. They beat me, too. I blacked out and next thing I knew, the paramedics were there. They rescued me but Peter they pulled a sheet over. I killed him, Em. Oh, God! What am I going to do? He's dead because of me."

"Hold on, Sam." Charles raised a hand and leaned forward. "Why is his death your fault?"

"Because he didn't want to go inside. Handball was his

thing, you know. But I was so fed up with it." Sam brushed a shaky hand over his face. "I told him he was being a big baby, always playing a kid's game. He got this hurt look in his eyes, but he followed me. He always followed me..."

"And?" Emma prompted.

"So I went to the dorms to chill. Something didn't feel right as soon as we entered. He felt it, too. He wanted to go back outside. But I kept walking to my bed and that's when I saw them." Beads of perspiration dotted Sam's forehead. He began tapping his hand on his thigh.

"Them?" Charles prodded.

"Gang members. Two I'd never seen before."

"What were they doing?"

"One of them was selling." Sam swallowed a couple of times. "One was buying and the others were using. They ganged up on us. The tall one told us not to snitch or else. But poor Peter didn't understand. I told you he was slow, right? He hollered for the guards, and that's when all hell broke loose. So much blood, and that terrible slapping sound their boots made when they kicked him. I keep seeing his eyes looking at me, hoping I'd save him. But I couldn't. I screamed and screamed but nobody came."

"Where were all the guards?" Emma asked, horrified.

"The Unit 3 sergeant apparently had some chest pain at that time so most of the officers were with him." Sam clutched at his hair and put his knees to his chest. "I killed him. I killed him."

"How did you kill him?" Charles calmly asked. "Did you kick him? Did you beat him with your fists?"

"Of course not." Tears streamed down Sam's face.

"Then you didn't kill him. They did," Charles said. "Don't blame yourself. You had nothing to do with it."

"But I led Peter in there. If I'd played handball with him, like he wanted, none of this would have happened."

"Maybe." Charles spread out his hands. "But you didn't know the gang members were there. You didn't plan on walking in on a drug deal, did you?"

"Of course not."

"Then none of this is your fault. It's theirs. You have to stop blaming yourself."

Sam gulped down several deep breaths. "It's hard. I keep seeing him whenever I close my eyes. I can't sleep sometimes."

"I know." Charles put the tips of his fingers together and brought them up. "That's why we have at least nine sessions and not just one. But you see the processing part of the therapy? I'm trying to reset your thinking. You didn't commit a crime. They did. They killed your friend, and they should be punished for it."

"Ha." Sam gave a grotesque imitation of a laugh. "They told me to keep my mouth shut or else I'd wind up like Peter. So I didn't say anything. By the time the guards came, they'd all run off. It was just me and Peter. His eyes were open, but I don't think he saw me. I think he was already dead."

"So you didn't tell Custody who did it?" *Surely her brother knew better.*

"No, I didn't." Sam glared at her. "I didn't want to die, okay? You don't know what it's like in prison, Emma. One wrong move and you're toast."

"What did Custody do?" Charles asked.

"Thank God they didn't blame me or else I'd have at least ten more years added to my sentence." Sam wiped the sweat off his forehead. "I told them I didn't know who did it. That it was too many of them to count."

"It's not too late. You can still tell them," Emma urged. "I'm sure the warden can help you. You can't let them go like that, Sam. Those inmates need to be punished so they won't do it again."

"They're going to kill me if I snitch. No way. I'm not doing it." Sam shook his head vehemently and dried the rest of his tears away.

"It's okay." Charles rose from his chair. "You don't have to do anything right now. Let's sleep on it. I'm glad you opened up about Peter. That took a lot of courage."

"I think so, too." *Charles was right. There was no need to push her brother so hard.* She laid a hand on his arm. "Thanks for telling us about what happened."

"And it didn't hurt you, did it?" Charles's eyes were full of sympathy. "You survived, Sam. Thinking about it isn't going to bring it back. For homework, I want you to do the rebreathing exercises and read this CPT handout."

"Okay. What about my meds? Should I keep taking them?"

"No. They don't seem to be helping you, so I'll taper them off. The lower doses will be at the pill line starting tomorrow. Let's give CPT a shot."

"Okay, cool." Sam shook Charles's hand. "Thanks, Doc."

"My pleasure. We'll set up an appointment for next week." Charles opened the office door. "Go with the guard out there. He told me he'd escort you back to your dorm when we're done."

Thank goodness it was a different guard and not Smith. No way did she want him attending their sessions. She hoped his replacement wouldn't insist on being there either. "How did you get the officer to stay for so long?" Emma asked as she waved good-bye to her brother.

"Bellamy is assigned to the pill line and they already passed out their meds." Charles locked the outer office door. "Nice guy. We've known each other since I came here."

Darkness had fallen by the time they made it out to the yard. A multitude of brilliant stars twinkled overhead, and the full moon lay like a golden offering in the sky. Was it only yesterday she'd been searching for the comet at Maxim's house? It seemed like forever, almost like another lifetime.

Charles walked quietly by her side as they approached the hill to go up to the Eagle gate. They passed a row of dilapidated buildings and dorms. *What were the inmates doing now?* According to Smith, dinner was usually around six p.m. Did they have their nighttime routine like everyone else? Brushing their teeth, changing into pajamas, showering? Or were they using drugs, getting high? Or were they itching to start another fight, tired of being cooped up for so long?

"Are drugs that prevalent in the prison?" Emma huffed out as they climbed the hill. *It'd been a long day. Too bad there wasn't a taxi around.*

"I think so, but no one knows for sure except the inmates." Charles guided her around some rocks in their path. "Several times a year, someone overdoses."

"Two already since I've been here."

"I know. Sometimes they come in clusters. It could be heroin, meth, morphine, whatever the flavor of the month is."

"And Custody does nothing?"

"They try." Charles shrugged. "But there aren't enough guards. They do the best they can with the limited resources available."

"Which means not much, right?"

"It's hard, Emma." Charles's face turned solemn as they showed their IDs and passed the Eagle gate checkpoint. "You know, these men are criminals. They're locked up to protect the public. Rehabilitation isn't anyone's top priority."

"That's too bad."

"I know. My sister is a counselor in a drug rehab program. She says they're always scrounging around for funding." Charles gave a rueful shake of his head. "The government doesn't have enough money to fix everything."

"I wish it did."

"So much idealism. You remind me of my sister." They were now in the brightly lit parking lot and he was escorting her to her car. "Don't burn yourself out trying to fix the world. Do what little bit you can, whenever you can."

"What a good philosophy. Is that what you do?"

Charles gave a self-conscious shrug. "I try. When are you free next week for another session?"

"I'm usually done by four so any time after that is fine." Emma touched his arm and gave him a grateful smile. "Thank you for doing all of this."

"You're welcome." Charles's charming smile was back in full gear. He pulled out a business card and scribbled something on the back before handing it to her. "Call me when you get home. I want to make sure you get there okay. My number's on the back."

"Alright." He was so sweet. Underneath that playboy demeanor existed a heart of gold. *How many psychiatrists would have volunteered their free time to treat an inmate? Nil or at most one, and lucky for her that one was standing right in front of her.* She leaned over and gave him a fierce hug. "Thank you. From the bottom of my heart."

"Can I get that after every session?" Charles asked, his voice light and easy.

"Let me think about it." Emma laughed in spite of herself. She was sure the man had to beat away women with a stick the way he flirted so effortlessly.

"Oh no. It's Chambers." Charles pulled back from her hug and frowned. "I swear the man sleeps here."

"What? Where is he?"

"Going to his car, behind you. Damn. He sees us." Charles gave a mock shudder. "We're in for it now. God. He needs an anger management class."

"Stewart. Dr. Edwards." Maxim's peremptory voice rang out a couple of seconds later.

Emma turned and sucked in a breath. Maxim's face looked like thunder, those silver eyes blazing at them like bullets.

"This is where you've been? All this time?" Maxim pointed to his watch. "You realize it's almost eleven o'clock?"

"And your point is?" Charles asked in an insouciant voice.

"You should have left hours ago."

"We were working." *What the heck was wrong?* The man was glaring at her as if she'd committed some great sin.

"This late?" Maxim scoffed. "Come on. I wasn't born yesterday."

"Fine. Believe whatever you want but it's the truth." Emma turned to Charles. "So next week, same time maybe?"

Something like a growl emitted from Maxim's throat.

"Sure." Charles cast Maxim a wary look. "You want me to stay?"

"No, I can handle it." Emma waved good-bye and rounded on Maxim as soon as they were alone. "What's wrong with you? You told us it was okay just this morning."

"I never—" Maxim sputtered. "Never gave you permission to use the prison as a dating ground."

"Dating?" Emma reared back. *Had he lost his mind?* "What are you talking about? We were doing CPT sessions."

"Don't even try to deny it. I saw you throwing yourself at Stewart a minute ago." He gestured to Charles's retreating back and then swung back as if he'd been hit. "Wait. CPT?"

"Yes. Cognitive processing therapy." Emma glared at him. "With a patient at the mental health building. We finished fifteen minutes ago. And I wasn't throwing myself at Charles."

"Sure looked like that to me," Maxim said, stretching his shirt collar.

"I was thanking him." Emma fished the keys out of her purse. "Not that it's any of your business."

"Of course it's my business. You and Stewart were reported as missing."

"Missing?"

"Nobody knew where you were. All we knew was that you hadn't returned your keys yet." Maxim clasped his hands behind his back. "Which meant you were still in the prison somewhere. Unaccounted for. You could have been mauled by an inmate for all we knew."

"Well, why didn't you tell me that in the first place?" *No wonder he was concerned about them. But did he have to act like such a boor about it?*

"I got carried away," he said.

"Yeah. You get that a lot, don't you?"

"What's that supposed to mean?"

"You know what it means." Emma clicked open the

car with her remote. She had to leave now before she said something she regretted.

"If this is about last night, that was a totally different situation," he said.

"Yeah? How? You do things without thinking and then regret it afterwards."

"I do not regret it. Not last night, at least."

"What?" Emma breathed out, not sure she'd heard right.

Maxim dug a hand through his hair. "Never mind." He shook his head, stepped away but then swung back.

"Here." He reached inside his inner coat pocket and handed her a large yellow envelope. "These are for you. I hope you like them."

Emma took the envelope, her fingers trembling. *What had he meant by that no regret comment? Did it mean he enjoyed their kiss?* If that were the case…she bit her lower lip. It didn't even bear thinking about. She shook out the envelope's contents.

Pictures. Dozens of them. Of the sky last night. Most were of Holmes but some were of her favorite constellations she'd told Maxim about on that car ride back to her studio from the emergency room. Cassiopeia. Canis Major and Minor. Andromeda. And best of all, Perseus. All laid out before her in their splendid glory.

"Oh, Maxim, they're perfect," Emma whispered.

"You like them?" he asked in a hesitant voice.

"Yes. I love them." She hugged them to her chest. "How did you develop them so quickly?"

"I put a rush on it." Maxim cleared his throat. "I knew you wanted them fast."

Aw. Actions spoke so much louder than words. *Did this mean what she thought it meant?* He'd even remembered her favorite constellations. "How did you know which constellation was which?"

He tugged at his tie. "I just knew."

"You're a closet astronomer?"

"No. I looked them up, all right?" He brushed a hand through his hair. "Listen, it's late. You should go. Give the pictures to your brother next time you see him."

"Alright. Thank you." A warm and fuzzy feeling blossomed in her chest. Maxim surely hadn't had enough time to look up the constellations in that brief dash upstairs to get the camera. Which meant he must have researched them sometime after their car ride from the ER the other day. Which meant...Emma's heart somersaulted. She turned to him, hardly daring to breathe.

He stood all silent and grim, waiting for her to enter the car. *So he wasn't going to make it easy for her. That was okay, for now. She had the pictures for proof, didn't she?* She got inside the car and rolled down the window.

"Thanks again, Maxim. I love the pictures."

"I heard you the first time."

"I know. It was very thoughtful of you."

"Come on, Emma. They're just pictures," he said. "You look like you've won the Lotto or something."

Maybe I have. Emma smiled and drove off.

CHAPTER 22

"That's the fourth jaundiced patient we've had this week."

"I know. Same story each time." Emma finished the OHU admitting orders and handed them to Madison. "It's either a dirty tattoo needle or they're shooting up." It was three o'clock, toward the end of their shift. Sam had already left for the day.

"But none of them admitted to it." Madison began noting the orders.

"It's obvious from their labs. All hepatitis C, same genotype 1a." Emma tapped her pen on the table. "All from dorm 207. You told Sergeant Peterson, right?"

"Yes. He searched the dorms but came up with nothing."

"That's because he didn't have our friends with him," a familiar voice said from the doorway.

Emma's breath hitched. "Hello, Maxim."

There he was, dressed in a pristine gray suit, looking as distinctive and formidable as ever. He'd left for a conference in Sacramento right after his father's funeral last week, and Emma hadn't seen him since. But she'd thought about him, every single day or even more often than that, if she were to be honest with herself. He blinked at her smile as he approached.

"Hi." His silver eyes were locked on her face.

"How was your trip?"

"Good."

"Friends?" Madison threw Emma a funny look. "What friends are you talking about?"

"What?" Maxim frowned, finally breaking his gaze.

"Searching the dorms…you said some friends may help us?" Madison prompted.

"Oh. The K-9 unit. I was able to get them back from Bakersfield. They're right here." He pointed to the door.

Dear God, they looked so vicious. Emma jumped up from her chair and clutched Maxim's arm. Two huge dogs with their tongues hanging out of their mouths prowled into the room. Her hands started shaking.

"What's the matter?" Maxim's eyes were lit with con-cern.

"The dogs…" Emma pressed against his side. *They weren't going to bite, were they?*

"They're expertly trained." He put an arm around her shoulder. "It's okay. Jesus, your face is all white. Breathe, Emma."

"Are you okay?" Madison's anxious voice came from nearby.

"Banding!" Maxim hollered. "Get those dogs out of here. They're scaring the doctor to death."

A stern-looking blond sergeant rushed into the room and fastened a much-needed leash onto each dog. "Sorry about that."

Thank God. Emma exhaled. "What are they?" The creatures were secured now but still looked as if they might lunge at her at any second.

"One's a Dutch Shepherd and the other a Belgian Malinois," Maxim said. "Don't worry. They won't hurt you."

"Sorry, Doc." The sergeant tugged on their straps. "Drake and Prince look scary but they're pretty docile."

The larger of the beasts strained against its leash. Emma's heart almost jumped out of her chest. Before she knew it, Maxim had shoved her behind him, shielding her from the dog's line of attack.

"Search 207." Maxim turned to Madison. "That's the dorm I heard you talking about, right?"

"Yes."

"Look for needles, drugs, even tattoo equipment."

"All right, sir." The sergeant finally departed with the dogs.

"It's okay. They're gone." Maxim gently touched her arm.

"Sorry." *She was such a coward.*

"Sorry for what?"

"Adults aren't usually terrified of dogs." Emma forced out a wan smile.

"Sit." He pulled up a chair, blunt and abrupt as usual. "You don't look very good."

"Bad experience with a dog?" Madison handed Emma a cup of water as she sat down.

"Yeah. A pit bull bit me when I was a kid." Emma gulped down the water, savoring the way the cool liquid slid down her throat.

"No wonder you're scared," Maxim said, his voice soft. "I'll tell Banding not to bring the dogs near you next time."

"Thanks." She put down her cup. *Time to pull it together.* No point dwelling on her phobia when there was so much more at stake. "So you heard about 207 and the hep C outbreak?"

"Yes." Maxim refilled her cup and handed it back to her. "I'm going to have the K-9 units do more random searches. At least several a week. Sacramento approved five more units during our conference."

"That's good, I guess." *She'd somehow have to get used to those dogs.* "What about encouraging the inmates to talk to ID the source?"

"Doc, they're scared. They're not going to say anything," Madison said.

"If I promise them extra protection, they might talk," Maxim announced. "I could send them to SNY."

"That's a great idea." *He was being quite understanding. And he'd rushed to defend her against the dog. How awesome was that?* "The inmates up there won't hurt them for snitching, right?"

"They shouldn't." Maxim's eyes were back on her face.

"I'll head down to the OHU to talk with Mr. Rodriguez now." Emma's face felt like a furnace. *God, those silver eyes were going to kill her.* Why was Maxim studying her so intently? It was as if he was trying to memorize her every feature. She cleared her throat and tried to focus on the problem at hand. "Mr. Rodriguez is the first inmate who turned yellow. He can tell us if he used a needle or did a tattoo."

"Or he may clam up." Madison shook her head. "If he admits to anything, time will be added to his sentence, you know."

"Just like that?"

"Yes. Drugs are illegal and so are tattoos," Madison said. "They have to get their punishment somehow."

"How about in exchange for info, I grant them immunity?" Maxim raised his eyebrows. "No prosecution if they spill the truth."

"You'd do that?" Emma's jaw almost dropped.

"Yes. It's worth it to stop more patients from getting hep C." Maxim frowned at her open astonishment. "What? This is a public health emergency. Got to deal with it somehow."

Emma turned away, a lightness seeping into her soul. First, the constellation pictures and now, the help with the hep C patients. *How could her heart help but melt a little bit more?* "Great. I'll tell Mr. Rodriguez right now."

"I'll go with you." Maxim ushered her out, putting his hand near the small of her back, its heat seeping through her white coat. She bit her lip, knowing she was in serious trouble. He wasn't even touching her and her body was already humming with excitement.

"Code 1 just came in over the radio," Madison suddenly called from behind them. "Looks serious. The dogs found some cocaine. An inmate swallowed a condom of it."

Emma rushed back into the clinic. "Is he stable?"

"For now. They're bringing him in a minute."

"Damn. I'll go check what's happening." Maxim cast her a worried look. "You'll be okay here?"

"Of course. Go. I'll be fine." Emma waved him off, touched by his concern but a little glad to get some distance between them. It was hard to concentrate with him so close. She turned back to the nurse. "Get the crash cart ready. He could go down fast if the condom bursts."

Madison hurried to check the cart while Emma

gowned up, anticipating the worst. Cocaine was bad news if there was a massive influx to the body. Who knew how many grams were in that condom? Once, at the county ER, she saw a man die of a massive heart attack within minutes of ingesting the drug.

"They're here." Madison dashed toward the entrance-way.

Ms. Carter and two officers pushed in a gurney with a huge inmate hunkering on top. Sergeant Peterson huffed his way behind them.

"He won't say a thing." The sergeant wiped a hand over his damp forehead. "But I saw him swallowing that balloon. Come on, Henderson, fess up."

"Didn't do nothin'." The man was enormous, over six feet tall and at least three hundred pounds. He had oily black hair and the usual tattoos littered all over his arms and face. Beads of perspiration dotted his forehead.

"Can we get some vitals?" Emma gulped down her unease. *Please let him stay stable.* Nothing worse than trying to resuscitate a morbidly obese patient. The airway was going to be a killer as the man had no neck.

"We couldn't in the field. Blood pressure cuff not big enough." Ms. Carter clucked her tongue and shook her head.

"I have a bigger one here." Madison wrapped the cuff around the man's arm while Ms. Carter hooked him up on the monitor.

"Blood pressure one eighty over one hundred, heart rate one twenty."

"Damn. Call 911." Emma's heart rate spiked a notch. "He definitely took something."

"Didn't take nothin'," Henderson grunted. His pupils were huge and sweat started to pour off his face.

Definitely sympathomimetic ingestion. "Your vital signs are sky high. Was it cocaine? Meth? We need to put in an IV."

"No IV," the man bit out. "Get the hell away from me."

"Heart rate one forty, Doc," Madison said.

"Get the crash cart ready." Emma's gut clenched. *Had the condom burst already?* "Do you have any chest pain? Trouble breathing?"

"No." Henderson began picking at his skin, his eyes bouncing back and forth.

"Pull up some Ativan," Emma ordered Madison. Thank goodness the nurse seemed as calm as a cucumber. "Five milligrams. Get ready to push it IM since we don't have a line. You called 911, right?"

"Yes. They're on their way," Sergeant Peterson said.

"Mr. Henderson, we need that IV. It'll be quick." Emma gingerly approached the man, who was now yanking at his hair. "We'll give you medicine to make you feel better."

"No." He suddenly bent over and clutched his chest.

"See? Your chest hurts." Emma swallowed down her rising panic. He was going to crash. She could feel it in her bones. "You need help."

She fumbled with the gurney's railing. *Damn. Where was that latch?* Finally it clicked. She swung the railing down and beckoned Madison to bring over the IV equipment. Henderson let out a groan and swiped at his arms and legs. "Get them away from me. They're crawling all over me!"

"Visual and tactile hallucinations. He probably took crack, right Doc?" Madison asked.

"Sure you want to do this, Doc?" Peterson nervously said from her left. "The paramedics are on their way."

"They won't be here soon enough. We need to stabilize him now." *Before they lost the airway.* "It's okay, Mr. Henderson. Madison will place the IV and give you the Ativan. You'll feel a lot better. You won't see those things anymore."

"He may have taken PCP, too." Maxim's voice. He must have just returned from the dorms.

Emma swung around, her anxiety picking up a notch. "PCP?"

"Yes. His bunkie told us he was mixing the crack with PCP. We found both in his locker."

"Jesus. PCP can make them really violent." Emma scanned the room. "We need more officers in here. Now. As many as you can get. Ms. Carter, pull out ten milligrams of Haldol."

"Get away from me!" The inmate screeched as Madison approached with the IV.

Henderson looked like an enraged bull, his eyes bouncing up and down as well as sideways. Suddenly, he heaved out of the gurney. *All three hundred plus pounds of him.* And he was hurling straight at her. Emma turned and found herself wedged between the gurney and the wall. She screamed. *This was it. Her last moment. Crushed to bits against a wall.* Someone seized her arm and flung her out of the way.

"Maxim!" Emma screeched.

But it was too late.

Maxim's head made a sickening thud against the sink as Henderson's enormous body slammed into him. Both men crashed to the ground. A group of officers jumped on top of Henderson and finally managed to pull the man off. But Maxim remained motionless on the floor, his eyes closed.

"Oh, God!" Emma ran to his side. *Please. Please don't let him be dead.* "Maxim, are you okay? Wake up!"

It took ten officers to restrain an infuriated Henderson back on the gurney before Madison could slip in an IV. At least she thought it was ten. It could have been twenty for all Emma knew. She was too distracted with Maxim to notice. There was a nasty gash on his posterior scalp where his head had smashed against the sink. Emma applied pressure, her hand shaking as she scanned the rest of his body for further injuries.

Thank God the paramedics arrived at that moment to push some Ativan and Haldol into Henderson. The man stopped howling and calmed down enough to be wheeled off to the hospital.

"Is he okay, Doc?" Peterson asked, his eyes wide with concern as he squatted beside Emma on the floor.

Madison was trying to take Maxim's blood pressure. So far he'd only moaned incoherently, not fully waking. *Dear God, should they call 911 again?* Emma's stomach felt like it was on fire and her left hand couldn't stop shaking. *Don't die on me, Maxim. Don't die on me, please.*

"I hope he's okay." Emma's voice cracked. "He has a tough head, doesn't he?"

"Yes, but that guy was like a sumo wrestler," Peterson said.

"I know." Emma bit her lip, drawing blood. She was never going to forgive herself if something happened to him. "Can you hold pressure on the wound, Sergeant? I want to do a brief exam."

"Sure."

Emma listened to Maxim's chest and found his heart rate a little fast but nothing alarming. Breath sounds both present. Now, for the most important part. Emma pried one eye open and shone a light in.

"Ow. What are you doing?" Maxim shoved the light away, his silver eyes snapping open. "It's too bright." His voice was a little sluggish but there could be no mistaking the glare in those gorgeous eyes.

"Oh, thank God," Emma whispered, scanning his face. "You're alive. You scared me half to death."

"Not as much as you scared me," he growled, sitting up abruptly.

"Take it easy. Your head took a major hit."

"I'm fine." He brushed her hand away and yanked off the blood pressure cuff. "Where is that refrigerator? He knocked me flat."

"One forty over ninety," Madison said at Emma's pointed look.

Thank goodness the blood pressure was okay. Now if only the stubborn man would stay still so she could make sure the rest of him was okay.

"The paramedics took him," Peterson said. "It took nearly a dozen of us to restrain him. You shouldn't have jumped in like that."

"Somebody had to." Maxim glared at Emma. "She would've been crushed by that monster."

"We were calling for reinforcements."

"Too little, too late." Maxim stretched his arms and groaned. "God, I feel like I've been hit by a truck."

"You were," Emma said, glad her hand was steady again. "Can you get on the gurney? I need to examine you."

"No, you don't. I'm fine." Maxim jumped up. His face turned pale and he swayed a little to the left before clutching the gurney's railing.

"Lie down." Emma reached out her hand. "You might have a concussion."

"She's right," Peterson said. "You should take it easy."

"I need to get back to ISU. See if they found any other drugs."

"That can wait." *His color didn't look good at all.* "Your health comes first."

"Go check the cameras, Sergeant." The stubborn man ignored her as usual. "Maybe the videos captured something. How Henderson got his stash."

"Will do, sir. Listen to the doc, Maxim. She just wants to make sure you're okay," the sergeant called over his shoulder as he took off.

"I'm fine." Maxim finally noticed the officers hovering close by. "What the hell are you all doing here? Go search 207 again. Maybe there're more drugs in that dorm."

The guards fled to do his bidding.

"They were concerned about you. No need to yell at them like that."

"Useless, the lot of them." Maxim flicked a disgusted glance at the doorway. "Where's Gonzalez? He should've been guarding you today."

"He was. He had to step out to help with the pill line."

"He's assigned to you. What the hell was he doing at the pill line?"

"They were short. And we were done seeing patients." Emma made a sweeping motion for him to sit down. "I need to examine you."

"He should've been with you." Maxim glared at her, refusing to budge.

"Hey. We have to go, Doc." Madison held out the

phone. "An inmate fell in the shower in SNY. They need us up there."

"Go ahead. I'm fine here."

Ms. Carter and Madison left, taking their emergency bag with them. Maxim's face turned paler and he swayed again. Emma rushed to his side and put an arm around his waist. He stiffened up like a board.

"Let go. I'm not that weak."

"Let me check." She gently pushed him onto the gurney. "I need to look at your head. It's probably bleeding again."

He let out a long-suffering sigh and settled his large body onto the stretcher.

CHAPTER 23

She was going to be the death of him, Maxim was sure of it. God, he'd lost at least ten years of his life when that bastard had hurled himself at her. He'd acted on instinct, knowing he had to save Emma at all costs. Thank God she was okay, every maddening precious inch of her.

The woman was fussing over him as if he were a mere child. He was fine—just got the wind knocked out of him, that was all. How embarrassing could it be? He got leveled flat right in front of her. *Way to go, Max.* He sure knew how to impress a girl. Damn, but his head did hurt.

"Stop being so stubborn," she told him as he lay down on the stretcher.

"I'm not." *Must she stand so close?* He could hardly breathe without taking a whiff of that delicious rosewater scent. And he'd been so good keeping his distance from her. True, he'd been in Sacramento the whole past week but he hadn't thought about her very much. *Oh hell, who was he kidding?* The woman had been constantly on his mind, ever since well…ever.

And when he'd finally seen her again, she'd smiled. And he'd been lost as usual, even forgetting temporarily about the K-9 units. Damn, but she'd been afraid of those dogs. He'd wanted nothing more than to wrap his arms around her to reassure her she was safe. But they were at work, for heaven's sake. She was his employee. An employee who wasn't even interested in him. He was the last man she'd ever want to date, she'd told him. He was never going to forget those words.

"Ow. What are you doing? That hurts." His wound felt like it was on fire.

"I'm washing your laceration with Betadine," she said from the head of the bed. "Don't worry. The stinging should be over in a second."

"Jesus, Emma." A probe was gouging through his skin. "What the hell is that?"

"It's a Q-tip. I'm exploring how deep the wound is."

"How bad is the damage?" he gritted out through the pain.

"About an inch and a half long and a few millimeters deep." The torturous digging continued.

"Do you hate me or something?"

"What?" she breathed out, the soft breath fanning his cheeks. She popped her head over to his right side, her beautiful green eyes wide with anxiety. "Why would you say that?"

"You're torturing me. Stop with the probing," he said. "Sew it up already."

"I think you should go to the ER."

"For what? Can't you fix it here?"

"You may need a CT. You were out for a few minutes."

"But I'm fine now," he insisted. No way was he going to the ER. He wasn't that hurt.

"Better to be safe than sorry."

"I'm fine. Maybe it doesn't even need stitches. Let me go. I need to deal with ISU."

"You're not going anywhere."

Her slim hand had the audacity to grab his wrist. His massive wrist. Sure, she had gloves on but her touch burned all the way down to his bone. He shook her hand away. A man could only take so much. "Fine," he bit out. "Just fix it and let me go."

"I'm going to use staples. That's our standard." Some papers rustled and then another cool blast of liquid singed through his scalp. "You want lidocaine or can I forge ahead with the staples?"

"Just get it over with." *Damn, but the room was starting to spin.* He clutched the railing when some instrument gripped the back of his head. *Click. Click. Click.* And so it went. Six in total. At least they hadn't hurt as much as that damned probe.

"All done," Emma said, her voice absurdly cheerful. "You did really well, Maxim. How are you feeling?"

"Great." *If you didn't count his throbbing head and the spinning room.*

"Good. Let's get you up," she said. "The nurses are going to need that bed for the SNY patient."

He stood and almost keeled over with dizziness.

"Maxim!" Emma's tiny body wedged itself to his side as her left arm curved around his waist. *God, but it felt wonderful having her so close. If only his cursed brain would stop spinning.* "What's wrong?" She pushed him back on the gurney.

"I'm a little dizzy," he managed to get out.

"Why didn't you tell me?" Her voice rose. "You're so stubborn, you know that?"

"That's the pot calling the kettle black, isn't it?" he shot back.

She ignored him and shined another light into his eyes. "Good, they're reactive. You know where you are? What's the date? Move your arms and legs for me. I have to test your strength."

And so the torture continued. Emma took what seemed like hours to finish the neurological exam. As long as he lay with his head back, the spinning didn't bother him.

"You have a concussion, Maxim," she announced when she was done. "Here, take a meclizine. It'll help your vertigo." She handed him a cup of water and a small white pill she pulled from the medicine dispenser. "Your exam is good but it's better if you get a CT."

"No." He swallowed the pill in one gulp.

"It's either that or constant neurological observation over the next twenty-four hours." She put her hands on her hips. "You have to have one or the other."

"I need a good night's sleep. I'll be fine tomorrow."

"You may not even wake up tomorrow." Her voice softened. "Get the CT, Maxim. We'll both sleep better knowing you're okay."

"We?" His eyes flew to her face. *Had he heard right?* His heart thundered at the possible implications. *Was that why she was fussing all over him?*

"Yes. I feel so responsible." She shook her head. "If it hadn't been for me, you wouldn't even be hurt."

"Don't be silly." His heart settled back to normal even as a pang of disappointment shot through him. *She felt guilty about what had happened. Nothing more than that.*

The phone rang, pulling Emma thankfully away, finally

leaving him some breathing room. Maxim gingerly brought himself upright. He couldn't lie here forever, especially with the recent drug bust. He needed to talk to his officers, and the spinning wasn't bad if he took things slowly. There, he was even standing now without any problems. He attempted a few steps, feeling his strength come back.

"What are you doing?" she hollered as he was about to make his escape.

"What do you think I'm doing?" he called back. "I'm going to check 207. See what's going on with the drug situation."

"Maxim." She ran to his side. "You can't work right now. You need to rest."

"I'll do that later." He focused his eyes straight ahead, knowing sudden movements could worsen things fast. Unfortunately, his left leg tripped on something and next thing he knew, his face almost hit the doorknob.

"See? You can't work like this." Emma latched to his side, her arm wrapping around his waist.

He was a fool twice over but it felt too wonderful with her next to him to raise any objection. And it seemed she was right. Maybe he needed to lie down. "I'll ask one of the officers to drive me home," he admitted begrudgingly as they headed out of the health care building.

Gonzalez happened to roll by at that moment, saving him some phone calls.

"Where have you been?" Maxim demanded.

"Sorry, sir. I just heard." The burly guard shuffled his feet. "The pill line needed me."

"Dr. Edwards needed you more." He felt Emma stiffen beside him and consciously lowered his voice. "Don't leave her next time."

"Yes, sir."

"I need an officer to drive me home," Maxim said. "You think you can manage it? It's an hour away."

"Uh, sure." The officer cleared his throat and then swallowed a couple of times.

"What?"

"It's…uh…we're really short-staffed today. A lot of the officers called off."

"Why? What happened?"

"I think it's the Las Vegas boxing match." Gonzalez swallowed again. "Jones versus Keller."

"Of all the stupid, idiotic…" *Goddamn it.* He couldn't believe his officers could be so irresponsible. Sure, it was a big fight but work was work. He'd just flown in from Sacramento and hadn't heard anything until now. "How many called off?"

"Around fifty, sir."

Maxim swallowed back another curse. He was going to discipline the lot of them on Monday. "Just drive us to the Eagle gate. I'll make it home on my own." No way was he going to drag an officer away to babysit him now.

Emma made some sort of distressed sound but he chose to ignore her. Or ignore as much as he could with that delicious body pressed against his. *Damn.* He was going to have to take a long cold shower when he got home. They settled in Gonzalez's golf cart and not surprisingly, the doctor wouldn't leave him alone even when they reached the Eagle gate.

"You can't drive home by yourself, Maxim. I'll drive you," she said as they walked into the parking lot.

She was no longer holding him and Maxim found himself foolishly missing her support even though he knew it'd been only temporary.

"Thanks but no thanks."

"Why not?"

"The drive is completely out of your way. It'd take at least two hours for you to get back with the traffic."

"I don't mind. Oh, wait." She snapped her fingers. "I'm on call. I can't be that far from the prison in case there's an emergency."

"There you go." Maxim sighed. "Don't worry. I'll be fine. I'll drive nice and slow. Haven't felt dizzy since I left the clinic."

"Who's going to watch you tonight?"

"Why do I need someone to watch me? Your head was hit pretty hard by Ransom, remember? You didn't need a nursemaid that day."

"Because I had a CT and it was clean." That determined look came back in her eyes. "You want to get one? It's not a bad idea. The ER is close by."

"No way. The wait alone would kill me."

"Okay, fine. So we have to find someone to watch you then." Her eyes suddenly lit up. "What about your friends? You know, the parents of your godson?"

"They're in Hawaii, celebrating their anniversary."

"I guess there's only one solution left." She bit her lip. "We'll have to bring you to my place."

"What?" His heart did a peculiar leap. "No way. Why would we do that?"

"Someone has to monitor you tonight." She shook her head. "Didn't you pay any attention to what I've been saying? I thought one of the officers could but if you're so short-staffed and you don't have anyone else, I don't mind doing it. I know my studio is small but it's closer to the prison in case I have to be called back."

"You're not doing this," Maxim tried to protest, despite the queer thrill in his chest.

"Come on, Maxim. Please." Her green eyes pleaded with him. "It's the least I could do. You got hurt trying to protect me. I'd feel awful if something happened to you."

"You really want to do this?"

"Yes. Please. I'd love to take care of you tonight."

"Really?" He raised his eyebrows suggestively, knowing what she meant but he couldn't help teasing her. She needed to laugh more, this beautiful maddening doctor.

She didn't laugh, though. No. Her cheeks flushed a delicate pink and she tugged on her necklace, not looking at him. "I didn't mean it that way."

"I knew that." The peculiar feeling was back in his chest. She looked adorably confused and a little embarrassed at the same time. And dare he say it? She *seemed* attracted to him. Or was that just the concussion giving him ideas? Whatever the case, it was clear she wanted to help him out. Which in itself was such a gift. He wasn't that much of a fool to refuse it.

"Okay. Let's go back to your place," he finally said, the feeling in his chest expanding by the minute.

CHAPTER 24

*D*ear God, how obvious could she have been? Emma shuddered. *I'd love to take care of you tonight.* Yeah, you bet she did, but did she have to say it out loud? Her subconscious must have been working overtime. Thank goodness the man knew what she had intended to say.

"So, let's go then." She licked her dry lips. "My car's this way."

Maxim walked beside her, not saying anything until he saw her Honda Civic. "I don't think I'll be able to fit in there," he said with a wry expression.

"You'll be fine. We'll push your seat all the way back."

"Let's take my car instead."

"I can't drive stick." Emma opened the door of her car. "And I don't like convertibles."

"What?" He sounded offended. "What's wrong with convertibles?"

"Too fast. And too bumpy." She waved him in. "Come on, Maxim. I live only ten minutes away. You can fit. I'm sure of it."

"If you say so."

He slid in and Emma knew she'd have to eat her words. Even with the seat pulled all the way back, his knees were touching the dashboard. "It's a little bit of a squeeze."

"You think?" His eyebrows shot up comically.

Emma bit back a grin. "Sorry. We'll be home before you know it."

They stopped by Maxim's car to fetch his overnight bag before hitting the road. He said he kept it for the days when he had to stay overnight at the prison. Luckily there was hardly any traffic. They made it back to her place all in one piece, with Maxim squeezed tight the whole way. He got out and stretched as soon as she parked the car.

"I think I hurt more now than before." He groaned out loud. "My back is killing me."

"Sorry. Was it really that bad?" She felt a tad guilty.

"Yes. I'd get rid of your car if I were you." He gave an exaggerated shudder. "It's a deathtrap in there."

"That's because you're huge." *How dare he insult her Civic?* She'd had it since medical school and it ran just fine, thank you very much. "You wouldn't fit in most cars."

"You're right. Most isn't good enough. I only drive the best."

"Oh. You are so arrogant," Emma began before noticing the twinkle in his eye. "Is that a joke?" She laughed. "I never thought I'd see the day."

"What? I'm not that bad, am I?"

"Let's just say you won't be winning the Mr. Congeniality Award anytime soon."

"Too bad. Another huge failure on my part. My father must be rolling over in his grave."

His father. How could she have forgotten? Emma felt like

a heel. "I'm sorry. I forgot to ask about the funeral. How did it go?"

"Well enough." He glanced over and forced out a smile. "Don't worry. I'm doing okay. I wouldn't have joked about it otherwise."

"It still must be very hard."

"He'd been sick for a long time." Maxim took in a deep breath and exhaled. "I'm glad he's at peace now."

"Me too."

"Too bad he never knew you. I think he would have liked you a lot."

Aw. How sweet was that? "Thanks," Emma said, her heart skipping a beat. There he was, giving her that look again.

As they entered her studio, a certain lightness blossomed in her soul. Emma glanced at Maxim, suspecting the reason for her happiness. What a lovely compliment he'd given her, especially as she knew how much his father had meant to him. And he didn't look as sick anymore. He was going to be okay.

"How's your head?" she asked, ushering him to the sofa.

"Much better. The pill must be working."

"Good. Thank you for what you did today. I'll always be grateful."

His eyebrows drew together. "I don't want your gratitude."

"Well, you have it," Emma insisted. "Whether you want it or not. Let me get you some ice for that wound. Does it hurt a lot?"

"It's fine. You don't have to baby me, you know."

"I'm not." She pointed to his head. "That's a nasty cut. I'll get you some Motrin too."

"Okay. Mind if I wash up? My head feels sticky."

"Sure. But don't scrub at the wound. Remember, the bathroom is that way." She pointed to the only room with the door a couple of steps down. Her five hundred square foot studio was tiny, and she was sure he'd much prefer to be back at his place. He looked disgruntled just now. But too bad. They had no other choice. He was stuck with her tonight. Those neuro checks were important. She'd seen enough patients die from head injuries to let him be on his own.

Emma pulled out three Motrin pills from the medicine cabinet and deposited them on a small plate. She grabbed an ice pack from the freezer and put it next to the pills. Next she placed the plate on the end table by the sofa. Now for dinner. She opened the fridge, scanning inside and finding nothing but milk, yogurt, a few fruits, and chocolate cake. They'd have to order. She pulled out the stack of takeout menus. Thai, Chinese, Italian…she'd just gotten to the Greek one when he reentered the room.

Forget the menus. *My God, he looked incredible.* She knew what she wanted for dinner and it definitely wasn't food. He'd showered and put on a tight black T-shirt, one that hugged every inch of his gorgeous, well-built chest. His biceps were huge and those forearms…those forearms were magnificent. Emma swallowed and hastily looked away. *God. Where was that ice pack?*

"Something wrong?" He came closer.

"No. Of course not. Why?"

"You look flushed all of a sudden."

"I'm fine." She fanned herself with a hand. "Do you want dinner? I was going to order something."

"What would you like?" He reached for a menu.

You. Anyway you like it. "Anything is fine." Emma threw the whole stash of menus at him and hastily darted around the counter as far away from him as possible. "I love all sorts of food."

"Alright." He gave her a funny look. "Are you sure you're okay?"

"Yes. Fine." He was in sweatpants, of all things. They were gray, soft, comfortable looking, something nice to lounge in. Not sexy at all. *Good.* She could breathe again. But then she imagined herself snuggling next to those pants, feeling those long, powerful legs of his pressed against hers.

"Um, excuse me for a second." She made a beeline for the bathroom. "Let me know what you want to order."

Oh, my God. What was wrong with her? Emma splashed some much-needed cold water on her face as soon as the door closed. *Get a grip, Em.* The man was her boss, here only because he was hurt. End of story. No point to be mooning all over him. She scrubbed off her makeup. *Was that a bloodstain on her blouse?* It must have been from Maxim's wound. She took off the shirt and changed into a pair of skinny jeans and her favorite pink sweater.

"So have you decided on anything yet?" she asked, glad she had herself under control again as she rejoined him on the sofa.

"How about Italian?"

"Sure. Sounds great."

"You like that, right?" he said, flipping to another menu. "Of course."

"I mean, we could try something else. Whatever you want is fine." He went to a third piece of paper.

"Just order, Maxim. I can eat anything."

He turned the menu over and glanced up at her, his eyes widening at her outfit.

"Is something wrong?" He had the most peculiar expression on his face.

"No." Maxim dug a hand through his hair. "So you want to order?"

"Sure. Let me see." She took the menu and did a quick perusal. Her stomach was growling, so anything would be good. "Vegetable lasagna, spaghetti with meatballs, chicken alfredo, lobster ravioli, two baskets of bread, two salads, and a strawberry cheesecake for dessert. Sound good?"

"Uh. My turn now?" He quirked an eyebrow.

"No. That's for both of us." *God, he must think she was such a pig. Or maybe not.* Maxim's lips were twitching.

"Just for that, I'm not letting you share." She laughed and swatted his arm with the menu.

"I didn't say anything." He chuckled, his silver eyes dancing.

It was as if someone reached inside her chest and squeezed out all the air. They were laughing together, she'd never thought it possible. This magnificent, wonderful, stubborn man who'd saved her life not once but twice. And those amazing eyes were stirring up her insides as nothing else. A warm feeling spread in her chest as her heart did a somersault.

Maxim cleared his throat and finally broke eye contact. *Was he noticing it, too?* This incredible pull and attraction between them? Dear God, she hoped it wasn't all one-sided. He stretched and rubbed his hand on the back of his head, suddenly wincing.

The wound! How could she have forgotten? "Let me look." Emma hastily leaned over. "It may have opened up in the shower."

"Please order the food." His voice was strained. "I'm fine."

"Turn your head the other way." Emma tilted his head with her fingertips and brushed aside his thick black hair. *Thank goodness, the staples were intact.* "It looks good."

"I'm sure it is. Stop hovering, will you? It's driving me crazy."

"Okay, fine." *What was wrong with the man? One minute he was joking with her and the next he was as tense as a board.*

Emma went to the kitchen to order the food and by the time she came back, Maxim was absorbed in his laptop. So he wasn't in the mood to talk, she could deal with that. She pulled out her iPhone to check if Charles had sent any updates.

Charles was supposed to conduct another CPT session with Sam today, but he had to attend a PTSD conference in San Diego so they'd tentatively rescheduled for Monday. He'd promised to confirm the time with her and to pass on any new information he learned at the conference. Sam seemed to be improving, not having a panic attack in over a week now but Emma was sure he still needed help. He seemed afraid of his own shadow sometimes.

Her cell suddenly rang. Maxim grunted at the interruption, not bothering to look up from his laptop.

"Charles. Hi." Emma smiled, recognizing the psychiatrist's voice immediately. "I was just thinking about you. How was the conference?"

"Productive. I learned some new data that may help Sam out."

"Yeah?" Emma brought the phone to the kitchen and lowered her voice. Hopefully Maxim wouldn't be able to hear from this far away.

"Yes. I'll brief you on Monday."

"What time on Monday?"

"Five thirty would be good."

"Great. I can't wait. Thanks so much, Charles." She hung up the phone, her mood lighter than even before. She returned to the sofa and found Maxim still hunched over the laptop. "What's taking so long with the food?"

"Beats me."

"I hope they come soon. Are you hungry?"

"No." He shrugged his shoulders and continued typing.

"Is your head okay?"

"It's fine."

"Did you take the Motrin I left out for you?"

"Yes."

"The ice pack is all melted. Do you want another one?"

"Jesus, Emma. I'm trying to work here." He glared at her, a ferocious scowl on his face as he picked up his cell.

"Fine. I'll get out of your way." She quit the sofa and camped out at the dining table. *What was up with the man?* He was like a grouchy beast all of a sudden.

"No, I need doctor's notes for all of them," Maxim demanded to a poor underling on the phone a few minutes later. "You bet. Fifty of them couldn't be sick at the same time. Give them a letter of instruction if they don't provide the notes. Yes, deduct their pay, too, if you have to."

He shook his head and stood to pace the room. "And question every inmate in 207. What else? About the drugs, of course. Pay attention, will you? No, no 115. If they can name names, they get protection. Yes, that's my order— deal with it."

He rolled his eyes and dug a hand through his hair. "I don't care if they're busy. The K-9 units need to patrol 207.

No, not once in a while. Didn't you get my email? Every day for the next week. And I want the dogs in the OHU and Urgent Care, too. I don't care if CIM needs them. Tell Banding we need them more."

He tossed the phone down and plopped back on the sofa where he promptly began rubbing his temples with his fingertips.

"Are you okay? Is your head hurting again?" *The man was working too hard. Why couldn't he rest like any normal person?*

"My head's fine." He threw her another scowl. "Stop hovering so much, Emma. It's very annoying."

"Jeez, fine." *Was it bad news he'd gotten from the prison?* One moment he was all good humor and the next angry as hell. *Or was it the meclizine?* She didn't know but she wanted the pleasant Maxim back, not this ogre of a man who seemed ready to bite her head off.

Dinner was a tense affair, to say the least. Maxim ate his salad and spaghetti from the sofa, refusing to leave his computer. Emma finished the alfredo and half of the lobster ravioli but couldn't finish the rest. She'd lost her appetite with Maxim being so surly. She put the leftovers, including the cheesecake, in the refrigerator.

Maxim had switched to surfing on his phone by the time she finished showering and brushing her teeth. The table was clean and the dishes she'd left in the sink were stacked neatly in the dishwasher. The man was full of surprises. He still looked upset about something, though.

"So you're done with your work?" she asked tentatively.

"For now." His eyes never lifted from the phone.

"Good. I want to do a quick neuro check." She picked up the big flashlight she used for emergencies from the kitchen drawer and walked over to him. "It'll be quick. Can you look this way? I need to check your pupillary response."

"My what?" He looked up, his silver eyes seeming to blaze with heat for a second.

"Your pupils." She shined a light in each one. "Lucky your eyes are so light. I can see your pupils easily. Good. They react perfectly."

Maxim was giving her that intense scrutiny again. Emma shivered, feeling hot and cold all of a sudden. *Had she forgotten to fasten her robe or something?* She glanced down. *No, thank goodness.* Everything was properly tied, covering her from head to toe.

"Now for the rest of the exam," she said, trying to get things back on track.

"There's more to this torture?"

"Yes. Just bear with me. They're questions to make sure you're thinking straight."

"Good luck with that," he mumbled under his breath.

"Do you know where you are?"

"Of course."

"Where are you?"

"Oh, come on, Emma. This is ridiculous."

"It's part of the neuro check. The sooner you do it, the sooner I'll leave you alone."

"Well, since you put it that way."

He easily answered the rest of the questions. She had him walk in tandem gait, touching his tiptoes to his heels to test his balance and he passed that as well. She, on the other hand, wasn't faring so well. Watching those powerful legs was a bit distracting to say the least. *Did the man have to be built so magnificently?*

"You're doing really well," she said, fanning herself as they sat back on the sofa.

"Good. Can I get back to work now?" He pointed to his laptop. "I have a ton of emails to catch up with."

"All right. I'll wake you up in a couple of hours to do another neuro check."

"Come on, Emma," he groaned. "That's overkill."

"I know it seems like that but we can't be too careful." She smiled and raised a hand. "I won't do the whole exam. Just ask a few questions."

"Fine."

Emma headed to the hall cabinet to pull out some extra sheets and a pillow. "I hope you can get some rest tonight," she said as she handed him the bed items.

"I doubt I'll get any." He rubbed the back of his neck.

"Sorry. I know the sofa's small."

"It's not that." He flicked her a glance. "Good night, Emma."

"Good night." She tugged at her robe tie. "Do you mind if I turn off the lights? I can't sleep unless it's really dark."

"No problem." His eyes were back on the computer.

"And wake me up if you need anything," she added.

He made an odd growling sound, not bothering to answer.

Emma turned off the lights and took off her robe before curling up underneath the covers. The room was dark except for a glimmer of moonlight filtering through the blinds at the kitchen window. The refrigerator's soft whir and the distant sound of dishes being washed by her next-door neighbor were reassuringly familiar. Occasionally she'd catch the soft clicking of Maxim's keyboard as he typed one thing or another.

Emma took in a deep breath and pulled the comforter up to her chest. It was cold tonight. *How nice it'd be to cuddle up next to Maxim.* His body was like a furnace. Too bad he seemed as approachable as a block of ice right now. Or more like a flaming ball of fire. Still, despite his gruffness, it was comforting knowing he was close by.

CHAPTER 25

The computer screen turned blurry after another hour of answering emails. Words and numbers merged into one another in no decipherable pattern. Maxim rubbed his eyes, sure Emma must be asleep by now. It hurt to pretend not to care, to shut her out with his work but what else was he supposed to do? His couple of attempts at a joke had earned a few precious laughs. She looked so beautiful when she laughed, like the sunrise peeking over the horizon chasing away the gray cobwebs of night. His world had brightened and for a moment he'd been foolish enough to hope. To dare dream of a time when she'd entrust her precious heart to him.

But then the phone had rung. And she was confiding in Stewart, whispering about plans to meet on Monday. He'd been such a fool. Emma laughed with everyone. Her generous heart reached out to all those in need. He was no one special, really, only someone she was grateful to, someone she felt obligated to take care of. Maxim sighed and stood, stretching his arms.

He moved to the kitchen to fetch a drink of water, careful not to peek at the bed in the corner of the studio. *Was that a snore?* He smiled. It wasn't anything loud or obnoxious, just a soft purr that was perfectly ordinary. Yet it called to him like a beacon. He couldn't help but look over.

Emma's arms and legs were flung out wide as she lay sprawled on her back with the comforter thrown back. Light cotton pajamas covered most of her delicious body but the shirt was riding up her abdomen, giving him a tantalizing glimpse of her tiny waist. Her dark hair spread like a black velvet curtain over the pillow. How he'd love to thread his fingers through those long, silky strands.

Her face was exquisite, softly lit by moonlight, young and innocent. Lovely. What would she ever want with a big brute of a man like him? He shook his head at the impossibility of it all. She would never and more importantly, should never settle for someone as bitter and tainted as he was.

Sighing, Maxim pulled the comforter up to tuck under her chin. She uttered a protesting sound and rolled onto her side, dismissing him in sleep as easily as she'd dismissed him in life.

As he was about to head back to the sofa, Emma suddenly flung both arms out. "Sam. Stop! Don't kill him!" she screamed, thrashing her head from side to side. "Sam! Don't leave me. Don't die! No! No!" She wailed and burst out sobbing.

"Emma, it's only a dream." Maxim sat on the bed and hastily turned on the light. *The poor woman. What was scaring her so much?* "It's okay. Wake up, Emma. You're having a nightmare."

Her eyes fluttered open and she gazed at him, the tears coursing down her cheeks. "Maxim? What are you doing here?"

"Remember, I needed the neuro checks?" How he ached to wrap his arms around her and chase away the tears. But that would frighten her even more. He was huge. His size intimidated most people, let alone a slip of a woman in the throes of a nightmare.

"Oh. I forgot." She wiped her cheeks with an unsteady hand. "How's your head? Is it time for the check already?"

"No. I'm fine." He reached out and brushed a lingering tear away with the pad of his thumb. *Even in distress, she thought of others. Was there no limit to her kindness?* "Don't worry about me. You had a nightmare. Do you want to talk about it?"

"No. Just hold me. Please." She threw her arms around him and buried her face in his chest.

His breath stilled as the world tilted. *What a gift to be bestowed her trust.* Something in his chest squeezed hard as he hugged her close and felt her delicate body tremble.

"I'm so scared." Her muffled sobs reverberated in the quiet room.

"It was only a dream," he whispered. "You're safe. I'm not going to let anybody hurt you."

Gradually her tears subsided and her breathing became more even. *Who the hell was Sam and why was she so scared?* He'd never felt so helpless in his life. "Who's Sam?" he asked.

"What?" Her body tensed as she pulled away, her green eyes shadowed with fear. "Why do you ask?"

"You were yelling out his name." Maxim's heart thudded. *Was Sam her boyfriend? Maybe even an ex-husband?* She seemed to care a lot for the guy.

"What else did I say?" Her tone was wary, afraid.

He hastened to reassure her. "Not much. You said you didn't want him to die."

"That's it?"

"And for someone to stop."

Emma rubbed her forehead with her fingers and backed farther away from him.

"Emma, what is it? Who's Sam?"

"Sam is my..." She swallowed and turned those haunted green eyes toward him. "He's my brother." The words were soft and barely audible.

"Your brother?" A certain weight lifted off Maxim's chest.

"Yes. In my dream, someone was beating him. He couldn't move. He screamed and screamed but nobody came." Her voice shook and her hand clenched down on the comforter. "I tried to run to him but something held me back. I don't know what it was. I tried so hard but I couldn't move. Finally I broke free. But it was too late. By the time I reached him, he was already dead." She burst into fresh tears.

"Come here." Maxim pulled her into his arms again and held her tight. If only he could chase away her demons. Those tears tore at his soul like nothing else. He would do anything for her. This incredible, kind, selfless, beautiful woman who held his heart in the palm of her hand.

"You love your brother a lot, don't you?" He gently brushed his hand over the silky mane of her hair.

"Of course. More than anything in the world." She hiccupped and choked back more tears. "He's the only family I have left. My dad died before I was born. Sam and I were so close when we were kids. We did everything together.

But then we kind of drifted apart and then something awful happened." She wrapped her arms tight around him, her light body shaking again. "Oh, Maxim, he died. It seemed so real."

"Don't cry, darling. It was only a dream." He kissed the top of her head. "I wish I can make it better for you somehow."

"Darling?" She pulled back, her green eyes still shimmering with tears.

"I mean…" Maxim swallowed. *Damn. Had he revealed his feelings so easily?* "It was just an expression. You needed some TLC."

"So you didn't mean anything by it?" she whispered, those gorgeous eyes burning into him.

"No. Of course not." He stood to get some breathing space. *Who was he trying to kid?* Might as well admit it to himself. He loved her. She was everything good in this world. Beautiful, kind, courageous. How could his heart withstand such an onslaught? But she was too good for him. No need to burden her with his feelings when he knew they couldn't be returned. And even if by some miracle she did return them, he wasn't the right man for her. He was still the warden. He couldn't get involved with an employee, no matter what his heart and soul longed for.

"I see." Emma stood up slowly and grabbed a Kleenex from the tissue box on her nightstand. She blew her nose and gave him a wobbly smile. "That's too bad."

"Too bad?" Maxim's breath hitched.

"Yes. Because for a moment there, I thought…" She swallowed and looked away from him. "I thought…never mind. Let's not talk about it."

"No. Tell me. What did you think?" His heart felt like it was beating out of his chest.

"I thought I was the luckiest woman in the world," she said, her voice barely audible.

"Luckiest?" He put both hands on her shoulders and took in a deep breath. *Dear God, what exquisite torture was this? Could she possibly mean what he thought she meant?*

"I thought you said it because…because you cared about me." She gave him a wistful smile.

"Oh, Emma. I do. You don't know what you do to me." He cupped her beautiful face between his hands and inhaled the scent of fresh clean soap. *God. Was there any sexier smell in the world?* He bent his head and kissed away every single tearstain. Her skin was as smooth as velvet. She tasted salty and incredibly sweet too.

"What do I do to you?" she breathed out as her lips parted in a sigh.

"Everything." He hugged her fiercely to himself, afraid to let the moment go, afraid she'd slip away from him somehow.

"Oh Maxim, I never knew." She rested her head against his heart. "I take it the darling still stands?"

"Yes." He pulled back though, remembering her words that night. "Are you sure this is what you want? Last week you said you'd never be interested in me."

"I did, didn't I?" She bit her lip. "Sorry. I kind of exaggerated back then."

"So you didn't mean it? All this time I thought you hated me."

"I'm so sorry, Maxim." She squeezed his hand. "I thought you didn't like the kiss. That you only did it to shut me up."

"Are you kidding me? That kiss kept me awake for days." *Was he dreaming? Had the concussion gone to his head? But no, there she was gazing up at him, her eyes full of tenderness.*

He'd been longing to do it for days. And here she was offering herself so freely. He leaned down. Her lips were soft, yielding, and tasted even more heavenly than he remembered. She came closer and wound her hands tight around his neck, opening her mouth for him. He caressed the velvety skin of her waist and brought his hand up underneath her shirt, gliding over the smooth, sweet contour of her back. *Dear God, she was so passionate, trembling at his every touch.* Her tongue tentatively touched his, and a bolt of fire lanced through his body. He grabbed her waist and yanked her closer. She moaned and tugged at his hair.

"Ow!" A tearing pain shot through his scalp.

"What is it?" Emma sprang apart from him, her eyes wide with anxiety. "It's your laceration, isn't it? Did I split it open?"

"No. I don't think so."

He touched his head but Emma was way ahead of him, already there inspecting the wound.

"The staples are still intact." She dabbed at the cut. "No bleeding. I think you'll be okay."

"Good." Maxim tried to pull her into his arms again but she pushed back, her eyes still worried.

"We shouldn't do this. Your head's still hurt."

"It's fine. It only hurt when you pulled at my hair."

"I know." She turned away and opened a kitchen drawer. "But it's better to be safe than sorry. Let me do a quick neuro check."

"Emma." He felt like laughing. "I've never felt better. Although my mind is kind of foggy."

"Really?" She grasped the flashlight from the drawer and shined it into his eyes. "Are you dizzy again?"

"I'm always foggy around you." He pressed a kiss to her lips, wrapping his hands around her tiny waist. "I can't think straight when you're close."

She laughed and kissed him back, her small arms encircling his neck. Maxim's heart soared. For some miraculous reason, Emma was interested in him. *Him.* Maxim Chambers, big barbarian and all. He didn't deserve her but he was too damned selfish to give her up now that he knew she cared about him. She felt so right in his arms. He deepened the kiss, tugging her up against him.

Suddenly the cursed phone rang. Emma pulled back, her eyes still hazy with desire. "I have to get that," she said. "I'm on call tonight."

"On call?" he asked, like a bumbling fool.

"Yes. Remember? That's why we're at my place. I'm the physician on tonight." She reached for her purse on the counter and pulled out her cell. "It's the Urgent Care."

Damn. Damn. Damn. How could he have forgotten for a minute about the prison? Maxim dug a hand through his hair, a sinking feeling growing in his chest. She worked for him. He was the warden. How were they going to make it work? It was going to be hard, but they had to keep their relationship a secret. That was all there was to it. They could do it; they had to. He couldn't imagine giving her up, selfish beast that he was.

Emma hung up the phone, her face pale. "I have to go."

"Everything okay?"

"Yes." She swallowed. "I mean, no. A patient has chest pain and I have to come in to see him."

"All right. I'll drive you. We can talk along the way."

"No. Just stay here and get some rest, Maxim." Her smile was strained. "I'll be back in a couple of hours."

"It's midnight, Emma." He located his overnight bag behind the sofa and pulled out clean slacks and a dress shirt. "I'm not letting you go there alone. It's too dangerous."

"We can't show up together in the middle of the night." Her eyes pleaded with him. "People are going to assume things."

"I show up at night all the time. Just to check things out." He shrugged. "They don't have to know we came together."

"Maxim, come on. I really can take care of this on my own."

"I know you can." He cupped her face with his hand. "But I want to make sure you're safe. I'm coming with you, whether you like it or not."

"You're never going to let me go alone, are you?" She leaned her cheek into the curve of his hand.

How trusting she was. He felt like a million bucks. "No. Get used to it. You're stuck with me for now."

A few minutes later, they were both changed and sitting in her tiny car. The night was chilly, so Emma cranked up the heat but the damned thing barely worked. She didn't seem to mind though, her eyes focused on the road. For some reason, the closer they got to the prison, the more anxious she became, her hands clenched tight on the steering wheel.

"Is something wrong?" She stiffened at his touch. "Emma, what is it? Are you worried about what happened back there?" *Was she already having doubts about them?* He had to reassure her somehow.

"Yeah. I'm a little worried." Her shadowed eyes met his across the seats. "What happened was a little crazy, don't you think?"

"A little." He smiled and squeezed her shoulder. "But I think we should give it a chance."

"I wish you weren't the warden," she said, her voice small. "I wish we were just plain Maxim and Emma, two strangers who met on the street."

"Well, we can pretend to be, when we're not at work." *If only he could tell her how much she already meant to him.* But it was too early for that.

"Maybe we got carried away." She bit her lip. "Should we forget what happened?"

"Is that what you want?" *How could she sound so calm when his heart was thumping out of his chest?* To his dying day, he would never forget what happened. Could never forget her.

"I don't know. It's so complicated." She exited the freeway and turned right into Fourth Street before glancing back at him. "How about you? What do you want?"

You. And only you. "I think we should date but keep it strictly out of the workplace," he said, trying to sound casual.

"Do you think that'll work?" Her voice was skeptical.

"I think it's worth a try."

After a few minutes of silence, she finally rescued him from the torture.

"Alright." She gave him a tentative smile and he could finally breathe again. "Let's give it a chance. But I don't want you hovering around me at work, Maxim. You can't interfere with how I see patients."

"Sure, as long as you have Gonzalez with you."

"Okay." Her eyebrows drew together. "Speaking of Gonzalez, how could you replace Smith so easily? He was a good guard."

"His brother was an inmate. He needed to go."

"Just like that?"

"Yes. It's strict policy."

"And if you kept him here, what would happen?"

"I'd get fired or at the minimum be in serious trouble." *Why the hell were they talking about Smith? He wanted to focus on them, not on some guard.* But Emma seemed determined to pursue the subject.

"What if Smith never told you about his brother? Could he have stayed?"

"No. We would have found out one way or another." They were only a few minutes from the prison now. Hopefully, the chest pain patient would be taken care of fast. It was getting late and they both needed to catch more sleep.

"What if you never found out?"

"You mean about the brother?" He frowned. "Don't you remember orientation? If Smith knows and doesn't tell us, he's in violation of the rules. He could get fired, too."

"Oh." Emma finally left off with the questions, but she looked more nervous for some reason.

"Don't worry. Smith called and said he's doing fine at RJD." It was just like Emma to be worried about the guard.

"That's good." She pulled into the parking lot, still looking a little forlorn.

Maybe she was tired. She'd barely slept earlier. He hoped they could leave soon.

"So who's this patient you're seeing? Is it going to take a long time?" Maxim asked.

"I hope not." Emma looked across at him, her eyes shadowed. "It's Morris, my porter. He's the one with the chest pain."

CHAPTER 26

Emma's heart thudded against her chest as Maxim drove them in his golf cart down to the Urgent Care. He was silent, looming like a solid mountain beside her. She longed to throw herself into his arms, to recapture the magic they'd shared back at her studio. Before the fatal phone call.

Sam. She should focus only on Sam. She dared not think of Maxim's kisses, his sweet words. She still couldn't quite believe what had happened. One minute she was crying and the next he was cradling her, kissing her, calling her his darling. Of course her heart had melted. He'd been everything she could have wished for. Patient, kind, loving. How she longed to tell him that Sam was her brother, to not have any secrets between them but look what had happened to Smith.

No, she couldn't risk being separated from her brother. Sam needed her. Charles had called from the Urgent Care, reporting that her brother had had a panic attack with crushing chest pain. Thank God he'd been the psychiatrist on call and had called her or otherwise she would never have known.

"How is he?" Emma asked as soon as she entered the Urgent Care a few minutes later.

Sam lay on the gurney with his eyes closed, an oxygen mask strapped to his face. Her eyes swung to the monitor. *Thank goodness.* His vital signs were all good.

Madison waved at her from the nearby sink where she was washing her hands.

"He's doing better. I gave him some Ativan. He's sleeping," Charles said, standing up from the nearby doctor's seat. He was in black jeans and a gray pullover sweater, different from his usual suit yet still as debonair as ever.

"Thanks so much for coming in the middle of the night. And for calling me." Emma sent him a grateful smile.

"He was just doing his job," Maxim said from beside her.

"Are you sure Ativan was necessary?" Madison said to Charles. "He was already getting calmer. You should have let me talk to him longer."

"And when did you get your medical degree, Nurse?"

"It's common sense, Dr. Stewart. But I suppose only doctors have that."

Jeez. What was up with them? Madison had never challenged Emma like that, and Charles was usually much more amiable. Before she could interrupt, the nurse forced out a smile and turned toward Maxim. "Are you doing one of your patrol visits tonight, Mr. Chambers?"

"Yes." *Why was he acting so remote and cold?* He seemed oblivious of the tension in the room, his eyes focused grimly for some reason on the psychiatrist.

Charles flicked Emma a curious look. "You came together?"

"No," Emma said hastily. "He gave me a ride from the gate. And you said you had other things to do, right, Maxim?"

"Right." Maxim finally looked at her, his silver eyes hard. "You'll be okay here without Gonzalez?"

"Yes. I have Charles and Madison."

"All right. I'll be down in the OHU if you need anything."

"What's eating him?" Madison asked as soon as Maxim left. "He's always so angry."

"He's just tired. And his head hurts. Remember what happened earlier?" *Poor guy. It was time somebody came to his defense.*

"His head is as hard as a rock," Charles said.

"Hey, give the guy a break, will you?" Emma looked at the nurse more closely. "Wait, why are you still here, Madison? I thought your shift ended hours ago."

"I'm doing a double. Vicks, the regular night nurse, called off."

"You look exhausted." Charles sounded angry for some reason. "You're doing too many shifts."

"And how is this your business?"

"You want to take a break in the lounge?" Emma interrupted, not wanting their sparring to escalate. And besides, she was desperate for alone time with Sam. "Looks like it's slow in here. I'll call if we need you."

"Alright. I'd love that. And before you go, do you mind checking on Mr. Nash? He said he was in more pain earlier."

"Sure." *Darn.* She should have checked on the old man before she left that afternoon. But it had been so crazy. First thing first though, she needed to make sure Sam was okay.

"What happened, Charles?" Emma closed the door behind Madison to give them more privacy. "It sounded bad. Are you sure he's okay?"

"I think so. He wouldn't tell me much." Charles pushed his chair toward her. "He was a Code 1 in the dorm. Maddy found him in his bunk, shaking uncontrollably. Luckily she knew about his panic history and called me."

"Madison knew?"

"Yes. Sam must have shared it with her."

"That's surprising."

A wistful look came into Charles's eyes. "Maddy's like that. She inspires confidences in everybody."

"Looks like the two of you don't get along for some reason."

Charles wiped a hand over his face. "Sam needed that Ativan. I hope you know that."

"Of course." Emma walked to the gurney and adjusted Sam's face mask. Her brother was still sleeping. "Does he still need the oxygen?"

"Probably not. Maddy threw it on as a precaution."

Emma slid off the mask. Sam groaned and opened his eyes, gradually focusing in on her.

"Hey," he said, his voice slightly groggy.

"Hi." Emma swallowed down the lump in her throat. While she'd been making out with Maxim, her brother had suffered a full-blown attack. "How are you feeling?"

"Okay." He sat up and yawned. "Can I go back to my dorm now?"

"Not yet. Tell me what happened."

"Nothing happened." His face closed up. "It was just one of those spells."

"Nothing set it off? Come on, talk to me, Sam. I drove all the way in–"

"I didn't ask you to, did I?" He threw back his blanket. "Can you push the railing down? I need to get out of here."

"What about your chest pain?"

"Gone."

"Something must have happened. You were doing fine in your sessions. Your attacks were getting better."

"I don't want to talk about it." Sam crossed his arms and glared at her.

"You have to if you want to get better."

"Emma." Charles laid a hand on her shoulder. "It's the middle of the night. Let's all go home and get some sleep. We can talk more on Monday." He pulled the gurney's railing down.

"Thank you, Dr. Stewart," Sam said, the relief evident in his eyes. "Jeez, give me some space, Emma. I'm not a little kid anymore."

"Is everything okay in here?" Maxim banged on the door before jerking it open.

"Everything's fine." Emma sighed, mentally shaking her head. *And he'd said he wouldn't hover.* "We were finishing. Morris was about to go."

"Good. I'll drive you back to the gate."

"The night officer can drive us," Charles said. "No need to go out of your way."

"I'm not." Maxim swung his scowl to Sam. "Why are you still here? Didn't the doctor dismiss you already?"

"Yes, sir." Her brother almost tripped in his haste to stand up. "I'm leaving right now, sir."

"Take it easy. You don't need to rush." *He'd received all that Ativan.* She hoped he wasn't going to keel over. Emma put out her hand. "Are you sure you feel better?"

"Yes, Doctor." Sam spared her one last warning look before shuffling out of the clinic.

"I'll call the night officer," Charles said.

"I said I'll drive her."

"It's okay, Charles. I need to check on Mr. Nash first." Emma quickly stepped between the two men. "You go first."

"Alright, if that's what you want." Charles flashed her his trademark smile. "So, I'll see you Monday evening? The session may run late so I'll order us dinner."

"That'll be nice. Thanks."

Maxim's nostrils flared. He looked like he was about to hit someone. *And here she'd been defending him earlier.* Emma sighed. Charles wisely gave them a wide berth before departing.

"What is wrong with you?" Emma said as soon as they were alone. "Why did you have to be so rude? You didn't have to yell at Morris, and Charles was only trying to be nice."

"Ha. I bet he was." Maxim dug a hand through his hair, his scowl deepening. "Do you really have to check on Nash? It's almost two o'clock. Can't it wait til morning?"

"He's in pain, Maxim. I need to see him." *Darn. It was really late. She should have checked on the old man already.* Emma hurried down the hall toward room eight.

"Wait. You can't go in there alone." Maxim was at her heels. "I'm coming with you."

"He's weak and dying. I think I'll be safe."

"Never trust an inmate, Emma. Haven't I told you that already?" Maxim followed her into the room but at least thankfully remained silent during the exam.

Mr. Nash's vitals were good but he winced as soon as Emma touched his abdomen. The poor man looked even more emaciated and jaundiced than before. She had to get him that compassionate release somehow.

"I'm going to up his morphine," Emma said as they proceeded back to the Urgent Care.

"Whatever. Do what you have to do so we can leave."

"He's dying, Maxim."

"Not my problem."

Jeez. What happened to the nice man who'd let her cry on his shoulders earlier? "Can you sign for his compassionate release? It's much better if he can die at home. Surrounded by his family."

"No way. He's not getting out early just because he's sick."

"Please, Maxim. He's been punished enough."

"He killed his own son-in-law."

"To protect his granddaughter."

"So he claims." Maxim snorted.

"How can you be so unsympathetic?"

"I'm trying to be fair to the victim here."

Emma kept walking, knowing defeat stared her in the face. She could understand where Maxim was coming from, especially with his parents' history, but did Mr. Nash deserve to die in prison alone? She didn't think so, but Maxim wasn't wrong either in his advocacy for the victims. If only he could bend a little just once. Maybe if she got to know him better, she could convince him.

When they arrived back at her studio, Emma still couldn't shake off the unbearable tension gnawing at her insides. Mr. Nash wasn't her only worry. Something must have happened to scare Sam tonight. He was lying about being fine. Why wouldn't he talk with her?

"You look exhausted, Emma. Let's get you to bed," Maxim said as she plopped down on the sofa.

"I'm alright." She swallowed a yawn. "How's your head?"

"It's okay." He sat down next to her, their shoulders touching. "Thanks for asking."

"You're welcome."

"I'm sorry I can't help you with Nash." Maxim reached over and clasped her hand. "You're so giving, you know that?" He leaned over and touched his lips with hers.

God, it felt so wonderful to be kissed by him. To be surrounded by all that power and strength. His warm spicy coffee bean scent wrapped around her like a drug. He was doing that wild thing with his tongue again, the maneuver that turned her insides to mush. She pressed closer, desperate for more but a brief vision of Sam suddenly flashed through her mind. Emma pulled back, the guilt clawing at her.

"What's wrong?" Maxim smoothed her hair gently back with his hand.

"I'm sorry. Can we take it a little slower? It's all so fast." *Actually it all felt right. Except for Sam.* Emma bit her lip. The only solution seemed to be to take things slow, one day at a time until she could figure things out.

"Of course." Maxim's hand dropped. "I definitely don't want to make you uncomfortable."

"I'm not uncomfortable," Emma hastened to reassure him. The poor man had stiffened up like a board at her comment. She clasped his large hand in hers and put her head on his chest. "I love being with you, Maxim. Please don't doubt that. It's just there're some things I have to work through."

"Are you interested in someone else? Like Stewart maybe?"

"No, of course not." She looked up, her heart clenching at the uncertainty in his eyes. "Trust me. You're the only one I'm interested in. Charles is a good friend. That's it."

"Good." Maxim let out a long breath and swung an

arm around her shoulder. "We'll take it as slow as you want. I'm willing to do whatever it takes."

"Hmm. I like the sound of that." Emma inhaled his wonderful spicy coffee bean scent again and snuggled closer. He was so warm, radiating comfort and security, everything that she craved. The sound of his slow and steady heartbeat reverberated underneath her ear as she drifted off to sleep.

CHAPTER 27

He'd give anything if he could spend the rest of his life with her nestled by his side like this. The incredible feeling of her soft body pressed against his, the rosewater scent from her skin, the way she breathed slowly in and out, her chest expanding and contracting…how precious it all was. He adjusted their bodies so they were lying side by side on the sofa. It was cramped but he didn't mind so long as she was next to him.

If only he could freeze time and lie here forever with her, his arms wrapped tight around her tiny, perfect body. She'd fallen asleep with her head on his chest. She'd bestowed so much trust upon him, easily curling up against him as if they'd been dating forever and not for mere hours. So she wanted to take things slow. He was fine with that. Sure, it'd be hard not to take things to the next level with the way his body so naturally reacted to hers. But Emma meant the world to him. He was willing to wait forever if that was how long it'd take.

If only they didn't have to keep their relationship private. It'd been agonizing to pretend she was merely Dr.

Edwards to him earlier at the prison. She was so much more and the whole world needed to know it, especially Stewart.

He'd seen how the psychiatrist had behaved around Emma tonight and he didn't like it one bit. Anyone with eyes in his head could see Stewart was interested in her. And somehow the man had finagled for them to spend time together during the CPT sessions, promising to buy Emma dinner at their next meeting. He trusted Emma. *Sure, she wasn't interested in Stewart, but why did she have to spend so much time with the man?*

If only she could love him a little bit, he'd take care of the rest. He'd shower her with everything she could possibly need and treasure her as she deserved. She was lovely and honest and kind. And generous to a fault. True, she was also stubborn and maddening sometimes, but he loved all of that about her. A big brute like him didn't deserve her but he was going to try his best to earn her trust and keep her happy. Perhaps he could leave all the bitterness and pain of the past behind him. With Emma by his side, anything was possible.

Maxim woke up the next morning feeling happier than he'd felt in a long time. His head still hurt a little but the dizziness was completely gone. He watched Emma for a few minutes, memorizing every freckle on her lovely face. Her dark lashes eventually fluttered open and she gave him a hesitant smile.

"Good morning." He leaned in and kissed the tip of her nose.

"Hi." She glanced at him and then away again, looking adorably shy. "How's your head feeling?"

"Great. Do you have any plans for today?" He stood

and stretched, hoping her answer would be no. He'd love to spend the day with her.

"I have to round in the prison." She brushed a hand through her tousled hair and sat up.

"The prison? What for? It's Saturday." A wave of lust hit him at her sexy and rumpled appearance. *She'd said slower. Slower.* He retreated a few steps.

"To check on the OHU patients. Make sure they're doing okay."

"Oh. Good idea." Good thing there was something to focus on besides Emma's bewitching appearance. "I need to talk to ISU about the drugs. And I should meet with the hep C patients, too."

"I'd start with Rodriguez. He's the first one who got jaundiced." Emma got up and walked into the kitchen, looking like a wood nymph just awoken from a deep slumber. She poured water into the coffee dispenser and lifted the lid to put in a filter. It was a mundane, everyday task but Maxim loved watching her do it, knowing it was the first time she made coffee in front of him, for him. He hoped they'd share many mornings like this in the future. Maybe they could try his place next time.

The morning passed quickly enough. Rodriguez, after almost half an hour of prodding, confessed to receiving a tattoo from an inmate named Greely. The other jaundiced patients admitted the same and Maxim had the pleasure of confiscating Greely's tattoo equipment.

"Thanks for not sending him to the hole," Emma said on their way up the hill to exit the prison.

"He got enough of a scare from me without resorting to it."

"What did you do?"

"Nothing as bad as you think," he said, proud she'd have nothing to complain about his behavior this time. "Next time we catch him doing tattoos, it'll be an automatic ninety days added to his sentence."

"I'm glad you didn't resort to violence."

"The case didn't need it." He frowned, remembering his discussion with ISU. "The drug situation is harder to control, though. None of the inmates is willing to say anything, even after I offer them protection."

"You have cameras set up everywhere now, right? I'm sure you'll catch the dealer soon enough."

God, to be given such trust. He sure hoped he wouldn't blow it.

Emma suddenly stopped dead in her tracks, entranced by a small bird chirping on a branch. "Maxim, that's him," she said, her eyes bright as her face broke out in a grin.

"I take it that's your blackbird." *Look at how captivated she was.* He couldn't believe he was feeling vaguely jealous of a bird.

"Yes. I named him Phineas. He's really rare." She gestured with her hand. "I know it's silly but I'm always happier when I see him. He reminds me of my brother. I hope Sam can meet him one day."

"I can arrange that. Where's your brother? I'll get clearance and he can come see your bird anytime he wants."

"Uh, I don't think that's possible." She lowered her eyes. "Sam's kind of not free right now."

"Okay. Let me know when he's free."

"Thanks. Believe me, you'll be the first to know," she said.

Maxim smiled. *Yes, he'd definitely want to meet her brother soon.*

CHAPTER 28

"A hunger strike?" Emma asked.

"Yes. The inmates won't eat til they get what they want. Pelican Bay organized it," Julien said. "They think thousands will join in. Last night, a lot of our Unit 2 and 3 inmates said they're on board."

"How many?" Kaye scowled from the head of the table.

Next to her, Maxim's seat stood empty. He'd missed all their morning meetings this past week because of teleconferences with Sacramento. Last night, they'd talked for hours on his balcony in his lovely mansion up the hill. Emma smiled to herself, feeling all warm and tingly inside.

She was in love with Maxim; no point in denying it any longer. Her heart practically sang with joy whenever he was near. The past week had been incredible. They hadn't met at work due to his busier schedule but they'd spent every evening together except for the couple of times when she attended CPT sessions with Sam. Maxim had been amazing…gentle, kind, tender, protective: everything she could have hoped for in a partner. And he'd been patient, too. True to his word, they'd kept it slow and hadn't taken things to the next level. *Yet.* But how Emma longed for that day to come. Perhaps soon. If only she could decide whether to tell him about Sam.

Her mind was still conflicted. If she told him, he'd either have to do the right thing and separate them or he'd have to go against policy and keep them together at Albatross. How could she tolerate being away from her brother? Yet how could she expect Maxim to jeopardize his job for her? He'd be violating his code of ethics. His very integrity would be compromised. She couldn't do that to him. But how long could she keep Sam's secret from him? Emma sighed, no closer to finding the answer.

"Yes, all the black inmates are on strike," Julien was saying.

"Really?" Emma tensed. *What about Sam?* Despite the last panic attack, her brother had actually improved in the past week. Hopefully the strike wouldn't set him back. "So they won't eat til they get what they want?"

"Something like that," Kaye said. "We're supposed to see anyone who hasn't eaten in twenty-four hours. This is going to mess up all our schedules."

"But we can't let them starve." Emma tapped her pen. "What do they want, anyway?"

"Constructive programs for those in the SHU and to end long-term solitary confinement," Julien said.

"What's the SHU again?" Emma asked.

"Security Housing Unit," Julien said. "It's the isolation facility of a maximum security prison."

"We don't have one, right?"

"No. It's only in Pelican Bay and a few other prisons."

"And what's so horrible about it?"

"Come on, Dr. Edwards." Kaye shook her head. "You've

been here for a while now and you don't know anything about the SHU?"

"The inmates are locked in solitary confinement all day in an eight-foot solid concrete cell," Julien explained. "They get at most ninety minutes to go outside a day. And they go out alone."

"Don't know what they're complaining about," Kaye sneered. "At least they get to exercise in a yard."

"But the 'yard' is not really a yard; it's less than twenty feet long and surrounded by concrete," Julien said. "There's no view except for a little skylight from way up top."

"So the rest of the time they're in their cells?" *No wonder they were striking.* Emma leaned forward. "Where do they eat?"

"Everything's done in the cell. The food trays are pushed through a little opening for them twice a day and there's a toilet in the cell. Three times a week they're escorted out to shower," Julien explained.

"Do they get to see anybody?"

"The cells are all concrete with metal doors so they can't see any other prisoner. They can't see the outside, the sun, the trees, or anything," Julien elaborated. "Once a week, they're allowed a visit for an hour but they have to talk through a phone behind glass."

"I used to work at Pelican Bay," Dr. Parker chimed in. "The SHU is awful. The men lose their sense of identity and often break down. Many get depressed and want to kill themselves. And the wait-list for mental health is so huge that a lot of them don't get treated."

"Don't feel sorry for them," Kaye said. "They dug their own hole and deserve everything they get. All of them are dangerous criminals."

"Yes, probably," Dr. Parker said. "But it's cruel to house them like that. They're like trapped animals."

"So that's why they're striking." *The inmates had a point, but why did Sam have to be involved?* He was thin already—a few days without food and Emma was sure he'd be a skeleton. "How long do you think it'll last?"

"Not long," Julien said. "Usually they go for a few days and then cave in."

"Are you talking about the strike?" Maxim's distinctive voice sounded from the doorway.

Emma turned her head, a blaze of happiness surging through her body. *Ridiculous.* She'd seen him last night but it seemed like forever. She smiled and ate him up with her eyes. He looked as striking as usual in a light-blue shirt, blue tie, and a pristine gray suit. His silver eyes scanned the room and stopped temporarily on her before moving on. His face, though, was remote, his eyes showing none of their familiar warmth. Emma's smile dwindled. *How could he be so good at pretending they were just business colleagues?* She, on the other hand, was a jittery mess.

"Maxim," Kaye purred from her seat. "We're so glad you could join us. The inmates are on strike. We need your input."

"Sorry I'm late." He sat down next to Kaye.

The CMO gave him a warm smile and placed her hand on his arm. *Why didn't he shake it off?* Charles had mentioned that they'd dated. *Was he still interested in the woman?* Emma looked away and tried to remind herself that they were at work. Maxim couldn't very well come over and single her out in front of everyone.

"So how many inmates are on strike?" Maxim asked.

He barked questions back and forth to Julien and

Kaye, instructing them to activate the hunger strike protocol. Then he reviewed a long list of policy updates he'd picked up from the teleconferences. The meeting dragged on and Emma had to stifle a yawn. She wanted to see how many meals Sam had skipped. None of what was being discussed was even relevant to patient care right now.

She sighed. *He was ignoring her. But she couldn't have it both ways, could she?* Business was business and she'd insisted on him not hovering at work. But did he have to look so chummy with Kaye? The two talked about some changes Sacramento had implemented with the TB testing procedure, their eyes only on each other. Finally, the torture ended. Emma packed up her bag and sprang out of her seat.

"Dr. Edwards," Maxim said. "May I see you in my office?"

"Uh, my clinic's starting." *And Sam was waiting.* "Is it important? Can we discuss it later?"

"No. I need to discuss it now," he said.

He ushered her to his office and swallowed her up in his arms as soon as the door closed. "Maxim!" Emma laughed and shrieked between his kisses. *The man was full of sweet surprises.* "The door! Someone will come in."

"Right." He backed toward the door and locked it with one hand, all the while never letting go of her. Emma pulled out of his arms reluctantly awhile later, her body tingling all over.

"We're so bad, you know that?" she said, straightening his tie.

"I can't help myself." He cupped her face with his large hands, his silver eyes aglow with tenderness.

"What about Kaye?"

"Kaye?" His eyebrows shot up. "What about her?"

"You two dated, didn't you? Looks like she's still into you."

"We had one date ages ago." He chuckled. "And I'm definitely not into her."

"You're not?"

"Of course not, Emma. Isn't it obvious?"

"What do you mean?"

"I love you. How could you think I'd be interested in someone else?"

"Really?" Emma's breath hitched. *He'd said it. The three magic words.* Her heart felt like it was going to jump out of her chest. "Are you sure?"

"Completely sure. Nothing will change my feelings." A hesitant look suddenly came into his eyes. "Is it too early to say it? I don't want to scare you off."

"Oh, Maxim, you're not scaring me off." Emma wrapped both arms around him and held on tight. "I love you, too," she whispered against his chest.

His big body tensed as he pulled back, those gorgeous silver eyes locked on her face. "Say it again."

She did and he tugged her in for another kiss, this time longer and even more passionate than the last.

"It's going to be tough pretending there's nothing between us," he said when they finally pulled apart.

"You did a good job earlier."

"I had to. But it's going to be even harder now. You shouldn't look so beautiful."

"Aw." She nuzzled his neck with her nose. She was beginning to love his scent above all else.

"You're killing me, Emma." He gave her a hard kiss before stepping back. "Let's save it for later."

"Alright." Emma smiled, amazed that she could affect him so easily.

"Do you need a ride down the hill?" Maxim put an arm around her shoulder. "I'm heading that way to speak to the Unit 3 captain. I can give you a ride if you want."

"Sure, but no touching, okay? I don't want people to start talking about us."

"Alright. Promise. I'll keep my hands to myself."

True to his word, as soon as they exited the office, Maxim's arms stayed by his side. About to get into the golf cart, Emma decided to check on Phineas. Strange but she didn't see him. He was usually out and about right now, pecking away at insects. She swept her eyes to the nearby bushes, an uneasy feeling stirring in her chest. *Come on, little one. Where are you?* She waited for his familiar bird-call but the air remained eerily silent.

"Maxim, can you hold on for a minute?" Emma gripped the seat handle on the golf cart. *Something was wrong. She could feel it in her bones.* "I need to find Phineas."

"Your bird?" He raised his eyebrows. "But he could be anywhere."

"No. He's usually right here. I know it's a lot to ask but can you help me look for him?"

Maxim luckily agreed and headed for the farthest bushes while Emma explored the grounds adjacent to the trees. A few minutes later, she spied something black at the bottom of a nearby bush. An ominous sensation prickled at the back of her neck as the uneasiness exploded in her chest. She swallowed against the rising tension and took a couple of steps closer. *No!* Her heart took a nosedive. *That couldn't be Phineas lying there crumpled on the ground. Not her precious blackbird. Anything but this.*

But alas, it was indeed her poor blackbird that lay dying amid the dirt. A jagged scratch mark streaked his chest and his left wing was bent at an abnormal angle. His usual bright eyes were squeezed shut as his breath came in sharp, quick bursts.

No! Sam hadn't even had a chance to meet him yet. *How could this be happening?* "Poor baby." She reached out her hand.

"Wait. Don't touch him." Maxim crouched beside her. "You may hurt him more."

"Okay." Emma bit her lip, trying to fight back the prickle behind her eyes. "But we can't leave him here. The cats will get to him. Can you bury him somewhere after he dies?"

"Sure. Where do you want to do it?"

"I don't know." Emma swallowed down the lump in her throat. "Just find somewhere safe. Where the raccoons and cats won't get to him."

"Alright." Maxim pulled out a large white handkerchief from his pocket and gingerly scooped up the bird in his giant hand, cradling it with the utmost gentleness. Poor Phineas looked to be gasping his last breath.

"I can't bear to look at him." Emma's voice cracked. "Do you mind doing it by yourself? I'll head down the hill first. My clinic's starting."

"No problem. I'm sorry, Emma. I know how much he means to you."

"Thanks." Emma wiped the wetness from her cheeks. "I know it's silly but don't tell me where you bury him, okay? I don't want to think about him lying in the ground somewhere. I want to remember him being alive and free, singing his little song."

"Alright, darling." Maxim squeezed her shoulder with his free hand. "Don't worry. I'll take care of him for you."

Emma plodded down the hill. Her feet felt like lead. *How was she going to break the news to her brother?* Sam would definitely be disappointed. But he had a thousand things to worry about every day already. Especially now with the strike. Would Phineas's death affect him as much as it affected her? She bit her lip, determined not to break down in front of her brother.

"Sam, are you seriously on strike?" she asked a few hours later when she finally got some alone time with her brother. Luckily the busy schedule had prevented her from dwelling on Phineas's death. Madison and Ms. Carter had departed on their lunch break and Sam was alone with her in the Urgent Care, stacking some oxygen masks in the closet. Sergeant Peterson was stationed across the hall from the clinic at his usual desk, so Emma kept her voice low.

"Yes." One of the masks fell down and he stooped to pick it up. "I can't stand the SHU. They should get rid of it."

"What do you know about the SHU?" Emma sat on the gurney and bit down on her apple. She'd decided to delay telling Sam about the blackbird. *No need to worry him more when he already had the strike to deal with.*

Sam threw a wary glance toward the entranceway. "I was there, Em. They sent me there after it happened."

"What?" *Her poor brother had been stuck in that horrible place?* Emma almost choked on her apple. "You were in the SHU? But why?"

"They thought I was part of the PALI gang."

"What's that?"

"It's the biggest African-American gang here."

"But you were assaulted," Emma said. "You weren't part of the gang."

"I'm black and they thought I was part of that drug deal with Peter." Sam began stacking some paper masks next to the oxygen masks. "Finally they cleared me. But I was there for a couple of months. I almost lost it. That's when I stopped writing to you."

"You should've told me." Emma got up from the gurney and reached out to squeeze his hand.

Sam immediately stepped back and gave a warning shake of his head. Peterson was looking at them from the doorway. The sergeant waved and she smiled back, hoping she didn't look as nervous as she felt. *Did he see her take Sam's hand?*

"Watch it, Emma," Sam whispered. "You're going to get in trouble. Don't talk to me when he's around."

"Alright." She settled back in her seat, glad the entrance-way was empty again. "You're too thin, Sam. You need to eat. I don't think the strike is a good idea."

"It's not just the SHU, Emma. If I don't do it, they're gonna get me."

"Who?"

"Who else? The PALIs. They rule here." Sam gave a defeatist shrug. "You have to do what they say or else."

"But that's so wrong. You have to tell Custody. I'm sure they can help."

"Nothing's going to stop the PALIs. That's just the way it is." His solemn eyes lightened up by a fraction. "But it's getting better. The K-9 units have been everywhere so the drug deals have stopped. At least for now."

"Good." Emma finished her apple and threw the core into the nearest trashcan. "So about the strike. How long are you going to be on it?"

"Until they tell me I don't have to anymore."

"So how many meals have you skipped?"

"Six."

"That's two whole days. Why didn't you tell me?" Emma jumped up from the gurney and rapidly scanned him for signs of dehydration. "I thought the strike started yesterday."

"They told me to stop eating Saturday."

"Are you feeling okay? Sit down." She ushered him into a chair. "Let's get your vitals. You're probably dehydrated. Are you drinking anything? No? Not even water?"

Luckily Sam's vitals and exam were good except for the mild tachycardia. He definitely needed more fluids. "You have to drink some water, Sam. You're already dehydrated."

"No, I can't. They said no water." His face was set, his eyes staring defiantly back at her.

"Come on, Sam. Drink. You're carrying this too far."

"I can't. They're going to kill me if I do."

"Sam, please." She touched his arm. "Let me talk to Custody. Who are these PALI inmates? I know the warden. He's really nice. I think he can help."

"Chambers? Nice? Yeah, right!" Sam scoffed. "No way is he going to help. And you better not tell him or I'll be toast. Nobody likes a snitch."

With a final warning glance, Sam wheeled away the supply cart and left the clinic. Emma pulled at her locket, cursing silently. *How the heck was she going to make him eat?*

"Everything okay here, Doc?" Sergeant Peterson sauntered into the room, holding his ever-present coffee mug.

"Yes. Why?"

"You don't look too happy." Peterson's kind eyes peered at her.

"I'm fine." Emma forced out a smile. "Morris is on the hunger strike so I was making sure he's okay."

"You care about Morris a lot, don't you?" His brown eyes never left her face.

"I care about all my patients." Emma tugged at her pendant again. *What the heck was the officer getting at? Surely he didn't know about Sam being her brother, did he?* "Sorry. I have to go to the OHU right now. Talk to you later, Sergeant."

Whew. That was a close one. Emma breathed out a sigh of relief. She'd have to be more careful with Sam. Only speak to him during the CPT sessions, which should be coming up soon. She went to see Mr. Nash and found him thinner and weaker than before. She'd heard from Julien that the compassionate release papers were currently in the warden's office, awaiting Maxim's input.

Emma squeezed the older man's hand. *She had to convince Maxim to sign the papers.* She'd failed before, but Maxim had been so kind and obliging the past week. Surely he could extend an ounce of compassion to a dying old man.

Later that night, Maxim hugged her as soon as she entered the door, reassuring her that Phineas had been well taken care of. He was so good to her, implicitly sharing her grief over the blackbird without reservations. *How many men would do that?* She'd lucked out for sure.

Dinner was a fantastic French meal of grilled seafood salad, oyster soup, and roasted lemon rosemary chicken, all homemade by Maxim. He served it on the expansive patio with a gorgeous view of the ocean as a backdrop. He wore jeans and a polo shirt, looking as striking as ever. His eyes rarely left her face, the love shining out of them quite evident to see.

She was so fortunate to have him in her life. *If only he could be a tad more understanding with the inmates.* How was she going to bring up Mr. Nash? Plus there was the hunger strike situation with Sam. Emma sighed and pushed the shrimp back and forth on her plate.

"What's wrong?" Maxim put down his napkin. "You don't like the salad?"

"No," Emma hastily reassured him. "I mean, the salad's great. I like it."

"You haven't eaten anything, and I know how much you love to eat."

"The food is wonderful." Emma smiled and reached over to hold his hand. "Thank you for doing all of this. You didn't have to."

"But I wanted to. To celebrate us being a couple." He caressed her cheek. "To let you know how much you mean to me."

"How much do I mean to you?" She leaned over, wanting to soak in his warmth.

"The world." He made an expansive motion with his arm. "And everything in it."

"Oh, Maxim." She threw herself into his arms. "You say the sweetest things."

He kissed the top of her head and the familiar warm tingly sensation pervaded her body. How nice to be surrounded with his love. She snuggled close, wishing she could stay in his arms forever. How wonderful it would be to spend the rest of her life with him. If only she didn't have to worry about the prison. It wasn't going to be pleasant what she had to say to him. Reluctantly, she pulled away and shifted back to her seat.

"Now I know something's definitely wrong," Maxim said. "Come on, Emma. Talk to me. What is it?"

"Okay, here goes." *It was now or never.* She sipped some wine and cleared her throat. "One of the inmates told me today that he was forced to do the hunger strike. That a gang threatened him. If he didn't do it, they'd kill him."

"This is what you want to talk about?" he asked, his eyebrows flying up. "I thought it was about us. Something serious."

"It is serious," she said. "Do you think it's true? That a gang can do that?"

"Probably." Maxim continued slicing his chicken into neat little pieces. "Can you pass me the salt? And the pepper, too? It's not that flavorful, is it?"

She pushed him the condiments. "That's all you can say? Just probably?"

"What? Oh, yes. The gang thing." Maxim twirled his wine glass around a couple of times. "There're several gangs in the prison. As long as they don't bother us, we don't bother them."

"You mean you let them intimidate the other inmates?" Emma almost dropped the glass she was holding. "My patient is scared for his life. He hasn't eaten because he's afraid they're going to hurt him."

"That's too bad." Maxim continued to chew his chicken. "Tell him to make a report. Name the people threatening him and we'll take care of it."

"He said the PALIs are making him do the strike."

Sorry Sam. She saw no other way around it. Maxim needed to know about the gang.

"That's a good start but it's too vague. Any specific individuals he named?"

"No, he's too scared to do a report. He doesn't want to be a snitch."

"Then there's nothing we can do."

"So it's either die by starvation or die by being beaten up? How can you sit there and let it happen?"

"I'm not just sitting here." Maxim's eyes darkened. "If they report it, we can protect them. It's their choice."

"But if they snitch, they can die, too."

"Yes. That's the way it is, Emma." Maxim sighed. "Why are you getting so worked up over an inmate? They're not worth it. Come on, finish your soup before it gets cold."

"I don't want to eat the damned soup." Emma tossed down her spoon. "I lost my appetite."

Maxim's eyes widened. He was silent for a moment before he picked up his fork and resumed eating. "I spent a lot of time on that soup."

"Sorry." So he was upset. *Who cared?* She was mad, too. She might as well speak about the other matter. Things couldn't wind up worse than they were already. "I also want to talk about Mr. Nash, the cancer patient."

"Again?"

"He's doing a lot worse, Maxim. Can you please reconsider? He has this cute granddaughter. She's only eight. And—"

"My mind's made up."

"He killed his son-in-law to protect his granddaughter. She was being abused," Emma said. "I don't think his crime was that bad."

"So he claims." Maxim shrugged his shoulders. "Who knows if it's even true?"

"I'm sure he told me the truth. Why can't you believe him?"

"Because he's an inmate. They're always lying."

Emma gripped the edge of the table and forced herself to count to ten. He wasn't ever going to change. He thought all inmates were bad. He wasn't going to help Mr. Nash. He wasn't going to help Sam. *What the heck was she going to do?*

"Come on, Emma." Maxim reached for her hand, his voice gentle again. "Let's not fight. We were supposed to celebrate, remember?"

"Yes." She blinked back her tears. As long as they didn't talk about inmates, their relationship was perfect. But how could they survive when Sam made up such a significant part of her life? Was she abandoning Sam by choosing Maxim? She needed time alone to think things over.

"I'm sorry. I don't feel very well." *Not by a long shot.* "Do you mind if I head home?"

"Now? But you haven't even eaten."

"I'm not that hungry." She kept her eyes down. "Please. I want to go home."

Maxim tried to persuade her to stay but Emma insisted. *No way was she going to be able to concentrate with him close.* She drove off, her mind swirling. True, they loved each other but maybe sometimes love wasn't enough. Her brother should be her number-one priority. She was at the prison only because of him. How could she abandon Sam for his jailer? How could she sit there enjoying dinner in a mansion by the ocean when Sam was hunkering down in his paltry bunk?

Yet how could she break it off with Maxim? She loved him and couldn't bear the thought of life without him. Toward midnight, Emma finally drifted into a fitful sleep, dreaming of Sam paroling, his gentle brown eyes shining with hope. She waited on the other side of the gate and initially Maxim was with her but then he disappeared. She ran through the thick fog in vain to find him, her heart pounding with fear.

When she turned back, Sam had vanished and she stood alone, trapped in the mystifying fog. Suddenly her attacker, nasty Ransom with the ugly tattoo, material-ized out of nowhere and grabbed her throat. She screamed and screamed but no one heard or responded. She woke up drenched in sweat, her heart beating a mile a minute. What did it all mean? *Was she destined to lose both of the men she loved?*

CHAPTER 29

"Where's Morris?" Emma asked Madison a couple of hours into her shift the next morning. The nurse had told her some of the inmates had eaten canteen food in the dorms so those inmates were now officially off the strike. Hopefully, Sam was among them but he hadn't reported to work yet.

"Not sure." Madison continued to enter their last patient's information into the computer.

The two were sitting in the back office next to the Urgent Care, taking a mini break before the next set of patients rolled in. Madison punched in a last number and logged off.

"I heard some of the inmates aren't showing up to work as part of the strike. Maybe he's one of them," Madison said.

"What?" Emma pushed her chair back. "We need to call him in. If he didn't eat yesterday, it'd be three days in a row."

"Don't worry. He's probably sneaking in some food. All of them are, you know." Madison gave her an odd look. "How come you're so concerned about him?"

"What do you mean?" Emma clutched her clipboard, her heart rate picking up a notch.

"Don't get me wrong. I like Morris. He's a great porter." Madison bit down on a granola bar as she relaxed back in her chair. "And he has to put up a lot with those panic attacks. So I'm kind of glad you look out for him. I wish more doctors did the same."

"Me too. Let me go check if he's okay." *Thank goodness the nurse didn't seem to suspect anything, but where the heck was Sam?* Emma walked out to the treatment area and flagged down Peterson. "Sergeant, can you bring me Morris, our porter? I want to know if he's still on the strike."

The sergeant gave her a strange look before scanning a large spreadsheet. He combed his finger down the page and then shook his head. "Looks like he hasn't eaten yet. You want Dr. Pan to see him? He's the regular PMD."

"No. I can see him." Emma forced out a smile. "I saw him yesterday, remember? It's better for continuity of care."

"Okay. I'll call him in right now." Peterson picked up the phone and started dialing.

About fifteen minutes later, Sam shuffled into the clinic, his hands clenched tight. There was a wild look in his eyes that Emma didn't like one bit.

"Morris, have a seat. Have you eaten yet?" she asked.

Sam shook his head and plopped down on the gurney. He stayed silent while Madison applied the blood pressure cuff and put the thermometer probe in his mouth. Emma's eyes swung to the monitor. The cuff expanded for what seemed like hours before the air finally hissed out. Ninety over fifty, heart rate one twenty.

"You're dehydrated." The familiar gnawing clutched at Emma's stomach. "How many meals has it been now?"

Her ever-present guard Gonzalez stepped closer. "Talk, Morris, before I make you talk."

Poor Sam dropped his head and hunched his shoulders, his knuckles white as he gripped the gurney's railing.

"It's okay, Morris." *Her poor brother. He was a complete wreck.* "You can tell me. I want to help you."

Sam kept silent, his eyes fixed on the floor.

"Can you give us some time alone?" Emma asked the guard. "Maybe he'll talk if you aren't here."

"Mr. Chambers won't like it, Doc," Gonzalez said, refusing to budge. "I'm supposed to be here when you see all your patients. You shouldn't have seen him yesterday without me."

"He's our porter, for goodness' sake. I don't need you in the room. He's not going to hurt me."

"No, I'm not moving," the stubborn man insisted. "If something were to happen, the warden would have my head."

"You're not staying." Emma raised her voice and headed to the door. "I'm the doctor here and I want you out of my patient's room. Now."

"Calm down, Doc. Fine, I'll leave. But if something happens…"

"Nothing's going to happen. And I'll take full responsibility if it does."

Madison shot her a sympathetic look and exited. Peterson and the other officers in the hallway shook their heads at her, looking none too happy. *Tough.* She didn't give a damn. Sam seemed like he was hanging on by only a thread. Emma slammed the door after Gonzalez and rushed back to her brother.

"Okay, Sam. Listen to me." She put both hands on his shoulders. "You have to eat or you're going to get very sick. It's been three days."

"I can't. They're going to kill me, Em. They're watching me all the time." Her brother's frantic eyes scanned the room. "Help me, Emma! You have to help me."

"Of course I'll help you. Come on." She ushered him into the back office, secured the lock, and sat him down on the chair behind the desk.

"They're going to get me." Sam licked his cracked lips, his eyes still darting around the room.

"Nobody's going to see you in here." She pulled down the window blinds. "See? We're all blocked off. Here, have some of my lunch." She grabbed her sack lunch from her bag and handed him the tuna sandwich and a can of apple juice.

"I can't."

"Come on, Sam. Eat. You need to get your strength back."

Sam stared at her for a moment before extending a trembling hand to grasp the juice. Slowly he brought the can to his mouth. He tilted it and finally swallowed. Emma exhaled. *At least it was a start.*

"Easy." Sam was guzzling down the juice. "Take it slow. Your stomach has to get used to eating again."

After that, Sam wolfed down the sandwich and drank half a bottle of water. His eyes appeared less dull by the time he finished, but he still looked scared and restless.

"What is it?" Emma touched his shoulder. "Nobody will know that you ate. Don't worry."

"Peterson was out there, right?" he asked out of the blue.

"Peterson? The sergeant? Yes." Emma handed him a napkin. "Why do you ask?"

Sam stood up abruptly, went around the desk, opened the door, looked out to the treatment room, closed the door again and locked it, his eyes wide. "You need to be careful around Peterson. He's in it with the PALIs. I didn't want to tell you but…"

"Sergeant Peterson? The older officer?" A shiver chased down Emma's spine.

"Yes. Peterson is a drug dealer," Sam hissed out. "He was the tall man Peter and I saw selling that day. They sold to a guy named Nate. You wanted names. Now you have them. Peterson's very dangerous, Em. Yesterday the PALIs cornered me in the bathroom and ordered me to stay away from you."

"What? Why didn't you tell me this before?" Emma tugged at her pendant, almost snapping at the chain.

"They threatened to hurt me if I tell you. But that's not the worst part, Em." Sam paused and took another gulp of water. "They warned me if I snitch, they're going to hurt you, too. And there's a third guy I saw that day too, remember? I don't know his name. He has a nasty snake tattoo on his arm. He's Nate's buddy—he said he'll be watching your every move. They got connections everywhere, Em, maybe even on the outside. You have to leave this place. Get away from here while you still can."

"I'm not leaving you." *No wonder the sergeant had been giving her those odd looks. How dare he wear that uniform and call himself an officer?* She was going straight to Maxim right now and get that man arrested.

"You have to go, Em. If you get hurt, I'll never forgive myself." Sam grasped her hand, his face bleak. "You're always trying to rescue me. And sometimes you just can't. Let me do the rescuing this time. Go. I'm begging you."

"I can't. Not while you're still here." Emma hugged

him with all her might. "I'm going to tell Maxim and he's going to help us. We'll be okay."

"Maxim?"

"Yes. Mr. Chambers." Emma bit her lip. *Should she tell him?* Maybe it'd ease his mind knowing the warden was in their corner. "We're friends. Actually, we're dating, Sam. I really like him."

"You're dating the warden?" Sam gasped. "Jesus Christ, Em. He's so nasty. What the hell are you doing with him?"

"He's not nasty." *Not by a long shot.* She had to make Sam understand somehow. "He comes across that way, but inside he's pretty decent. I'm going to tell him about Peterson and get that crook arrested."

"Chambers doesn't know I'm your brother, does he?" Sam gripped her hand.

"No. I haven't told him."

"Don't tell him. Everybody knows how he feels about inmates. He's going to go bonkers if he finds out."

"Don't worry. I'm not going to tell him." Emma handed him another bottle of water. "Here, drink this while you still can. I'll go up to his office right now."

"Are you sure? They're dangerous, Em. You should quit." Sam tightened his grip on her hand. "Get out of here before you get hurt."

"And leave Peterson to do more damage?" She squeezed his hand in return. "No way. I don't want you to be afraid anymore. You can't live like this, every day fearing for your life."

"It's the way it is." His voice was defeated, broken. "That's how our lives are in prison. The gangs control everything."

"Well, they shouldn't. Stay away from Peterson until you hear from me. I'll ask Maxim to transfer you to SNY."

"And be with those child molesters?" Sam visibly shuddered. "Are you sure, Em? I'll hate it up there."

"You know it's not just for the child molesters." Emma touched his cheek, desperate to reassure him somehow. "It's for anyone who needs extra protection. And you definitely need it."

"Alright." Sam let out a long sigh. "I hope we're not going to regret this."

"We won't." Emma hugged him again. "Now go. Don't worry. Maxim's going to take care of everything."

Emma opened the door, glad the main treatment area remained empty. She led Sam out into the main corridor. *Thank goodness, Peterson wasn't around.* Gonzalez, however, was there and scowled at her before turning away. The other officers at the table threw her nasty looks, too. *Great.* All she needed was for Custody to hate her. *Still, what else was she supposed to do? Abandon her brother when he needed her most?* She told the officers she had to attend an emergency meeting. They grunted and went on with their business.

At least Maxim was still on her side. He was in charge of all of them. He'd understand and help her out. Emma strode outside to the main yard and rushed up the hill.

Please let Maxim be in his office. God forbid if he was stuck in some long meeting. She raced up the steps to the administration building and ran down the hall to his office. It'd only been yesterday that she'd been here. He said he loved her. He had to help her out. He was her only hope.

At last she came to his door. The next few seconds felt like torture. Nobody answered her knock. *Darn it.* Was he out? She turned the knob and pushed the door open.

"Maxim, thank God." His dear familiar face met hers from behind the desk. "I need to talk to you."

"I'm in a meeting," he said, his tone frosty. *And why did he look so grim?*

Emma entered. "This can't wait."

"Hello, Doc."

That voice. Emma shuddered and took a step back. "Sergeant," she forced out. *What the heck was Peterson doing here?* The officer sat in a far corner of the room, his evil eyes gleaming at her.

"I'll head off." Peterson stood and shook Maxim's hand. "I didn't want to come, but I felt you needed to know."

"Thanks for coming." Maxim's voice was like ice.

Emma nodded at the sergeant as he waved good-bye. Her hands were trembling so hard she had to clasp them together.

"So you wanted to see me?" Maxim said when they were finally alone. He didn't get up from his chair but waved her over to Peterson's old seat.

Where was all the love he'd showered on her yesterday? True, they hadn't parted on the best of terms last night but she'd been certain of his affection. Now he looked as remote as a statue. Emma swallowed the lump in her throat and sat down.

"I need your help," she blurted out. "Please, I need a big favor."

"What is it?" His voice was curt, his eyes like chips of ice.

The gnawing began in her stomach. She pulled hard at the pendant. *What did Peterson tell him?* She swallowed and licked her lips.

"Last night you told me if my patient tells you who's threatening him, you'd take care of it." She dug her nails into the palms of her hands to still their trembling. "Well, he just told me, Maxim. And it's so awful. You wouldn't believe it. I need you to protect him. Send him to SNY or something."

Maxim continued to look at her, his face an emotionless mask. "Let me guess. Your patient is Morris, right? The porter?"

"Yes." She braced her hands on her seat. "He told me there's a guy named Nate who's dealing drugs, who's threatening to kill him if he snitches. Nate belongs to the PALIs, the same gang that's forcing him to do the hunger strike."

"I see. And why do you care so much about Morris?"

"What?" Emma squeezed her hands together. "He's my porter. My patient. I want to help him."

"That's it?" Maxim asked, his wolfish eyes unblinking. "He's just your patient? Nothing else?"

"What do you mean?"

"I'm asking you about Morris. Is he your patient or is he more than that?"

"I don't know what you're getting at." Emma bit her lip, the gnawing eating through her stomach.

"Just answer the damned question!" Maxim bellowed, slamming his hand on the desk. He came around and grabbed both of Emma's upper arms, pulling her up. "Is there anything going on between you and Morris that I should know about?"

Maxim's eyes bored into hers. *What did he know? Why was he so upset?* Maybe she should confess, let the burden off her chest, but she couldn't bear to be separated from Sam. Her brother was still her number-one priority. If she wasn't around to protect him, who would?

"No." She forced herself to stare Maxim in the eye. "He's my patient. That's it."

"Liar!" Maxim pushed her away, his face like thunder. "How could you lie to me like that?"

"What?" The breath whooshed out of her chest. "What are you talking about?"

"I saw the video. I know you're involved with him."

"Video?"

"In the closet in the OHU when you first started," he said, his voice bitter. "Before we even started dating. You were hugging him."

"It's not what you think." It was when she'd gotten those blankets. *What had she said? Dear God, what was on that video?*

"Don't lie to me, Emma." Maxim stalked away and looked out the window. "I can't even bear to look at you."

"Please." *He had to believe her.* She took three steps forward and touched his sleeve. "You have to believe me, Maxim. I love you. I would never betray you like that."

"Love?" He scoffed, swinging around to face her. "How could you say that? You lied to me. You cheated on me."

"I didn't cheat. Please, Maxim. You know me better than that."

"Peterson said he saw the two of you together. Making out." Maxim looked tortured and disgusted at the same time. "He's an inmate, for God's sake. What were you thinking?"

"Peterson's a liar," Emma said as calmly as she could. It was tough considering inside she felt like screaming. *The nerve of that weasel! How dare he spread such lies about her?* "He's in cahoots with Nate. He's part of the PALI gang and he's selling drugs to the inmates. That's what Morris told me just now. I ran up here to tell you. You have to get rid of him."

"Get rid of one of my best officers? Are you kidding me?" Maxim sneered. "He was my mentor. He taught me everything I know about the prison system. He'd never sell drugs. He's a grandfather, Emma. Your boyfriend is lying to you."

"He's not my boyfriend," Emma shouted, not caring if she sounded hysterical. "Can you trust me on that? Morris needs protection. Peterson and Nate ganged up on him yesterday. They threatened him. They told him they'd kill him if he snitches. Please, Maxim, you have to help him."

"I don't have to do anything," Maxim said, his eyes blazing. "I don't trust anything you say anymore."

"Please." *He didn't believe her. How could this be happening?* Emma choked back her tears. "I'm begging you. Please protect Morris. He's going to die if you don't help him."

"I don't believe you." Maxim straightened to his full height and glared down at her. "Peterson is accusing you of having sex with an inmate. Because he told me, I'm bound by law to launch an investigation. I'm removing you from all your clinical duties. You can't see any patients until the investigation is over."

"*What?*" A vise squeezed at her chest. *Was he serious?* "You can't do this. It's not true!"

"These are the conditions of the investigation. You have to stay away from Morris. You can't be in the same room as him. You can't communicate with him in any way. You can't talk with him, you can't call him, you can't write him," Maxim bit out. "Do you understand me? If you violate any of those rules, you'll be fired and reported to the board. You'll lose your license."

"Oh, my God." Emma clutched her middle. The pain was searing through her stomach. She bent over and grasped the edge of the desk. She couldn't get enough air.

How could this be happening? How could Peterson do this to her? And worse yet, how could Maxim not believe her? He was supposed to be on her side. *So much for his claim of undying love.* Her hand slipped from the desk and she sank to the ground, feeling wounded, beaten, and worst of all, betrayed. Betrayed by the man she loved. He stood above her, all grim and silent, his face as remote and cold as a block of ice. She had to get away from him, but what was going to happen to Sam?

"Maxim, please," she begged one last time. "At least move Morris to SNY. I promise I won't go near him."

"Still begging for your boyfriend? You must really love him," he tossed out at her. "I told you I'm not moving him. Now go. We're finished."

Finished? How dare he dismiss her like that? How dare he believe that weasel Peterson over her? Emma lifted herself up, all her misery transformed into a burning rage. "You're unbelievable, you know that? I hate you, Maxim Chambers. I was such a fool thinking we had something special." She let out a bitter laugh. "Love? You don't even know the meaning of the word. You treat the inmates like dirt. I don't know what I ever saw in you!"

She strode away and slammed the door on his proud, arrogant, loathsome face. A thousand needles poked at her. She hurt so much she felt like she was going to crack any minute now. They were going to investigate. She wasn't allowed to see patients anymore. And she may lose her license. Worst of all, poor Sam was still down the hill. What if something bad happened to him? She was never going to forgive Maxim for this.

CHAPTER 30

"Damn it all to hell!"

Maxim grabbed the nearest object and threw it as far as he could. Broken pieces of glass shattered on the floor. Pencils and pens flew in every direction. *How could this be happening?* He swept all the files off his desk in one violent motion, scattering papers everywhere. He sank into the armchair and grasped his head in his hands. Emma's wounded face kept staring back at him. She'd looked so frightened, so small and alone standing there, pleading with him. For a moment, he'd wanted to believe her, wanted to hold her in his arms and soothe her worries, wanted to tell her that he was going to protect her, let nothing bad happen to her.

He'd given her a chance to explain. He'd practically begged her for any sort of explanation. Maybe for her to even say that they were old friends reuniting. That wouldn't have been so bad. It was wrong but maybe he could have forgiven her for that. But she had lied straight to his face, had told him Morris was just a patient. When he'd known for a fact that they were so much more to each other. They were hugging in the video. And worse yet, the video had had audio. He'd heard her tell the porter how much she missed him, how much she loved him. The same words of love that had spouted so easily out of her mouth just yesterday. *What a cool liar she was.*

If he remembered correctly, it was the same damned inmate who'd visited her in the Urgent Care after she was assaulted. The same one they'd driven in the middle of the night to see. No wonder she'd been in such a rush to drive in that day. She'd been involved with him the whole time, even doing all those CPT sessions with him. *Did Stewart know about the affair?* Maxim was going to give that damned psychiatrist a piece of his mind. *How dare he facilitate their sessions? Was Stewart even there during the sessions?* Like hell it had been about CPT.

Peterson had said she'd tossed Gonzalez out by his ear and closeted herself with Morris today. And he'd trusted her all this time. Maxim pounded his head against the desk and let out a howl of rage.

He loved her so much it was like a piece of him had been torn off. *How could she do this to him?* He hadn't believed Peterson at first. He'd told his mentor that she cared about patients, that she often put their needs above her own. So what if she was friendly with Morris? She was like that with all her patients. The sergeant had shaken his head sadly at him and then dropped that bombshell about seeing them making out. Of course he hadn't believed the story at first. But then Peterson had played the video for him. That damned video that had shown so much. If it hadn't been for Peterson, Maxim would still be left in the dark, ignorant of all her transgressions.

And how dare she accuse his mentor like that? Had

she no shame? Or was she blindly swallowing whatever lie that bastard was feeding her? Morris probably had her wrapped so tight around his little finger that she'd do whatever he dictated. Like hell was he going to move him to SNY. Morris was going to stay exactly where he was, and Maxim was going to pay him a little visit soon.

He had to start the investigation first. *Christ!* His heart twisted at the implications. If they found Emma in the wrong, she'd be reported to the board. Worse yet, it was a felony to have sex with an inmate. She would go to prison. Dear God, he hoped it wouldn't come to that. She was exquisite and tiny—she'd never survive prison. *Who the hell was Morris?* How could she throw her life away for that jackass?

Maxim buzzed his secretary and asked for Morris's C File. He needed to find out as much as he could about the bastard before he called in the investigators. Too bad he couldn't ask for Stewart's files on the man as well. Those were confidential and only Morris's doctors had access to them. The C File would have to be it for now. He was glad for something to do at least, anything to keep his mind off the miserable empty existence that was now his life.

Emma drove back to work the following morning, dreading what awaited her. *How could Maxim believe such lies about her?* Her mind shied away from him or else she'd burst into tears or veer off the road in utter rage, she didn't know what. She parked the car in the usual spot and reached for her doctor's bag. And then it hit her. She wasn't allowed to see patients anymore.

She threw the bag in the trunk and discarded her white coat with it. Too bad she was dressed like a slob today. Loose black trousers and an oversized pink silk shirt. That was the best she could do. Her hair was a mess. She'd forgotten to clip it back that morning. Its thick curtain was constantly falling over her shoulders but heck, what did she care? She wasn't going to see any patients so she could afford to look like she'd just rolled out of bed.

Emma slapped on some red lipstick but couldn't stand the pale cheeks and hollow eyes staring back at her from the mirror. She hastily added some mascara, eye shadow, and blush. *There. At least she didn't look like a ghost anymore.* She usually never wore that much makeup to work but today she needed it. She hadn't slept all night and felt like hell.

"Good morning," she said to everyone as she entered the conference room. Maxim hadn't appeared yet. Hopefully, he'd never show up. She sat next to Julien and gave him a wavering smile.

The other doctors greeted her as if nothing were amiss. *So Maxim hadn't told them yet. Good.* She didn't know how she could face them with the accusations. It was so humiliating to not be trusted. Soon enough the door opened from behind her and she braced herself for more pain. She was going to ignore him, she decided. Not talk to him. Not even look at him. She kept her eyes on the table as he took his seat.

"Good morning, Maxim." Kaye's sultry voice again.

Emma shook her head in disgust and picked up a pen.

"Let's start," his loathsome voice said. "Any update from last night, Brown?"

"Updates?" A foreboding sense of doom washed over her. Emma turned to Julien and forced out her question. "Did something happen?"

"I got several calls. A broken ankle, an abscess that needed to be drained, and a low blood sugar in a diabetic."

"That's it?" Emma pressed.

"That's it besides the assault. Let's see." Julien flipped through a stack of notes. "Unit 3 guy assaulted in the shower. He got kicked pretty badly and stabbed several times in the chest and abdomen. 911 came."

All the blood seemed to rush from Emma's head. A weird buzzing sound began in her ears. *Please, please tell me it wasn't Sam.*

"He almost died. Got intubated by the paramedics and transferred to the trauma center," Julien continued. "He went to the OR a few hours ago. I think they're still operating on him."

It seemed like she was standing in a tunnel. Far off at one end was a bright light where Julien was reading his report. Yet everything else was dark. The buzzing continued in her ears. Someone asked for the patient's name. Julien answered. *No!* A crushing weight slammed down on her chest. She couldn't breathe. She tried to sweep away the foggy haze covering her vision but the mist only intensified. She felt herself falling. Falling further and further into the engulfing darkness.

"Jesus Christ! Is she okay?" someone said from far away.

"She fainted. Give her some space!"

Someone was carrying her across the room. She was pressed against something solid. A frantic thumping sound reverberated underneath her ear. She took in a deep breath and inhaled the scent of coffee beans. Her body stiffened. She twisted in his arms, trying to get as far away as possible. Her eyes snapped open.

"Put me down," she said to his hateful face.

"Not yet." He looked a little pale and out of breath.

"Let go of me," Emma bit out.

He placed her gently on a sofa. She glanced around and realized they were in his office. She pushed herself up but everything began to spin, so she dropped back down. She squeezed her eyes shut, trying to block out his face.

"What is it? Are you okay?" he asked, his voice strained.

"Just go. Leave me alone," Emma said, her body shaking. *My God. Sam! What had she done?* She'd trusted Maxim and now her brother was hurt. And the worst part was she couldn't show she cared too much or else they'd believe Peterson's lies. And Maxim was hovering over her, pretending he cared. Nausea roiled in Emma's stomach. She opened her eyes. He was leaning over her.

"I will never forgive you," she said.

His silver eyes flared. "That makes two of us."

She sat up and scooted as far away from him as possible. The light-headedness swept over her again and she hastily bent over, putting her head between her legs. *Get a grip, Emma.* She needed to go to the hospital and check on her brother. But she wasn't supposed to be around Sam. Maxim's hateful restrictions flew back at her.

"What's wrong?"

"Nothing." Emma pinched her upper arm hard. It worked. The light-headedness abated a significant amount. She slowly straightened. "Where's everybody?"

"Brown is calling 911. They should be here any minute now."

"I don't need an ambulance."

"You fainted. You're going."

No, I'm not. She rubbed her temple. *But wait. An ambulance meant a ride to the hospital.* They always took emergencies to the closest hospital, which happened to be the trauma center. Where Sam was. It was the perfect solution. She closed her eyes at the sound of sirens approaching.

"They're coming." She heard Julien's voice as he got closer. "Are you okay, Emma?"

"It was only a vasovagal." Evil Knievel's voice. "I don't know what the fuss is all about. Let her lie down for a few minutes and she'll be fine."

Probably true but there was no way she'd be left behind. She opened her eyes and clutched her stomach. "Oh my God. It hurts so much." She hated to fake the symptoms but desperate times called for desperate measures. She lay down on the sofa again and pressed her hand to her stomach. "I'm having so much pain," she gritted out. Mental pain but they didn't need to know that.

Maxim's hand gripped the edge of his desk. He was as white as a sheet. *Why the heck was he looking so worried?* It wasn't as if he cared. The man probably just didn't want her to die in his office.

"So what have we here?" The same paramedic, Garcia, she'd seen several times in the Urgent Care rolled in, his partner by his side. "Is it syncope or vasovagal?"

"What's vasovagal?" Maxim was still gripping the desk. "She fainted and isn't feeling very well."

"Vasovagal is fainting when you experience something scary," the other paramedic replied. "Like passing out when you're getting your blood drawn."

"Dr. Edwards!" Garcia said. "I didn't know it was you. Are you okay?"

"I think so." She hated to lie to the crew so forced out a reassuring smile. "But maybe I should get checked out."

Garcia slapped on the blood pressure cuff while his partner listened to her heart and lungs. "Vitals good except your heart rate is way too high. Are you having pain?"

"My stomach." She reluctantly let out another moan.

Thank goodness the questions soon stopped and before she knew it, Emma found herself strapped to the stretcher on her way to the hospital. The ER appeared as crowded as her first visit there. They placed her in the same stall as last time, when John had shown up at the end. *John. That was it.* Of course. Why hadn't she thought of it before? She grabbed her cell and texted him. *Please let him be in the hospital.* He was a trauma surgeon and of course would know about Sam's case.

All afternoon as Emma waited for blood test results and final clearance to go, she kept checking her phone. *Damn it. Had John changed his number or was he ignoring her?* She hadn't been very nice last time they talked. Her hopes dwindled toward mid-afternoon when her cell remained silent.

Finally, as she was checking out, the phone beeped. She read his text and her heart leapt. *Yes.* He was coming to see her. Emma camped out in the waiting room, glancing at her watch every few seconds. At last John appeared in the doorway and she rushed up, her heart hammering inside.

"Thanks so much for seeing me," she said, half out of breath.

"No problem." He was in full scrubs and still wearing his surgeon's cap. "Sorry I couldn't get back to you earlier. I was in surgery. Are you okay? I heard you fainted."

"Yes. When I heard the news about Sam, but I'm okay. It was just vasovagal." Emma looked around. There were people everywhere. Some of the patients could easily listen in. "Can we talk outside?"

"Sure." John led her out to the foyer and gave her a weary smile. "Your brother's okay. I operated on him. There was a lot of bleeding, so we had to take out his spleen. He had a few broken ribs on the right and a broken leg but so far so good. He's one hell of a lucky guy."

"Thank God." She couldn't believe it. *Sam was going to be okay.* Emma clapped a hand to her mouth and stifled back a sob.

"He lost a lot of blood but we managed to keep up with the transfusions."

"Oh thank you, John." She threw her arms around him, the tears coursing down her cheeks. "I know how you feel about him, so an extra thank-you."

"I'm sorry about that." John's blue eyes were filled with remorse. "I was such a jackass, wasn't I?"

"Well…" She bit her lip. "Yes, but it was a long time ago. I forgive you. You saved him today." And Emma realized she spoke the truth. It was all water under the bridge, considering how she hadn't thought about John for ages now.

"Just doing my job," he said, squeezing her shoulder. "I'm sorry I acted the way I did, Em. You know, you look a little like your brother."

"What?" Emma smiled through her tears. "How?"

"The way your eyes tilt at the corners." John took off his cap and brushed a hand through his hair. "Too bad I had to meet him like this. You want to go up and see him?"

Emma relayed to him what had happened at the prison and how she was forbidden to see Sam.

"But I just spoke to your boss before I came down. He seemed so concerned. He asked a bunch of questions. I thought he knew you guys were siblings."

"What? My boss? Here?" *Surely John was mistaken.*

"Yes, the guy who was with you last time. Big, scary-looking."

"You didn't tell him Sam's my brother, did you?" *Please tell me you didn't.* Emma dried away her tears.

"Relax. I didn't. He looked really worried, though."

"Yes, because it was all his fault." *Every last bit of it.*

"What do you mean?"

"He could have prevented the assault by moving Sam to somewhere safer." Emma was a little glad Maxim was suffering. She was suffering a hundred times as much.

They couldn't talk more as John had post-op patients to round on. Before he left, he promised to keep her updated on Sam's condition. Emma took in a deep breath and exhaled. At least her brother was okay. She had to concentrate on that. *Nothing else mattered.* She hailed a taxi and headed home, glad the awful day was drawing to a close.

From a corner of the parking lot, Maxim watched Emma depart and felt like wild horses were pulling him apart limb by limb. How he longed to hold her close. But she had hugged that ex of hers instead. How it killed him to see her in another man's arms. She belonged to him. And only him. *Why did he still love her?* It made everything so much harder.

It had been petrifying watching her faint that morning. He'd almost lost it when her head had lolled to the side and she'd lost consciousness. And she'd felt so fragile in his arms, like a tiny bird with a clipped wing. *Damn.* She hated him, he could tell. Had he been wrong in believing his mentor over her? But the video had been so clear. What else could it mean?

Yet Morris had been beaten up exactly like she'd feared. What had she said? That Morris had snitched and was going to pay for it unless Maxim moved him. That Peterson sold drugs to the inmates. *Impossible.* It couldn't be true. Yet Maxim couldn't be too careful. He had driven in last night and seen for himself the aftermath of the assault. He'd asked questions. The officers said they'd found Morris in the bathroom, blood seeping from a head laceration with several knife wounds to the chest and abdomen.

The man was beaten up pretty badly. He was lucky to be alive. *Was he actually Emma's lover?* Maxim's big body shuddered in disgust. How could she have betrayed him like that? It was clear she cared for the guy. *Look at the way she'd collapsed at the news of his assault.* She'd been devastated. Maxim's heart twisted inside. It hurt. It hurt like hell but he still had a job to do.

Nobody deserved to be assaulted like that. He was going to investigate and catch the men who did it. He hadn't learned much yesterday. Peterson apparently hadn't been on duty. There were no witnesses, at least none who would come forward. They'd attacked in the bathroom exactly at the camera's blind spot, so there weren't any videos.

Maxim drove back to the prison, determined to find out more. He needed to revisit dorm 308, the scene of the crime. Birmingham, the chief deputy warden, accompanied him to the dorm and briefed him on the latest updates.

"Got any new leads today?" Maxim asked.

"Cortez, one of the Hispanic inmates, told me in confidence that it was the blacks who did it," Birmingham said, sweeping a hand over his wild beard. The man looked like a mad scientist but Maxim knew his mind was as sharp as a tack.

"At least that's something. How many of them?"

"Five to eight. Cortez said they're part of the PALI gang."

Maxim froze, his heart thudding. Emma had said the PALIs were involved. *Was she telling the truth this whole time?* "The PALIs? Are you sure?"

"Don't know why Cortez would lie about it."

"But the gang has been pretty quiet for a while now," Maxim said, trying hard not to think about the possible implications. *If Emma had been right.* He clenched his hand and dared not go down that path.

"Well, you know how they are. They act up when they want to send a message." Birmingham shrugged. "Who knows what it could be about? Maybe Morris owed them some money and didn't return it. Or maybe he insulted one of them. You never know what sets them off."

"So who are we talking about? Do you have any names?" Maxim asked.

"Don't know yet. Cortez is too scared to tell us. I already moved him to SNY but he's not saying anything else."

They reached 308 and Maxim headed straight to bed 35 up, Morris's bunk. It lay stripped and bare without any personal belongings. The other inmates were in the chow hall eating, so they had the dorm to themselves.

"The officers already cleaned out his bed. They figure he won't be back for a while," Birmingham said. "I think his locker is still untouched. Do you want to see it?"

"Sure."

"Here's the key." Birmingham handed him the standard set of keys carried by the dorm officers. "Mind if I go check out 307? We're short-staffed in there today."

"Go ahead." Maxim crouched down and inserted the universal key that opened all the lockers. The latch stuck for a little bit but after a couple of jiggles, the locker door sprang open.

Maxim bent his head and peered inside. A bag of chips, four ramen noodle packages, and a stack of newspapers. Farther in the back lay a couple of books. *About birds, of all things. Blackbirds.* A prickling sensation crawled over Maxim's spine. Maxim rubbed the back of his neck. He reached inside and pulled out a vaguely familiar yellow envelope. *No. It couldn't be. It can't be. There was no chance in hell...*Maxim opened the envelope and shook out its contents. *Oh God.* Holmes, the comet, stared back at him.

CHAPTER 31

"I hope he's going to recover okay." Emma pressed the phone against her ear and threw herself on the bed.

"I'm so sorry, Em. Wish I could be there." Riley sounded so distant, all the way in Vietnam. "What does Maxim say about all of this?"

"Don't even bring him up." Emma shook her head in disgust. "He didn't believe me. Sam almost died because of him."

"How could he even think you'd have sex with an inmate? That's the most ridiculous thing I've ever heard."

"He doesn't trust me at all." Emma bit her lip. "I know the video doesn't look good but you'd think he'd at least have some faith in me."

"Maybe you should tell him Sam's your brother."

"No way. He'd separate us." The tears were starting again. Emma grabbed a pillow and hugged it tight. "And I can't see patients anymore. Maxim said he's starting an investigation."

"Aw, Em. That's horrible. You want me there? I can take the first flight out."

"No. It's okay." Emma dried her tears on the pillow. "Thanks for the offer. I'm going to have to deal with it somehow."

"Are you sure? I can book a flight. They have enough doctors here."

"Yes. I'm sure. Thanks, Ri. You're a good friend."

"Let me know if it becomes too rough. Get some rest. I'll call you tomorrow."

Emma hung up the phone and curled on her side, forcing herself to inhale and exhale. *Deep breaths.* That's all she should focus on. The breathing technique gradually worked. Charles was definitely onto something. She felt marginally better and closed her eyes, sending up a silent prayer for Sam.

As she was about to drift off to sleep, the phone rang. She seized it immediately.

"Emma?"

"John?" Emma sprang up, her heart in her throat. "What's wrong? Is it Sam?"

"Yes. His blood pressure just dropped," John said, his voice rushed. "You should come, Emma. He's not doing very well. He's in room 605 East right now but we may move him to ICU soon."

"Oh, my God." Emma clutched her pillow tighter. "What happened? He was okay an hour ago."

"I know. But he's post op. You know how things can change." John let out a long, frustrated sigh. "Just come, okay? I have to bring another patient to the OR right now but I'll find you when I'm done."

Emma slammed the phone down and shot out of bed. *No. This could not be happening.* She'd thought the worst was over. But there had been those broken ribs. *Had they punctured the liver? Was there more bleeding?* Maybe his bowels had been injured too. Whatever it was, it didn't sound good with the blood pressure dropping.

Emma grabbed her purse, rushed out of the house, and blasted on the car engine. Damn it. *Turn on, why don't you?* After the third attempt, the engine finally spluttered to life. She pushed hard on the accelerator. The tires screeched as she raced onto the street. *Don't die, Sam. You can't die on me.* She turned left and then right to avoid the freeway traffic, choosing instead to take the side roads.

Her cell suddenly rang again. *Dear God, that better not be John. Was Sam already worse?* Hand trembling, she picked up the phone. "Yes?"

"Emma? It's Charles. Where have you been? I've been trying to reach you."

"My phone's on." Emma glanced at the screen. Three missed calls. The side streets she took mustn't have had any signals. "Sorry, Charles. It's been kind of crazy."

"No worries. Where are you? I heard what happened to your brother. Are you okay?"

"No. Sam's crashing at Riverside Community. I'm heading there now."

"Crashing? What happened?" Charles's voice rose a notch.

"He got out of surgery and deteriorated. I don't know much else."

"Okay. I'll meet you there. Drive safely."

"You don't have to come."

"Of course I do. He's my patient. What room is he in?"

"605 East."

"All right. See you soon."

Emma hung up the phone, feeling marginally better.

Charles would be a great comfort, no matter what happened. Especially with Riley in Vietnam. And especially with the way things were with Maxim. *Maxim.* She couldn't bear to think about him.

At last the hospital's familiar structure greeted her. Emma accelerated into the parking lot and bolted out, snatching her purse in the nick of time. The security guard at the main lobby called out to her but she flashed her medical ID and dashed into the elevator, ignoring his summons. *Up. Up. Up.* Finally, floor six. Emma zipped out and hurried down the east hallway.

"Code Blue Team. Code Blue Team. Six East," an announcement blared overhead.

Was that Sam's room? Emma's heart took a nosedive. Her chest constricted. *Sam! Wait for me. Please don't die. Sam. Don't die!* She raced down the hall and veered left: 615. 614. 613. 612. 611.

"Code Blue Team. Code Blue Team. Six East. Room 622."

Thank God—622, not 605. It wasn't Sam. Tears pricked behind Emma's eyes. *Why was the corridor so deserted?* Everyone must have been in the code. She sprinted the last five yards. Room 605 at last. *Where were Sam's guards?* Two officers were usually assigned to watch over each hospitalized inmate, even if the prisoner was dying. *Oh God. Dying.* She threw open the door, her breath ragged.

The room was so dim it took a moment to get her bearings. Sam lay in the center bed. At least she hoped it was Sam. All she could see was a head swaddled in white bandages and a casted leg hanging off a swinging contraption. She cautiously approached the bed, careful not to disturb him. An IV hung from his left arm and a chest tube protruded from the right side of his chest, emitting a swishing sound with each breath. His eyes were closed, his face pale. Yes, it was her brother. She couldn't mistake that beloved face. Her poor, darling brother, once so vibrant and alive and now reduced to this. And it was all Maxim's fault. *How could Maxim have let this happen?*

Emma clutched at the white sheets covering Sam's body. Tears clogged at her throat. She tugged at her pendant and checked the monitor. Blood pressure ninety over forty. Heart rate one thirty. Pulse ox ninety-two percent. It was too low, the blood pressure. *Was he bleeding internally? Did he need to go back to the OR?*

A soft knock sounded on the door. Emma swung around, expecting to see the nurse. She had myriad questions for the surgical team. *Shouldn't they transfer Sam to the ICU?* His vitals were tanking.

"Hi," she said as the door opened.

"Hi, yourself," a familiar voice said back.

No! It couldn't be. Emma gasped and put both her hands out. Sergeant Peterson stood in front of her, his face set in ugly lines.

"What are you doing here?" Emma managed to breathe out against the rising panic clawing at her insides.

"I should be asking you the same question." The officer closed the door softly behind him and approached the bed, still in full Custody gear. His right hand was fumbling with something in his pocket. "Didn't Chambers order you to stay away from him? You're violating the investigation, Doc."

How could she ever have thought Peterson's eyes were kind? They looked as evil as sin right now as he glowered at her.

"Stay back." Emma grabbed the cord lying next to Sam and pushed hard on the call button. *Why didn't it ring? Where were the nurses? The guards?* Her eyes swung frantically to the door.

"Don't bother. I dismantled the call mechanism." The sergeant's hand stayed in his pocket. "Not that anyone's around. There's a medical emergency down the hall, and I already dismissed the guards."

"Get out!" Emma put a protective hand toward Sam. Her brother was still unconscious, his breathing slow and irregular.

Peterson took a menacing step closer.

"Stay away from him." Emma inched toward the head of the bed.

"Begging for your lover?" Peterson jeered. "It's too late. He won't make it out of here. I'm going to make sure of that."

"You'll never get away with it." Emma's eyes darted to the wall behind the bed. *Where the heck was that code blue button?* She had to find it. It was the fastest way to get help.

"Shut up. You've caused enough trouble, Doc," the sergeant ground out. "I'd leave fast if I were you."

"Never! Get out! Someone will be here any minute now." *There it was, the code blue knob.* Red. Round. Only three feet from her left hand.

"You get out." The sergeant suddenly whipped out a gun, pointing it straight at her.

Dear God. Could the situation get any worse? Peterson was only about two feet away from Sam. And he looked like a raving lunatic right now. She stepped closer to the button, swallowing down her fear. "Why are you doing this, Sergeant?" she croaked out, hoping to distract him. "Maxim trusted you."

"I have no choice," Peterson bit out. "Morris snitched on me. And I'm not going to let him do it again."

"They'll catch you. You'll never get away with it."

"Not if it's ruled a natural death. His lungs are already weak." Peterson yanked Sam's pillow out from underneath his head. "It'll be quick. Thirty seconds without air, I figure. Nobody's going to come in time."

"I'll report you. You'll be arrested."

"No one's going to believe you. You're under investigation, remember?"

Peterson slammed the pillow over Sam's face, pushing down hard with his left hand. Emma pressed the code button with all her might. A loud buzzing sound rang out.

"Code Blue Team. Code Blue Team. Six East. Room 605." The overhead speaker blared.

"You'll pay for that," Peterson hissed, bearing down on the pillow. "Stay away or I'll shoot!" He aimed at Emma with his right hand.

"No!" Emma screamed as the door suddenly flew open.

Sam was going to suffocate any minute now. She lunged at the sergeant. He pulled the trigger, igniting a deafening blast.

CHAPTER 32

He was her brother. Maxim could hardly breathe. A tidal wave of guilt washed over him. No wonder she'd fought so hard to protect the man. It explained so much: the video, the CPT sessions, the driving in at night to treat Morris's panic attack. She'd told him she loved her brother more than anything in the world. *And he'd failed to protect him.* No wonder she hated him.

He'd totally blown it. It was his responsibility to keep the prison safe and secure but he'd been too hung up on his personal jealousies to do the job. Because of him, an innocent man had almost been murdered. Maxim punched the locker, almost denting the metal. The pain unfortunately wasn't enough to keep his mind from roiling with self-disgust.

And Emma. He'd discounted her every word. Dismissed her every concern. Threw her under the bus as soon as Peterson had spread his poison. Thank God he hadn't started the investigation. He'd been tempted but in the end he hadn't done it. A subconscious part of him must have recognized Emma would never betray him like that.

How could he ever make it up to her? He hadn't trusted her when it counted. She'd loved him and he'd thrown it back in her face. Maxim let out a howl of rage and slammed the locker door shut.

And if Peterson lied about Emma, then he was the worst possible kind of criminal. Why would his mentor commit such a heinous crime? He'd lied to discredit Emma so no one would believe her accusations against him. He must have been desperate to get rid of Morris, just as Emma had warned. Which meant Emma was a potential target. Peterson would want to silence her exactly as he did Morris. *Oh God. Emma.*

Maxim shoved the pictures back into the envelope and rushed out of the dorm. She'd gone home in a taxi. *Christ. Was Peterson waiting at her studio? Had he already harmed her?* Maxim jumped into his Porsche and slammed his foot on the pedal. *Please let him get there in time.* He grabbed his phone and dialed a number.

"Banding?" he said to the K-9 sergeant. "Peterson lied about the doctor. I think he's the one who assaulted Morris."

"What? Are you sure?" Banding's voice crackled over the Bluetooth.

"Yes. I can't go over the details now." *Damn, there was too much traffic.* Maxim veered two lanes to the left and shot into the carpool lane. "Get some ISU patrol units to Peterson's house. Now. He's at 945 Ellis Lane. In Pomona. We have to watch him."

"What's your evidence, Mr. Chambers?"

"Just trust me. He's dangerous. Go! Call me when you locate the sergeant." Maxim hung up the phone, glad Banding was on board. The K-9 sergeant was great in an emergency.

No way was he going to tell ISU that Morris was her brother. He knew policy but this was Emma. It'd kill her to be away from her brother. He couldn't separate them, which meant he must keep her brother's identity a secret.

Why hadn't she told him about being Morris's sister? She obviously hadn't trusted him enough, scared he would ship her away as he'd sent away Smith. No wonder she'd asked all those questions about Smith. *Damn.* She should have known better. He would have kept her secret. Sure, it would have been wrong but he would've done anything for her. Hadn't she realized it? *But when it counted, you didn't help her, did you? You fed her to the wolves.* Maxim wiped an unsteady hand over his face.

What he did had been unforgivable. But he couldn't dwell on that now. He had to focus on keeping Emma safe. He dialed her house again. *Come on, pick up, darling. Pick up.* He gave up after the tenth ring, letting out a silent curse. Her cell also went straight to voicemail. *Where was she? Had Peterson gotten to her already?*

And why the hell was there so much traffic? The carpool lane was almost at a standstill. Maxim let out a string of curses and changed to the outer left lane. At least fifteen excruciating minutes passed before the traffic lightened again. A sense of doom washed over him. Emma needed him and he wasn't going to make it in time. Just like what had happened with his parents. He'd arrived too late to save them. Would it be the same with Emma?

A loud ringing rescued him from his morose thoughts.

"Chambers," he barked over the Bluetooth.

"It's me, Banding. We went to Peterson's house but he's not home."

"No? Where the hell is he?" Maxim clenched down on the steering wheel.

"His wife said he went to Riverside Community to check on Morris."

"That's what she said?" Maxim bit out. "Are you sure?"

"Yes. You want us to head there?"

"Yes. Immediately. I'll meet you there."

The sense of doom thickened as he clicked off the phone. Peterson could be heading to Riverside Community for only one reason: to finish off Morris. No way was Maxim going to let that happen. He dialed the hospital. Morris's nurse said there was no sign of the sergeant but she promised to keep an extra eye out for him.

At least there were guards watching Morris. Surely he wouldn't come into any harm. He was in the hospital. Nurses and doctors were in and out of his room all the time. And Maxim had witnessed Emma leaving the hospital earlier. She was safe. Maybe even in the shower back at her place.

Or maybe Peterson had hurt her already. Maxim took in a deep breath and exhaled through his mouth. He needed to get a grip and calm down. Everything was going to be okay. No point to get ahead of himself and think of worst-case scenarios. Emma was probably home right now. He redialed her number. Still nothing. Her cell didn't pick up either. A heavy knot clutched at Maxim's chest, refusing to let go. He veered off the Lincoln exit and turned right. At least the traffic didn't extend to here. Maxim sped to over eighty miles per hour and swerved sharp into the hospital's parking lot.

He sprang out of the convertible and soon was racing up the main stairs in the east wing. The elevators weren't available due to some medical emergency. Finally he finished climbing and bolted down the Six East corridor.

"Code Blue Team. Code Blue Team. Six East. Room 605."

Jesus Christ. That was Morris's room. Maxim sprinted the last ten yards and flung open the door to 605. He screeched to a stop, his heart in his throat. Peterson was pointing a gun at Emma, who for some inexplicable reason wasn't ducking. She threw herself at the sergeant instead. *No!* Maxim jumped between them as a loud shot rang out.

"Run, Emma!" Maxim tackled the sergeant and knocked the gun out of the man's hand. Peterson's head made a sickening thud on the tile floor. Maxim's shoulder hurt like hell but no way was he going to release the death grip he had on Peterson's arms. Suddenly a slew of white coats and nurses flew into the room.

"What's happening in here?" one of the nurses yelled out as most of her colleagues rushed to Morris's bedside.

"Let go of me!" Peterson shouted, his eyes bulging.

"Not in this lifetime." Maxim felt like throttling the man. "I trusted you. How could you do this?"

"It's not what you think. Let me go, Maxim," his mentor had the effrontery to say.

"Never," Maxim bit out. "You're under arrest, Sergeant."

Morris's two assigned officers finally made an appearance as they ran into the room, clutching their batons. *The damned guards. They'd come too little, too late.* Maxim was going to skin them alive for this. "Where the hell were you?" he yelled.

"The sergeant told us to go on a break," the taller guard replied, his voice cracking. "Sorry, sir. We didn't know."

"Mistake. You should never have left your post." Maxim

shoved the sergeant their way. "Take him and bind him up. Hand him over to the proper authorities."

Peterson spluttered his outrage as he was led out, but Maxim didn't give a damn. He scanned the room, searching for Emma. *Where the hell did the woman go?* His eyes swung frantically to the hospital bed. At last, her dear face came into view amid the sea of white coats. Maxim finally could breathe again. *She was all right. She wasn't hurt.* But she looked terrified, her face as white as a sheet.

"John, save him please," she was saying to her ex. "Why's he so hypotensive?"

"I think he lost more blood. I'll do my best. What's the hematocrit?"

"Twenty-five," a blonde nurse said.

"Christ. I was right." The surgeon glanced at his watch. "Let's bring him back to the OR. Stat."

"Sam." Emma squeezed her brother's hand. "You have to fight, Sam. Don't give up. Do you hear me?"

The nurses retook Morris's vital signs and disconnected the various tubes from the walls. "Miss, we have to go now. You have to give us some room."

"Please don't die. I need you, Sam." Emma backed away, her eyes stark with fear. "I love you, Sam. Don't leave me." She clamped a hand over her face as the staff pushed Morris out of the room.

Maxim came over immediately, but Emma pushed him away, her eyes shooting daggers at him.

"Get away from me," she sobbed. "It's your fault. You did this, Maxim."

Maxim turned away, his body breaking out in a sweat. He rubbed the nape of his neck, his hand trembling. *She was only speaking the truth.* He knew it had been a risk to get involved with Emma, that he could drag her into his dark world but he'd never imagined this. *What was wrong with him that everyone he loved met with violence? First his parents and now Emma and her brother.*

"You love Morris?" a stern voice called out from the entranceway. "You have some serious explaining to do, Doc."

Damn. Banding had to show up now of all times. The sergeant was standing by the doorway, a grim scowl on his face.

"Yes. I do love him." Emma declared, her voice rising.

"So Peterson was right?" Banding entered the room. "You know it's a felony to be involved with an inmate."

"Sam Morris is my brother. So stop with your stupid accusations. I love him. And he's hurt." Emma swung an angry glare at Maxim. "All because of your damned prison. All because of you, Maxim. It was your job to keep him safe. Why didn't you? Why didn't you listen to me?"

She flew at Maxim and pelted him with her small fists.

He deserved her condemnation. *All of it. How he'd failed her.*

"I'm sorry, Emma. I'm sorry," he said over and over again but Emma kept pummeling him, her tears back in full force.

"Step back, Doctor." Banding dragged Emma away.

She collapsed into a nearby chair and buried her face in her hands.

Banding shouldn't have pulled her back. The pain she inflicted was nothing compared to what was eating at Maxim's soul. One punch, though, had landed right smack on his aching shoulder. A dark stain was beginning to form there. *Damn. Was that blood?* He must have been shot earlier. No time to take care of it now, though. Emma was breaking apart. He had to help her somehow.

But it looked like she wasn't going to require his assistance after all, for Stewart suddenly appeared in the room, running to her side. "Emma! What's wrong? Where's Sam?"

Emma threw herself into Stewart's arms. The knot in Maxim's chest tightened. He should have been the one holding her, the one providing comfort, not the psychiatrist. But how could he blame her for turning away from him? He was the cause of all her heartbreak. She was better off without him. The realization was a punch in the gut, all the more deadly because of its accuracy.

"They know Sam is my brother," Emma told Stewart, hiccupping at her last word.

"You should have told us earlier," Banding announced. "You violated policy, Doc. I'm going to have to tell Sacramento about this. They're not going to be happy."

"Let me deal with it." Maxim drew Banding out into the hallway.

Suddenly, a wave of light-headedness swept over Maxim. The ache in his shoulder became a raging fire. He swayed and leaned back against the wall for support. The stain on his shirt seemed a little bigger. *Maybe he was getting what he deserved after all.*

CHAPTER 33

"I'm sorry, Emma." John's exhausted face stared back at her. "We couldn't save him."

"What?" Emma gasped. "He's gone?"

"We tried our best."

"But he was doing well." Emma shook her head, a haze of blackness swimming at her periphery. "What happened?"

"The surgical bed was diffusely oozing, probably because he'd been coagulopathic." John squeezed her shoulder.

"You mean he couldn't clot? But why?"

"He'd lost a lot of blood earlier. You know when that happens, the clotting factors and platelets become dysfunctional. Patients bleed more easily."

"Did he get FFP?"

"Of course. More than ten units but we still couldn't control the bleeding. I'm so sorry." John swept off his surgeon's cap. "Do you want to see him? He's still in the OR. They're cleaning him up right now."

"Yes. Please, I need to see him." Emma bit her lip, the haziness increasing around her. *Sam couldn't be dead. Not her darling, precious brother.*

"All right. Come with me."

Emma stepped through a set of double doors and down the short corridor to another set. Someone was walking next to her. *Maxim?* For a moment, her treacherous heart longed for his reassuring presence. His comforting arms, his solid and warm body. If only he could hold her and chase away this nightmare.

"Emma. This way."

Emma blinked. It wasn't Maxim walking next to her. No, it was Charles. Charles, who'd been so solicitous. He'd sat with her through the night in the waiting room without complaint, getting up to buy her coffee every hour, feeding her snacks, reassuring her that things were going to be okay. But they weren't okay, were they?

And why the heck had she been longing for Maxim? The man was responsible for her brother's death. And to make it worse, he'd disappeared as soon as Sam had left for the OR. He hadn't had the decency to wait to see if her brother was okay. But that wasn't surprising in the least, was it? Sam was an inmate, so why would Maxim care what happened to him? No, Maxim was probably back in his mansion, lording it over the world.

"He's in here," someone called.

A blast of cold air slammed into her as she entered the OR suite. She shivered and tried to rub the goose bumps off her arms. A few techs were putting away the surgical instruments as housekeeping scrubbed the floors.

Emma placed one foot in front of the other, telling herself to keep breathing. At last she reached the center table. She gripped the table's edge and blinked away her tears. *Yes, that was Sam.* She couldn't mistake that frizzy hair anywhere. They'd removed the bandages from his head. Some matted blood clung to his right forehead. A white sheet covered his body.

The trembling first started in her fingers. Then it traveled up her arms into her chest and then down her legs. Little shudders at first, they gradually picked up steam and transformed into violent jerks within minutes. Emma collapsed on the cold floor. Bright light blazed down at her. *Did Sam see the same light? Was there a heaven that welcomed him? Did heaven even exist?*

Oh, Sam. Take me with you. Emma curled her knees to her chest. *Why did you leave me?* Someone lifted her onto a gurney. A rushing sound buzzed in her ears. She couldn't hear, couldn't speak. Her body kept shaking. She closed her eyes. Phineas flapped his wings as he danced in front of her from one branch to another. *Dear Phineas. Take me with you. Take me with you.*

A while later, Emma awakened in a strange room. She wasn't sure how much time had passed. Minutes, hours, days—did it even matter? The room was small and sparse, holding only her bed and a tiny sink in the corner.

"You're awake." Charles sat on a chair next to the bed, his gray suit rumpled, his eyes bloodshot. "Thank God."

"Where am I?" Her mouth felt fuzzy and her voice cracked.

"In the ER. You've been asleep for almost the whole day." He leaned in, his worried eyes scanning her face. "How do you feel?"

"Groggy. My throat's dry."

"The attending gave you some Ativan." Charles gently

brushed a lock of hair from her forehead. "Do you feel any better?"

"No." She bit her lip. "Sam? Where is he?"

"At the morgue." Charles clasped her hand in his. "Emma, I'm so sorry."

"Can you take me home?"

An hour later, she was finally able to crawl into her own bed. Her body felt bruised and shattered, as if a truck had struck her. Charles offered to stay but she dismissed him, wanting nothing more than to be alone.

The next few days flew by in a blur. Emma spent most of it in bed trying to sleep but usually failing. Charles arranged for the cremation. Too soon, she stood at the crematory with her friend, staring at Sam's cold, lifeless body before they wheeled him back.

"I think those are perfect," Charles said, pointing to Sam's personal belongings.

Emma smoothed a shaking finger over the blackbird picture she'd taken from her wall. "You think he's going to feel any of it?"

"The cremation? I don't think so." Charles put an arm around her shoulder. "His soul is already gone, Emma. I'm glad you also included the comet pictures. Where did you get them?"

"A…A friend gave them to me." Emma swallowed down the lump in her throat. "I kept a few and gave the rest to my brother."

"That's why he was always talking about comets." Charles squeezed her shoulder.

She touched Sam's cold hand and pressed a kiss to his face. "Good-bye, brother," she whispered. "I'll always love you."

"I'm leaving as soon as the typhoon is over," Riley said on the phone.

Emma pulled up the bedcovers and focused on the new addition to her room. She'd picked it up yesterday and had placed it on her nightstand. "You don't need to. I'm fine."

"You don't sound fine. Are you eating enough?"

"Yes."

"What was the last thing you ate?"

"Oatmeal, I think." Emma scrubbed a hand over her face. It must have been at breakfast. She didn't remember having lunch or dinner. But she wasn't even hungry. "I have to go, Riley. I have a lot to do."

"Like what?"

"This and that."

"Emma, it's noon over here in Vietnam. Which makes it ten p.m. where you are. You can't have that much to do."

"I can sleep." *Not easily but she could try.* Or she could look over Sam's photo album one more time. Or reread some of the letters he'd sent her ages ago.

"You told me you slept half the day away."

"So, I'm tired. I need rest." The same nightmare about Sam being beaten kept rearing its ugly head at night. She'd barely slept a wink the past week. Just naps in the daytime, but Riley didn't need to know that. Her friend was worried enough already.

"Have you stepped out of your studio once during the last seven days?"

"Of course."

"I'm not talking about for the cremation."

"I don't need to go anywhere." Emma rolled over in the bed and curled her legs to her chest.

"Has Charles come by?"

"Not since Thursday. He's away on a trip."

"Oh. What about Maxim?"

"What about him?"

"Has he called?"

"Just once." Emma reached over to the nightstand and dragged Sam's urn onto her bed. It felt cold and smooth. Like the way Sam's forehead had felt the last time she'd kissed him good-bye.

"Only once? I thought he would have tried more than that."

"I told him to stay out of my life. That I never want to see him again." Emma hugged the urn to her chest. *Her poor, vibrant brother, reduced to this.*

"Maybe you should talk to him." Riley let out a long sigh. "I'm worried about you over there all alone."

"I have nothing to say to him." Emma smoothed a hand over the urn. "Nothing polite, that is." She threw out a humorless laugh.

"You loved him once."

"He killed my brother." Emma shivered and huddled underneath the comforter. *Not that it would do any good. She was always cold these days.* "Every time I think about him, I feel so guilty. Like I'm betraying Sam's memory."

"Don't be ridiculous. Peterson and his gang killed Sam. Maxim just didn't protect him enough."

"Same thing as killing him."

"No. It's different." Riley blew out a breath. "All I'm

saying is that people make mistakes, Em. And I know his was a big one. But he thought you and Sam were involved. Jealousy blinds people sometimes."

"So what are you saying? That we should kiss and make up? For God's sake, he had me investigated, Riley. He didn't trust me one bit."

"But he threw himself in harm's way three times to protect you. It's obvious he's crazy about you."

"Three? There was Ransom and then Henderson. I don't remember a third."

"Hello? Didn't you tell me he tackled Peterson to the ground?"

"Yes. But that didn't count." Emma shook her head, not wanting to relive that horrible day.

"Didn't count? How can you say that? The sergeant had a gun. You bet it counted."

"Whatever. The man didn't even stay to see if Sam survived." Emma gritted her teeth. *How could he desert her like that?* "I'm done with him."

"Maybe he had a reason for not staying."

"Like what?"

"I don't know, but you should talk to him. How long did he let you have off?"

"As long as I need, he said." *He'd sounded contrite. But it was too little, too late.*

"It's dangerous in there, Em. Maybe you shouldn't come back."

"I don't know what I'll do yet." The days stretched ahead of her, empty and meaningless.

"I'll be back by the weekend. I'm sure they'll let us fly as soon as the typhoon clears."

"You don't have to rush back, Riley." Emma rubbed

the urn with her thumb. "I'm doing okay and Doctors Without Borders needs you more."

"I'm coming back and you can't stop me, Em." Some foreign language erupted in the background. "Listen, I have to go. Clinic's starting. Get some sleep. I'll call you tomorrow."

Dear Riley, always looking out for her. Emma wrapped her arms around the urn, careful to hold it upright. Maybe she'd finally get some sleep tonight if she kept Sam by her side. *But what if she knocked it over during the night?* Sighing, she kissed the urn and placed it back on her nightstand.

"Good night, Sam," she whispered, closing her eyes.

In her sleep, Sam came to her, walking tall and straight, his limp gone, his big brown eyes solemn and watchful. He sat on the rocking chair next to the bed and held her hand, not saying much. Just stayed there, rocking the chair and holding her hand.

"Why did you have to die?" she asked him toward morning time.

I guess it was my time.

"What's it like up there? Is Mom with you?"

She's always with me. Just like she's always with you.

"Take me with you. You're all I have."

I wouldn't say that. Give him a chance.

"He killed you, Sam. I'm not going to betray your memory."

I want you to be happy.

"Take me with you."

I can't. It's not your time yet.

"I miss you so much."

I miss you, too.

"I'm so sorry, Sam. Why did you have to die?"

The prison's dangerous, more than you know. Don't go back there.

"It won't be the same without you."

So find another job, please. I have to go now.

"Don't go." She squeezed his hand. "Sam, don't leave me. Stay a little bit longer."

I saw Phineas. He's beautiful, like you said.

"Is his wing still bent?"

He's recovering pretty well. Just like you will. Good-bye, Emma. I love you.

"No. Sam. Don't go!" Emma woke up in tears, her hand still outstretched toward the rocking chair. She expected to see Sam sitting there but no, the chair was empty. It had only been a dream. She closed her eyes, hoping to float back into the dream, to be with him again one more time. But her mind remained blank. All she heard was the ticking of the clock and the call of a blackbird heralding a new morning.

Emma checked the time. Eight a.m. *Amazing.* She'd slept through the night. The nightmare hadn't come. Maybe Sam had something to do with that, too. Emma brushed a finger over the urn and made her way into the shower. *Why had Sam visited her?* The thought of never seeing him again was unbearable but perhaps he was right. He wasn't all she had. No. She had her career, her job...Riley.

And perhaps even Maxim, too. It'd be so heavenly to feel his arms around her one more time. She was always cold these days, and he was a living furnace, definitely able to keep her warm. But how could she forgive him for all that he'd done? Her brother was gone because of him. But Sam had told her to give Maxim a chance, hadn't he? Sam wanted her to be happy. *Could she be happy with Maxim?* She had thought so once. Ages ago, it seemed.

Emma turned off the shower and pulled on some jeans and an old T-shirt. Oatmeal didn't seem as appealing this morning. She took out a pan, poured in a dash of extra virgin olive oil, took two eggs out of the refrigerator and cracked each one on the pan. The oil fizzled and sprayed. She flipped the eggs over with a spatula. An oil drop splattered on her hand, stinging her, but she welcomed the pain. It was better than the perpetual numbness she'd felt for the past week. She pushed her hand under the kitchen faucet, welcoming the rush of cool water that splashed against her skin. She turned off the water a minute later and took out the loaf of bread Charles had brought over before his trip.

Emma toasted two slices of bread and scooped the two eggs out onto a plate. *Good, the yolks were still runny the way she liked them.* Next, she poured herself a glass of orange juice. She could do this. It wasn't hard if she took it one step at a time. Breakfast today. Maybe tomorrow she could try grocery shopping. Her feet still felt as if lead were weighing them down but any little progress counted, didn't it?

The buttered bread tasted like sawdust, but Emma chewed anyway. *Baby steps.* That was what she needed. She cut the eggs into square pieces and forced down ten pieces before her stomach rose in protest. She next tried the orange juice, welcoming its sweet fresh flavor as she sipped a few mouthfuls.

It wasn't the entire meal but it was enough. More than she'd eaten the whole day yesterday. Emma put plastic wrap around the plate of eggs and placed it in the refrigerator. She was about to do the same with the orange juice when the doorbell rang. Her hand shook as she placed the glass back on the table.

Could it be Maxim? Was she ready to face him again? Her heart rate spiked. She swallowed down the lump in her throat and walked to the door. She peered through the peephole. Her hand unclenched.

"Julien." She smiled as she opened the door. She hadn't seen the chief since he'd reported on Sam's assault at the physician conference.

"Hi, Emma. May I come in?" His kind eyes crinkled up at the corners as he gazed down at her.

"Sure." She closed the door after him and ushered him to the sofa.

"Sorry I haven't stopped by before. Mary and my kids got chickenpox so our house has been kind of crazy." He swept her an uncertain look. "You're immunized, right?"

"I got it as a kid so I'm protected. Is your family doing okay?"

"Yes. Thank God. How's it going with you?"

Emma shrugged and forced out a half-smile. "It's going."

"I'm sorry about your brother." Julien extended his hand. "If it makes you feel any better, they arrested Peterson and the gang members."

"You mean the PALIs?"

"Yes. Some of them confessed to the assault in exchange for less time. Peterson is in jail, waiting for his hearing."

"Good. Does anybody know why he did it?"

"Nobody knows for sure." Julien shook his head. "But there're rumors going around that he was broke. And you can make a lot from selling drugs."

"That's so despicable."

"I know. Nobody's more shocked than Chambers. He just got out of the hospital."

"What?" Emma's heart thudded. "Maxim was in the hospital?"

"Yes. He had surgery to remove the bullet."

"What bullet?" The room suddenly dimmed as Emma's legs buckled. She dropped down on the sofa and clutched its armrest.

"Peterson shot him. The surgeon thought it nicked his lung but luckily it was only in the shoulder. They operated right away." Julien touched her arm. "Hey. Are you alright? You look real pale."

"Maxim was shot? Is he okay?" Emma croaked out against the rushing in her ears. *No wonder he hadn't stayed to check up on Sam. He'd been in the OR.* And all this time, she'd been cursing him for his callousness.

"Yes. He's fine. Recuperating at home." Julien got up and brought back her half glass of orange juice. "Here, drink, Emma. You look like you need it."

Emma gulped down the orange juice, her mind spinning. "Why didn't anyone tell me? I didn't know he was shot."

"He told us not to tell you. Said you had too many things to deal with already." Julien sat down next to her. "But I thought you'd want to know. You're close to him, aren't you? Are you guys dating or something? There're some rumors floating around."

"No, we're not dating." Emma bit her lip. *At least not anymore.* "Why do you ask?"

"Well, he knew about Morris being your brother and didn't say anything. You must have been close."

"What? What did you say?" Emma's fingers clamped down on the glass.

"Don't worry. Sacramento was going to fire you for not telling us about your brother." Julien leaned back on the sofa. "But Chambers took the blame for it. Confessed he knew all along Morris was your brother. So now all their wrath is on him."

"Maxim said what?" The rushing in Emma's ears amplified into a loud roar.

"That he knew about your relationship with Morris." Julien took the glass from her hand. "You could have told me too, you know. Although I don't know what I would've done. It took a lot of guts for Chambers to keep your secret. And even more guts to admit he knew about it."

"I know," Emma forced out through the lump in her throat. *He'd lied to save her. The poor, darling, wonderful misguided man.* "I feel so horrible about the whole thing."

"It's okay. Water under the bridge and all that." Julien gave her a sympathetic smile. "They're only giving you a letter of instruction. You can come back any time."

"But what about the investigation?"

"Investigation? What investigation?"

"He said he was going to have me investigated. For being involved with Sam."

"There's no investigation." Julien shook his head. "Peterson must have lied about it to scare you off."

"No. Maxim said he was going to launch one."

"Nothing was launched. He knew all along you were Morris's sister. Why would he start one?"

Oh my God. He had never launched the investigation. He was protecting her all along, even when he thought she was involved with Sam. But he'd told her he was going to call for one, didn't he? Maybe he'd meant to start one but couldn't go through with it. Because he cared about her.

Because he loved her. And what had she done with that love? She'd cursed and screamed at him, throwing it back in his face. She'd been so awful.

"Anyway, I wanted to let you know you can return to work anytime," Julien was saying. "You're a good doctor, Emma. The patients miss you. They keep asking about you."

"Thanks." Maybe she should go back to Albatross. It felt nice to be needed. But Sam had warned her to stay away. It was going to be tough to decide.

"Thank goodness Sacramento didn't fire you. They suspended Chambers, though."

"No! For how long?" A cold vise gripped at Emma's heart.

"Two months."

"Jesus. That long?"

"Yes. They were pushing for more but his officers spoke up for him. So it's only two."

Poor Maxim. He had done it all for her. How unjust his punishment. She should have been the one suspended, not him. She had to fix that, if he'd let her. "Where is Maxim right now?" Emma forced out through the knot squeezing at her chest.

"Most likely at home." Julien stood and put on his jacket. "I tried to visit but he turned me away, being his usual grim and silent self."

"He's a really good guy when you get to know him."

"That's what all his officers say. Sorry I can't stay longer. Mary needs me back at the house." Julien leaned over and gave her a hug. "Take care of yourself. Call me if you need anything."

"Thanks." Emma waved good-bye, her mind reliving their conversation. *How could she have been so mistaken?*

Maxim had loved her all along. He'd given up so much for her. Sacrificed his job, even lied for her. True, he hadn't protected Sam but he'd done everything else, including taking that bullet for her. She owed her life to him. She was always going to miss Sam. But blaming Maxim wasn't going to bring her brother back.

She needed to thank Maxim for all he'd done. And she had to reverse his suspension somehow. But most of all, she had to beg for his forgiveness. She'd been downright cruel to him. Funny, Sam had said to give Maxim a chance. Her brother had it all wrong. It was Maxim who should be giving her another chance.

CHAPTER 34

The drive to Maxim's house was interminable. Traffic was light but the winding road up to his driveway took forever to climb. Finally she stood outside the door to his mansion, her heart in her throat. She looked down and winced at her outfit. Faded jeans and an old college T-shirt. In her rush, she hadn't stopped to change. And she had no makeup on. *Great going, Emma.* She tugged at her pendant and rubbed her palm on her jeans. *Oh well. It was now or never.* She pressed the ringer.

A pleasant, plump middle-aged woman opened the door. "Yes?"

"Hi." Emma licked her dry lips. "You must be Maxim's housekeeper." Maxim had wanted them to be alone during her previous visits so she hadn't had a chance to meet the housekeeper yet.

"Yes. I'm Ana. Can I help you?"

"Is Maxim in? I have to see him."

"I'm sorry. Is he expecting you?"

"No, not really. But I think…" Emma swallowed. "I mean, I hope he'll see me."

"What's your name?" The woman darted a look over her shoulder before turning back.

"Emma. Emma Edwards."

"The doctor from the prison?" Ana's face broke out in a smile. "Well, why didn't you say so before? Come in. I'm sure Mr. Chambers will be happy to see you."

Emma exhaled a small huff of air, the tightness in her throat easing by a fraction.

"At least I think he'll be happy." Ana shook her head and smoothed a hand over her white apron. "He hasn't asked about you for a while now. Come with me. He's in the back."

The constriction in Emma's throat slammed back in full force. Maxim used to ask about her, but not anymore. *Was she already too late?* She placed one foot in front of the other and stepped onto the marble tiles. They were pink and white, easily twenty inches by twenty inches with a gold edge around each border. Nothing but the best for Maxim. The vast array of sculptures and paintings along the sweeping hallway still intimidated her, screaming wealth and elegance. Emma plucked at her worn T-shirt and bit her lip. *She definitely should have put on something more presentable.*

Too late. Ana was already opening the French doors to the back gardens. Emma inched forward, her hands clenched. A light fragrance of roses permeated the air. She took in a deep breath and held it before letting it out through her mouth. She forced her breathing to slow. *She could do this.* Maxim had sacrificed so much for her. She'd be willing to do anything to win him back.

"It's okay, Ana. You don't have to announce me. I'll find him." Emma put a hand out to stop the housekeeper.

"Are you sure?"

"Yes. I've been here before."

"All right, Doctor." Ana gave her a friendly wave before heading back into the house.

Emma stepped past her favorite koi fishpond. There were more fish than she remembered. Maxim must have bought more. Most of the water lilies weren't blooming but the pond still shimmered with peace and beauty. A big yellow fish swam to the edge followed by two smaller ones in different colors.

On-ke-kaaangh. On-ke-kaaangh. Emma stumbled. *Was that what she thought it was?* She shook her head. Of course not. She must have imagined it. But no. There it was again, somewhere from the direction of the gazebo. It sounded so much like Phineas. *It couldn't be. There was no possible way.*

Emma veered left and dashed past the bright courtyard of rosebushes. Down the trail she ran, shooting around another corner before she screeched to a halt. She blinked a few times. *Surely her eyes were playing tricks on her. But no. There he was. Phineas! Alive and well. Her beautiful blackbird.*

He perched on a bar in a large wooden octagonal birdcage hanging at the front of the gazebo. Maxim stood next to him facing away from her, dressed in loose jeans and a light-blue dress shirt, a white sling covering his left arm. His right arm was raised to the birdcage. Emma brushed away the wetness from her eyes. *Phineas was alive.*

"Hello, Maxim." Her voice cracked.

Maxim's arm froze in midair. For a few seconds, he did nothing, his body unnaturally still. Finally he turned.

"Emma. What are you doing here?" His voice was

hoarse and there were dark shadows circling beneath his eyes. Still, he looked as magnificent as ever.

"I can't believe it. You saved Phineas?" She wanted nothing more than to run to him but his expression was grim and almost unwelcoming.

"Yes. I brought him to the vet."

"Why didn't you tell me?"

"It was touch-and-go for a while so I didn't want to get your hopes up. Luckily he pulled through." Maxim indicated the birdcage, his gaze softening. "He has a dressing on his wing but the vet thinks he'll recover okay."

"He looks wonderful." And indeed her blackbird's feathers were extra glossy today, providing quite a contrast to the white bandage he had wrapped around his left wing. He swung his eyes back and forth between Maxim and her before letting out another loud chirp. "Thank you for saving him."

"You're welcome." Maxim's tone was formal, his face still remote and cold.

"So how are you doing?" She forced some false cheer to her voice and clasped her hands in front of her to still their trembling. "How's your shoulder?"

"Fine."

"I'm sorry you were shot." Emma stepped closer but he retreated, his form rigid. "I didn't know. Nobody told me."

"I told them not to tell you."

"Why? I wish I'd known."

"Your plate was already full with your brother." Maxim's mouth twisted. "And I was pretty sure I wasn't your number-one priority at that moment."

"I'm sorry, Maxim. I treated you so horribly."

"No more than I deserved." He sighed and shoved a

hand through his hair. "I'm the one who should be sorry. I should have protected your brother."

"You didn't know our relationship."

"Why didn't you tell me?" he asked, his eyes bleak. "I would've tried to help somehow."

"I wasn't sure what you'd do." Emma paused. *If only she could find the right words to make him understand.* "I didn't want you to compromise your job for me, and I couldn't bear it if Sam and I were separated."

"You didn't trust me enough to keep your secret."

Was that the gist of it? The guilt clawed at her. "You're right. I'm sorry, Maxim." Emma swallowed and took a cautious step forward. "Especially now when I know all that you've done for me. You didn't even launch the investigation."

"I'd planned to." He gave a bittersweet smile. "But in the end I guess I couldn't go through with it."

"I wish you'd told me. I was so worried."

"I know. I should've been more open with you. Maybe you would've trusted me more. And none of this would have happened. Your brother might still be alive." Maxim pulled at his sling, his face twisted in remorse.

"Please. It's not your fault." Emma tried to reach for his hand but he moved back again.

"I heard they suspended you," Emma said after a few more seconds of excruciating silence. "Thank you for what you did, but you shouldn't have lied for me. I'll talk to Sacramento and tell them the truth. That you never knew about my relationship with Sam."

"No. Don't do that."

"But it's not right. They'll probably reverse your suspension and then you can go back to work."

"Leave it alone, Emma. Giving a false confession will get me suspended, too." Maxim thrust a hand into his jeans pocket. "And besides, I'll use the time off to think about things. To reevaluate. I've been so blind. I couldn't see how corrupt my own staff was."

A painful knot squeezed in Emma's chest. He was trying so hard to make up for his mistakes. And he refused to let her take the rightful blame. "You'll come back stronger and better than before, Maxim. I am confident of that." She gave him a watery smile.

"Such faith. You know I don't deserve it."

"You do deserve it." Emma stepped closer, longing to chase away the uncertainty in his eyes. "I love you, Maxim. I believe in you with all my heart."

He sucked in an audible breath. "Are you sure? Even after all that's happened?"

"Yes."

"But you said you wanted me out of your life."

"I was in shock, grieving. I didn't know half of what I was saying." She tentatively touched his sleeve. "Please, I was horrible to you. Can you forgive me?"

"Forgive you? Don't be ridiculous. There's nothing to forgive." He scowled down at her. "I'm the one who killed your brother. I'll never forgive myself for that. And I don't expect you to either."

"But I do forgive you, Maxim. You didn't kill Sam. Peterson and the PALIs did."

"God, Emma, you are too generous." Maxim turned away, his voice cracking. "I don't deserve your forgiveness."

"Well, I'm giving it. Stop telling me you don't deserve things." She forced him to face her. "You're a good person. You're worthy of a lot."

"Right. Your brother died because of me and you almost did, too."

"Peterson is the main culprit here, not you. You did the best you could, given what you knew."

"But it wasn't enough," he said, his eyes anguished.

"Maxim, you have to let it go." Emma cupped a hand over his dear face. "I love you. I don't want you to suffer like this."

Maxim turned his cheek into her caress and pressed a soft kiss to her palm. "So many times I've dreamed of you coming to me like this." He lifted a hand to her hair, his face almost reverent. "Telling me that you love me. That you want to be with me."

"Well, you don't have to dream anymore." Emma wrapped her left arm around his waist and put her right hand over his chest, careful not to touch his sling. He was so warm. She buried closer and inhaled his familiar wonderful scent. "I love you," she whispered. "Tell me that we can be together again."

His big body trembled and his heart rate accelerated under her hand. *At last she was home. It felt so good to be in his arms.* Emma tilted her face up, sure she'd finally reached him. Her glow of happiness though was short-lived.

"What's wrong?" Maxim's face had that remote expression again. And his arm was hanging by his side, no longer touching her.

"I'm sorry, Emma." He gently pushed her away. "Your love means the world to me. I'll always treasure it, but I'm not the right man for you."

The familiar knot returned to her stomach. "What are you saying?"

"I'm no good for you." Maxim shook his head. "You deserve someone better. Someone good and kind and noble. Not a beast of a man like me."

"You are not a beast." Her heart constricted at his self-doubt. "You are good, and kind, and noble. And so much more. I love you. We can make it work."

"We can't." He pushed her away more forcibly this time.

"We can." A horrible thought seized Emma's mind. "Unless you don't love me anymore?"

"As if that were possible." He gave her a wistful smile. "I will never stop loving you."

"Then what's the problem?" The tears welled up in her eyes. *He loved her but didn't want her in his life?* Her heart and soul screamed at the senselessness of it all. "How can you love me and let me go? Take a chance on us. Take a chance on me. We belong together."

"No." Maxim's voice rose. "I love you enough to let you go, Emma. Trust me, I'm doing what's best for you."

"No, you're not," Emma said, her heart cracking inside even as a blaze of anger scorched through her. *How could he throw away their love like that?* "You're doing what's best for you. Love is about sharing, about taking a leap of faith, taking a risk. But you're not doing any of that. You're shutting yourself away from me. That isn't love."

"That's all I can offer," Maxim insisted. "I know it isn't enough. That's why you should find someone else. Someone who can give you what you want. What you need."

"I don't want anyone else."

Maxim shook his head again and took another step back. "Just go, Emma. There's nothing here for you."

He was dismissing her. Just like that. Kicking her out of his life. *How could this be happening?* Emma blinked back her tears. The man was so stubborn she wanted to scream. He was the only one she needed, the only one she wanted. *How could he not realize that?*

Phineas suddenly chirped, jumping from one bar to the next in his cage. Maxim had brought this bird back from the brink of death for her. Who else but a kind and noble person would do that?

"Please, Maxim. Are you sure?" She must pierce through his armor somehow. "I think you're perfect for me. I want to be with you. No one else."

"Don't make this harder than it already is." Maxim clenched his hand, refusing to budge. "Go. I've made up my mind."

"Fine. But I'm taking Phineas with me," Emma said, coming to a sudden decision. She was not going to leave without that blackbird. She had lost both Maxim and Sam. No way was she going to lose Phineas, too.

"You're taking Phineas?"

"Yes. You don't mind, do you?"

Maxim cast a longing glance at the bird. "Of course not. He was yours to begin with." He touched the birdcage with one finger. "But make sure you give him plenty of fresh water. And he likes berries. But only the black ones."

"Black?"

"Yes." Maxim cleared his throat. "He likes them over-ripe and cut into little pieces."

"For someone *not* good and *not* kind, you know a lot about what pleases a bird," Emma said, her heart overflow-ing with love for the stubborn, pigheaded man. An idea suddenly took root in her mind. A brilliant notion of how to have Maxim stay in her life.

"It's what he eats," Maxim said, clearly not liking her

comment. "Here. Take him if you want." He gently lifted the cage and handed it to her. "Make sure you don't drive too fast. You might scare him."

"Okay. I'll drive extra slow." *The poor man looked like he was giving up his firstborn child.* "He'll be fine, Maxim. But in case I run into problems, do you mind if I call you? I've never taken care of a bird before."

"Sure." He paused and brushed a hand through his hair. "Wait. No. It's better if we make a clean break."

"I see. You're right." Emma faked a deep sigh. "I guess I'll depend on the vet or maybe the Internet. The Web's always full of good ideas of how to do things. I'm sure I can scrounge around for information on bird care. And I could always wing it if I have to."

Maxim's face turned a peculiar pasty color. "His vet is Dr. Geary. On River Street. Corner of Lincoln. I'm sure he can help you out."

"Thanks." Emma forced out a smile. "Good-bye, Maxim. Maybe I'll see you around sometime."

"That's it?" he asked, his face tight with emotion.

"I guess so." How she longed to throw herself into his arms and kiss away the desolation etched on his face. But she had to be patient for her plan to work. She gripped the birdcage and straightened her shoulders. "Take care of yourself."

"You, too."

Emma turned and put one foot in front of the other, flicking a glance at Phineas now and then as she walked out of the garden. It was tempting to look back, to check if Maxim was watching her but she had to keep moving. To let him know she was willing to follow his lead. To appear to cut him out of her life the way he wanted. Would the stubborn man run after her? Would he realize that no matter what, they belonged together? That she was never going to give up on him?

Oh, how her heart yearned for him to chase after her. To raise a protest, to tell her he couldn't live without her, to gather her back into his arms where she belonged. But no. None of that happened, of course. Maxim was too honorable and hardheaded for his own good. Emma made it back to her car without any hindrance. She placed Phineas in the front passenger seat and snapped a seat belt around his cage. Her plan had to work. She had to win Maxim back. Any other outcome didn't bear contemplating.

CHAPTER 35

Watching Emma walk away from him was the hardest thing he'd ever endured, Maxim was sure of it. He'd never expected her to visit. Sure, he'd had some wishful thinking, instructing Ana to let her in if she called on him. But that was in the beginning, right after he'd gotten out of the hospital. Before his hopes had crumbled during the last few days of endless waiting.

She'd looked so lovely, young and innocent. But she was thin. Even thinner than he remembered. Maxim cursed, wishing he'd reminded her to eat more. The grief had caused her to lose weight. Another fault to add to his long list of sins. And how could she have forgiven him for her brother's death? She was too generous, too selfless. And definitely too good for him. He'd almost killed her because of his inability to trust. Maxim rubbed a hand over his bandaged shoulder and grimaced. *Christ.* The bullet had been meant for her. It was only by the sheerest of luck that he'd arrived in time. His body broke out in a cold sweat.

No way was he going to tempt fate again. Violence and death followed him everywhere. How could he live with himself knowing he was a risk to her very safety? The pain of losing her would be unbearable. Why take the risk? It was safer to let her go. She deserved to find happiness with someone else. She loved him, which was a miracle in itself, but she was still young. Her whole life lay ahead of her, a life better off without him.

But dear God, how he'd been tempted. Especially when she'd wrapped her arm around him. When she'd rested her lovely head on his chest, when she'd confided she wanted him and no one else. *Yes!* He had wanted to shout. He'd felt on top of the world, stronger and taller than the highest mountain. But one glance at the blackbird had dashed all his hopes. That had been her brother's bird. And he'd killed her brother. He'd failed her. He had no choice but to push her away. It was for her own good.

But she'd absconded with the blackbird. *How could the woman be so cruel?* Phineas was his single link to her, the only part of her he'd allowed himself to have. And she'd taken Phineas, snatched the bird right out of his life. So he was left with nothing, just distant memories and an aching heart.

"Come on, Phineas," Emma pleaded later that night as she tried to coax some berries into the bird's mouth. "You haven't eaten anything for hours. The vet said you should get at least two meals a day. I got it overripe like Maxim said. And I chopped it, too."

Phineas perched in his cage, his eyes dull and lifeless as he stared blankly ahead. His little bowl of water lay untouched on the cage floor. *What the heck was wrong?* She'd only been kidding when she'd told Maxim she needed his help. She thought she could play it out. Make him wait a few anxious days, letting him see how much he missed her before she made that phone call. Before she'd ask for his help with Phineas.

Of course he would have come over. He loved the bird and would have rushed over in a heartbeat if she'd told him Phineas needed help. She'd felt bad about the ruse but she was desperate. She had to try something, anything to keep him in her life.

At least that had been the plan. A stupid, childish one, Emma admitted but it had been better than nothing. Still, how could it have unraveled so quickly? It wasn't days but hours and she didn't have to fake any symptoms. No, indeed, her poor blackbird looked miserable and sick right now. Where were his bright eyes? His sweet birdcalls? Nothing. Not even a chirp had he let out since she'd carried his cage into her studio that afternoon.

Emma had even visited the vet to obtain some advice and bird food. She'd bought the seeds Dr. Geary had recommended, but Phineas had soundly rejected them. The little pieces of fresh berries she'd chopped also lay untouched on his dish. She'd even attempted feeding him with her hand, all to no avail.

"Come on, little one." Emma touched his bowl of water. "At least drink something."

Phineas didn't pay any attention and just shut his eyes, his body completely still. Was he sleeping? Or was he sick? Dr. Geary had instructed to give him at least a few drops of water every few hours. But he'd ingested none. Had she hurt him by removing him from Maxim's care? He'd been so lively that morning, chirping and hopping from one place to the next. Now he looked the opposite, all worn out and beaten.

She had no choice but to call for help. This was all her fault. She shouldn't have taken the bird away from Maxim.

He picked up on the fourth ring.

"Maxim?" she asked, her voice breaking.

"Emma? What is it?"

"Please help. I think he's dying. Can you come?"

"Who's dying?" Maxim's voice rose a notch. "Emma, what is it? Are you okay?"

"It's Phineas. He's not eating or drinking anything." Emma bit her lip and tried to steady her voice. "I should have left him with you."

"Don't worry. I'll be right there."

But he lived far away, not arriving until a full hour later. One of the longest hours of her life. At last, he knocked. She yanked the door open and pulled him into the studio, her heart pounding. *Dear Maxim.* He looked so solid and dependable, dressed in the same jeans he'd worn this morning. He'd thrown a gray sweater on top of his shirt but was still wearing the sling. How she longed to bury herself in his arms, but poor Phineas needed him more at the moment.

"He hasn't moved since I called you." Emma hastily led Maxim to the birdcage. "Is he sleeping or do you think something's wrong with him?"

"I don't know. It's hard to tell." Maxim opened the cage and placed two pieces of berry onto his index finger. "I used to feed him like this when I first brought him home from the vet."

Phineas snapped his eyes open, blinking at the sight of Maxim's finger before swinging a long look at Maxim's face. Slowly but surely, he bent his head and pecked at the first piece of berry.

"Oh, Maxim, you did it!" The breath whooshed out of Emma's lungs. "He never did that for me. I tried everything."

"Seriously?" Maxim lifted the bowl of water and coaxed Phineas to drink a few drops. He deposited more pieces of berry on his finger and over the next ten minutes patiently fed the blackbird all the tiny bits.

"He obviously prefers you to me." Emma smiled as Phineas swallowed the last fruit bit.

"Well, it's your first day with him." Maxim stood and watched the bird for another few moments. "He looks okay now. Do you have enough blackberries for him?"

"Yes."

"Good. You can feed him later." Maxim glanced around the room before clearing his throat. "It's pretty late. I should head off."

"But what about Phineas?" Emma asked, her heart sinking.

"What about him?"

"I can't take care of him." *And you can't go. Not yet.* She tugged at her pendant. "Can you stay and help me?"

"Stay?" Maxim's eyebrows drew together. "No, of course not. Feed him the way I showed you. I'm sure he'll be fine."

"But I tried that today. He wouldn't eat."

"Then let me take care of him. I'll bring him home and keep him until the vet takes the dressing off."

"But I'll miss seeing him every day." *And I'll miss seeing you even more.* Emma's heart felt like it was going to crack.

"You'll see him again. As soon as the bandage comes off, I'll release him back to the wild. I promise."

Emma let out a little whimper. Her plan wasn't working on so many levels. Here they were, alone in the middle of the night. She'd shown Maxim how much she needed him and still the man wanted to leave. *Was there no hope for them?* If he departed with Phineas, she was sure that was the last she'd ever see of him except for maybe at work, where he'd probably do his best to stay out of her way. And she wasn't even sure she'd be returning to Albatross. This might be her last time with him.

Emma stumbled to the nightstand and brushed an unsteady finger back and forth over the urn. *Sam. Help me. What am I going to do? Should I let him go with Phineas?* She knew in her heart the answer was yes. Phineas deserved the best chance to recover and fly. *The best chance.* Her finger froze. *That was it. She'd found the answer. It'd been right in front of her all along.*

Emma swung around, her heart pounding.

Maxim stood a mere two feet away. "That's your brother's urn?" he asked, his voice strained.

"Yes. I didn't know where else to keep it."

"Most people bury it or scatter the ashes."

"Well, I haven't decided what I'll do with it yet."

"I see." Maxim scrubbed a hand over his face. "I really need to go. Can I take Phineas with me? I promise I'll take good care of him."

"Can we talk about us first?"

"I already told you." Maxim shook his head, a shutter falling over his face. "There's no us."

"Didn't you say you wanted to take care of Phineas, at least until his bandage is off?"

"Yes. So? What does that have to do with us?"

"Everything, Maxim." Emma swallowed. *She had to make him understand.* "You're the only one who can take care of Phineas. I can't do it. Even the vet didn't offer much help."

"What are you trying to say?"

"Don't you see? Phineas needs you like I need you. You're his best chance of survival. He responds only to your voice, to your touch. No one else will do. It's the same with me."

"You're being overly dramatic." Maxim's voice softened. "You'll find someone else, Emma. Someone who can make you so much happier than I can."

"Phineas opened his eyes and ate because you were the one feeding him. He won't respond to anybody else."

"He's a bird. He doesn't know anything."

"Are you sure?" Emma placed a hand on Maxim's arm, praying she could get her point across. "Animals have instincts. They know who's good and who's bad. Who they can trust and who they can't. Phineas obviously knows he can trust you. Because you're good. And kind. And worthy."

"You're being ridiculous. He's only a bird." Maxim stepped back but his voice was uncertain, as if he dared not believe what she was saying.

"Look at him. His eyes are following you everywhere you go." Emma ushered Maxim toward the cage, hoping to demonstrate exactly what she meant. "All afternoon, he barely moved. He just kind of stared ahead, not eating or drinking. As soon as you step in and he hears your voice, he chirps up. See how bright his eyes are now? And look, he's even drinking more of the water. He knows you, Maxim.

You've taken really good care of him the past couple of weeks and he trusts you. Like you've taken great care of me and I trust you. You have so much good in you, Maxim. I wish you could see it."

"Do you really believe that?" For the first time, a sliver of hope dawned in Maxim's eyes.

"Of course I do. I love you, Maxim. You're the only man for me."

"Oh God, Emma." Maxim pulled her up against him, his face raw with emotion. "Are you sure? I'm so afraid of hurting you. I'd die if anything happens to you."

"You'll hurt me more if you let me go." Emma wrapped her arms around his waist and squeezed with all her might. "I need you, Maxim. I couldn't survive without you."

"But what if something happens to you? I'd never forgive myself," he murmured against her hair.

"That's the risk I'm willing to take." Emma cupped his beloved face between her hands. "Something bad can happen to me anywhere, anytime. But with you, I believe I have the best chance of survival. The best chance of happiness. You're strong and kind and everything that I need. Everything that I want."

"Christ, Emma. You bring me to my knees, you know that?" Maxim lifted her against his body and leaned his forehead against hers. "Thank you for giving me your heart. It's more precious to me than anything in the world."

"So don't give it back," Emma whispered against his lips. "It's yours. For now and always."

"Mine." Maxim pressed his lips hard against hers. "I'm never going to let you go after this. You know that, right?"

"Right. I'm counting on that."

On-ke-kaaangh. On-ke-kaaangh.

"Looks like our friend's counting on it, too," Emma added.

They turned as one to look at the blackbird and found him gazing at them, his eyes now bright and full of life.

EPILOGUE

Freedom at last. The day had finally come. Maxim drove Emma up Skyline Drive to hike the nearest mountain surrounding the prison. She usually didn't like to backpack but this wasn't going to be just another hike, much as she loved spending every minute with Maxim. He'd planned it perfectly, he said. Up they trekked along the winding trail, each carrying his and her special cargo. Maxim no longer needed his sling and had full use of his shoulder again.

Emma's heart thumped hard with each passing minute. When they reached the pinnacle, she inhaled the clean, crisp air and soaked in the beautiful scenery. Snow-peaked mountains rose majestically around them while far below, a small stream wound its meandering course through the thick woods. Bursts of marigolds and bright yellow and orange poppies dotted the hillside. Off in the distance, a cloud of blackbirds sailed through the air.

"Ready?" Maxim asked, his beautiful eyes shining softly at her.

"I guess so." Emma swallowed the lump in her throat and uncapped Sam's urn. The ashes felt like fine sand as they coursed through her fingers. She lifted a handful and tossed it high into the air. Some of the ashes drifted down but most were carried away by the strong wind. "Be free, Sam," she whispered. "I'll always love you."

Maxim unlatched the cage he was carrying and swung open its door. Phineas perched still for a moment, his eyes darting back and forth between the two of them. He finally spied the strewn ashes and cried out a loud chirp before lifting his wings and gliding out of the cage. His black wings glistened in the golden sunlight. For a brief second, he turned and looked back at them, his bright eyes blinking rapidly.

"Be free, my friend," Emma said, scattering the rest of the remains into the air. Phineas sang his trademark bird-call before soaring away between the falling ashes.

Maxim embraced her from behind, pressing a kiss to her hair. Emma blinked away her tears and leaned back into the warm shelter of his arms.

ABOUT THE AUTHOR

DB Michaels is a life-long reader who fell in love with the field of medicine during college. Double boarded in internal medicine and emergency medicine, she enjoys using her skills to help those in need. Working as a doctor in the prison system inspired her to write *Song of the Blackbird*, the first installment in her Albatross Prison Series. Though the book is fictional, it illustrates the power of love, hope, and second chances.

DB's first passion has always been books and she is happiest when she is absorbed in a great novel or writing. When she has time off, she likes to watch old movies, dally in the sun, and spend time with her family.

DB loves to connect with readers on her website http://www.dbmichaels.com and on her Facebook page http://www.facebook.com/DBMichaelsAuthor. You can also sign up for her newsletter at http://eepurl.com/bQOaZL.